Unsung Warriors

Ann Mc Gowan

First Published in Ireland, in 2014, in co-operation with Choice Publishing,
Drogheda, County Louth, Republic of Ireland
www.choicepublishing.ie

ISBN: 978-1-909154-59-9

Cover Design by Erne Print, Ballyshannon, Co Donegal
Tel 071 98 58004

Printed in Ireland by SPRINT-print Ltd

Belfast

Of all the places I have been
There's only one to fill my dreams.
The place that lingers in my mind
Is the town I've left behind.
I've been away now for too many years
I've read all the papers they told of your tears.
Though I've left you with a heart that's been torn,
I'm coming home now
To the place I was born

Chorus:
That's Belfast you call to me
When I am far away
I think of thee
Your Black Mountain, Cave Hill, City Hall
Shaw's Bridge, River Lagan
I'm going home to them all.

I'll meet friends and relations
Each one I'll embrace
We'll pass round the pictures
Which time can't erase
And it won't be long now
'Til I see them all,
Then I'll walk round the old streets
And good times I'll recall

Chorus;
In Belfast, you call to me
When I am far away
I think of thee
Your Black Mountain, Cave Hill, City Hall
Shaw's Bridge, River Lagan
I'm going home to them all.

Words and Music Alex Quinn 1984

Dedication

Dedicated to the women of West Belfast.

Thank you

Thanks goes to Mary Duggan and my daughters Amanda and Leanne who gave me their time and advice voluntarily.

1

The winter sun was brightening the sky over West Belfast as Tess stirred, subconsciously fighting the emergence of reality, knowing instinctively it was not a good place to be. But her body clock was in control and she woke at her usual seven thirty.

Eyes closed she turned in the bed, stretching out a hand she met empty space. Barry wasn't beside her. Once more she was plunged into the horror that was now her life.

As her brain kicked into action, the events of the previous three days hit her like a tsunami. Moaning aloud she wrapped her arms around her body and fought to hold on to her sanity. Each memory sent shock waves through her.

"What am I going to do?" she cried. The future stretched before her like a canvas filled with horror.

"Here I am, three children, no job, no money and now no husband. How did we get here? How does a wee family with no political or paramilitary connections find themselves in this situation?" she cried.

She felt she was going crazy, all these questions and no answers. She'd just turned twenty five, her family and home had been her life for the last seven years. She knew nothing else nor wanted anything else.

She cursed the country she lived in and how a man like her husband could be lifted off the street and interned just for being in the wrong place at the wrong time.

But for now, she knew she had to stand up and start living, her children were her number one priority and she had to make sure they were okay.

"They poor wee things have no other parent to rely on now and I may be the only one they have for years to come."

One minute at a time," she told herself. "Put your feet on the floor and walk to wee Jimmy's bed and lift him before he starts crying and wakes the other two."

Reaching for her dressing gown, she pulled it on over her shaking body and struggled to her son's room.

Looking at the three little blonde heads sleeping on the pillows, she knew they were her world. She had to keep going for their sake and make life as good as possible for them.

"Will their daddy be here to see them grow?" she asked herself.

A little voice came from the bed beside the window. "Mammy, I'm hungry."

Tess smiled at her little man. "Are you, Pet? Well! We better get you breakfast then."

She bent down and kissed his forehead. Lifting him she held him close as she carried him downstairs. Putting him gently on the couch she tucked a cot blanket around him and gave him his little lorries to play with.

"My daddy gave me this yellow one," he said as though he knew something was wrong. "Will he buy me another one, a blue one like the coal man's?" he queried.

"I don't know, wee man. Daddy is going to be away for a wee while, maybe when he gets back."

As she stood at the kitchen worktop her mind returned to three nights before, when she and Barry were getting ready to go to her friend, Margaret's, birthday party. They were in great humour and delighted to be going out for the first time in months even though they worried about leaving the children with Tess's mother.

Like all young children they could be a handful. Their development, the good as well as the naughty was something both she and Barry were proud of and laughed about. They spent hours talking about what they did or said and took great joy in watching them grow up.

"He's going to miss so much if they keep him in. He will hate not being with them. What will I do without him? He's my first boyfriend, my best friend, my support, he means everything to me - we're a partnership." She put her head down on the kitchen worktop trying to get strength to carry on.

She'd met him when she was fifteen and there had been no other man for her before or since. They got married three years after they met and hadn't been separated since.

Their life was very much a joint effort. Barry worked six days a week and brought home the wages. Tess cooked, cleaned, paid the bills, kept the home and looked after the children. He spent time with the children in the evening before he went out and patrolled the local area to stop paramilitaries or others creating trouble. Now her life had been torn apart, their future looked very bleak and she was falling to bits.

2

It was strange to think that three nights before they were in their bedroom after putting their youngest child to sleep with Tess's mother giving the other two their supper downstairs before they too would be tucked up for the night. They'd wanted them settled before they left so it would be less trouble for her mum.

Barry was kidding about having another five or six and Tess told him in no uncertain terms;

"Tie a knot on it. I have bought an economy pack of condoms and you're not coming anywhere near me without at least three of them on you."

He knew she was half kidding but deadly serious at the same time. She'd had a rough time giving birth to all her children and it wasn't easy rearing three of them in a small council house where you could hardly swing a cat.

But they loved the little house and spent every spare penny doing it up. Barry, with Tess's dad, had built an extension a few years before, creating an area where they could sit around the kitchen table for evening meals, where their friends could chat or for them to be together over a cup of tea.

He claimed evening was the best time of the day for him especially as Jimmy was old enough now to feed himself and he didn't end up covered in goo. He'd teach the children how to use their knife and fork properly, cutting the meat for them and chatting to them as they ate. Afterwards he would read stories and he was now teaching Grainne, their oldest to tell the time.

"Well! He won't be doing that for a while," she sighed

Tess loved her kitchen too because it meant she had her own space while the children played in the living room.

Barry worked with his father-in-law in the construction business. It wasn't a big firm but they made enough to get by. She'd met him when he'd come to the house with her dad for tea a few times.

Her father would laugh, "I can't think what the attraction is but that fella's always making excuses to come up here. I'd better watch him in case he is after the family jewels."

"The only jewels that boy is after has blond hair and gets all giggly when he's about," laughed her mother.

"If he'd ask her out we might all get a bit of peace," said her brother Sean, from behind the newspaper "All we hear is Barry this and Barry that, when he's not here and she won't say a word to him when he's here," he teased.

They eventually got around to talking to each other and within a short time they were engaged and married. It was a small wedding and she and her mum made her dress. All she cared about was that they'd be together. The money they saved went into buying their little council house with a little help from her parents. In a short time she was pregnant and in the following four years the three children were born.

"Oh Yeah! Watch the quiet ones," her brother would tease them.

Their dream was to own a house in the country with a bedroom each for the children and enough land for a few animals. The plan was that Barry and her father plus a few friends could build it for next to nothing.

Then he would laugh; "All we need is for some kind soul to give us a plot to build on."

"And the money for the bricks and mortar," Tess would laugh back.

She loved the thought that they would move out of the city and live in open green fields one day with a few animals to take care of and a dog, especially a dog. She felt it would be unfair to keep one where they lived now with no space for it to run but she would love one.

"One day," she would say and smile at the thought.

She'd once seen a documentary about llamas on TV and read that they made good pets and their wool was highly prized and told him she could see a field with half a dozen in it. She would sell the wool or learn to weave and knit with it and Barry would tease her about it,

"I could always get you one for the back yard for Christmas. You could shear the wool off, weave it and knit jumpers for the children to wear."

They joked about putting it in the shed with the coal. Their dreams and sense of humour got them through the days of Belfast during the Troubles at the beginning of the seventies.

3

Barry had taken his bath earlier in the day as it took ages to reheat the water with the back boiler in the range. Tess waited a few hours to have hers so the water would be reheated. When she'd finished she could bathe the three children in the same bathwater as she'd used before they went to bed. Everything had to be economised.

On other evenings she would steep Barry's work clothes in the water she had washed the children in. This would loosen any heavy dirt before she put them in the top loading washing machine, run them through the mangle and hang them in the shed in the back yard to dry.

But that was for other evenings; this evening she got the older children into their pyjamas, took them downstairs where she dried their hair by the fire and bundled them off to bed. She had pulled her nightdress over her slip so the children wouldn't know she was going out. Her fingers were crossed they wouldn't notice the little bit of make-up she was wearing.

For a change they were as quiet as mice and promptly went off to sleep once she had read them a story. She collected her coat when she finished dressing and tip toed down stairs again.

"That long walk in the park today certainly tired them out," she remarked to her mother.

"Nothing like fresh air to wear the wee ones out," smiled her mother back as she helped tidy up the kitchen.

"Wow! You scrub up nicely," Barry laughed as she came into the living room. "I haven't seen you dressed up like that in ages. Nice dress, nice legs. You look great."

"Cheeky!" she smiled back, pleased he still noticed her.

She wore a black and white mini dress she hadn't worn for years and felt almost like the young woman she used to be.

"Very nice, dear," said her mum. "Your hair looks lovely." Ignoring the dress as Tess knew she would. Her mum had very old fashioned ideas about how young people should dress and mini dresses did not come into it.

"You'll be all right?" she asked her mum as they headed for the front door.

"Of course I will," she replied "Your dad will be over after for a while to keep me company and haven't I reared you lot? I know what I'm doing. Go on out and enjoy yourselves."

Tess hugged her and they headed off in a taxi to Margaret's house where the party was being held.

4

A few other guests had arrived before them and the craic was starting. Some guys were tinkering with guitars, banjos and a fiddle or two in the corner, debating about songs they should sing. As usual, as in most Irish conversations there was a lot of banter.

Tess and Barry relaxed into the atmosphere of the night and the next couple of hours were spent mingling and chatting with others, some of whom they saw most days but others who only made the occasional appearances at weddings and funerals. Old school friends or work colleagues dotted the groups.

With the segregation of Catholics and Protestants in many areas in Northern Ireland most people knew each other in their own area and the night was spent catching up on what was happening in each other's lives. Since the introduction of internment the Troubles were never far from any discussion - who had been lifted or shot, what premises had been bombed, who had been raided, what damage had been done, what fire damage sale was on and what had been bought at them were regular topics? Some areas were getting the worse of the Troubles and many of the people present were badly affected by it.

"They call it 'The Troubles' but to me it's an all-out war!" one man said.

Barry put his arm around the man's shoulders and said;

"That's a discussion for tomorrow; let's not let them spoil Margaret's party tonight with it."

"You're right, Barry. Let's not spoil Margaret's party discussing the Brits, they have spoiled enough of our lives already," slurred the man, a little the worse for the wear.

Around ten thirty Margaret mentioned that they would run out of drink shortly if someone didn't go to the off – licence before it closed. Barry, overhearing this, laughed and said;

"God forbid that would happen at an Irish birthday party, we'd hate to ruin your birthday, Mags, especially for the price of a few bottles of booze. I haven't got the van with me but if someone can run me to the off-licence I'll get something we can drink."

"I'll go with you," said Tess

She didn't want to drink too much as she had the children to look after in the morning and didn't fancy waking up with a hangover. Going to the off-licence would take her away from the party and the drink for a while. Someone was always topping up her glass as she stood around chatting and she wasn't used to so much alcohol.

Owen, one of the other men in their circle agreed to drive them. He had just arrived and hadn't had a drink yet and Owen's wife Mary decided she would go with them too so the four of them set off.

The craic was good in the car as they drove. It was a good night to be out and they felt young and free again. Like a lot of Irish men and women Owen and Mary were good story tellers and they chatted away about different people they all knew and most of the stories were funny. As Barry said laughing;

"They lost nothing in the telling."

Just as they were half way down the Springfield Road there was a check-point with soldiers stopping cars but no one seemed too bothered about it? They were so used to being stopped when they went out, it was almost second nature to them and another everyday practice they had to put up with in their lives now.

If you were going into the city of Belfast any day you could be searched five or six times. If you were driving you could be stopped anywhere at any time and searched. Sometimes you were taken out of your car and the door panels and other parts taken off.

With internment now in place the fear of being lifted was a worry in the back of everyone's mind. People knew they could be lifted off the street at any time just by being in the wrong place at the wrong time or being in the company of the wrong person.

Like a lot of things that were happening in Northern Ireland now, people had to put up with it. They accepted it as just another obstacle to add to the many others that they hated having to live with. While knowing it was happening to others they prayed it would never happen to them or anyone belonging to them.

But this time, as soon as they pulled up at the check-point, they knew it was different. When Owen stopped the car the door was yanked open and both men were pulled out of the car on to the street and frog marched up a side alley by the soldiers. The women were left stunned in the car.

Within seconds Mary was out of the car and called after the soldiers;

"What are you doing? Where are you taking them?"

At this point Tess was also out of the car. After a minute or so they could hear the soldiers beating the two men. The thumps and kicks echoed down the alley to them. Other soldiers then dragged the women along the street and held them at gun point by the side of the road for ten minutes. All the time they could hear the brutality going on up the alley. The moans and cries of the men in pain and the shouts and taunts of the soldiers were audible.

Tess was horrified and started shouting;

"Why are you doing this to Barry? He's done nothing wrong. Stop that, please stop that, leave them alone! Our husbands haven't done anything! There is no need for all this cruelty! My husband is the father of three young children! He has done nothing wrong!" she screamed.

The soldier threw Tess on the ground and told her to shut her fucking mouth or she would get the same.

Of course she had heard stories of the brutality meted out to different people but never passed any remarks about it. She didn't really believe it could be true. Now she was hearing and witnessing it at first hand and she was shocked beyond belief.

They called her a lot of filthy names and she was horrified that someone could treat her or Barry like this. She was a decent person and so was Barry, they were good parents and came from good families, how could they be treat like this? What was happening to their world?

She kept shouting at the soldiers to leave Barry alone. While she was shouting Mary was pleading with her to be quiet.

"Say no more, Say no more, please! You have the children to look after. They might lift all of us! These boys don't care about you, Barry or your children. They'd as soon shoot you. Please stop shouting, Tess."

At that the two men were dragged out of the alleyway and bundled into the Land Rover that was parked at the checkpoint and it tore off up the street with some of the soldiers in it.

Tess was in shock, she couldn't believe what was had just happened. She had seen Barry's face and it was covered in blood.

"Where are you taking our husbands?" she shouted at the soldiers left behind. She jumped up off the street and stood shouting and running after the departing Land Rover.

They caught her and she was once again forced face down on to the street with Mary alongside her. They put the barrel of the guns to their heads and told them to shut up or they would be sorry. Then they laughed, ran off and got into the other Land Rover parked further up the road.

Shouting obscenities back at them about their families and what they would do to their husbands and to them when they saw them next they drove off. The two women dragged themselves up off the street.

Tess was frantic and shouted repeatedly to Mary;

"What are we going to do? What are we going to do?"

Mary put her arms around Tess and held her. She had become very quiet and now seemed to be taking it all very calmly.

"Owens's brother lives up the road and I can drive the car to his house, I think. We'll go and tell him what's happened. He'll know what to do," she replied to Tess' frantic pleas.

"How the hell can you be so calm?" Tess shouted, pulling herself away from Mary.

"I can't let them bastards see me upset. You shouldn't either," said Mary.

"But this is horrifying. Are they going to intern them? Why did they just target our car? What about the men in all the other cars they stopped? Why didn't they lift them? What are we going to do?" shouted Tess continually, clearly in shock, repeating everything and rambling.

"I've no idea what they are going to do with them," replied Mary "Calm down, Tess, we've got to think. I've no licence to drive but I think I can get us to Ballymurphy where we'll decide what to do. I've only had a couple of driving lessons from Owen for a bit of fun but I know how to change gears and brake so we should get to Owens' brother's house all right."

"How the hell can you be so calm?" repeated Tess "That's your husband too that they've battered and carted off."

"Someone has got to keep control here, now get into the car. As long as the RUC don't decide to stop us and find I have no licence, we might get away with it."

"It's just as well you can nearly drive because I can't, I feel so helpless! What are we going to do?" she kept repeating, while running her hand through her hair. "I just don't know what I'm going to do," she was panicking and crying all at the same time.

"The first thing you do is stop panicking. It's not helping. We need a plan," said Mary sternly as she put her arm around Tess's shoulder again and shook her "We'll get through this. They won't beat us and you can't let them think they are going to beat us. Come on! You're stronger than this."

The two women got into the car with Tess calming down a bit. After a few very bumpy stops and starts they reached Mary's brother-law's house without further mishaps. Luckily there was very little traffic on the road. For the rest of the night they tried to find out where the men had gone.

"We'll go to the nearest barracks and check if they were taken there," said Mary.

When they got to the first barracks they were told they weren't there and they were sent to another. When they got to the second one they were told they had been moved on again and at the next one they had been moved to somewhere else. This went on for hours and by morning light they still hadn't found them.

Tess had frantically called in at home and spoken to her mother to tell her what was happening. She and her father were staying with the children while the women were driven all over Belfast by Owen's brother.

By dawn the women were exhausted and numb with shock. When her solicitor's office opened Tess was at his door first thing, to get him to find out where Barry was being held. He was used to dealing with problems like this over the previous few years and didn't hold out much hope for him not being detained and possibly interned.

The first question he asked Tess was;

"Do you think he will recognise the courts if he is charged with anything?"

"Oh God! I don't know. But what could they charge him with if he hasn't done anything?" asked Tess worried.

"There are a lot of men in Long Kesh who have done nothing to deserve being there but nevertheless they are there," replied her solicitor.

Tess's heart sank when she heard this for two reasons. She knew now they could intern him without taking him to court and keep him for as long as they liked but if they choose to charge him with whatever trumped up charges they could come up with she had a feeling Barry would not recognise the courts. He had often spoken about it and agreed with other men who had been charged not doing so. He claimed he could not recognise a court which was there to quell the Catholics and the Nationalist community with no justice for them in it.

If it came to Barry going to court he would do time. It would be expected of him by the community and he would do it. She just knew it in her heart.

Something changed in Tess as she thought this. She could feel her skin crawl and the shock spread through her system. She now felt sure in her heart that this was what was going to happen. No matter how she tried to deny it, the feeling stayed with her.

The solicitor said he would let her know when he had any news and she left a very troubled young woman. Eventually she got word of where he was being kept and she went to see him. But when she got to the barracks she was told she couldn't see him as he was being interrogated. Once again she was turned away.

When she told her mother this she said,

"Barry won't speak to them and if he doesn't, they'll just lock him up."

"But he has done nothing wrong," she kept insisting.

"It doesn't matter, love. He comes from a Republican area and we are all tarred with the one brush," remarked her mother.

Tess couldn't understand any of this and wouldn't believe it could be true.

"But Barry has done nothing wrong. He's never been involved in anything," she cried again and again but no matter what she said it made no difference. She was at the end of her tether!

When she left her mother she hauled herself home and threw herself on the couch, totally spent. Her mother came in later and made her a cup of tea and insisted she go to bed where she cried herself to sleep, exhausted. A few hours later she was up and out again trying to find some way of getting Barry home. No one seemed able to help.

Next day Tess got word that a detention order had been served on him and the following day Internment Papers came through her letterbox saying he was being sent to Long Kesh.

This was the worst case scenario Tess could have envisioned and it was something many women throughout Northern Ireland feared and experienced. Long Kesh? Everyone knew that this meant it would be months at least before their loved ones would be out again.

"God only knows how long they will keep them," said Mary when they met up later.

She had called constantly on Tess to give her updates and to find out what was happening with her. That morning she'd received the same papers as Tess.

"What are we going to do?" cried Tess almost delirious with lack of sleep and worry.

"You're going to take one day at a time, the same as me. You are going to pull yourself together and look after yourself because your children need you now more than ever and you are not going to let them bastards destroy you," she exclaimed.

Everything was going through Tess's mind. She could see so many problems arising and didn't know how she was going to cope.

"We've spent most of Barry's wages on renovating the house and the present and drink for Margaret's birthday. What am I going to do for money for food, heat and light?" she asked.

"Stop worrying about the future and take each day at a time. You are well capable of getting through this. You don't know how strong you are until you come up against serious problems like this," returned Mary. "You have to believe in yourself. The first thing you do is sign on for Social Welfare! That will get you a few pounds."

Barry always brought his wages home and gave them to Tess for the family's needs, keeping very little back for necessities for himself. They had very few luxuries and practically no savings. All their money went into the family and the home. She had given up her job to rear the children and couldn't see how she could get one now with them still so young.

"Dear God! I can't believe my husband has been interned," Each time the thought struck her the shock hit her again anew. "Interned, Interned" seemed to scream in her head.

She had heard many stories of people being interned but it had meant nothing to her until now.

Outside of Tess's little home things were very different for many.

'Internment was introduced in 1971 by the Unionist Government primarily to suppress Republican opposition. Men and women were lifted off the street regularly and interned without trial and often without crime. Their only crime often being that they were Catholic.

The Nationalist community was very angry at this and their anger grew when news of ill treatment of the internees became public. This anger increased support for the IRA and ushered in the start of a campaign of civil disobedience that had overwhelming support in the Nationalist communities.'

Tess couldn't understand why it had impacted on her family as the Troubles had never touched their immediate circle before. They had attended a few protest marches and other demonstrations but that was the most involvement they'd ever had. Barry was a quiet man and wasn't involved in any paramilitary activity that she knew of. She believed she would have known if he had been.

As a member of the neighbourhood watch he worked with others to try and control the violence in the area and to safeguard the population of West Belfast but that may very well have been all it took to get him arrested and interned. She never knew him to have anything to do with violence. He was a real family man and spent the majority of his time working or with the family. Now it was as though her whole world had been turned upside down and gone crazy.

Tess did a lot of thinking over the next few days and kept remembering what Mary had said; "We need a plan!"

"That's it! I need a plan to get me through this," she thought. But her mind was too stunned yet to think sensibly or to plan anything.

She would never understand how they could possibly think her husband was involved in the IRA or any other paramilitary activities. But whether they did or not she knew she was on her own with three young children to rear. She had no idea when she would have her husband home again and she was terrified.

"How can I get a job to earn enough to pay a babysitter and run the house?" was one of her first sane thoughts for many days.

This was her dilemma on a cold October morning as she made breakfast for the children and tried to stop herself crying when they asked where daddy was.

She quietly told them, "Daddy is gone away for a while. I'm not sure when he'll be back."

They were too young to understand what internment meant and Tess didn't want to explain something so terrible to them. How could she expect them to understand when she couldn't understand herself?

5

Continually she held long conversations in her mind about what had happened and what people said. Then she remembered something else Mary had said to her, “don’t let them think they have beaten you.”

She felt her backbone straighten, somehow her strength was returning and she focused her anger on the security forces. She was now very angry;

“I will show them. They won’t defeat me, I won’t let them.” She stormed as she went around the house like a whirl wind cleaning and polishing.

“Come on girl, stick that head up, you’re going to get through this,” she told herself. “The first thing you do is go up to my mum’s and ask her to keep the kids until you find out what is happening and what you have to do to survive,” she continued to herself.

Shaking herself she finished putting the breakfast things away and got the children ready for the road.

“Come on. We’re going to granny’s house,” she told them.

As she was heading out the door her brother Sean called to see if she was all right. “Ma sent me down to bring you and the wee ones up.”

“I suppose there’s an inquest going on in the house up there and everyone knows what has happened.”

“Of course we all know, Ma and Da are worried sick about you and the wee ones and the girls want to do what they can for you. We’re here for you. And you know this place, everyone knows the news nearly before it happens or before you know it yourself. Come on sis, we’ll get you through this,” he said as he hugged her by the shoulders.

“Of course there has to be a family conference on what to do with Tess!” she snapped.

Then she shook her head and said, “I know there’s no reason to be angry at the family, they are the only ones now I can rely on now. I’m just so angry with the injustice of it all!”

“Of course you are and where else would we be but supporting you through this?"

Sean was anxious to help, he had seen it all before with many other women whose men had been lifted. The feeling of desperation and loss was clearly etched on his sister's face as it had been on all of theirs. Now he put young Jimmy on his shoulders and took the other children's hands as they walked up the road to their Ma's house.

"We're all there for you, Tess! We'll do what we can!"

"I know you will," she replied "It's just that I feel so helpless."

"We'll sort something out for you. Don't give up!"

"Oh! I won't give up, I can't. I have to look out for the children and as Mary said I can't let the Brits think they have beaten me."

"That's the girl," said Sean.

When she arrived at her mother's it was obvious the family conference had already begun. The bad news had obviously spread fast and a few neighbours had called to add their penny's worth. Her two sisters were there and both had their own ideas of what she should do.

Sean and Tess let them chat on for a while about different people they knew that had been lifted, saying very little. Her mother was also quiet. It was clear they were all worried about Tess. She was not seen as being the strongest of the sisters and they wondered how she would cope with Barry's internment. They knew how close they were and how much Tess relied on his support.

After the tea was made Sean stopped all conversation and told Tess;

"This is what you will do. Go to the Sinn Fein Office and tell them what has happened. They will tell you the procedures you have to go through. They're used to it by now with all the other men and women who have been lifted. Tell them you have no money and you need some for rent and food until you get the Social Welfare for yourself and the kids. It's important you do this now so they will get it to you before you run out of money for food. When you come back I will go over and chat to you. Ma will keep the kids for the day and we will work out a plan. Get Mary and take her with you. She knows a lot of the men there and she'll have to sort her own situation out too!"

"How does she know these men?" asked Tess.

"It's a long story," replied her brother.

"And how do you know all these things?" Tess snapped.

"Ah! Don't be silly, of course I know these things. I'm out on the streets every night looking after the area and people get lifted all the time and we have to deal with the families left behind. I'm just sorry it happened to Barry. He's done nothing to be lifted for."

"What about Owen? Has he done something to be lifted for?" asked Tess quietly as it occurred to her the soldiers might have been looking for a specific person when they'd lifted the men.

"Ah! Well now, that could be a different story," replied her brother.

Tess was stunned and she knew immediately why Barry had been lifted.

"Damn him, damn him and whatever he was up to! He got Barry lifted as well as himself," she said angrily.

"Now Tess!" Don't start blaming Owen! Barry knew Owen's history as well as I do. He took his chances. I'm sure Owen didn't aim to be lifted either," said her mother.

"For God's sake! Do you know all about him too? What kind of a gobshite am I that I know none of these things?" shouted Tess as she whirled around to face her mother.

"The only thing that was important to you in your life for the last eight years was your family and home and that's how it should be," said her mother calmly "You had enough on your hands having your babies and rearing them to be bothered about what was happening outside your home."

"But if I had known about Owen I wouldn't have let Barry go with him in the car. Why wasn't I told?" she asked angrily.

"You know we don't gossip about these things in this house," said Sean "It wasn't anything to do with you."

"Well! It certainly is now!" she returned.

"Look! These things happen and we have to deal with them the best way we can when they do," said her mother "Now go and get Mary and go to the Sinn Fein office and see how that goes. Come back here and I'll make something to eat. Then you and Sean can go and find out when you can visit Barry and we can work from there. We'll get through this together. We're all here for you, Tess."

"I know, Ma! I'm sorry but I'm so worried and so angry," she said as she gave her mum a hug and left the house.

She went down the street fuming with the injustice of it all. Barry was an innocent man who happened to be in the wrong place at the wrong time with the wrong person. Now she and the children had to suffer the consequences. She knew now, in her heart, that neither she, her family nor Barry had any involvement with paramilitary activities.

"What a fool I am?" she thought.

She had been beating herself up that maybe there was something she didn't know about Barry, that got him lifted. She had even started to blame herself and him.

"Maybe it was because I marched down the Falls Road?" she had thought to herself.

"There is no way they would lift Barry because I marched down the Falls Rd with a couple of thousand other women," she thought to herself "How would they pick me out of that crowd? And if they were going to lift anyone for that it would be me not him!"

One of Tess' abiding memories of the Troubles would always be the women breaking the curfew of the Falls Road where Noreen, one of her sisters, lived.

6

The British Army carried out house to house searches in what was known as 'The Rape of the Falls' for IRA members and ammunition in July 1970. A curfew was brought in for three days and all movement of people was restricted. House searches lasted for two days with a lot of destruction to homes and the contents which angered the community.

The army uncovered a small amount of arms and explosives but the manner in which the searches were carried out broke any remaining goodwill left between the Catholic community and the Security Forces.

During the curfew there were gun battles between the IRA and the Army. Two people were killed by the British Army during the violence. One of those was killed deliberately when run over by an army vehicle. Another person was shot by them and died later.

7

Even this had very little impact on Tess. Of course she was sorry for her sister who lived there because she couldn't get enough food to feed her children but Barry went over with the necessities to her at night, taking to back lanes and in and out of houses to avoid the security forces because no one was allowed in or out of the area. Food vans and lorries, including milk men, were stopped at the barricades and not allowed in either.

Then children became sick and doctors weren't allowed in to treat them. One morning the word spread like wild fire around the areas in West Belfast that women from all over the area were to march on the barricades. They knew they had to do something about it and a decision was made to break through the barricades the army had erected to stop the deliveries and services into the area.

It was as though the word was spread by smoke signals or drums because within a short time hundreds of women appeared from streets and houses all over the place spewing out from Lenadoon, Andersonstown, the White Rock, Turf Lodge, Ballymurphy Ardmonagh and down the Falls Road.

Tess joined her sister and thousands of other women and they marched without stopping, pushing prams and push chairs and collecting others as they walked to the bottom of the Falls Road. Here they hauled aside the barricades defying the British Army to stop them. In doing this they broke the curfew while the British army stood by astonished and helpless.

She had been really impressed with the power of the women that day but didn't really think it included her. She was only there because of her sister and her children and because her mother and sisters had asked her to come. Each time she thought of that epic march down that road the hair stood on the back of her neck. Women, pushing prams and carrying toddlers, hundreds of them, mothers, daughters, grannies and great grannies all together, singing, "We Shall Not Be Moved". She couldn't hold back the tears as she thought of it; she was so proud of those women and now she wanted to be strong like them.

It was an impressive sight, all bravely marching on the military blockades, pushing the barricades aside and walking through with their prams and children, ignoring the soldiers with their guns and tanks. They women needed food and care for their children and they were going to get it, one way or another and to hell with the army or anyone else.

Like every woman there she was glad and proud of what they had done. But then she went home to her nice little house, closed the door and locked the world outside once again. She saw herself as one step removed from all that was going on. It wasn't relevant to her immediate family so nothing for her to worry about.

Barry was really impressed she had taken part but Tess didn't think much of her role. For some reason she seemed to see herself as separate from the other women, not at all significant. Even when the Ballymurphy Massacre occurred, it didn't seem to impede much on her psyche.

In the thirty plus years of the Troubles it was possibly the greatest atrocity meted out to the people of Belfast. In August 1971 eleven ordinary civilians were shot dead on the street in the Ballymurphy area of West Belfast by the British Army Parachute Regiment as though they were picking off pheasants or grouse as they hunted, without respect for human life. That the army could do this and get away with it, in a modern western country, defied belief. People now knew that it didn't matter who or where you were: if you were Catholic you were seen as fair game by the British army and liable to be shot without compunction at any time.

Included in the eleven victims of this atrocity was a Catholic Priest who was waving a white flag aloft while going to rescue a young man wounded and lying dying on the street, a mother of eight looking for some of her children who were out playing, a young man who was trying to reach his friend lying wounded on the ground and a father who had been up to his daughter's house to check if she was OK.

None of the victims had guns and most were shot in the back. Their only crime was that they were on the street at that particular time. These incidents happened over a period of two days and changed the thinking of many: if these were permitted actions by the army then they knew there was no hope of getting justice from the British. They had put themselves above the law. They had shot eleven human beings dead on the street and the people knew now it could happen to any of them. Human or civil rights didn't apply to the treatment they could expect from Britain.

The regiment that carried out this atrocity was the same regiment responsible for the Bloody Sunday shootings in Derry five months later on 30th January in 1972.

Many saw only one answer to these actions; all-out war, a war that would last for over thirty years.

8

Tess had heard all about these atrocities but she didn't let it in. She could hear the bombs going off in the distance and the shootings; she listened to stories from others of the traumatic incidents occurring daily but seldom questioned why they were happening. It hadn't touched her family so it was not relevant to her! She was immune to it.

"No!" she thought "Not relevant to me then but by God it is relevant to me now. And all of this was not my fault or Barry's!"

"Well! I'm not taking this lying down!" she thought "Nobody messes with my family and gets away with it. I will go to the Sinn Fein office and I will get some funds to see me through. I'll then go to the Social Welfare Office and sign on for the Bru so I'll have regular money coming in to feed the kids and I'll try and get to see Barry in Long Kesh and see how he is. Then I'll work from there. From the looks of things I need to educate myself too on what is going on around here."

She carried on down the street to collect Mary with sparks almost flying from her feet. Mary hadn't even mentioned that Owen was involved with the IRA. She was furious with her now as well as with Owen and her attitude was very frosty towards her as they walked to the Sinn Fein office while she wondered what to say.

"They will all know by now that they were lifted and they will know what we want too when they see us there. Unfortunately we are not the first women they met looking for help after one of the family was lifted," remarked Mary realising that Tess probably knew about Owen by now.

"You would know all about that, wouldn't you?" snapped Tess.

"I'm not the enemy," said Mary quietly "I'm not the British army nor am I involved in the IRA."

"No! But Owen is."

"What Owen does is not my responsibility," Mary said quietly.

"Obviously not but it certainly is Barry's and my responsibility now!"

exclaimed Tess.

"If I could change anything about that now I would do it but I can't and I'm very sorry."

"You could have done something the other night about it but you didn't. All you had to do was say it might not be safe to travel with you."

"Do you have any idea how many times I've wished I had said something, I didn't know they would be waiting for Owen. I didn't know they were stopping on the Springfield Road!"

Tess ignored her and stormed on down the street.

As they approached the building Tess realised the windows had iron grills on them. She'd never noticed this before. When they got to the door they had to ring a bell and there was shuffling heard from the inside before the door was eventually opened.

"What the hell are they doing leaving us standing here like paupers with everyone looking at us?" demanded Tess.

"They're checking to see who's here and that the Brits aren't on the street. Now they're opening the metal door on the inside," said Mary.

"It's like a jail!"

"Yes! They have to suss out who's at the door in case they might attack them before they open it and the grills are to stop intruders or bombs being lobbed into the building."

"What a way to live! You seem to know a lot about their activities?"

"I did a bit of cleaning in there one time some of the top boys were visiting."

"Christ! I've heard it all now. How bloody involved are you with what is going on around here?"

"I was only cleaning the bloody place, Tess. I wasn't making bombs!" snapped Mary.

"I don't know what to believe any more!"

Tess felt she had learned a lot in the few days since Barry had been lifted and the more she learned the more she felt she didn't know what was going on.

"How's it going, Tess?" a familiar voice asked as the door finally opened.

Looking up surprised she saw her neighbour who lived two doors away from her holding the door and waiting for her to step into the hall. She was so shocked to see him there she didn't know what to say and just walked past him.

When she went into the office she was greeted by name by a number of men she knew fairly well. Leaning on a table was a cousin of Barry's chatting to Helen's brother, Jody, whom she had known since they went to school together.

She hadn't known what to expect when she decided to come to the office but she hadn't expected she would know nearly all the men in the building by first name.

"I'm terribly sorry about Barry," said her neighbour. "Maybe they won't keep him too long."

"What are you doing here?" she whispered.

"Arragh! I give them a hand out every now and then," he replied.

"A hand out at what?" she queried.

"Oh! This and that!" he replied evasively "Maybe we can see what we can do for you today?"

Tess wanted to tell them all to 'shove it' but she realised she needed their help and beggars couldn't be choosers.

Standing casually around, someone made a cup of tea and they all chatted for a while like they were standing in someone's kitchen. Two seats were produced for the women and the men stood leaning on filing cabinets and other furniture.

The conversation mostly concerned the weather and what had happened to their two husbands, all very understanding and agreeable. It was decided the office would look after the two women with a few pound here and there when they had an emergency and pay for heat and food for both families until their Social Welfare came through. Although, they emphasised, they had very little money and could only give a little to all the families with fathers or husbands interned.

Tess felt demoralised standing there trying to make polite conversation. She had never had to beg for anything in her life but she did not know how she was would cope if she didn't take what she could where she could get it now. She had to look after her children. She knew her family would help where they could but they didn't have much either.

She hated it even more that it was from people she knew, her neighbours and family friends. Her face was burning with embarrassment, she couldn't look the men in the eyes while they spoke to her and she headed for the door as soon as she could, vowing she would never put herself in that position again.

"Jesus! Is everyone involved in the Troubles except me?" she murmured to herself as she left the building.

"We'll not get rich from that lot anyway," said Mary. "And to think of all the time Owen spent fighting their bloody war for them!"

"Yeah! And if he hadn't been fighting their bloody war Barry would still be here with me and I wouldn't be begging for a pittance from them!" said Tess angrily "And my children wouldn't be without their father."

"Well! Don't blame me!" snorted Mary "I didn't send him out and he wouldn't listen to me. And quite frankly someone has to fight the British injustices and I couldn't expect others to do it if I wouldn't let my husband do it."

"Well! I hope you think it's worth it."

"I'm sorry, Tess. I really am! If I could turn back the clock I really would. I know you're suffering for something that is neither you nor Barry's fault but I can't change what happened."

Tess said nothing for a while. She knew it wasn't Mary's fault and she was in the same situation as she was but with twice as many children. She had enough on her plate without her taking strips off her for Owen's behaviour. She finally calmed a little.

"I know it's not your fault. I'm just mad that I didn't know Owen was involved or maybe I could have stopped him driving the other night and they wouldn't have been lifted. Why didn't you stop us going with him?" replied Tess.

"I wish I had but what was I supposed to say?" "Hey you know Owen is in the IRA and the Brits may have their eye on him so don't go to the off-licence with him!" I didn't know there were up the street waiting to lift him!"

"I don't know! You could have said something, anything, so Barry didn't end up being lifted with him!"

"I didn't know it would happen, Tess. And how do you think I feel? Before it happened I spent night after night waiting to hear if Owen had been shot dead, blown up or arrested and not being able to do anything about it. He wouldn't listen to anything I had to say. I had to put up with it. My children are without their father too but at least now I know where he is and it's unlikely he'll be killed in there. I love that man but it doesn't mean I have to agree with everything he does or even know what he's been up to!"

"But damn it! If I had suspected anything the other night Barry wouldn't be in jail now. Owen should have gone himself, why did he take us with him?" shouted Tess frustrated.

"What's the point of shouting at me? I didn't have them arrested; it was the Brits who arrested them. Blame them if you want to blame anyone!"

"Damn the cruel bastards!"

"Exactly! It's them your anger should be directed towards, not me!"

"You're right! I'm just so upset. I shouldn't be blaming you. You're in the same situation as me and you have more mouths to feed."

"I will survive as long as I know Owen is safe and not running about the place trying to take pot shots at the Brits."

"How long do you think they will keep them?" asked Tess anxiously, too worried to have any sympathy for her and too exhausted to be angry any more.

"Years!" said Mary "There are boys in there already who have done two or three years and it doesn't look like they are going to get out any day soon. They are taking a lot of them to court and sentencing them to years imprisonment instead of keeping them interned."

"Oh! Jesus! I thought you were going to say weeks, maybe months," said Tess. "This is worse than I thought. That means I could be a lone parent for the next four or five years. The wee ones won't know their daddy when he gets out. They'll grow up without him."

"You can take them to visit him," said Mary.

"For Christ's sake what good is half an hour a week to them? How could they build a relationship with him or keep the relationship they have with him going on a half hour a week?" said Tess stunned, as the reality of the situation finally dawned on her.

"It's all we have now," replied Mary.

Each hour seemed to bring another blow for Tess.

9

Over the next six months life found its own routine for Tess. Each day was a struggle to make ends meet, running from office to office trying to get money from Social Welfare, children's allowance, Charity Shops, looking after the house and children and arranging visits to Barry.

Running the home was a game of robbing Peter to pay Paul and vice-versa the following week. She met other women in the same situation whose husbands, fathers or brothers were interned and in a very short period of time she learned further how very little she knew about what was happening around her. But she was learning fast.

The women took to dropping into each other's houses and offering support wherever they could. They swapped clothes when going on visits to Long Kesh so they would look well and not let their husbands down. They shared the children's clothes and hand-me-downs were the order of the day for all the families.

It was a struggle every visit for Tess to get the children ready. They didn't like going to Long Kesh, all the security and searches scared them. They couldn't understand why their daddy couldn't come home and there was many a crying match when it came time to leave him.

Her heart broke each time she had to walk away and leave Barry sitting there with a look of devastation on his face. As hard as it was for her she felt Barry was getting a much worse deal. He had done nothing wrong and yet he was locked up and not allowed home to be with his young family who he loved dearly.

She felt too as if she was losing him with each visit. He was changing and his conversations were peppered with remarks about what should be done with the security forces and the Brits.

This was not something she would have heard from him before and it worried but didn't surprise her. She knew from listening to the other women that many innocent, peaceful men went in the gates of Long Kesh and in a short time, as a result of their treatment there, they developed militant tendencies.

The women put every penny they could spare into food and clothes parcels for their men so they wouldn't go without and would always look clean and well-dressed while they were locked up. They men didn't wear prison uniform as they had political status which differentiated them from the 'ordinary decent criminal' as the security forces called all other lawbreakers. They sent their laundry home and the women washed and ironed it and took it back to them on their next visits or they would send it in with some other women if they couldn't go themselves.

They had two visits a week, each for half an hour and the men expected a letter every day which meant finding someone who was going on a visit to a relative or get the drivers on the mini buses to take them.

One day after returning from a visit Tess was talking to her best friend Helen and mentioned, "Sometimes those boys on the bus are a bit saucy. Last week when I was going to Long Kesh the driver made a smart remark to me. It was really sexual and ignorant and one of the other women shouted at him."

"What did she say to him?" asked Helen. She was very protective towards her and annoyed that someone would target Tess for harassment.

"As though what she was going through is not enough for her to cope with," she thought.

Tess laughed, "Oh! She let him have it with both barrels blazing about him being a bloody pervert and what did he think he was doing harassing a lovely young woman who wouldn't spit on him if he was on fire."

"Here boy!" she shouted at him "You should be given bromide to curb them urges of yours like the soldiers in the last world war. Do ye really think a fine looking young woman like that would have anything to do with an ugly auld codger like you?"

"I laughed but I felt terrible. Is it not bad enough to have to deal with our husbands being interned than to have to put up with sexual innuendoes and insults from auld boys driving the bus?" asked Tess.

"What happened then?" asked Helen.

"The other women gave him a lot of stick too."

"When I was getting off the bus I said to one of the women 'Thanks for that', I don't know how to deal with boys like that."

"I know! But you better learn quick and the sooner the better. They don't really mean any harm and think they're being funny," she told me "and you're a bloody innocent! You could be travelling this road for many years to come so don't let them away with anything, just give as good as you get."

"I told her I didn't know how to answer him and just got embarrassed!

"You better learn then, I won't always be there to fight your corner," she told me

"She's right! You're too timid with people and if you keep it up they will walk all over you. You can't afford that when you are responsible for three children, it's time to toughen up. Between now and your next visit get a few smart remarks ready for the driver and make them funny. The women will laugh and he will back down. You can make this your next project," replied Helen laughing.

Tess smiled and remarked;

"Yes, I could, that's what I need to do, start to toughen myself up. I can practice on those boys and I think the women will back me. It could be fun! I have a feeling my education at this 'University of Life' is about to begin."

Helen laughed and she laughed with her. It was the first time she could see any hope in the future. Just a little glimmer but never the less, hope that she could and would survive.

Over the next few months many things came up which threw Tess into turmoil. Apart from paying bills and getting necessary repairs done to the house, one problem gave her more sleepless nights than others.

Although she was a married woman with children she was also very innocent and shy regarding anything of a sexual nature and she began to dread her visits to Long Kesh.

Barry, still being only twenty six years of age and with the natural urges of any young man was frustrated. He felt she should try and oblige him with what he called a 'quickie' and enjoy it while she visited. Tess was horrified that he would assume she would even think of having sex with him in an area where anyone passing could hear.

There was only a small cubicle where they sat and a warden could walk past at any time. She could not and would not feel comfortable getting intimate with him. Barry didn't seem to care about what she saw as blatant sexual exhibitionism but she certainly did.

"I can't let anyone undermine my dignity like that," she thought "I could not lower my self-esteem by acting like a cheap hussy just because he feels randy!"

It put her in a very compromising position. Although they would be separated from the other prisoners and their visitors by a thin wall, everything could be heard. Barry wasn't the only one who was frustrated but it still didn't help the feeling of embarrassment she felt by the pressure he was exerting on her.

She started to bring her children with her on every visit that she could and if they were at school and couldn't come she would cancel the visit.

She decided to discuss this with Helen one evening as she didn't know how she could go about telling Barry how she felt without hurting his feelings.

"Knowing my husband wants to make love to me and is frustrated is tough but I can't deliver what he wants because my pride wouldn't let me and knowing the screws would be listening or maybe even watching is enough to put me off anyway."

"Hey! Don't you worry about him and his urges, if he knows and loves you he will know this would be one step too far for you," said Helen "I bloody well wouldn't whip down my knickers for my boy knowing one of the screws might walk past. Wouldn't they just love that?"

"Would you not?" asked Tess surprised as she started to giggle "I thought you'd be fit for anything?"

"Not bloody likely. Can you hear the smart ass comments I would get going through check out?" retorted Helen "Oh! No! I wouldn't give them the satisfaction and they would probably enjoy it and fantasise about it. I wouldn't give them that pleasure. I would imagine they were lying in bed with their wives and fantasising about me. Ugh! Having said that, I hear there have been a few Long Kesh babies born."

"Good luck to them if they can do it but I'm so worried about it now I bring the children with me on most visits to avoid pressure from Barry," laughed Tess "And on other visits I let friends who have requested a visit go instead of me. I'm only too happy to oblige."

"That's crazy! I think you need to be honest with him. Stress on him that it is not going to happen," replied Helen "If you don't do this it is going to stand between you and cause further problems."

"I know I should face him and be honest about it but I don't want to hurt him, I just need to get the courage up to do it," said Tess.

"If you feel so strongly about something you cannot let someone else make you do what goes completely against your nature. You have a right to feel as you do! Now tell Barry how you feel. I'm sure he knows you well enough to know that this is against your nature," insisted Helen.

Tess was surprised that Helen felt as strongly about this as she did and got courage from this thought. On her next visit, later that week, she explained to Barry in detail why she could not behave intimately with him. He was really surprised at how strongly she came across about it.

"Hey, Tess! I didn't know you felt that way! I'd forgotten what a timid wee thing you are," he said "I just thought it would be a bit of fun. But now I understand how you feel, I'm sorry for pushing the point. I should have known you wouldn't be up for it. I just heard some of the boy talking about having sex with their wives and I thought I would like to try it."

"Well! If you do, it won't be with me!" said Tess, delighted she had sorted that problem out.

Barry laughed, "I'm afraid they don't supply that kind of service in here. You were the only candidate for the job."

"Well! This candidate does not appreciate the environment you expect her to work in and is rejecting your offer," she retorted laughing.

"Well! Can I have a hug instead?" asked Barry.

"Anytime," laughed Tess relieved.

Tess left Long Kesh that day a much happier woman. It had been hard to broach the subject with Barry but she was very glad she had. She was getting stronger every day.

"Maybe I need to believe in myself and express what I believe in more," She pondered.

A few days later she met Helen and told her about it and how embarrassed she was.

Helen retorted laughing, "You want to hear about embarrassing? Listen to this one. My hubby's mother was visiting him the other day and it was her first time because it breaks her heart that he is locked up. Anyway she didn't understand the search procedure. When she arrived at the camp she went into the room to be searched, you know the one where you go in one door and out the other?"

"Oh! Yeah! I know that room intimately," said Tess.

"Well! God love her! She was wearing one of those old fashioned corsets with all the bones in it and they ordered her to take it off. Then the screws took every one of the bones out of the corset. The air turned blue. She was raging! It's a wonder she didn't end up in the cell next to her beloved son, she created such a fuss."

"I don't believe you!" said Tess, bent over laughing "Oh! Poor Minnie!"

"It gave everyone such a good laugh that day. She came out of the prison with all the bones in her hands and the corset over her arm and everyone saw her and they thought it was hilarious. Not that she saw the funny side of it for a while. She sat on the bus the whole way home trying to put the bones back in and you can't put those things back in properly once they've been taken out," laughed Helen

"Ah, Bless her! The poor thing," said Tess.

"Poor thing, my backside! She was lapping up the attention. She'll live on that story for many years to come! She's talking about sending the bill for a new corset to the Governor of Long Kesh," laughed Helen.

The craic was better for Tess going to and from the internment camp after that. She tried to think of something smart to say to the driver on every journey and to get over being quiet and shy. Helen told her it was her re-birth and she was growing a backbone finally. As the months went by she grew bolder and braver and she enjoyed it.

The people of Belfast, surrounded with the Troubles on all sides, used humour as a safety valve to stop themselves from going mad or to cover up the desperation they felt.

Helen said many times, "If we didn't laugh we wouldn't stop crying. It's pure 'Gallows Humour'; we know we should be crying but we laugh, otherwise they could just lock us up and throw away the key!"

"There are many times I feel ready for a strait jacket and sometimes I think it would be a relief if they put me in one," said Margaret, one of the other women whose husband had also been interned.

"I don't care what kind of humour it is, it's keeping me going," exclaimed Tess "I spend my time now thinking of some smart crack I can use on the bus instead of worrying and crying. I feel so much better because of it too! I'm building up a great repertoire."

"Whatever gets you through the day, girl!" laughed Helen "Humour, it's the only thing that keeps us sane! If we didn't have it we would probably burn the Kesh down or get locked up in an insane asylum."

Many evenings the women spent an hour or so together in one or other of their houses, sitting around the kitchen tables chatting. All problems were discussed and solutions debated. This evening in Helen's house Tess said;

"Do you know what Barry handed me last week when I went to see him?"

"Oh Please! Don't tell me. I haven't had a wee bit for years and you're going to discuss your sex life with us," laughed Lucy, whose husband had already done a couple of years inside.

Tess laughed; "You may not have had a wee bit for years but your dirty mind hasn't improved," she said "Terribly sorry to disappoint you but I'm not going to disclose my closet sexual practises. The eejit handed me a big lump of rock."

"What are you talking about? Where did he get the rock?" asked Helen with an incredulous look.

"I think they watch too much TV in there. The great escape must have been showing," laughed Tess "I asked him what it was and he said a paper weight or a door stopper. He had written Long Kesh and the date on it in marker and let me tell you, he's no artist."

"When I asked him what I was supposed to do with it he told me to shut up and just take it! My face must have been a picture, Barry never ever told me to shut up before. I thought he must be upset that I didn't appreciate his artistic genius," laughed Tess

"I only asked!" I replied "Don't take my head off!"

"Sorry!" he muttered "Please just take it!"

"I then thought maybe he wanted me to start building a wall at home or something with bits of Long Kesh for when he comes home so he won't miss it too much."

"Your wit is really improving." laughed Helen.

"I must have looked confused because he started to explain in whispers that it was a piece of a tunnel they had started to dig and they were passing bits of it out to their visitors as paper weights or door stoppers or anything we choose to use them for."

"But don't they know Long Kesh is built on an old airfield with reinforced concrete so it will be impossible to dig a tunnel there?" asked Helen.

"I think they do now but they still had to get rid of the rocks," laughed Tess.

"They're mad," laughed Mary and Lucy

"I think it's just another way to annoy the screws. They're always trying to find ways to keep their morale up and create a bit of diversion and humour," said Tess.

"Mick wanted to see what the one nurse and only woman in the camp looked like last week, so he told the screws he had a toothache. They took him to the clinic and he was prepared to sacrifice a good tooth to get a look at her. He said it wasn't worth it as she was a long way from the Mona Lisa," laughed Helen.

"They're like little boys!" exclaimed Tess "I suppose given their circumstances if I was living in such cramped conditions in old Nissan huts I would try anything to lighten the monotony too. It must be difficult for them. They have to keep their minds occupied doing something."

"Those huts were once used for the airport authorities a long time before internment began. Winter must be tough in them with very little insulation in the walls and with concrete floors," said Helen pensively.

"That's why they are fighting to get the conditions improved. I'm sure we don't know the half of what goes on in there. Just like we don't tell them about the conditions we have to live with out here," said Lucy.

"Yeah! I'm sure they keep a lot from us as well," remarked Tess.

10

Internment

With the introduction of internment on the 9th August 1971, the RUC and British Army raided homes looking for suspects and arrested three hundred and forty two Catholics all over Northern Ireland. Word spread and the IRA were tipped off and most of them escaped capture. Some Protestants were arrested. One hundred and four of those arrested were released when it was discovered they had no paramilitary connections.

The Army and RUC were accused of using out-of-date information, bungling the operation and arresting the wrong people. All it did was create more anger in the Nationalist areas causing a huge influx of young people to join the ranks of the IRA.

By 1972 nine hundred and twenty four men and women were detained without trial and many without crime. By 1975 and the end of internment, one thousand nine hundred and eighty one people had been interned. One thousand eight hundred and seventy four or 95% were Catholic and one hundred and seven or 5%, were Protestants.

Long Kesh, was known as the H Block or the Maze and built in the Maze, an area outside Lisburn, nine miles from Belfast. Previously it had been a Royal Air Force base. The prisoners were held in Nissan huts which were freezing in the winter and like ovens in the summer.

It became an Internment camp in 1971 and three years later, a prison. The inmates played a prominent role in the history of Northern Ireland during the 70s, 80s and 90s with many protests, including the Dirty Protest and the Hunger Strike.

The Nationalist SDLP party ran a campaign of civil disobedience due to the introduction of internment and withdrew its representatives from a number of public bodies.

Sixteen thousand households withheld rent and rates for council houses also as part of the campaign of civil disobedience. One hundred and thirty non unionist councillors refused to sit on district councils.

Five members of the Northern Ireland Parliament including John Hume, Austin Currie and Bernadette Devlin began a forty eight hour hunger strike, against internment, in London, near 10 Downing Street. Protests continued until internment ended in December 1975.

The conditions in Long Kesh deteriorated and prisoner were constantly subjected to brutality by the wardens. This led to the prisoners taking action in 1974 by burning the Long Kesh cages and taking over the prison. The British Army came in and over two days of fighting, hundreds of prisoners were seriously wounded by rubber bullets fired at point-blank range and beatings by batons.

Then the British used helicopters to drop highly toxic CR Gas on the prisoners. As the fighting continued, the prisoners were driven into the centre of the camp and helicopters flew over and dropped the CR Gas on them. The operation was codenamed 'Snowdrop' and described by the British Army as "the contingency plan developed to deal with hi-jacking and other serious armed terrorist incidents". Members of the SAS were transported in helicopters trained to carry out the operation.

Many of those gassed had experienced the effects of CS gas from previously rioting on the streets of Northern Ireland but described that gas as a completely different sensation than the CR Gas used in Long Kesh.

Scientific research reports on the effects of CR gas says; 'It is six to ten times more powerful than CS gas. It causes intense skin irritation, in particular around moist areas, causing temporary blindness and coughing, gasping for air and panic and incapacitation. It is a suspected carcinogen and toxic but less so than CS gas, by ingestion and exposure. It can be lethal in large quantities and in poorly ventilated spaces an individual can inhale a lethal dose within minutes. Death is caused by asphyxiation and pulmonary oedema. The effect of CR gas is long-term and persistent. CR gas can persist on surfaces, especially porous ones, for up to sixty days'

Many ex-prisoners suffering from leukaemia and other carcinogenic diseases in later years blame their illnesses on being subjected to the gas in Long Kesh. It is reported that twelve to fifteen per cent of prisoners who had been subjected to the CR gas contracted different forms of cancer and other lung diseases.

In the weeks following the fighting, prisoners had their blood tested by the British Ministry of Defence who refused to explain why they were doing this.

Medical records for 1974 mysteriously disappeared never to be seen again. Some prisoners were able to get their medical records for the time they were in prison except for those from 1974. No one in the British Government admitted to taking blood samples from the prisoners.

For many years the internees and prisoners fought for justice in Long Kesh, for improvements in the conditions of the Nissan huts and to retain their status as political prisoners.

In 1972 there were one thousand one hundred Special Category prisoners in Long Kesh which gave them the same privileges as internees previously and included free association between prisoners, extra visits from family and friends, food parcels and the right to wear their own clothes rather than prison uniforms.

The British Government's policy on criminalisation coincided with the end of internment and the new Secretary of State for Northern Ireland, Merlyn Rees, ended Special Category Status on the 1st March 1976.

Those 'convicted' of 'terrorism' after that date were held in the eight "H-Blocks" in Long Kesh. The existing prisoners remained in separate compounds and retained their Special Category Status with the last prisoner to hold this status released in 1986. Some lost their Special Category Status when convicted in courts as ordinary criminals.

11

In 1974 Helen, Tess and Mary discovered that their husbands were being taken to court and being prosecuted for being members of the IRA and for their parts in 'subversive activities' and murder.

This came as a huge shock to Tess. She never thought for a second that it could happen. She'd always believed that Barry would continue his time in Long Kesh as an Internee and would be let out in a short time like a lot of other men. But it seemed the security authorities thought otherwise and would make him pay for being in the wrong place, at the wrong time, with the wrong person. They were going to hold on to him as long as they could.

Helen said "I can understand them prosecuting Mick because he's a known member of the IRA but they have nothing on Barry. He's one of the innocents in there."

"It doesn't seem to matter whether you're innocent or guilty," said Tess "Being Catholic is enough. All I know is we may now just get used to the ideas of them doing a lot longer inside than we thought."

The three women were sick with worry and didn't know what to do. This disturbing news brought up a lot of issues. They knew the men would never recognise the Diplock Courts, as this was the norm in Northern Ireland at that time for the majority of Nationalists.

"It's bound to go against them when sentencing," said Tess.

"The judge will throw the book at them and they will get years in jail," insisted Helen.

Nationalists did not get a good hearing in these courts. The British judicial system saw the prisoners as being in contempt of court and the prisoners saw the courts as being biased and corrupt. This point of view was shared by many across the world.

The Diplock Courts were established in 1973 and did not have a jury. Cases were heard by a judge and convictions could be decided on a confession and there are many stories of these confessions being extracted through torture and brutality. Although abolished in 2007, the system is still seen as a very sordid legacy of the Troubles in Northern Ireland.

When the court cases came around, Helen, Mary and Tess attended together on the different days of the men's trails. They were filled with trepidation every time. They sat stiffly on the hard seats trying to catch their men's eyes and let them know they supported them, no matter what happened.

The men refused to recognise any of the officials including the judge and wouldn't answer when addressed. The trials took place in different weeks with Helen's husband being the last to be sentenced.

To Tess's shock and horror, Barry got life with the recommendation that he do no less than fifteen years. With the time he had already done in internment this brought the sentence he would serve to at least twelve years.

He was accused along with Owen of the murder of a UDA man. Tess knew he had nothing to do with it but no matter what she said to anybody it made no difference. The men refused to hire a solicitor to fight their cases and they told the women they would not recognise the court no matter what they said or did or how they pleaded.

It was as though they were living in different worlds to the women with different priorities. The women worried about how they were going to cope with rearing their children on their own or keep the home going while the men worried about the political connotations connected to their cases. Fighting the British in whatever way they could was their number one priority, everything else took a poor second place.

Tess spoke to a solicitor who told her if the men didn't want to be represented than he could do nothing about it. The court got a solicitor for them but because the men wouldn't speak to him there was very little he could do.

Mary's husband Owen got the same sentence as Barry and they were taken away. It took a long time for the women to recover from the shock of such severe sentences.

Tess especially found it unfair. She knew Barry had nothing to do with murder and she couldn't understand why he did not fight to defend and save himself.

"What about me and the children?" she often asked herself.

"He has done no wrong!" she repeated to anyone who spoke to her, she felt helpless to change anything and she found the whole procedure beyond belief. It was all a horrible nightmare.

Although she was furious with the courts, she was also furious with Barry:

How could her interests and the interests of their children get pushed aside while they played the game of who was cock of the North? But even though she felt very strongly about it all, she knew she had to support Barry because at the end of the day he was innocent and he thought he was doing the right thing.

Mary took things a little better because she had known from the beginning what could happen and was half expecting it.

Helen was almost as shocked as Tess as she now knew for sure it would be a long time before she and Mick would be together again.

"Knowing it could happen is one thing but the reality is devastating when it comes and knowing we can do nothing about it is the killer," she told Tess.

There were many tears in the following weeks. Over and over they analysed what could or couldn't be done until they finally came to the only conclusion there was: there was nothing they could do except carry on as best they could. They would have to accept the situation as it was and learn to live with it. The men were not going to change, neither was their sentences nor the court.

Tess looked at the future without Barry as a very dismal option and the only thing that kept her going was the children.

"I have to make their futures my priority now," she kept telling herself as she tossed and turned at night in her bed, not able to sleep with worry. "One day at a time" became her mantra.

12

This, now it had come, was like a wakeup call for the three women. They knew what their situation was and would be for many years to come. Their future and that of their children was, now, all down to them.

Until that moment they had been in limbo waiting for the men to come out, take control and get on with the rest of their lives together. Now they knew they wouldn't be coming home any time soon or for a long time to come and it was up to them what was to happen in their lives. They would be the only earners and the only parent present in the families and they had to make the best they could of it.

They continued their regular visits to the men in jail and they were always plotting and planning what they could bring them in to keep them amused and their spirits up.

Many times Tess thought it was her and the other women who were doing the sentence, not Barry, Owen or Mick. They were getting looked after and many of them were getting educated inside. But she wouldn't criticise them, they had to stick by their men.

With this in mind they spent a lot of time wondering what they could do for them besides the usual visit. One Christmas they bought bags of oranges and a bottle of vodka between them, they got a syringe from a pal with diabetes and sitting around Tess's kitchen table and giggling like young girls, they injected the vodka into the oranges as a treat for the men.

When the men got the oranges they were thrown into a homemade still they had hidden in the prison. Mick told Helen they did this with nearly everything they could get their hands on including medicine they got from the prison nurse - Long Kesh's answer to Poitin!

They claimed they got the same medicine for rubbing on their feet as they got for pains in their stomach and some of this went in too.

Long Kesh was not known for looking after the health of its prisoners.

13

Internment lasted from 1971 to 1975 and it was a great relief to both the families of those interned and the Nationalist community when it came to an end.

It had created a bad time for Northern Ireland and was seen as a big black mark against the British Government around the world. Many men were badly treated by the British Army and the warders while interned.

Reports of them being verbally and physically abused, threatened, harassed by dogs, denied sleep, starved, forced to run gauntlets of baton-wielding soldiers, heads forcefully shaved, being kept naked, burnt with cigarettes, sacks put over their heads for long periods, ropes around their necks, barrels of guns pressed to their heads, being dragged by their hair, trailed behind armoured cars barefoot and tied to armoured cars as human shields were rife.

Outside the jail, in ordinary little homes, soldiers smashed their way into houses and fired rubber bullets through doors and windows of families of men who had been lifted.

In retaliation widespread violent protests broke out around Northern Ireland and the British Army came under sustained attack in Nationalist areas especially in Belfast. Vehicles were hijacked and factories were burnt. Roads were blocked and many streets had burning barricades to prevent the British Army entering their neighbourhoods. Many places became 'no go' areas.

In Ardoyne, soldiers shot three people dead and around two hundred Protestant families fled, burning their homes as they left, to stop them falling into Catholic hands.

Catholic and Protestant families fled to what became segregated, one-religion enclaves, which would become the demarcation line for the Peace Wall which even now continues to exist over forty years later.

Around seven thousand people were left homeless, most of them Catholic. Around two and a half thousand refugees crossed the Border to the South into the Republic of Ireland. Refugee camps were set up for them around the Border counties including Finner Army Camp in South Donegal.

Violence eventually began to ease off. Reports said it was due to the exhaustion of both the IRA members and Security Forces.

14

With Internment ending men started to arrive home. At first it was just a trickle but then it speeded up and almost every day you heard of someone else being let out. When all internees had been released, there was, once again, a great surge of Paramilitary activities.

Internment did not have the desired effect as foreseen by the British Government. If a man had not been involved in paramilitary activity before he went into jail he certainly was when he came out.

"For God's sake!" remarked Helen. "Do they not know that the Irish have been fighting for their freedom for eight hundred years and if you try to put them down they just rise up stronger?"

"They're not called the fighting Irish for nothing," agreed Tess.

"It says something for the stupidity of those in Westminster," remarked Mary. "Can they not analyse a situation or a people?"

Tess said; "Instead of scaring the people into submission, the brutal treatment meted out to Catholics by the British army makes them angrier and they fight back, seriously organising their military force. Each act of atrocity by the British is another recruitment advertisement for the IRA.

"And rightly so!" said Helen.

The women of Northern Ireland were getting as angry as the men with the brutality that was being experienced by the ordinary people from the security forces and many were joining the IRA. Helen and Tess often spoke of it but their children were always their first priority, though as time went by their anger increased as did their thinking.

"They cannot expect to treat us as less than animals with no rights and think we will become lap dogs to their regime!" said Tess angrily.

Looking back on all that had happened in her life over the last few years, she couldn't believe how much she had learned and how she had changed.

The Loyalist strike of 1974 was the first event that saw her finding her place in the community. A few short years before, the Troubles had little or no impact on her. At the time of the strike she found herself with other women organising food and its distribution for all who couldn't fend for themselves in the locality.

The power stations were shut down by Loyalist extremists. Electricity only came on for two hours a day and everyone had to improvise. People became very resilient. They built brick structures in the back gardens creating makeshift fires to cook soup, sausages, stews, and other food available. Potatoes were wrapped in tin foil and put in the hot ashes.

They burned wood or coal if they were lucky enough to have any. Otherwise they got sticks and other combustibles from around the areas. They made communal pots of food for everybody including the elderly and sick.

Everything had to be cooked as quickly as possible as most of the time it was raining. All ingredients went into one pot while somebody stood over the fires with an umbrella stirring it. The results were that all pots and pans had the backsides burnt out of them and everything was black, including clothes, faces and hands.

Cooking their food in the back yards and sharing saucepans with their neighbours seemed like a big adventure to Tess and she discovered she was a good organiser. The strike lasted two weeks and created further community solidarity.

Everything was shared. People with new babies were given small Primus stoves from neighbours to cook on. The elderly and sick were brought their meals and there was a great feeling of comradeship and community. She got to know a lot more people and it gave her a sense of purpose.

Strangely, there seemed to be no open resentment against the Loyalist extremists, everyone just got on with it.

One of Tess's priorities at this time was to get clothes washed for the children in the few hours the electricity was on. As she put on the washing machine one day an idea came to her. Maybe she could use the hot water for other things? After a bit of thought she decided that while the water was boiling in the top loader and before she put in the washing powder, she would boil some eggs in it. She got a wire clothes hanger and an onion net and hung the eggs over the side of it. She had the supper and the washing done in the same water. When the washing was done she used the warm water to wash her floors.

She laughed as she told the women, "it's lucky for the children they don't fit in the machine or they could have had their baths as well."

This was still the most important thing to her, looking after her children and home, but now the wider family and the community were getting a lot of her attention.

The strike wrecked the power-sharing deal in Northern Ireland and caused the collapse of the Sunningdale Agreement. It was later enforced by blockades by Loyalist paramilitaries.

15

Tess often thought that the best thing to happen to her was having Helen as her best friend. She couldn't remember a time when she wasn't in her life. They started school on the same day and were friends right through their school years. She always had her support and wisdom. Even though they had very different personalities they got on very well together. Tess absolutely believed she was her life saver.

Now with Helen being in the same situation as she found herself in helped enormously, not least because she understood all her problems but more so because her continued influence helped Tess to see herself in a more positive light and to grow in confidence.

She refused to let Tess feel sorry for herself while she was around and she had a wicked sense of humour. She would chide her for her lack of interest in the place she was born and lived in and the insular life she had lived before Barry was lifted. It helped make Tess look outside her home and see what was happening in her community.

"The more you are down and crying the more the Brits have won." Helen told her "A smile on our faces and laughter will really annoy them. And the more you do it the better you will feel so it's a win, win situation. Don't let the bastards get you down!" she would laugh swinging her arms around.

And Tess found herself laughing a lot more with Helen around. Through her influence she was getting braver and opening up to more people.

A lot of her life was still spent behind closed doors but she was often persuaded to go out to one or two events a week with the rest of the women.

At times she thought she was still in shock, finding herself on her own with the children with no partner's support. What happened to Barry still traumatised her. It was something she could never have foreseen. She was now just another one of those women caught up in the Troubles in Belfast and gone forever was her safe little family life she had so loved.

She became more knowledgeable about what was going on around her through meetings she went to but also from personal experience with raids on her house by the security forces. This invasion of her home, without thought given to her or her children, was such a shock to her she found it very hard at first to believe it was happening. She now couldn't believe she had lived for so long with her eyes, ears and mind closed to what was happening all around her.

But one of her biggest problems was still finding money to survive on a daily bases and lately she began wondering if she could find work and if it was possible to do so with the children so young.

"I have to find something or some way to survive," She repeated often "If the Conway Mill was still open I might have had a chance of getting a start there. But even that is gone,"

The Conway Mill, on the lower Falls Road closed in 1975 with the loss of two hundred jobs. It had been opened in 1842 by James Kennedy to spin flax. It is believed that he was also responsible for building many of the mills in Manchester. Later the weaving of linen was added to the work done in the Mill. It had given employment to generations of women and men in West Belfast and was sorely missed.

Some of those women were her mother before she had her children and some of her aunts. She often spent night listening to them tell stories of their times there and although times were hard she could also hear a kind of nostalgia in their voices as they spoke.

Now she wished she could find something similar so she could earn a few pounds to make things easier for her and the children.

16

Something in Tess turned around this time. She knew the men had not got justice in the courts and she felt that no one cared and she became angry on their behalf. She also became angry by the invasions of her home by the security forces because she knew they had no reason to do this and it was purely harassment of the wives of the men that were inside.

She started listening to the news reports from a different perspective and was disgusted with the attitude of the British. She thought to herself;

"Maybe I'm growing up and getting a backbone finally and I'm seeing the regime we live in for what it is. We haven't a hope of getting any form of justice until we get rid of the Brits!"

Helen would laugh at her; "You're only finding out now what most Catholics in Northern Ireland have known for a lifetime or many life times?"

She'd been really shocked at the injustice of Barry's sentence. She knew he had never been involved in subversive activities, he had done his best to protect the local community from harm and to work with groups trying to find a solution to the Troubles. He did not deserve to spend what would be, at the very least ten or twelve years in jail.

She started to go out more and look around her and get to know people who were actively involved in various projects in the locality. She would talk to them and question them on civil and human rights and she discovered that the law concerning these rights did not include treatment of Catholics in Northern Ireland.

She joined groups with men and women who had strong ideas on what was happening and she listened and made her own mind up. And of course Helen was always at her side. One evening, coming home from a local community centre, they discussed the difficulties women were coming up against. Some mothers in the centre, who had taken their children to visit their fathers in Long Kesh, said they hadn't being allowed in because their ID cards were slightly faded. One of the women had her house raided again that morning at six o'clock and all her children had been pulled out of their beds and terrified. This was the second time in a fortnight.

The raids were nothing new to them but hearing about it from the other women emphasised how prevalent it was and how unjust. The women and families were being targeted because the father, son or husband was jailed.

A lot of damage was being done to their houses including gas and electric being cut off by the soldiers. It could sometimes take weeks for the council to get it switched on again. Sons and daughters were getting angry and they worried what they would end up doing if it continued.

Tess and Helen felt very frustrated at the abuse women were being subjected to by the security forces, there seemed to be no place they could turn for help to stop it. If they objected to the security forces it only escalated. It all stemmed from their husbands being interned or jailed and was another stick to beat the men with. The majority of women only wanted to rear their children, keep a roof over their heads and keep their kids safe, yet they were being victimised on a daily basis.

The women became involved in helping other women who were raided or otherwise abused to repair their homes and clear up after the damage was done. Tess roped her father and brother in on this. They were both handymen and helped get repairs done and homes back together again.

Around this time Tess also began smuggling messages in to Barry from people on the outside with information for members of the IRA on the inside or from him to others on the outside. She was seen as a safe bet as she was so quiet and unlikely to be suspected by the security forces.

"But this worm is turning," she thought to herself.

The messages were written on tiny pieces of paper or toilet roll. Some were like works of art they were so small and so neatly written you needed a magnifying glass to read them. These were passed surreptitiously back and forth from the men and women when the screws weren't looking, sometimes by hand but often by a quick kiss from mouth to mouth. They were sown in the hems of clothes they took home for laundering or concealed on pieces of art the prisoners made.

On one occasion when Tess had returned home and was just sitting down to have a cup of tea there was a very loud knocking at her door which was very insistent. On opening it a man flew past her into the kitchen shouting,

"Where's Barry's shirt?" Tess got really annoyed and told the man he wasn't getting the shirt and to get the hell out of her kitchen.

He was completely out of breath and bending over he began to laugh and gasp.

Tess was getting worried as she never set eyes on this character before. When he eventually got his breath back he explained that Barry had forgotten to tell her there was a message from the OC in Long Kesh to one of the OCs on the outside in the hem of his shirt. Another women visitor had rang him and told him to get to her before she stuck the clothes in the washing machine.

The other woman had travelled to Long Kesh by car from near the Border and didn't know Tess or where she lived. She rang the only man she knew in West Belfast to see if he knew her. He rang around and eventually found someone who told him where she lived and this was the panic. He had to leave work and run half a mile to her house in case she put the laundry into the washing machine immediately after arriving home and it would be destroyed.

"It's very important," gasped the man "I was afraid it was going to be destroyed before I got to you," he said, bending over with his hands on his knees trying to catch his breath, panting. Some of the top IRA men were in jail but were still running things from their cells.

He rooted through the clothes Tess pointed him to, took the missive out of the hem of Barry's shirt and went on his way.

"Mother of God!" laughed Tess to herself, slightly stunned "This is sometimes like the Mad Hatter's tea party. The flipping White Rabbit has just left the building! It's certainly not boring around here."

17

Life became particularly difficult for Tess around this time when Jimmy became very seriously ill and had to be hospitalised. She felt the full burden of her responsibility of running the home and rearing her children on her own and she was desperately worried. It hit her very clearly that she was now the only one responsible for her little son's life.

He had a very high temperature and was having fits and doctors couldn't find the root of the problem and were very concerned about him.

Tess decided to send a petition to the Secretary of State to request they let Barry out on compassionate leave. Many phone calls and arguments later he was allowed six hours to visit the hospital after the doctor verified to the security forces that the little fellow was definitely very seriously ill.

Within another forty eight hours Jimmy's temperature disappeared as quickly as it had appeared and he was up and about again as though it had never happened.

But it had been very hard for both of them when Barry had to go back to the prison, especially when the little fellow was still on the critical list. Tess felt desperately alone and could not hide from him this time how hard things had become at home. He could see there was very little food in the house and all the children's clothes were well worn or patched.

Things were definitely not like they were when he had a job and all his pay went on the family. He could see that Tess was doing her best but now she had to get most of the children's clothes in the Salvation Army shop and sewed or darned everything that was torn so it would last longer.

Nonetheless there was no question of Barry not returning to prison. It was 'an honour thing' among the men inside. If any of them had not gone back it would have been more difficult for someone else to get compassionate leave.

At this time the men were refusing to eat prison food and the women had to send parcels of food in every week in order to keep them fed. These would often include roast chickens, steak and fruit. The women felt it had to be good food or the men would feel let down otherwise.

If any of them smoked cigarettes, these had to be sent in also. Barry didn't smoke but he got Tess to take them in to use as bets when playing cards.

As Tess and Helen were discussing it one day she told her, "I boiled the chicken and parcelled it and sent it in to him. All we had to eat for two days was the water it was cooked in and some potatoes I threw in!"

"Look! Woman! If you do that again I'll kill you myself!" said Helen "Half that chicken would do that boy of yours. The children and you need nutrition. You're skin and bones already. You need to put on a bit of weight."

"There's more than me doing this. Many families are going hungry just to keep up appearances."

"All I'm worried about is you and me. You are going to look after yourself and the children and Barry can have what you can afford afterwards! Do you hear me? You have to stay healthy to rear your children and the children need their food to become strong and healthy! Barry can do with mince stew, it will be good for him!" Helen shouted at her one morning as Tess was getting another steak for Barry with very little in the cupboards for herself and the children.

Tess often resented having to take the food into the prison to Barry and many mornings before she left the house she would storm about talking to herself.

"The bastard knows how hard things are for us but he has to keep his bloody head up in front of his mates in prison while we do without at home. How the hell am I going to keep this up?"

But once she left the house she was all sweetness and light and she would not betray her thoughts to anyone except Helen. Because of all the extra expenditure she was finding it harder to make ends meet and as time passed it got more difficult with the children growing and more demands on her purse and her own clothes were hanging off her. Her mum made sure the children had at least a good dinner every day, for which she was very grateful.

"Keeping up appearances is bullshit. It will be a lot of good to your children if they are left without a mother who starved herself because of what others might think. Don't be an idiot, feed yourself and your kids first then think about others," stormed Helen.

She was given three pounds fifty pence a week from the Prisoner Dependants Fund to help with going on prison visits and to bring in the parcels. Sometimes it was hit-and-miss with this money as it had to be raised from donations which included door to door collections.

Everyone was expected to give to it and when they came to the doors, even the women who had men inside and could be recipients the following week, felt obliged to give. So they gave what they could manage to a collection that was ostensibly for people like themselves.

This was a further strain on her budget. They organised fund raisers to try and supplement the money collected which included football matches, dances and raffles but few had much to give at this time.

At the weekend, dances were held in the local school and were fun for the women. A man at any of these events was a rare sight. Most of them were in jail or interned or patrolling the local area to prevent attacks. But it was a good way for the wives, mothers and sisters to release some tension and support each other. The dancing got their frustrations at life of out of their system. These occasions were often the only thing which kept the women going. Getting together and seeing what they could organise to get more money to support 'The Cause' was the only social outing many of them had.

Helen told the others, "Only for that awful 'Gallows Humour' of the women I'd be hanging from them. I only go to get a good laugh. Some are priceless comedians."

No one had anything during these times and there certainly was no money for drink except maybe at Christmas when they would save up for a few weeks and buy a couple of bottles of cheap wine between them and get dressed in any good clothes they had left and go to one of their houses, stick on the record player and dance around the kitchen or living room. With a few drinks the women could relax and enjoy a bit of craic.

They did not want the men worrying therefore there was no mention to them of the many nights they fell asleep crying and worrying about the next bill or where they were going to get money for shoes for the children or decent clothes for them going back to school.

Her brother promised he would lend her money if she was stuck but she didn't want to ask him. He had been shot a few months previously as he was coming home one evening and hadn't been able to go back to work yet. He was living on the Bru too.

Her mum and dad would give her their last penny but they had given her so much already she couldn't ask for more. She wouldn't borrow money anywhere else as she didn't know if she would ever be able to pay it back.

Although the women rarely spoke about how hard they were finding life trying to survive on their own Tess often angrily thought that Barry had forgotten all he had learned when he was out on compassionate leave when wee Jimmy was sick. As soon as he went back inside he expected her to carry on bringing him the best of food, take his clothes to be laundered and provide cigarettes for him to gamble with, cigarettes that he didn't smoke.

But she, like most of the other women, was afraid she might be seen as betraying her husband if she ever spoke to anyone about the situation. It was very frustrating. On the one hand she didn't want to let him down but on the other she had nothing to give and the children needed so much.

18

"The women have been left behind to cope just so the men can go out and play their bloody war games," she cried to herself many nights.

Thinking of all these things as she walked along the street one day and praying for a solution she bumped into Helen. Both her father and husband were now interned so she knew well what a struggle it was to cope without their pay packet coming in and worrying about her mother as well. But she had a good job and was making a few pounds for herself which really helped.

"Now there's a face that could haunt a house if ever there was one." she laughed as Tess came near her "What's up with you, you look so glum? Are you practicing for Halloween and just trying to scare people?"

Tess started to laugh and was half way through telling her all that was bothering her when Helen stopped her and said,

"I'm your Fairy Godmother, my lass!" she exclaimed with a deep bow and an extravagant flourish of an imaginary wand, "and I have the solution to your problems."

"Oh Yeah! I hope it doesn't mean walking down darkened streets with fishnet stockings and a mini skirt because I couldn't afford the price of them?" laughed Tess "It's too bloody cold at the moment anyway but the way things are going it could seem like the only thing left to do in a week or two if I want to clothe and feed my lot!"

She knew Helen was capable of coming up with some imaginary hare brained scheme for making a quick pound for the craic, so Tess wasn't taking her too seriously.

"Well! You could always try that if it's what turns you on!" she laughed "Or you could apply for the part time job that has become vacant in the electrical shop I work in? I'll put in a good word for you."

"How could I apply for a job?" retorted Tess "What would I do with the children and I know bloody nothing about electrical goods" retorted Tess surprised.

Many women worked outside the home at this time even after they had their family. But in Tess' family it was seen as women's work to have the children, rear them, keep the house clean, make the meals, look after their husbands and stay at home. The husband brought in the pay packet.

"That's enough for any women to get on with," her father would say.

"I suppose I don't have a family?" retorted Helen sarcastically "We all have to compromise and do what we have to do to make ends meet! Get with it, girl. This is the 20th century and we are no longer tied to the kitchen sink and we don't have to carry our children on our backs anymore."

"For God's sake I haven't worked outside the house for years and I wouldn't know what to do with an electrical gadget," exclaimed Tess.

"You have to sell the damn things not operate them and you worked in a shop before you got married. It's only part time and your mother or sisters could look after the wains for you. They're all at school now so it will be no great hardship. Stop making excuses and let's see some action!" said Helen as she pushed Tess in the shoulder. "You need to get out of the house and away from the kids for a while. Your brain is seizing up! I'll ring my boss and tell him you'll call in first thing in the morning to see him."

"But, but," started Tess thinking of a thousand reasons for her not to do it spinning through her head.

"No buts, do it!" ordered Helen "Go up to your mother now and ask her if she'll babysit for three days a week and you'll give her a few pound for it! I'm sure she could be doing with it too."

"But what would Barry think?" asked Tess

"What the hell does it matter what he thinks?" stormed Helen "He's not out here trying to rear three children on his own. He's very comfortably installed in Long Kesh, getting three meals a day, plenty of buddies to support him and not a bill to worry about. Now let me know on your way home what your mother said and I'll ring my boss and arrange an interview for you tomorrow. Then you turn up in the morning and chat to the manager. He's sound! Easy-peasy! Now go on. It's a better way of making money than what you were suggesting earlier," laughed Helen as she walked away waving her hand in the air. "But if that's what you really want to do, feel free. I'll think about doing pimp for you."

She laughed and walked on.

Tess stood for a second on the sidewalk, stunned.

"I can do this!" she told herself as Helen walked away. "I know I can do this. All I have to do is what Helen said."

She started walking slowly towards her mother's house, planning.

"What will my mother say? Would she be able to look after three active children? Shut up!" she muttered to herself "You're only putting obstacles in your own way! You can do this! You will do this!" she emphasised to herself as she carried on talking to herself. "Well! It's only about three hours on three days a week when the children come from school so it won't be an all day job for me Ma," she thought.

Entering the house she headed straight to the back yard where she knew she'd find her father. She watched him for a while standing tying beans to supports in what he laughingly called his glass house. It had been built from scraps of wood and old windows that had been taken out of houses he and Barry and Sean renovated.

"It does the same job as a fancy one." He would say if anyone mentioned it.

He was in his shirt sleeves which were rolled up past the elbows. His old blue and grey patterned braces held up his gardening trousers which had once been his working trousers but were now too patched to be seen out in. He had a thick black belt around the waist of them too. His working boots finished his outfit. His body was very slim but hardy from many years of hard graft.

As well as working in the building trade he did the maintenance for all the families' houses including fixing roofs and chimneys and sealing windows. The family didn't know what they would do without him. He could turn his hand to anything and you never heard a cross word from him. He was a quiet man!

Tess smiled as she watched him for a few minutes. He hadn't heard her come out he was so engrossed with his vegetables. He created such a familiar picture; it was one that would stay with her all her life.

She loved him a lot. A man of few words and all of them wise so she knew she could talk to him about anything and not be criticised. She now needed to talk out Helen's idea with him before she spoke to her mother.

"Dad, can I chat to you?" she said softly.

"Any time, love," he replied with a smile.

"What would you think of me going back to work and asking mum to look after the children?" she asked.

"Where were you thinking of working?" he asked.

She told him about Helen's idea and they chatted about it for a few minutes.

"Well! I think it's a good idea but you will have to talk to your Ma about it," he replied.

"Do you think she'd be able to look after the children? I don't want to burden her," said Tess

"All I can say about that is, ask her. She has to make that decision herself."

When she spoke to her mother later she surprised Tess by being delighted at the idea.

"I'll get one of the girls to come over every day after school and give me a hand. They'll be away during most of the day and it's only a few hours in the evening and the weekend. Triona and Grainne have grown up a lot in the last few years and wee Jimmy will be grand out the back with your Da pottering around the garden. It will do you the world of good to get out of the house and you need the money."

"Oh Mam! You're a brick, what would I do without you?" asked Tess as she hugged her "I can do this, can't I? I'll be able to cope now!"

"Of course you will, love! Look how well you're doing already on your own with three children and Barry inside? A few extra pounds will make all the difference. You can do anything you put your mind to! You're a tough wee tyke underneath it all," smiled her Ma as she hugged her back. "Go on now and tell Helen you'll go for that interview!"

She walked back towards her home a different woman.

"I have a feeling things are going to get better," she smiled to herself as she called in on Helen and told her she was going to try for the job.

"The job's yours, if you want it," said Helen "I've talked to the boss and told him you're a friend of mine, you are reliable and hardworking and he'd be a fool not to give it to you."

Tess laughed; "Thanks, Helen! But you're as cheeky as anything! He will probably be scared not to give me the job now in case you tear strips off him."

"Go on with ye!" laughed Helen. "You're perfect for the job."

"I hope you're right," sighed Tess "I just think I have the jitters because I haven't worked outside the house since I got married and I'll have to deal with people in a line of business I know very little about

"You're a quick learner. I've watched you over the last few years and you catch on quickly," said Helen as she pushed her shoulder "Anyway haven't you been looking after the family and home since Barry went inside and doing a grand job with very little, why wouldn't you be able to sell a food mixer or drill to someone who needed it."

"It sounds very simple when you put it like that."

"It is very simple! It's just your mind that makes it more difficult than it is! Go home and sort out something to wear and if you need anything give me a shout. I'll chat to you tomorrow after you confirm you got the job!"

Tess went off down home thinking to herself;

"That could be the biggest dilemma I have to face, finding something suitable to wear."

19

Everything seemed to be slipping into place and looking easier with everyone helping. Now all she had to do was ensure she got the job. On waking early the next morning she dressed and packed the kids off to her mother's with her sister who had called to collect them.

"Well! Here goes!" she said to herself as she put on her one and only good coat. "If you could call it that?" muttered Tess as she checked herself in the mirror and went out the door.

She'd bought the coat while she had been pregnant with Grainne and with the other two children coming so quickly together she had put on a bit of weight. Now the weight had gone and the coat was worn, stretched and hanging off her.

It really annoyed her not having money for essentials like a decent warm coat for the winter. A few years before she would have thrown the coat out and she certainly wouldn't have been seen outside the house in it. Now she had no alternative but to wear it.

"At least it's clean and with a touch of make-up it mightn't be noticed. I'm still not bad looking so maybe if I smile nicely and show him I'm not an idiot, he might give me the job. I'm good with people too! I've learned a lot about getting on with people since I started to stand up for myself on the bus to the prison. I'm sure a bit of humour will help to sell stuff too. I like helping people so that should help when selling too," she kept thinking positively trying to convince herself she could do this.

No matter what Helen had said or what she tried to tell herself, Tess was terrified. She had very little knowledge of anything electrical, except the kettle and iron, so she could not see how she would have the knowhow to sell them. Helen had tried telling her it was lack of confidence that was wrong with her but she wasn't fully convinced.

She continued the walk to the interview lecturing herself. She knew she had grown in a lot of ways in the years since Barry had been interned and she was beginning to appreciate that she could take on and cope with a lot more than she would have believed possible. Maybe she would be OK with this job too.

Nevertheless, going into the store a little later she was still very nervous as she asked to see the manager. She believed if she got the job it would be the beginning of things changing for the better so she stood stiffly with her fingers crossed behind her back and praying to God to help her through the next half hour.

All she wanted to do was make enough money to be able to provide proper meals for the children and herself and not always relying on her parents. She longed to be able to bring the children shopping to buy them some nice clothes and she would love to be able to get new curtains for the kitchen. All her ambitions were centred round her children and her home.

"And maybe I might be able to get a new coat for myself," she smiled to herself.

She was left standing around waiting for the manager for a few minutes which made her even more nervous. It was getting so bad she was on the verge of walking out again when she saw a man in a suit striding purposefully towards her down the shop aisle. As he neared she realised she knew him. It was Eugene Barron. He and Barry had been at school together and they had met him several times over the years when they were out socially.

"Hello Tess!" he said "I was delighted when Helen told me you were the woman I'd be meeting regarding the job?"

"Good God Eugene! Are you the manager here? I didn't know you worked here," laughed Tess all her nerves vanishing "I'm standing here terrified about the interview with the manager and you come along!"

"Helen only told me initially a friend of hers was the right woman for the job and she was sending her in tomorrow. Then she told me this morning it was you and I was delighted. It's hard to work out who you can trust in this business these days and I knew I could trust you implicitly. It was such a relief," laughed Eugene "She gave me my orders I had to employ you and you know you don't argue with Helen, she is always right, even when she is wrong."

"I wished I'd known it was you I was going to see but that brat never told me," remarked Tess "I wouldn't have been so nervous."

"The job is yours, girl! I'm delighted it's you who wants it, you're very capable of working here," he told her stretching out his hand and shaking hers. "I'll see you on Monday at nine o' clock and we'll take it from there."

Regarding her worries about knowing nothing about electrical goods he reassured her, "Read the back of the box, most of the information about them is there. Customers come in and usually they know what they want themselves anyway, you will learn how to work them by reading the instructions as you go along. Not that you'll need to work them but the more you know the easier it is to sell them. I'm available if you or a customer has any questions. You'll be good with the customers with your personality. You'll pick it up without any bother. You're a bright young woman. I'm delighted to welcome you on board," he enthused.

The interview she had been so worried about ten minutes before turned into a chat about Barry and what had happened to him and how unfortunate he was to be in the wrong place at the wrong time. Eugene asked how she was coping since he had been interned. Then she asked about his family and within a few minutes all her nerves had disappeared and she was a very happy woman.

She left the store twenty minutes later with a much lighter step and a feeling that things were really changing for the better. What she had been so worried about half an hour before had been so easy. Eugene confirmed again with enthusiasm that she had the job, that he knew her work history and was delighted he had found someone he knew he could rely on.

Now as she walked along the road with a spring in her step that hadn't been there for a long time she looked at how much she would earn, calculating how much she could save each week and what it would mean to her and the children.

She felt as though a great weight had been lifted off her shoulders. She was getting her life back together again. Come Monday morning she would be a working woman making her own money. She wouldn't make a fortune, it was only three days a week but she could sign on the Bru for the other two.

"I will be able to cope now! I want to dance with joy!" she thought as she swung her arms and smiled as she walked along the street. She longed to reach her mother's house and tell her parents. She ran the last few yards and flew through the door. She swung her mam around the kitchen shouting;

"I got it, I got it! I got the job!"

"Of course you did, I had no doubt you would," laughed her mam.

"Oh, Mam! I have a feeling everything is going to get better!"

"Of course it will, pet! Now you're going to work and get a few extra pound, it'll make all the difference!"

It was the first time in a long time Tess could see a way forward into a future that would not be filled with despondency and poverty. She had a premonition that she and her life were changing and things would never be the same again and she promised herself she would do all she could to improve her and the children's lot.

"This is just the first step!" she silently promised herself.

The following week she signed up for night classes in Business Management. Two months later she was taken on full time in her job.

Barry wasn't too impressed with her working outside the home. But after she told him;

"When you can supply enough money for us to live better than paupers then you can decide what I do to rear our children when you are in here!"

He was shocked she'd spoken to him like that but he understood what she was saying and she heard nothing more from him on the subject. She was amazed she had stood up to him and vowed it wouldn't be the last time.

Helen laughed when she told her what she said, "The little worm is really turning! Watch out world!"

20

Instead of the political situation improving there was a marked increase in the unrest all over the North of Ireland. The security forces were continuing to come down very hard on those in the Catholic areas and huge resentment was building up. There was an everyday diet of tanks and rubber bullets on the little streets of Belfast and elsewhere. Little houses with only mothers trying to protect their families in them were being wrecked by the army and police on a regular basis. This only added to the resentment of the people and the long line of youth and those not so young wanting to join the IRA, was growing daily.

The British army seemed to have lost control and the IRA was carrying out an increased number of bombings and shootings aimed at the destruction of anything British. The British Government were coming out of it looking very bad and they were losing face all over the world. The abuse that was being meted out to the ordinary person on the streets and in their homes was escalating. The International News reporters covered it all.

Newsmen and women were based almost permanently in Northern Ireland for many years dispatching bulletins all around the world to America, Australia, Africa, Europe China and elsewhere. They got to know the people and the situations in which they were living and told the human story as well as the political one.

The war in Northern Ireland was gaining support left, right and centre. The harder the British came down on the people the more they fought back. They had no compunction with using the media to broadcast the cruelty and brutality that was being experienced by the ordinary families and they became experts at doing so- even though the Government of the Republic of Ireland banned all IRA supporters from broadcasting their views under Section 31 of the Broadcasting Act.

Instead of realising that their heavy handed behaviour and their brutality was achieving nothing except making the people more determined to retaliate, it was also ensuring the IRA became one of the most exceptional guerrilla armies in the world.

The British seemed incapable of recognising this and they kept upping their bullyboy tactics. They continued putting curfews in place and barricades of concrete and wire around the Catholic areas. Check points were on almost every corner. It was a war zone in Belfast and in many other areas throughout Northern Ireland but they refused to recognise this also. If they had recognised the situation as a war zone they would also have had to comply with and implement the recommendations of the Geneva Convention for war.

The Geneva Conventions of 1949 collectively form international humanitarian law, a series of conventions and protocols that regulate armed conflict. The Geneva Conventions specifically detail a number of protections which states must extend to enemy combatants from the opposing country captured during times of war. These include prohibitions against all forms of violence including torture, humiliating and degrading treatment, and the passing of sentence without a properly constituted court hearing. In addition, medical treatment must be provided to those who need it and prisoners must be allowed to send and receive letters, enabling continued contact with their families. However, these protections only apply to soldiers of recognised armies.

Had the British Government acknowledged the situation in Northern Ireland as a war zone they would not have been allowed to carry out Internment, the Diplock courts would not have been recognized as legal, they would not have been able to use CS or CR gas or destroy the homes of the wives and mothers of internees or prisoners and they would not have been allowed to torture prisoners, carry out a shoot to kill policy or many of the other atrocities they carried out.

The British Government would never recognize the IRA as a legitimate opposing army so therefore would never recognize the situation in Northern Ireland as a war zone.

Nevertheless ordinary people were living in terrible circumstances and things were getting worse. Tanks meant only for warfare sped up and down the little streets of Belfast and soldiers fought running battles with the IRA on a daily bases there.

People were not allowed out of their houses after six in the evening which meant everything they needed had to be brought in before this time and any work that needed doing had to be done before then. Children were not allowed outside to play. It was six or seven weeks before people eventually rebelled against curfews and brought it to an end.

Belfast was torn apart by political and sectarian violence. Women tried hard to hold the families and the communities together but it was a tough and an on-going battle.

Few people were immune to the horrors occurring. Daily, the sordid brutality and hardships were reported across the world in the newspapers, TV and radio. There wasn't a day when Northern Ireland didn't make the news. Thousands of emigrant Irish people became involved overseas, sending money home`to help especially to those on the Nationalist side.

21

Women were widowed all over Northern Ireland either through shootings, bombings or rioting. Young mothers struggled to bring up children on their own without the love, support or wages of their husbands. Others spent their days caring for loved ones seriously injured. Many paid the ultimate price with their lives.

The years went by and many of the men remained in jail. Some lifted, interned and later brought to court, found guilty of various crimes with very little evidence and jailed, many for years and many innocent. Very little had changed in the judicial system!

There were years of protests in the prisons by the men, especially for their rights to be recognised as political prisoners. Many on the outside ran protests and marches to raise awareness of the issues.

In 1978 some prisoners refused to leave their cells to wash or use the toilet because of attacks by prison officers. The brutality continued and the men were always looking for ways to prevent or highlight it.

In April that year a fight broke out between a prisoner and a prison warden which left the prisoner in solitary confinement. News reached the other prisoners that he had been badly beaten and they responded by smashing the furniture in their cells.

The prison authorities removed the rest of their furniture leaving the prisoners with only blankets and mattresses. They then refused to leave their cell and the prison officers were unable to clear them. Three hundred prisoners took part and it quickly escalated into the 'Dirty Protest' and into completely inhumane conditions.

"I wish I had been there, I could have used the wood for kindling for the fire," said Lucy when she heard it, "I had no money last week for coal and I had to break up the dressing table and burn it to keep the children warm. I wouldn't mind but it was the only dressing table I had left in the house!"

"For God sake why didn't you come to us and we would have got the money between us for a bag of coal," asked Mary "We may not have much but we will make sure we all have heat and a bit to eat."

"Mary is right," said Helen. "We have to help each other and make sure all of us and the kids are looked after. Myself and Tess are working so we can afford a bag of coal for you."

"I will definitely help you out any time," agreed Tess

"It's good to know that. Sometimes I'm so desperate I'm pulling my hair out!"

"You can stop that right now, I don't want my friend going around half bald because she has too much pride," laughed Tess.

After that Tess would sometimes get the coalman to drop a bag of coal at Lucy's door and say nothing about it.

22

Treatment of the prisoners in the jail got worse and the dirty protest escalated. Visits stopped and the women worried about how the men were and what was going to happen next.

Many of those in public office spent their time on the television and radio speaking or preaching hatred and violence as the situation deteriorated. Others tried to find a solution through peaceful methods but with little results.

Fr O'Faich reported to the Media after visiting prisoners in Long Kesh;

"One would hardly allow an animal to remain in such conditions, let alone a human being"

"It seems the prisoners prefer to face death rather than submit to being classed as criminals. Anyone with the least knowledge of Irish history knows how deeply this attitude was held in our country's past. In isolation and perpetual boredom they maintain their sanity by studying Irish. It was an indication of the triumph of the human spirit over adverse material conditions to notice Irish words, phrases and songs being shouted from cell to cell and then written on each cell wall with the remnants of toothpaste tubes. "

The protest continued with no sign of the British Government agreeing to the prisoners' terms. By late 1979, nine out of ten new prisoners choose to join the protest. In January 1980 the prisoners issued a statement outlining what became known as the "Five Demands",

These were;

- *The right not to wear a prison uniform.*
- *The right not to do prison work.*
- *The right of free association with other prisoners and to organise educational and recreational pursuits.*
- *The right to one visit, one letter and one parcel per week.*
- *Full restoration of remission lost through the protest.*

The British Government continued to refuse the prisoners demands. Outside the jail everyone waited with bated breath.

23

The seventies were over and nobody was sorry. Tess, Helen and the other women prayed that the eighties would be better for everyone.

"Jesus! It couldn't be much worse, could it?" she asked one day as she stood with her eyes to the heavens and prayed.

The thought had hardly time to reach the heavens when the worst happened.

In February 1980 over thirty prisoners in Armagh Women's Prison joined the dirty protest following disputes with the Prison Governor. There were allegations the women had been ill-treated by male prison officers.

In October 1980 some IRA and INLA members began a hunger strike for the restoration of political status and securing the five demands. After a fifty-three day hunger strike and one of the prisoners on the brink of death, the British Government 'supposedly' conceded to the prisoner's demands with a thirty page document detailing the settlement.

When the document was on its way to Belfast, on the 18th December, the decision was made to call off the strike after fifty three days.

In January 1981 it became clear that the prisoners' demands had not been conceded to.

On the 4th February the prisoners issued a statement saying that the British Government had failed to resolve the crisis and they were going on hunger strike again.

The 1981 Irish Hunger Strike began on the 1st March. Bobby Sands was the first to refuse food.

The dirty protest ended the following day.

During this time thousands attended protest marches and meetings all over Ireland. Every woman with a son, father or husband inside worried in case they would join the Hunger Strike.

Margaret, one of Tess's women friends who she met up with regularly, was very angry with it all,

"We, the mothers," she stormed one day "we gave birth and reared them children and now they want to throw it all away. Why? So they can wear their own clothes and eat different food. Food that we take into them that we and our other children have to do without to provide for them."

"Shut up, Margaret!" said Helen "It's the only way they can protest and get their rights."

"Ah! Leave her alone, Helen!" Tess replied "She's as worried as the rest of us about it all!"

"I don't understand how they can throw their lives away for those five demands. How can they expect their families to watch them starve and let them die?" cried Margaret "Every time I think about it I want to scream "Somebody do something to stop this! For God's sake, somebody do something to stop it!' she beseeched.

"I know how you feel! We all know how you feel! And the worst thing is nobody seems to be doing anything," said Helen "Every mother who's given birth to a child must feel so much compassion for the mothers and wives of the Hunger Strikers."

"Yeah! Everybody but that bitch in Downing Street!" said Margaret.

"And we feel so much terrible frustration at not being able to do anything about it either," cried Tess "It's all so inhumane!"

Protest marches became prolific and were held all over the world. Thousands took to the streets in America, Australia, Europe and elsewhere but to no avail. Margaret Thatcher was 'not for turning'. Mo Mowlem, British Home Secretary at the time, fought hard for the prisoners but she was only one woman.

To anyone with the least bit of interest in Northern Ireland it was a tragedy on a massive scale and a huge disgrace on the British Government.

Bobby Sands was elected as a Member of Parliament during the strike, prompting even more media interest from around the world.

By the time the Hunger Strike ended on the third October 1981, ten men were dead,

Bobby Sands MP - 5th May 1981- 66 days
Francis Hughes - 12th May 1981- 59 days
Raymond Mc Creesh - 21st May 1981- 61 days
Patsy O' Hara - 21st May 1981- 61 days
Joe Mc Donnell - 8th July 1981- 61 days
Martin Hurson - 13th July 1981- 49 days
Kevin Lynch - 1st August 1981- 71 days
Kieran Doherty - 2nd August 1981- 73 days

Thomas Mc Ilwee - 8th August 1981- 62 days
Mickey Devine - 20th August 1981- 60 days

Two days later, the incoming Northern Ireland Secretary, James Prior, announced a number of changes in prison policy, including that all paramilitary prisoners would be allowed to wear their own clothes at all times.

A victory, but much too late for too many.

24

On the days she was not at work Tess would drop in for a chat to one or other of her women friends. They would natter about the cares of the day over a cup of tea and all gossip was shared around the kitchen tables. Often they would look back to their childhood and reminisce on the difficulties that had occurred down through the years.

One morning in Margaret's house they were discussing how living from day to day with barricades, checkpoints, strikes, raids, bombings, riots, shootings, the burning of homes, personal searches as well as curfews was now seen as normal.

"I hate to say it but it's true you can get used to anything," Tess told the women. "You even get used to death being an everyday thing!"

"Yes! Including the death of those close to you," said Lucy, who had lost so many people in her extended family that she had lost count. Brothers, brothers-in-law, cousins and uncles had all died in tragic circumstances.

"Isn't it amazing?" she asked. "That big bomb that went off the other day on the Falls Road was just a wonder for a few hours and then we carried on as usual."

"I stop now, just for a moment, when I hear one going off and wonder where it was, then do an inventory in my head as to where my close relatives or friends might be and if any are in the direction the blast came from. I say a wee prayer that no one was killed and carry on with what I was doing," agreed Tess.

"Even shooting, when it is close by, doesn't bother me like it used to," said Helen. "I check if all the kids are accounted for and just hope it wasn't someone I knew."

"It annoys me when they close off the streets and I can't get up them to do my shopping. I'm losing interest in the reasons for it anymore, I just want to get my shopping done and get back to the house and carry on with my house work," remarked Margaret.

Each day it seemed another relation or a friend was lifted, shot, found with a bomb or buried. Young people on the streets were shot with rubber bullets and many children were injured and killed by them.

As well as dealing with all this, they had to feed, clothe and educate their children and many women they knew still had to resort to the services of charities to survive.

Tess and Helen often spoke of this and were grateful they both now had good jobs with enough money for a decent standard of living. They could also help out the other women when needed.

Jobs were another thing that was scarce. They were few and far between especially for Catholics and it was dangerous to travel outside your own area.

Men and women were lifted regularly and they disappeared behind those high wire fences and concrete walls only to be seen for half an hour once or twice a month, often for years at a time.

Helen claimed that seventy five per cent of the men in their area were jailed.

As they chatted that morning about all of this, Margaret looked back to her childhood and reminisced about what she could remember of her life when she was young, before the Troubles started and the difference in her life now.

"I grew up in a mixed part of the Ormeau Road," she told them "just above the bridge. I remember my childhood as being very happy. It was a normal fun loving life, playing in the street with neighbouring children, skipping, swinging around lamp posts, going to football matches and visits to the Ormeau Park and the playground. We collected wood and tyres for the twelfth of July bonfires with the Protestant children. They were carefree days! I had no idea about different religions. All I knew was that my best friend and next door neighbours went to Sunday School, while we went to Mass. She was a good friend! She had a great wee bicycle and we took turns to ride it. We explored all around the area together. Her family came on the St Patrick's Day celebrations with us.

"But in the early seventies the Troubles heightened and the Ormeau Road was being ruled, mostly, by young Protestants. They congregated along the road and it became a 'no go area' and a very scary place. We had to take to the back streets to get to our Youth Club instead of passing them. We were afraid they would attack us and we would be beaten up, as many young Catholics were! The youth club was the highlight of our week. We would meet up with other friends for 'Top of the Pops' which we loved.

But life was changing and our neighbourhood became segregated. Catholics one area! Protestants the other! Eventually we had to pack up and leave because of the threats and attempts to burn us out of our house. I never saw my friend again but I often think of her and wonder where she is now."

"I often think of friends I had who were Protestants," Mary said "We would play on the street and they would be in and out of our house. They had to move because someone poured petrol through their letterbox one night at three o' clock in the morning and set it alight. It would have burned them all in their beds if they hadn't heard the noise and checked it out. They were just ordinary people, working like us to make ends meet and had nothing to do with the Troubles. Their only crime was that they were a different religion to the other people on the street. I don't think it was anyone in our area that did it because that family was well liked and good neighbours."

"Our whole world has gone mad and all because we Catholics want to be treated as equal citizens. Where is it all going to end? I never thought my husband would end up in prison. He's a good man and he shouldn't be jailed. I know I keep saying this but God knows what this is doing to him and our children!" exclaimed Tess.

"I wonder how many of them will still be 'good men' when they get out?" remarked Lucy "I know I would want to get my own back if I was locked up for years and I had done nothing wrong!"

"Yeah! And there are a lot of bloody boys running the streets who I think need locked up instead of some of the fellas who are inside!" said Helen.

"What are you on about?" asked Lucy looking at her surprised "It's not like you to be so cynical."

"I have damn good reason to be cynical! After what happened to me last night." retorted Helen "I'm hopping mad that I let myself be taken in by the toe-rag!"

"Good God! What's up with you? Where's all this coming from? I had a feeling there was something wrong with you today," remarked Tess. "You're like the wicked witch of the West and if the wind blows on that cross face you have on you, you'll stay that way," she laughed. "Spit it out, what's happened that has you boiling?"

"A certain boy called at my door last night. He was a friend of Mick's. I would have said before yesterday he was a friend of mine too but not anymore. He told me he wanted to hide for twelve hours because the security forces were looking for him and someone was smuggling him to Dundalk this evening. Of course I let him in and left him sleeping on the couch with a blanket thrown over him and a pillow. At one o'clock this morning I woke to find him trying to get into my bed!"

"Jesus Christ!" said Mary "You did not!"

"And he was not taking no for an answer!" said Helen fuming.

"What did you do?" asked Margaret.

"Some friend of your husband's that boy is!" remarked Tess.

"Exactly what I thought," returned Helen.

"What did you?" chorused Lucy and Margaret

"I told him to fuck off out of my room and hit him a wallop!" said Helen "What do you think I did, threw back the blankets and invited him in? I don't think so!"

"Not unless your taste in men has gone to hell! No decent man would try to take advantage of you like that!" stormed Tess "I hope you had a good shot at him and gave him something to remember you by."

"This boy was not going to be put off so easily," said Helen "He was very persistent and not taking no for an answer he tried to drag the bedclothes off me while I was hanging on to them for dear life and shouting at him to leave me alone. I'm sure he was going to assault me. That is until I grabbed the alarm clock off the bedside locker and cleaved him on the side of the face with it. I then started shouting and woke the kids because I thought he was going to murder me."

"Jesus Christ Helen! That's terrible!" said Tess shocked. "What happened then?"

"I bashed the clock into his face again and nearly blinded him. I then jumped out of the bed and grabbed the hurley stick I keep at the side of my bed to protect me and let him have it."

"Good for you! I hope he felt every wallop!" said Mary.

"Well he roared enough anyway," grinned Helen. "There I was standing on the bed in my long flannelette nightie, taking every slap at him I could with the hurley stick."

"What happened then?" asked Lucy agog.

"He took off running down the stairs with the blood pouring out of his face and me after him roaring and waving my broken alarm clock in one hand with springs hanging out of it and the hurley stick in the other. I hopped the clock off the back of his head as he was going out the gate and I probably woke half the street roaring after him," replied Helen.

"Jesus! I would have loved to see that," laughed Tess, holding her side. "I bet he won't come back for another rub of the relic off you!"

"Good God! You must have looked a sight running after him waving the clock," laughed Margaret. "Fair play to you, that's the way to treat them!"

"I was very proud of myself and that was a great shot with the clock. I think I might take up darts now, it was so good," laughed Helen.

"I hope you knocked some sense into him!" said Margaret "I'm sick of creeps leeching around me when I go outside the door. Auld feckers standing on the corners with lecherous looks and undressing you with their eyes! Just because the men are inside, the eejits that are left outside think we're desperate enough to take them on."

"Jaysus! Any boy that would undress me with his eyes or anything else would be in for a shock when he came to the navy pantaloons and the stays in my corset. He would need oxygen to go any further! He'd start putting my clothes back on again pretty quick," laughed Mary.

"You paint a very pretty picture there, Mary," laughed Tess.

"Do you know what's really funny and I can't stop thinking about it, he was wearing dirty old grey underpants that were hanging off him! I think if I was going to try to have it off with someone I would check my knickers were decent before I went out," laughed Helen "Maybe he thought he would get into my bed quickly in the dark and I wouldn't notice."

"Oh God! You're joking! Did he run out of the house with just them on him?" asked Tess.

"He didn't have time to pick up his clothes on the way past the living room with me after him with the hurley stick and clock," replied Helen.

"What did you do with his clothes?" asked Margaret.

"I gathered them up and threw them up the street after him when I came back in and saw them lying there in the living room. I didn't want anything belonging to him in my house" said Helen "They were gone this morning!"

"It would be some craic if someone else lifted them!" laughed Lucy.

"If he put them on he will probably have his death of cold by now because I threw them in the drain and it was teeming rain and the water was running in torrents down the street."

"I bet he's regretting going anywhere near your house now and thinking you were a soft touch!" laughed Tess.

"I'm wondering all day what tall tale he told his wife with the blood running out of him, one eye nearly shut and maybe a spring or two from the clock still stuck to him. I would be surprised if I haven't broken his arm too," said Helen.

"I hope he has a couple of broken ribs as well. It should curtail his shenanigans for a while," said Lucy.

"I wouldn't mind but he is nothing to look at. I wouldn't even take him on a string of herring to make a dozen. How he came to think I'd entertain him in the first place is beyond me? Do I look so desperate that I would stoop so low to pick so little? It is so insulting," replied Helen.

"Oh! There are boys out there who think they're God's gift to women with nothing to back it up. I think all this fighting for 'the Cause' is going to their heads. They see themselves as Che Guevara or some other bloody hero!" replied Margaret.

"Ah! They're all bloody studs in their own wee legends in their heads and they think we should throw ourselves at them," said Lucy disgusted.

"I have enough to do to put up with one bloody hero without taking on any more," laughed Helen "I wonder how brave they'd be if I went to the IRA hierarchy and reported them for trying to screw their comrades wives while they were inside doing time for 'The Cause'?"

"Is it not bad enough that we have to do with very little to keep our husbands in the style they are getting accustomed to, without toe-rags like him trying to take away the little bit of dignity we have left?" said Margaret, "Jaysus! If Mick gets wind of this, Helen, the walls of Long Kesh won't hold him!"

"That's what I'm afraid of. We'll have to keep this quiet or it will get back to him and he'll go crazy. As if it wasn't bad enough I have to worry now about keeping the creep safe. That is so insulting! Protecting the bastard who tried to destroy my dignity!" snorted Helen.

"There is no way that that boy could destroy your dignity, Helen. You turned the tables on him well and truly. I don't think he had much dignity left running up the street half naked with an old pair of dirty grey underpants hanging off him," laughed Tess.

"When I came back in my two boys were standing at the front bedroom window looking out and Chris shouted, "Good shot Ma! Maybe they jailed the wrong parent in our house. My father couldn't hit a barn door with that clock."

Kieran said, "You looked like the charging avenger down that path after that creep in your long nightie. Nice one, Ma!"

"They thought it was great craic. I was so embarrassed they had seen it all. The both agree they're safe in their beds while I'm protecting them. They're threatening to get an arsenal of clocks for me to use in riots," she laughed.

"And to think you nearly lost your 'born again virginity'!" laughed Mary.

"Are you going to tell us who he is?" laughed Tess "Maybe we could all pay him a visit?"

"Yeah! Now that's an idea! Especially as his wife would not be too impressed." laughed Helen.

"The prig! Tell us!" pleaded Tess "We'll have a quiet word with him together."

"It was Paddy Davis," said Helen.

"Doesn't surprise me!" exclaimed Tess.

"Yeah! I heard something about him harassing some other woman, not too long ago!" said Lucy, "It's a pity we don't have 'an auld boy' between us who would give him a good seeing to!"

"We don't need 'an auld boy' to give him a seeing to when we have five good women to cool his heels," replied Tess.

"You're really getting out of your box this last while," laughed Helen "A few years ago you wouldn't have thought of confronting anyone. You were such a mouse!"

"You can blame the British Army for that," laughed Tess back.

"Sure why not blame them for that too, everything else is their fault," remarked Margaret, tittering.

"It wasn't the British Army who was creeping into Helen's bed last night!" snorted Tess.

"Well! Let's deal with him," said Lucy.

"Can you imagine his reaction when he sees us all standing at his door? I think we should pay him a visit on Saturday night on the way to the dance. We'll let him know he's not wanted at the dances anymore too and if he goes near any other woman he'll be looking for the police to protect him, not hiding from them, because we'll report him to a few friends of our husbands who are on the outside and they will deal with him. That will curb his heels and keep him away from the door of the club and ogling up all the women going in and out," said Tess.

"I'm game!" said Lucy "We need to look out for each other."

"Count me in!" came a chorus from the other women.

"Men are a rare enough sight at the dances these days but we can live without boys like that. I never thought I'd see the day when I'd be looking forward to dancing with a crowd of women," laughed Margaret.

"We have to get our exercise somewhere when we're not getting a 'bit of the other' with the men inside," laughed Lucy "Jumping around the floor to Elvis Presley and the Beatles does me the world of good."

"I draw the line when Tess wants to slow dance with me just because she hasn't had a hug in ages," laughed Helen.

"I just like the song 'Honey' and I wanted to close my eyes and float around the floor," Tess sighed "You're just afraid I might make a pass at you. Sorry! You're just not my type. You don't have the equipment I need."

"Never mind your messing. What are we going to do with that gobshite Paddy Davis?" asked Mary.

"We're going to pay him a visit," said Helen "If you're all game. I have to face him and ensure he doesn't come near me again or I'll be waiting for a return visit every night. With your backing he should think twice about coming back for more of 'how's your father' or anywhere near me in the future."

"I don't think he'll dare come back for another crack of the alarm clock but it would do no harm for him to know we all know about his shenanigans and put a stop to them," said Tess, "I don't want to open my door and find him there either or any others asshole like him."

On Saturday night the five of them got dressed up in their 'finery', which in most cases were dresses that were years old, and they met at Helen's house. Leaving the house they marched along the road in their high heels and big hair styles. Like women on a mission they stopped at Paddy Davis's house. The five of them stood like sentries outside it as Helen knocked. He opened the door almost immediately. He had seen them coming up the path and didn't want trouble.

"Oh dear! Paddy! Your face is really a bit of a mess," remarked Tess sweetly "Have you been in an accident? You really should be more careful!"

"What do you want?" he snarled with a look of terror on his face.

Mary stepped up to him, stuck her index finger in his chest and pushed while he grimaced.

"We want to speak to your wife for a moment," she replied with a smile.

"She's busy!"

"Oh! We won't keep her long!"

"Go away! You can't see her," Davis said through gritted teeth with the sweat running off him.

Helen stepped in and said, "This is our message to you and her, if you attempt to come near any other woman's house or invade any other woman's privacy within our vicinity again, like you did mine the other night, we will be back here and we will not stop at this door. We will march right in and tell your wife exactly what you have been doing, in person and you won't stop us."

He started to stutter, "I'm going to sue you for assault. You attacked me with a clock and a hurley stick."

"You weren't expecting that, were you?" she laughed "I saw the surprise on you face when you first saw it and it was even better when I hit you with it."

"You shouldn't have hit me with that clock, look at my face, look at my eye! I'll sue you! I can't see through my left eye!"

"Sue me for hitting you with a clock that was sitting on my bedside table! A hurley stick that was at the head of my bed to protect me from scum bags like you! How will you explain that to your wife or maybe I'll just tell her now?" She went to walk past him.

"No! Please! No!"

Helen smiled; "No! I thought not! And I want the cost of that clock from you too." she snapped.

"You destroyed my clothes," he retorted.

"You're lucky I didn't burn them in the range and send you home with nothing on but your saggy grey drawers hanging off you," retorted Helen.

"You are nothing but a bitch," he stuttered.

"And don't you ever forget it!" returned Helen.

"I'm not paying you for the clock. You smashed it yourself," he argued.

"That's fine," said Helen "I'll get it myself from your wife," and she went to push past him again.

"No! Don't tell her, please, don't tell her! I'll give it to you!" he begged as Helen continued to push past him again.

Helen stuck out her hand, he looked at her still debating whether he should give it to her or risk not. They could see the realisation dawning on his face that these women were not messing about. They would carry out their promises.

Mary then stepped up and said in a menacing voice; "Pay up, you slime ball! And if we hear of you preying on wives of other men jailed we will tell the IRA about you pestering their comrades' wives. I guarantee you will be hobbling around on crutches for six months at least if we do."

"But I didn't, I wouldn't, it was a mistake," he stammered.

"You're right! It was a big bloody mistake and I would advise you not to repeat it. You picked the wrong woman!" said Tess.

"And a mistake you better not make again on any other decent women," retorted Helen.

With that the five women turned in unison and walked off down the street. As they rounded the corner from the house they stopped, looked at each other and doubled up with laughter.

"Oh my God!" squealed Tess holding her sides "Wasn't his face a picture?

You really made a mess of it, Helen. It will be a week or five before those cuts and bruises clear."

"I thought he was going to have a seizure trying to get us away from the door before his wife heard us," laughed Lucy.

"It's just as well she was bathing the kids," said Margaret "You could hear them making noise in the background. She has enough on her plate being married to that useless toe-rag!"

"I bet he tells her we were collecting for something or other and that's why he had to give us money," laughed Lucy.

"And I bet he will not be calling at any other woman's house again late at night, with his fairy tales in the foreseeable future." laughed Helen, pocketing the money for the alarm clock.

"Did you see the shiner he has? By God! Helen, you certainly went to town on him!" laughed Margaret, "remind me never to stand on your corns."

They walked on to the club laughing.

"Imagine the fecker trying to deny it?" said Tess "And threatening to sue you. He really is a brainless gobshite."

"If that eejit's in the IRA I think we better tell them not to give him a gun or a bomb or he'll blow his own goolies off, he's such an eejit," said Lucy.

"That's one of the best evening's work we've done in a long time!" exclaimed Mary laughing.

"It goes to show what we can do on our own if we stand together," remarked Helen

"We don't need anybody to fight our battles," smiled Tess "We're perfectly capable of fighting them all by ourselves as you could see clearly from that boy's face."

"But it is good to have the support," returned Helen.

"Indeed it is," mused Tess.

Paddy Davis wasn't seen back at the dances again after that and of course the story of the women's visit to him was too good not to make the rounds. It caused quite a bit of hilarity, especially among the other women.

25

After this episode Tess felt herself growing stronger and began to recognise her own strength of character. She knew she could rely on the other women to look after her and no matter what; they would always protect her back.

Also around this time she got around to progressing her education. She had already completed a Degree in Business Studies and was anxious to go further so she applied to do a yearlong course at night in advanced facilitation. She felt she needed to gain more confidence in herself and this was another step in the right direction. She was also promoted to shop manager with much better money. Everything was coming together for her.

She'd become very proactive in the community and had learned a lot more of what was happening around her in everyday life and began to form her own opinions and plans. As a volunteer in the women's centre a couple of nights a week she gradually became involved with other groups and began organising events and projects and coordinating anything from education, training and trips abroad for youth groups.

Unfortunately everyday there was another atrocity perpetrated on her community and more and more women ended up suffering as a result. She found herself dealing with the fallout from this and the more she learned or was subjected to, the angrier she became!

It was as though all natural law was suspended and did not pertain to the Catholics in Northern Ireland. People were mowed down in the middle of the streets. No one was safe, man, woman or child.

The only law available to them was the dubious convictions in the Diplock Courts and a security force that was seen as anti-Catholic.

Anyone and everyone was being lifted off the streets and subjected to brutal treatment in the Police and Army barracks. Stories of atrocities being committed by the Army and the Police were growing daily.

After Bloody Sunday, the Ballymurphy Massacre and the Hunger Strike, the women knew that anything was liable to happen. There was no limit to how low the British security forces would stoop. They had no respect for human life and they were getting away with blatant premeditated murder on an epic scale.

26

Margaret was becoming more angry and unhappy and the women were worried about her.

"What the hell do they think we are doing or hiding from them is beyond me?" she said one morning after she had been raided again for the umpteenth time "Why the hell do they disconnect my electric and gas when they search my house? I couldn't even make my kids their breakfast before they went to school this morning and last time I had to wait for days to have it all connected again. Oh! I suppose it was the same reason they tore up my family allowance book and took a jack hammer to the living room floor. The last time they raided the house I could see right down through the floor into the arch over the entry to the back yard. They did so much damage in the back bedroom it was like a junk yard. When I asked them what they were doing I was told "searching"! Searching for what? I'm a lone woman with kids and my husband is locked up! What the hell do they think I'd be hiding? And they do this time after time, as though I'd be so stupid as to hide anything in or around the house with them raiding continually."

She was being targeted more often than the others, possibly because her husband had, supposedly, shot a soldier, although he denied the allegations he had been convicted of this in court. They security forces came early in the morning and turfed all the children out of their beds with total disregard for them or their home.

"I have been raided at least seven times in as many months. Last month they raided me twice. Every time they caused so much damage I wanted to throw in the towel. The Housing Executive often don't get out for weeks to fix the damage," she said "They took a jack hammer to the kitchen wall and living room floor on at least three occasions and left big holes in them. I'm at the end of my tether!"

All the women continued to have to tolerate the frequent early morning raids. Tess' house was now being raided as often as the other women's but since Margaret's family allowance book and other documents had been shredded during the raids she had bundled all her documents into a tin box and left them with her parents.

But she felt one of the lucky ones. When her house was raided, she rang her parents and they came immediately. Her mother took the children to their home while her father stayed with her. This way the children wouldn't witness the abuse to Tess and the destruction of the house.

Helen claimed they had all developed built-in radar and could hear the army heading their way even before they entered the street. Many nights Tess stood at the window watching to see if they were heading her way. If they were, she ran downstairs and opened the door so they wouldn't break it in, then she lifted her phone and rang home. It was one of the first things she had installed after she started work, one phone in her living room and one in the bedroom.

When it was all over her father, brother and she cleaned up the damage and the children knew very little about it. She had become very adept at wallpapering and painting and could even tackle a bit of carpentry. Her father was a great believer in helping yourself so he took great patience to teach her all he could in case one day he wouldn't be there to do it for her.

When her electricity was cut off she got one of the men she met through work to come and reconnect it for her. Her brother had a friend who worked for the Gas Board who dealt with the gas disconnection. All was dealt with as quickly as possible.

The other women then began to develop the same support system around them. When the raids happened a neighbouring man would come and support any women who hadn't got a man in the house. This seemed to lessen the damage done slightly.

But unfortunately, no sooner would they have the house fixed than the next raid would take place. Their nerves were always on edge waiting for the next invasion and some of the older children were very upset and getting angrier.

This worried the women even more than the raids, particularly Margaret. What would they do to retaliate? She ruled over them like a sergeant major and they couldn't get out of her sight or she was after them to see what they were doing. It was wearing her and them down visibly.

The stress was affecting all the women in the area badly, both mentally and physically. Many were on tranquillisers and sedatives. It was having an increased detrimental effect on the children of the area also. Those in their teens often became involved in riots on the street and attacks on the British army and others became active in the IRA.

Even though they tried to keep their children away from the Troubles they understood their anger and them wanting revenge.

All the women spent time patrolling the streets when rioting started. Tess would march her lot up to her parents and join the other women looking for children that were missing from homes and drag them back.

And still one or other of the women were left with rooms full of rubble at least once a month. Margaret had been taken to the barracks and thrown in a cell three times when she objected to the army disturbing her children in their beds early in the morning.

"Is it not bad enough we have to hold everything together with our men inside, without them harassing us like this? I am on the verge of cracking up. I don't think I can take much more. They can keep the bastard in there for all I care, just leave me and my children alone," cried Margaret.

Helen put her arms around her as she cried. "You're going to have to toughen up, Margaret. It looks like these raids are going to continue."

"Do you not think I know this and I'm just waiting for the next one and do you not think I went through enough hell the last three times?" she shouted back as she pushed Helen away. "I have now spent three days in jail because I object to them taking my kids out of their beds at five or six o'clock in the morning when they're sick. It's just as well you live near me and keep an eye on my kids. Otherwise they would have been left to look after themselves the last two times they lifted me. My eldest is looking for revenge and I'm worried sick he'll do something drastic. It's no way for them to be treated."

She had tried to stop the army going into her children's bedroom and taking them out of bed because her eight year old daughter was ill and she had just got her off to sleep at three o' clock in the morning. They arrived two hours later. She was exhausted herself and had stood with her arms out across the door to stop the soldiers. When she wouldn't move they arrested her and kept her for two days. The second time she tried to stop them they kept her for a day and the third time they kept her for a few hours. Each time when she got back her home was shattered with carpets lifted and torn, services disconnected, wallpaper off the walls and furniture broken.

"Them boys don't give a damn about the likes of us or our children," she said angrily "The time they dug up my front garden path they thought it was amusing to say they were looking for one of the hunger strikers. Then one of them laughed and said, Oh! That's right, we won't find him here! He's dead, he died this morning? Then they all laughed."

"They're the best recruitment agency for the IRA ever," said Lucy "They'll get their comeuppance one of these day."

"Isn't that what is worrying us all? It will probably be one of our children who will carry it out. What will the children turn out like after being subjected to this harassment and trauma? How will we keep them safe?" said Helen worriedly.

"Every time one of mine leaves the house, I ask them where they are going, they say something smart like, "Out for a dander round a salt herring barrel" like all cheeky teenagers. But I worry myself sick that they'll come home in a box. God only knows what they are getting up to when I can't see them! If they are not back in a couple of hours I'm out looking for them. I'm driving them silly with my behaviour but if it gets them home sooner and makes them think and not get into trouble then I don't care," said Margaret.

"We're all the same. It's hard enough rearing them in good times but with all this mayhem happening all around us it's nearly impossible," sighed Lucy.

27

From first thing in the morning to last thing at night the lethal cloud that was the Troubles in Northern Ireland hung low and heavy, waiting at any moment to drift down and sweep more of their children and family into its destructive environs.

As the women thought about it, a feeling of helplessness and fear swept through them.

“Come on, stop being so maudlin,” chided Helen “We have to try and stay strong and positive or we’ll end up in the loony bin. Did you hear about the freezer van that was hijacked yesterday over the street? The whole content of the van, mostly chickens, were handed out to anyone who wanted them by the young ones who hijacked it. Two young lassies were going around with a shopping trolley door to door giving out the frozen chickens. There were three turkeys in it and I got two of them because I was the only one with a deep freeze.”

“The kids around here are getting as cheeky as anything,” laughed Margaret.

“They thought it was fair game, it’s an English company,” smiled Helen.

“The peelers came down the road in their jeeps and said they were taking fingers prints,” continued Helen “We could imagine them taking the dabs and then looking for the chicken. Sure the whole lot would be cooked and ate long before they’d finished!”

“That is so silly, sure the bloody things would be melted anyway and the dabs washed off,” snorted Mary.

“Anyway we hid the turkeys at the bottom of my freezer and decided we’d be all right because the peelers were only looking for chickens. They’re so stupid they’d never work out that there were turkeys in the van too. Nearly every family got a chicken for dinner, some for the first time since last Christmas. It was brilliant, the whole street smelt of roast chicken!”

“Ah Jaysus! I missed that,” said Margaret “You should have given us a shout. What I wouldn’t give for a decent bit of home cooked chicken with crispy skin?"

"I still have the turkeys," said Helen "We'll cook them tomorrow and have a dinner for us all tomorrow night. I'll defrost them tonight and you all bring the spuds and vegetables and some one of you bring dessert. Jelly and ice cream will do. The kids love that. We'll have it in your house Tess because you have a bigger kitchen table."

"That's a brilliant idea!" replied Tess "Bring your guitar Helen and we'll have a sing song."

Mick, Helen's husband had started learning the guitar in jail and after buying some books for him she decided to teach herself. She was getting quite good at it, although her sons were always joking about the squealing and screeching noises coming from her bedroom.

"I'll never get a big head in that house of mine," she remarked as she left the kitchen.

Next evening they all gathered at Tess's house. There were children all over the place, on chairs, the floor and the stairs while the women sat around the kitchen table preparing the meal. All five women and their children squashed into the little house caused quite a din.

Helen gathered the wee ones on the stairs with herself at the top and she played and sang every song they could think of to keep them quiet.

A lot of laughter came from the kitchen where Lucy and Margaret's cooked turkeys were, with great rivalry as to who had cooked the better one. After dinner the children went out into Tess's backyard to play. Helen and Mary's sons, being the oldest took control and kept the younger ones occupied.

Meanwhile the women sat around the table chatting and plotting and planning. Whatever was left of the turkeys would be made into soup the next day and shared.

Margaret asked; "Did you hear my nephew was caught firing Marleys (marbles) at the soldiers with a slingshot a few weeks ago. When the soldiers came after him he ran into a house down the road where the woman of the house was 'having-it-off' with someone else's husband. He thought it was hilarious but they were so upset at being found out they were grovelling for their clothes to cover their modesty. He was caught by the soldiers and they confiscated a Marley he had left in his pocket. They took him to court and the woman was there to give evidence against him."

"Stupid woman!" laughed Lucy. "He'll probably tell her husband on her!"

"I've warned him to keep his nose out of it and his mouth shut but I have a feeling it may get back to him anyway, my nephew had already told everyone he knew before I got to him, he thought it was so funny. Anyway when we went into the court the evidence table was filled with Armalites, AK47s and other big guns and there among them was my nephew's wee Marley, a wee glass ball in the middle of the table with all this heavy artillery!"

"It looked ridiculous. When it came to my sister giving evidence in the dock she was so nervous when the judge asked her name she shook, stuttered and mumbled so much the judge threw the case out of court and told her to go home and take her son with her and put manners on him. It was hilarious."

"I hope the bloody Brits felt as foolish as they looked, wasting time and money to bring a wee Belfast cub to court for playing Marleys on the street," said Helen "If they weren't making targets of themselves on our streets, our children wouldn't be using them for target practice."

"I suppose that's one way of looking at it," laughed Tess.

"Maybe the IRA should take up Marleys if they can create such a disturbance," laughed Helen. "I must chat to some of the boys I know about it."

"And they wouldn't be as hard to hide as a gun," laughed Lucy.

28

The women continued to do all they could to make their men's stay inside comfortable. They never let them down but most of the time it was a huge strain. Along with all the aggravations in the outside world they were trying to live as normal a life as possible in a very abnormal situation and it was getting harder all the time.

Tess was still doing 'post woman' getting reports in and out from the prisoners for some of the top men in the IRA. She told the women; "I've become an expert at talking with my mouth full," she laughed, "With a quick kiss Barry delivers the post and I have to make sure I don't swallow it."

"It gives a whole new meaning to French kissing," laughed Helen.

"Getting a note covered in spittle is not my idea of good news," laughed Margaret.

The women could find humour in anything. But all of this had a very serious aspect too. There were many men in jail who had a lot of influence in the IRA and needed to get word in and out of the prison. As Barry kissed her he would slip a small rolled up note he had been holding in his jaw into her mouth.

As she was receiving messages from him orally she would quickly be delivering another into his hand or down the back of his shirt.

"If he's that good?" laughed Lucy "Make sure he doesn't deliver anything else. You have enough to rear!"

"If I thought there was the least chance of that happening I would sew it up!" exclaimed Tess, "If there is going to be another child in our family it will be Barry who carries it for the nine months and rears it!"

The women all laughed except Margaret; "I hope you know what you are doing, Tess?" she said "If you're caught, what would happen to your children if you wound up in Armagh Gaol with the rest of the women that were lifted?"

"I just feel I have to do something to help. If the only thing I can do is deliver a few messages to some men out here, then that is what I will continue to do. The security forces have me so angry with their unreasonably brutal behaviour I could spit fire," replied Tess.

"That would be a good trick. We could have our own dragon and parade her up and down breathing fire on all the jeeps as they speed up and down our streets at night," laughed Helen.

"I'm serious," said Tess, "It makes me so angry. I try not to let the kids see my reaction but it's burning inside me!"

"It's bad enough when they attack the parents but I draw the line when my children are harassed every time they pass a patrol on their way to and from school," said Helen "Their school bags are continually being dragged off them and dumped on the ground in the rain and their jackets pulled off them by soldiers. Apart from that they get awful verbal abuse about me and their Da!"

"It's very hard on them and you can see the effect it is having on them," returned Mary "They speak about it with real hate for the soldiers."

"You're right. Instead of getting used to it all everyone is getting angrier," said Margaret. "I cannot control my temper with the security forces when they come to my house anymore. I'm so afraid I will end up in jail and my kids will have to fend for themselves. I don't know what to do."

"Just be careful," said Helen "When they know they are getting to you they get worse. They hardly ever bother Tess because she is so nice to them. Yet she is the one who is doing postman for the IRA and she gets away with it because she bites her tongue."

"Maybe I need to learn how she does that, because I can't."

"They'd get the quare shock the next time they knocked and you opened the door with a big smile and escorted them around the house and opened doors for them and woke the kids and lined them up in the hall for inspection. At least maybe your possessions might be safer from them and your wee home mightn't come off as badly as it does," said Tess.

"And they wouldn't get the satisfaction of seeing you angry and upset," said Helen.

"I'm so nice because I know there are boys out there who will sort them out one of these days," said Tess "As I go around the house with them I'm thinking, One day your time will come, boy. That keeps me calm and sane."

Margaret now looked as though she was on the verge of a nervous breakdown and she was getting more anxious as time went by. Lately when the women talked about the Troubles her reaction was often:

"For God's sake, I can't take anymore! Can't you talk about anything else? I have it for breakfast, dinner and tea. I'm fed up with it all, I'm going to ban everyone from speaking about riots, bombs and raids and what is happening on the streets or in the prisons from now on. What about the rest of our life or even about the rest of the world?"

Tess looked at her seriously and said; "You know something Margaret, you could be right. There is more to life than the men in Northern Ireland and what they get up to. Maybe we should think about our own place here and other women's places in Northern Ireland and what they are doing. Maybe we should try to get something going that will give us some amusement and entertainment."

"That's a good idea," remarked Mary "Maybe I'll get out my red flannel shift and start singing on the corner. It would entertain the neighbours anyway."

"I'd go to watch you," laughed Tess.

"The kids would probably use you for target practice and throw stones at you and I wouldn't blame them with your voice," grumbled Margaret.

"But, you know! That's not a bad idea," said Lucy "Why not think of entertaining ourselves and leaving the whole 'Troubles' outside the door for a couple of evenings a week?"

"I agree with Lucy," called Tess from the kitchen where she was making more tea.

"OK!" said Helen "We will have two evenings a week when we won't mention men or the 'Troubles'. You'd never know what else we could be planning if we weren't plotting visits to them and making their lives better. Let's try to make our own lives better for a change!"

"Do you know what I've always wanted to do?" asked Lucy "I want to write a play, a comedy, about the women in the Troubles."

"Oh! Yeah! That'll be very funny," sneered Margaret "What part of our lives do you think is funny?"

"There is plenty of fun in our lives," replied Tess "How many times have we been laughing so hard in the last few weeks that the tears have run down our faces?"

"That's true," said Helen. "We've been in some very funny situations."

"As a matter of fact I have written quite a bit on some of our experiences. I think a lot of it is very funny. I want you to read it and see what you think."

"I read some of it last week and I think it's hilarious," said Mary.

"Well, that's good enough for me. If you can get the rest of it together I'll arrange for a venue in one of the Community Centres to rehearse it and we will get some of the women from around her to take part in it," promised Tess.

"I want you lot to have a role each in it," said Lucy. "It will be great craic and you are all fit for anything."

"Count me out as an actor!" said Margaret. "But I'll help with the costumes and backstage."

"Every little helps," said Lucy.

Lucy had written some articles for the local paper over the years and she was always writing short stories for the children. Some of these had also been published. She had a real talent for it. The women knew she was very capable of doing this and were excited to be involved in something so different.

Through working on the play, which turned out to be a hilarious comedy, they became further involved in the community. Lucy continued writing and getting different youth and women's groups to act in them. Apart from staging them she also brought them to the schools to teach children about life. One or two of the women went with her when they were available to give their input.

After the news got out of how successful her plays were she got funding to expand on this, she'd found her niche and loved it and continued to do it for many years.

The plays based in comedy were a great success and through laughter helped many to forget for a short time about their situation. They were shown in community centres all over the Nationalist areas and got other women involved in telling their stories through drama. It opened up a new life for her.

Tess and Helen spent a few hours each week as volunteers in any way or place they were needed. Apart from occupying themselves it created further social interaction and kept them up to date on what was happening in the greater Belfast area.

Tess changed a lot over the following years. The more she became involved with the community and the more she learned about what was happening and the more she wanted to do her bit. She and Helen started to do little jobs for the IRA. They would smuggle passports, money and other documents as well as letters around the country.

As well as managing the store she worked in she travelled to different stores owned by the company throughout the Province. This allowed her the legitimacy to travel, without questions asked, to various other areas.

29

Over the following years some of the long-term serving men were released. There were mixed emotions from the women of the area waiting for their husband's return. They were going to get their men home but what would it mean for their families? Many of them had been without men for four or five years or longer. What would they expect when they got home? How would they fit in? They had been gone so long it would seem strange having them home again. Their biggest worry was how the children would react to having their father home in a role of authority when some of them barely remembered him being there in the first place.

Fridays evenings were the worst. If your husband's name hadn't been announced by then the women knew that they would have to wait until Monday before they heard anything else. Even though they were delighted for the families of those who were being released, Tess, Helen and Mary couldn't help a pang or two of jealousy and fear.

Fear because they knew they had changed as people and become so independent it would be difficult to take another person into consideration especially when they themselves had been solely responsible for everything that happened in their families' lives since the men had been jailed. Tess felt she had grown a lot more mentally than Barry had in this time. He appeared to still be the same young man who had entered the prison with very little concept of how things had deteriorated since he had last walked the streets of West Belfast.

Anyway, there would be no happy homecoming for them for a long time yet. But if they felt that way now, how were they going to feel six or eight years down the line? It would be that many years at least before their men would be released and they had to look at what life had to offer them in the meantime and continue to seek what the future might bring on their own.

They watched it all evolving with mixed feelings. Their husbands had got such long sentences that their mind-set was different to that of the other women whose husbands had received shorter sentences. They tried to be happy for them but they could see trouble brewing from the outset.

Margaret, who had been finding it harder to tolerate the fall-out from the Troubles, was, increasingly as time went by, getting very nervous about her husband, Liam, arriving home.

"I don't think I even like him anymore," she confessed to Tess one day "He's a totally changed man. One minute he's dictating to me about the changes he will make when he gets out and how he will control the children. The next minute he is crying that he doesn't know what he will do when he comes home."

"We all have our doubts at times," said Tess, "It's a scary time for everybody. You are both as worried as each other about his home coming."

"I wonder if things will be as they were before he was jailed or has he changed like I have? I feel as though I don't know that man in Long Kesh. Will I finally get a long earned rest from the responsibility of the children? How will they take to him being home and will they have to change to fit him in or fit in with him? Will he take over as boss and be critical of how I managed things when he was away and will his feelings have changed towards me in a physical sense or in any other sense? Damn it! I can't stand the thought of being physical with him."

All of this came tumbling out of her. But Tess knew she was asking all the questions the other women waiting for their partners to be released were asking themselves.

She had told Tess some time before that she no longer wanted to visit her husband anymore. She was tired of worrying about her children and what was happening to them. The kids were the pivot on which her world revolved and she was very scared that one of them would die as a result of a bomb or a bullet. All of them were teenagers now and getting harder to control. And all this worry was making her ill.

One night she said to Helen, "The thought of having to kiss him never mind having sex with him, is horrifying to me!"

"I can't see that relationship surviving if Margaret doesn't have a complete change of heart after Liam comes home," Tess told Helen one evening after talking to Margaret.

Helen couldn't understand this. She loved Mick and couldn't wait to have him home. "Damn it!" she told Tess; "I would give anything to haul him up the stairs and have my wicked way with him."

They both laughed.

Margaret's husband was ironically the first of the five to get out. His turn came a few weeks after the releases started. At about four o clock one afternoon as she was walking along the street coming from the shops, a neighbour stopped to inquire about Liam and when he might be getting out.

"I've no idea," she told her. "You know how these things are: we are the last to know."

As their conversation ended and she was walking on a car pulled up outside her house. It took her a minute or two to recognise the man alighting from the taxi. She got such a surprise she yelled; "Liam" and rushed up the street leaving the woman standing gazing after her.

Tess was teasing her later about the reception she gave him and she retorted, "Liam walked towards me and threw his arms round me; it was a lovely moment and all the neighbours came out to shout their greetings and to express their delight at him getting home. But the moment didn't last much longer than that."

She had been genuinely delighted to see him. Not least because it meant she wouldn't have to travel to Long Kesh to visit him anymore. She would also not have to buy expensive cuts of meat to take into him in his twice weekly food parcels which cost her a lot more money than she could afford.

She continued, "I was panicking a little bit really. All I kept thinking was, had I enough food in the house or was the house tidy enough. I really didn't know how to behave towards him. Should I make a fuss of him and let him have his moment in the spotlight, the little bit of hero worship that's bestowed on all the prisoners that are released. Or should I steer him to the house? I needn't have worried; he only stayed on the street a few moments! He couldn't wait to get into the house."

She was very nervous and not really sure how to deal with the whole scenario she found herself in. When Tess met her a few days later she looked very unhappy.

She told her; "He's not himself anymore. He's become very quiet. He doesn't seem to know how to react to me or the children and they don't know what to say to him. Six years is a long time to be away from home. We seem to have grown totally apart and we have nothing in common and even less to say to each other. He can't stand the noise on the street and if one of the children raises their voice he takes off to the bedroom where he stays for the rest of the day. We're all tiptoeing around him as though waiting for an explosion! It's nerve wrecking!"

As time passed the situation got worse and Margaret was unable to deal with Liam's extreme reactions to ordinary life. If someone came to the door he ran to the kitchen. She couldn't have the radio on as he couldn't deal with the noise. Any loud noise or chatting sent him running for the stairs. She asked the women not to call as he reacted very badly to anyone coming to the house, even his own relatives.

"Give him time," replied Tess. "He'll get used to being out again soon."

"It's probably post-traumatic stress," said Helen "A lot of men are suffering from it!"

"If he doesn't get over it soon he'll be visiting me in the 'big house' because I can't take much more of it!" exclaimed Margaret.

A few days later the security forces raided Margaret's house and her husband went berserk. He ran into a corner in the kitchen, hunkered down and started screaming. They had to call the ambulance and he was sedated and taken to hospital. He had a nervous breakdown. Margaret told them he would be there for a while.

"He's totally demented. I think he scared the bejaysus out of the soldiers. He certainly scared me and the kids. Bloody Hell!" she swore "I didn't think this was how things were going to be when he came out! I've been through enough!"

"I know it's rough on you," said Tess.

"I'm telling you the truth, Tess, I really don't think I can take anymore. I'm not martyr material!"

A few days later Tess and Helen met her again.

"What about Liam?" asked Tess "Is he any better?"

"He's like a bloody zombie! Filled to the throat with tablets and muttering to himself!" she declared.

"We're sorry, Margaret!" said Helen. "You're having a tough time!"

"I'm not sure I want to deal with any more of this!" she told them angerily "It was him who got involved with the IRA but it was me who had to cope while he was inside in a cushy cell getting himself educated. I was the one carrying in his food to him because he didn't want to eat prison food or wear prison clothes. I had to eat shit and wear my clothes until they became nothing more than rags while his children did without too, sometimes even the very basics."

She was very angry.

"I had to worry about everything out here and now the 'poor dear' can't cope with the noise or the raids or even his own children speaking. So where is he? In hospital being looked after once again while I'm out here with all the responsibilities. Again! What about me? Who has had to put up with everything for years? I had to? Who worried themselves sick about the kids in case they got into trouble? I did! I've had enough!" she exclaimed "I just want myself and the kids to get on with life and not have to deal with any more shit. And now it's him who has a nervous breakdown. I didn't have the luxury or the time to have one and by God I could easily have had one!" She started to cry

Tess put her arms around her and rocked her.

"It may be all right when he comes out of hospital. They'll probably sedate him until he gets used to things outside again."

"Arragh! Feck it! I don't give a damn anymore! I'm too tired," said Margaret crying and throwing up her hands "I didn't sign up for this lark and neither did his kids!"

She walked away from Tess and Helen.

"I want a man who can support me and be by my side to carry some of the weight of the shit that life is throwing at me. After all these years of caring for him I think I deserve it," she called back to them.

She stopped again a little way down the street, turned back to them and said; "Everyone says we should stand by the men when they come out. Let me ask you something, who is standing by us? Tell me that! Who is standing by us?" she repeated. Then she walked on.

Tess called after her to come back but Helen said; "Let her go! She's right, you know! Nobody gives a damn about us and what we have been through. The men are treated like heroes when they come out and we have to continue holding the families and the community together. They sit in the bars and clubs being feted as though they're great men, bloody heroes, with young lassies throwing themselves at them. She's right! I wouldn't blame her if she let him paddle his own canoe!"

Tess stood on the street thinking with a worried frown on her face. She seemed miles away. Helen asked her if she was all right.

"I know what you're saying," she said turning to her "And I know it's hard! And I don't know what I'm going to do when Barry comes home! I can't go back to being the nice, quiet, wee housewife he left and probably expects to come home to. He has no idea about half the things I get up to or what we have been through. And I have no intention of stopping any of my activities when he comes home. This is my life now! I have moved on and he can move with me or be left behind. But I won't be putting up with any of this kind of shit from him!"

Helen put her arm around her shoulders and said; "It's not easy being a woman, you know! But you and I are stronger than most! Don't forget that, we'll cope, we always do!

Tess nodded; "But is just coping enough?" she asked.

They walked on, deep in thought.

30

For a few weeks Margaret went back and forward to the hospital visiting Liam. Tess met her a few times on the street and was pleased to see she didn't seem as stressed as she had been.

"Hopefully things are changing and getting better?" she thought to herself.

But when she spoke to Margaret she was being told nothing. When asked how things were she would reply, "Never better!" and make an excuse and walk on.

Tess felt as though something wasn't quite right but she couldn't put her finger on why she thought something was wrong. Margaret had stopped spending time with the women and Tess found this strange and upsetting. When she visited her she was very polite but was always on the way out. It was as though she grabbed her coat and put it on when she saw Tess coming to the door so she wouldn't have to answer any questions.

Tess discussed this with Helen and Mary and they wondered how they could help. Margaret seemed very secretive when either of them spoke to her and started evading questions about Liam.

All was finally revealed one morning at about two thirty when Tess, who was sound asleep, answered an incessant knocking on the door. After checking out the window it wasn't the army she cautiously opened it to find Margaret outside.

"Well Girl! You're late or maybe I should say early on the road," she said puzzled

"Can I come in and talk to you for a minute?" Margaret asked.

Tess opened the door wide and said; "Of course you can! For God's sake come inside! What are you standing out there like a stranger for?"

Margaret timidly entered the hall, looking worried. After a minute she said; "I need to speak to you and I know I should have spoken to you before now but I just knew you'd try to stop me!" she stammered with what sounded like panic in her voice.

"What's wrong, Mags?" asked Tess gently putting her arms around her. "Whatever it is, we will work it out."

She was really worried now. Margaret did not seem herself at all.

"Oh! You won't be able to work this one out. It's all done and dusted and there's no going back now," she replied.

Tess was shocked at the vehemence expressed by her and was afraid of what she was going to hear. Looking closer at Margaret she realised she looked very harassed and unkempt.

"Good God! What have you done, you haven't shot him, have you?"

"No!" laughed Margaret. "But that was the other alternative."

"You have me really worried now. What have you done?" asked Tess.

"Don't shout at me, promise!" she beseeched Tess "If you don't promise I won't tell you"

"Of course I won't shout at you. What made you think I'd do that?" asked Tess.

"You might when you hear what I've done!" smiled Margaret.

"For God's sake please tell me what you have done. You really have me worried," pleaded Tess.

Margaret looked at her for a few seconds as though debating how to tell her what she was up to, then she said very quickly,

"I have a van outside; it's filled with everything out of the house I could get into it. We've been packing since early evening. The kids are all up the street in my brother's car and we are moving away from here and all the hell that is going on around us here," she gushed out breathlessly as though glad she had got it out "And I'm not coming back!"

"Oh, Margaret! Are you sure?" asked Tess, not really surprised.

"I've never been surer of anything in my life! I can't take anymore. When I made the decision it was like a great weight had lifted off my shoulders. I have felt that way since and I know it's the right thing for us."

"So that was the change I saw in her that I couldn't put my finger on," thought Tess. "She had made the decision to go and was planning it all along and she was afraid we would stop her."

"You are obviously certain about this?" said Tess.

"If I stay here any longer I will go insane. I don't know that man in the hospital and I feel no responsibility for that stranger. I owe him nothing!" she told Tess "My brother has a house rented for us near where he lives in Kerry so

I have somewhere to go. I'll be near him and not have to cope on my own anymore. I can't wait to get out of here. I feel like a ton weight has been lifted from me since I made the decision. I can't wait to get over the Border and out of Northern Ireland. I feel I won't be able to breath properly again until I do. I'll send you my address in a few months and you can come and visit. I'll not give it to you now so you can't be held responsible for knowing where I am and not telling."

"Why didn't you tell us what you were planning and we would have helped you?" asked Tess.

"Then what I was planning would probably have got out and got back to Liam or his family. Someone would have tried to stop me!" she exclaimed. "I'm leaving and I don't want anything to do with that man or this place any more. I don't love him or even like him now. I did all I could. I have the children to look after and I don't need to be responsible for anyone else. I need to get them away from here before they get into trouble or maybe murdered. He is no help going into his hysterical mode. The next thing that will happen is one of the children will be shot dead. I couldn't take that."

Tess didn't know what to say to her. She knew she was right. There had been rumours about her kids being seen in different riots lately. She knew one of them was definitely running around with a very militant group.

It said a lot about her as a mother that she got them to agree to leave with her. Maybe they knew they were skating too near the edge now and realised they needed to get away.

"I hate to see you go," she told her. "We've been friends for so long. I'll really miss you."

"I know you will and I'll miss you but you also know I'm right, if I want to keep my kids safe. I have had a long talk with them and it hasn't been easy but my brother has promised to see them right. He has his own building business and a small farm. He will train the older lads in a trade. They'll get a chance there they wouldn't get here. They'll be able to breathe fresh air that doesn't have the smell of tanks, bombs and gun powder in it. They'll be near the sea. They're coming with me but they could be back in six months but at least I'll have tried to protect them and get them away out of here."

She threw her arms around Tess and gave her a hug and held on to her tightly.

"Tell the other women I'm sorry I didn't see them before I left and tell them I said thank you to all of them for getting me through the last few years. You have been great friends. I'll be in touch with you when I'm settled and we'll meet again when times are better."

She turned on her heels and walked out Tess's path waving her hand in the air as she went.

Tess called, "Margaret? Margaret?"

She turned around and the tears were running down her face.

"Take care of yourself, Margaret! God bless you!" Tess said to her and blew her a kiss.

"I love you, Tess, you're a good friend," she sobbed. "I pray things will get better for you soon. They'll be better for us tomorrow!"

Then she walked on down the street and got into her brother's car. The children waved from the car windows as they passed calling goodbye and they drove away with their little home following behind in the removal van.

Tess ran after them for a little bit waving then she stopped and with tears running down her cheeks she wished them all the luck in the world and breathed a little prayer for them. As they turned the corner she walked back to her house and closed the door.

Going into the kitchen to make of tea before she went back to bed she smiled to herself.

"She doesn't need to send me an address. I could find her easily if she's going to live near Barney in Kerry. Didn't I stay in his house myself once?"

His was one of the houses she had visited over the years when she was doing runs for the IRA. Only she and Helen knew about this. They both had another life that very few people knew about except the chosen few. Barney had access to a man they often used to get false passports and other documents and his house was seen as a safe place for men on the run. The two women had gone on a few occasions to collect these documents and had also driven a man in the trunk of their car there who was important to the IRA and who needed to leave Northern Ireland in a hurry.

"I hope he keeps it to himself that I stayed there," she said to herself. "Margaret may be hurt I didn't confide in her if she finds out."

Next day she rang him and warned him to say nothing to her. He told her not to worry, that was all behind him now. He laughed and said, "There was no money in that carry–on, I'm concentrating on making a fortune now to keep myself and the wife in a style we'd like to become accustomed to. It's harder work but with less risk to life and limb and I'd like to be around to see the kids grow up."

His building business had become very successful and he was making a better life for the family and himself away from the Troubles. He promised Tess that Margaret would be better off with him and he would look after her and the children and keep them out of mischief.

"I'll give them plenty to keep them occupied. They'll have no time to get up to anything. It's a great place here for young ones and my lot will bring them around and introduce them to other young ones. Don't worry your pretty head, I'll have them fishing and playing sports shortly and they won't have time to think of the Troubles. It's a different world here for kids. They can be kids here without any of the pressure they came up against in Belfast."

"Look after them all for me, Barney! I'll be thinking and praying for them."

"Pray for yourself, darling," he replied. "You need all the prayers you can get up there!"

"I'll do that," smiled Tess as she said goodbye.

She felt a lot happier after that.

"At least she won't be on her own anymore and she'll have a bit of support to cope now. Barney's a good man; he'll look after her and the kids."

31

A few days after Margaret left Belfast, Lucy's husband, Dessie, came home. She was delighted to have him back and things seemed to be going fine for a while. Then Tess noticed that Lucy was getting more ill-tempered and stressed as time went by. One day taking her aside she asked her gently what was wrong.

"I don't really know!" she said "Maybe it's me! But it's as if he never grew up. He's the same man who went into Long Kesh, he hasn't changed a bit. He's still twenty three in his head with no sense of responsibility and he keeps finding fault with me, how I look and how I run the house. He can be downright insulting on occasions, commenting on my appearance or my clothes. He seems to forget the fact that we have three children and very little money. He wants me to be the young carefree girl I used to be but I'm not or can't be that person for him. Sometimes he treats me like I'm his mother, not his wife. I'm supposed to lift and lay him. He doesn't think the rearing of the children is his responsibility or indeed anything to do with him. It's as though they are total strangers with no connection to him. When I ask him to talk to them he asks me, "What do I say to them?" I told him to talk to them like young adults but he doesn't want to know and they want nothing to do with him!"

"It takes time for them to adjust," said Tess.

"He doesn't want to adjust!" snapped Lucy. "And now he has taken to mocking my work and asking the kids: "Who does your mother think she is, teaching drama? What the hell does she know about drama? She's full of bullshit!"

"The kids are not impressed; they are proud that I'm recognised as a playwright and my plays are enacted by some good drama groups."

"We're all proud of you, Lucy. You've really done well and put a lot of hard work into your writing and classes!"

"And I'm proud of myself too. I pulled myself up by my bootlaces to get where I am and I'm not letting him spoil it. I was really worried how he would fit back into the house after being inside for four years but I needn't have worried. He was no sooner in the house then one of his friends called to take him for a pint. As the invitation didn't extend to me, it was the same old story: I was left at home with the children. I don't begrudge him a drink after so long in prison but not every night of the week and sometimes during the day too at the weekend. We can't afford it but he thinks it's his right after all those years inside."

"Everything is very difficult when the men come home at first, trying to fit in with each other's expectations," Tess told her.

"I took it for granted that I would be treated with a certain degree of manners even gratitude and respect by my husband when he got out. I have been a loyal wife and I did my very best with the family and home in very difficult circumstances when he was away. Not all women fitted into that category, as you know," she told Tess. "Some couldn't resist the temptation of other men when their men were inside. They had a good time to themselves. I used to criticise them, now I'm beginning to think they were right because we get no respect for what we did from them."

"Ah! Come on! Lucy! Not all the men are like that," said Tess.

"Most of them are. Look at Margaret and many others we know," she cried. "I really believed that I would be treated like a queen and looked after when he came out after what we've been through. How stupid and trusting was I? He doesn't care about me or his children or what we went through at all."

Tess and Helen spoke to Lucy a lot over the following weeks trying to calm her but more rumours were reaching them about Dessie's behaviour. It was getting harder to justify what he was getting up to.

A couple of weeks later while having a cup of tea with the two women, Lucy was still very unhappy about her husband's continuing bad attitude and behaviour. All of a sudden she said; "I know exactly what that bloody man is!"

Tess raised her eyebrows and smiled, "And what have you decided he is this week?" she laughed.

"I'm deadly serious!" exclaimed Lucy.

"Don't keep us in suspense," smiled Helen as she poured the tea. "Spit it out! I can't wait for this pearl of wisdom."

Lucy continued, ignoring her sarcasm; "I was talking to a man who Dessie knew the other night in the club. I knew he wasn't impressed with Dessie and of course I wanted to know why. Dessie was at the bar chatting to the barman and some other men about horses and he'd left me sitting with this man I hardly knew; he'd been his ex-cell mate at one time in Long Kesh. His name is Joe

Harris. We were having a drink and trying to make conversation and I kept pushing him to tell me why he wasn't Dessie's number one fan when after a while he said to me.

"Because he's a bit of a bollocks, isn't he?"

"And you know what? That's exactly what he is! Not a bit of a bollocks but a full blown one! I never saw it before that minute," said Lucy with firm conviction. "But I can see it as plain as day now."

"Good God, Lucy! That's a bit rough," remarked Tess, shocked.

It wasn't like Lucy to use such strong language. Herself and Helen and maybe Mary, but not Lucy; Which made it all the more shocking.

"I could do without friends like that," murmured Helen.

"The guy said he was never a friend of Dessie's," said Lucy. "As a matter of fact he said Dessie was so far up his own arse he can't see the light of day."

Helen laughed out loud. She disliked Dessie intensely, especially when she saw how he was treating Lucy. But she had another reason for disliking him even more so now. The previous week she had met him on the street and he had insinuated they should get together some night. When she told him to 'dream on' he wasn't impressed and when he started to push himself on her Helen said;

"Next visit to the prison Mick is going to hear about this!"

When she told Tess about it she said; "There was a look of shock on his face and he scarpered. I knew I would have no more trouble from him. He's scared of Mick and his connections. He'd obviously forgotten who I was married to when he approached me."

Now she thought to herself; "that man's description about sums him up."

But Tess was still trying to patch things between Lucy and Dessie.

"Give him time," she told her "Talk to him about the things you've told us and see if you can work it out. Don't do anything drastic."

"Ah Tess! I did talk to him about all these things but he's not listening. All he wants is a good time. He's either in the pub, club or the bookies. He dresses up on a Friday and Saturday night to go out as though he's single and he wonders why I get upset at him going out on his own, dressed to the nines without a thought for me. He uses the excuse that he was inside so long he should now have his freedom to do what he wants."

"I don't know what to say to you, Lucy!" said Tess. "I wish I could help you!"

"I know what I would do. A quick castration would solve the whole trouble," laughed Helen

"Can you not think of anything more drastic than that?" said Tess cynically "Maybe hang, draw and quarter him, too?"

"You could line up a few other boys I know with him and we'll do them all as a job lot," laughed Helen

"You don't have a magic wand, do you?" laughed Lucy cynically, "Because I think that's what I need now and it's the only thing that might work. Unless he has a complete change of character he'll find himself looking for permanent board and lodgings in one of them clubs he's so fond of, very soon!"

A few weeks later Lucy was rushed into hospital with a burst appendix. Tess and Helen spent hours trawling the pubs and clubs to find Dessie, who was nowhere to be found.

His sister met him later that night and told him what happened. She suggested he visit her the next day and bring her some toiletries and a night dress from home. He started making excuses about why he couldn't go and she lost her temper and ordered him to go. Reluctantly he agreed.

Lucy told the women afterwards, "He couldn't wait to get out of the hospital when he arrived. It was as though he couldn't care less about me. I was of no importance! He had something else on his mind. I was very ill and they'd put me in a ward by myself and he told me he hoped we didn't have to pay extra for me lording it in a private ward. He hasn't paid a penny for a bloody thing since he came home and spends as much money as he can get his hands on in the pub or on the horses, the cheeky fecker!"

"He arrived with a nightdress and toiletries. I asked him where he'd got them and who had bought them and I was told 'a friend'."

"I knew none of you had bought them, you have better taste. I knew he hadn't bought them either because he wouldn't go into a woman's shop. To say my suspicion was aroused would be an understatement! When he left to go home I dragged myself out of the bed to look out the window to see if I could see him in the car park and there, just beneath the window of the ward I was in, was our car. As he got into it I saw a girl sitting in the front seat and I recognised her. She works in one of the clubs he goes to. Of course everything started to click into place. I had been told by various people, in a roundabout fashion, that something wasn't right. Just hints from gossips who delight in other people's misery. I was still willing to give him the benefit of the doubt but how can you fool yourself when the truth smacks you in the face like a wet dish cloth like that?"

Lucy was in a very fragile state after the visit but decided to ring Dessie anyway. She told him what she had seen but was told by him that she was imagining everything. She then told him not to bother coming back to see her but he returned the next night as if nothing happened. He proceeded to tell her a tissue of lies and because of both their families she tried to believe what he said.

After a week she was allowed home but was still very weak, both mentally and physically. After a day or so the same old pattern began again. The excuses came one on top of another. He had to go here or there, to do a favour for a mate or to cover the door at the club or help his uncle.

Lucy told the women, "He told me not to be so suspicious that it was all in my head. I was accusing somebody in the wrong and that poor girl who was in the car was completely innocent and I should be feeling sorry for her instead because she couldn't have a family and I was so lucky to have one. He was spouting the greatest load of rubbish at me and expecting me to believe it."

A few months later Lucy could take no more and threw her husband's clothes into a couple of bags and left them in his mother's house. She hid the keys of the car; she had bought it when he was inside and it was in her name and paid for by her. She sent a note to the club he was working in that she had changed the locks on the doors and not to bother coming back to the house.

"He didn't even come to check if this was true. He took his freedom and followed the nearest skirt!" she told the women "He's acting like the man about town running around with younger women. He wasn't even hiding it anymore. He'll get the quare shock when I go looking for maintenance especially as I know where he's working and he's collecting the Bru too."

The women tried half-heartedly to talk to her and get her to take him back but they knew what he was up to. They had seen him on various occasions with different women. As Lucy said, he was making no bones about what he was doing and didn't care if she knew. She was adamant he was not coming back and he obviously agreed with her.

"Myself and the kids are happy now, back on our own and there's peace again. I'm doing the work I love and there's no one criticising it," she told them. She definitely seemed more at peace with herself and no longer hurt and humiliated.

Six or seven months later, she rang Tess, arranging to meet her, Helen and Mary later that day.

"Come over to my house and I'll make something nice for tea at about seven," Tess told her. "I might even stretch to a cheap bottle of wine."

"I have a couple of bottles; I have something special to celebrate."

"That's what I like to hear. Good news I hope?"

"I think it is!"

Tess smiled and thought; "Maybe we're going to find out what has put the spring back in her step lately?"

When she arrived there was an air of mystery about her but she refused to say anything until they were all seated with a glass of wine in their hands.

Mary was getting impatient.

"Spit it out, Lucy! Who are you sharing your crumpet with these days?"

"You better start talking, woman, if you don't want strangled!" laughed Helen.

"I've got some news for you and I thought I'd better tell you myself before someone else does," she laughed embarrassedly "I have got myself a new man and he's moving in with me next week!"

Mary spluttered her wine.

"Bloody hell, child! I was only joking! That's a bit fast, isn't it? You've only got rid of the other parasite!"

Rumours of her seeing someone had reached Tess and Helen long before Lucy told them but they'd said nothing and waited to see what she would say or if anything developed from the relationship or whether the new man in her life was serious or not. Now it seemed they got their answer and he certainly was!

"Are you sure about this?" asked Tess. "Do you not think it's a bit sudden?"

"I'm as sure as anyone can be about these things," Lucy replied. "There are no guarantees with these boys but I think this one is a good one!"

"Who is this mystery man we are hearing about anyway?" asked Tess.

"Has he got a name?" asked Helen.

"Joe Harris."

"Don't I know that name from somewhere?" asked Tess.

"Is that the same Joe Harris who told you Dessie was a bollocks and shared a cell with him for a while inside?" smiled Helen.

"Well! Doesn't God work in mysterious ways?" questioned Mary.

"Indeed he does," laughed Tess.

"That's what I call poetic justice," murmured Mary.

"At least he has good taste," laughed Helen, "He knows what Liam is and he knows that you're a diamond."

Lucy was delighted the women didn't think badly of her for going out with another man.

"I was so worried about telling you about him. I thought you wouldn't approve."

"Why the hell would you worry about us approving or disapproving? It's your life and you are entitled to live it whatever way you like. Who are we to judge?" asked Helen.

"For goodness sake haven't we been through thick and thin together. Why would we turn against you now, especially after what you've been through with that other boy of yours?" asked Mary.

"I'm just jealous. Go off and bonk your brains out and give him one for me. I have to wait a few more years to do that to my man," was Helen's next comment.

The others laughed.

"Give him one for us too," they chorused through the laughter and the wine.

"Imagine keeping myself pure and chaste for him while he was inside and within eighteen months of him coming out I'm sleeping with a guy he shared his cell with?" laughed Lucy.

"Lucky you!" said Tess. "Enjoy it! These things don't come too often and I believe you should grab every little bit of happiness you can."

"I will," replied Lucy laughing now with relief. "I think I have a good one this time, at least he's mature and can speak to my kids!"

"That's a good start," laughed Helen.

Lucy hugged them all as they left. "You are such good friends. I should have known you would support me!"

Joe moved into her house the following week and she began a new and different life with him.

Helen told Tess and Mary; "At least they agree on one thing so that's a good start" she laughed cynically "The other boy is a bollocks!"

"Indeed that's a good start, they have that much in common at least," laughed Mary.

"I hope it works out for her," said Tess. "She seems to have got a new lease of life from being with him anyway. They're always out and about together and they seem to really care for each other."

"That's all any of us need, a wee bit of love and affection, TLC. Maybe she found that magic wand after all?" laughed Helen.

"I don't know what she found but it's done her the world of good and she looks great," replied Mary.

32

Walking home one evening after a meeting, Tess, deep in thought, ran into Helen.

"Good God what have we here?" Helen laughed "Mother of Sorrows?"

"I've been thinking," started Tess.

"Sometimes that can be very painful," mused Helen.

"Shut up, ye eejit! I was thinking of what I can do to contribute more to the fight we have on our hands here in Belfast against the security forces. You said we should be planning our lives instead of giving them all over to worrying about our men. Well! I need to have some impact on the Troubles and the shit we have to put up with."

"We have developed a right wee rebel in you, haven't we? Where's the quiet wee woman that wouldn't say boo to a goose all those years ago gone to? The wee woman who went in and locked her door and didn't want to know what was happening in her community?" asked Helen.

"Oh! She's well and truly gone, a long time ago," sighed Tess. "The Brits made sure of that!"

"You can say that again. I was supposed to be the rebel but I wouldn't hold a candle to you now."

"But it's not enough! I'm really pissed off! They raided our Rose's house the other night and they destroyed the place! Neither she nor her husband were ever involved in the Troubles but because of her connection to Barry and other relatives of ours they are targeting her now. They live in a quiet wee area where no one gets raided and she's all embarrassed!"

"That's what they do!" replied Helen. "No one belonging to any of the prisoners are safe – parents, sisters, brothers and children, especially the children."

Working in community projects was a real eye opener for her, a further education was received chatting to the men she delivered the notes to from the jail and listening to other women who had been through the mill or were active in the IRA. She had become very cynical.

"Now, maybe I know too much," she said to Helen "I feel so angry and sometimes so old. I have lost count of all the bodies I have seen shot dead in our wee city. How many bombed places are there? How many people do I know who have been jailed, how many children killed with rubber and metal bullets? How many women are left heartbroken after a husband or son was murdered? How many families are divided? The whole community is torn apart and I blame the British for it all."

Then she stopped and thought for a moment with a very worried look on her face.

"How are we going to fix this? How the hell are we going to fix this?" she asked desperately.

They walked on deep in thought.

"I lived with my head buried deep in the sand for years," she added eventually, "I got such a shock when I awoke and looked up and found I was sleepwalking all my life until then."

"I'll say you did!" smiled Helen "It was a fairly rude awakening!"

"Sometimes when I think of that woman I'm amazed at how little I recognise of her now and how little she knew about the people she was living among or what was happening to them. How could I have shut it all out? Now I know things I shouldn't know and I see things I shouldn't see. People tell me their most intimate secrets and I can tell no one. Some of them are horrendous."

"I know the feeling," said Helen "I feel like the oracle of West Belfast. I'm supposed to have a solution for everyone's problems!"

"They need someone to talk to and sometimes, just to have someone listen is all they need," replied Tess "If we don't listen and do what we can, who will?"

"We both know there are some who could do a lot more but don't," sighed Helen, "Anyway let me know what you're going to do when you decide. Then I'll tell you what I'm prepared to do or capable of doing with you. At the moment I can't think of anything else I can do, unless you want me and you to be Belfast's answer to Annie Oakley and Calamity Jane."

"Jesus! I wouldn't like to see you let loose with a gun. No one would be safe," laughed Tess.

"And I can see you opening up in the city centre and indiscriminately spraying all and sundry with your little temper when it blows!" Helen waved her hand, laughed and walked on, "Chat to you soon and we'll put together our dastardly plan and action it."

Tess knew she had changed out of all recognition. Now she was working full time managing the store and she really enjoyed the feeling of accomplishment at achieving this. She laughed when she thought of how worried she was at having to sell electrical goods when she first started. Now she had control of all the orders and this gave her a legitimate excuse for travelling the country.

She was proud of herself. The only worry she had was the harassment she and her family were still getting from the security forces.

"Me and every other family I know who have men inside," she thought "It's just not on! They are pushing us all the time into retaliating and we will!"

As well as everything else in her life she was still volunteering in the community and loved it. Her kids were involved in community groups too and it helped to ensure she knew where they were.

Grainne, her eldest daughter was really good with the younger children in the childcare centre and was often to be found there. Triona, her other daughter, spent a lot of time at art courses and Jimmy, her youngest, was going into high school and all were very involved in sport.

Her dad had become the kid's usual chaperone to sports events and many other places and he loved it. It gave him a new lease of life. Some evenings her mother would come over and take charge so Tess could visit families who had been badly affected by the Troubles, especially those who were having a hard time coping. She and some of the other women were trying to find ways to help.

There was a lot of work being carried out in the communities and more projects opening up all the time. Women had found their niche and were doing great work involving everyone from children to the elderly. As often happens in hard times the community was pulling together and women were at the helm.

33

Tess continued her visits to see Barry and in between his family and friends visited him. Between them they made sure he had everything he needed.

Working full time she was making good money and having worked hard to get where she was she took care not to jeopardise her job. As the only breadwinner, she needed to ensure she had enough saved to put the children through college. Barry still wanted his food parcels, cigarettes and clothes to keep up with his cell mates next door: It was a lot easier now with the money she was making to provide what he and the children needed. She was also her own boss and could work the hours she choose which was very handy.

Still she felt there must be something more she could do.

The solution to her pondering came one evening when a woman she knew asked her to go with her to check on her son who had been lifted and was being held by the police. While sitting with the mother in the barracks she spent her time looking around the reception area and later a waiting room they were brought into. She asked to use the toilet and realised the police had placed no restrictions on her and she had plenty of time to suss out her surroundings. Nobody seemed bothered as she walked around.

Later that week she was delivering a note from Barry to an IRA activist and she happened to mention to him where she'd been and what she saw. He asked her to sketch what she remembered on the back of a book he was holding and she was surprised at what she could remember. It was possibly because she had been so surprised at having so much freedom to walk around that somewhere in her subconscious she knew this knowledge would come in useful.

A few weeks later she heard that the Barracks had been blown apart. She guessed it was due to the information she had given. She felt a real sense of achievement, as though she had succeeded in hitting back at the security forces for all the humiliation she had experienced at their hands, for the destruction of her home and the humiliation of every other woman she knew.

"Now let's see how they feel about living in rubble!"

Although she was a little afraid the information she supplied would be traced back to her she felt no regret at all. After talking to the man she was supplying the information to, he told her they couldn't hit every barracks she was in and could now hit a few she hadn't been in due to other information they'd received, she felt better about it.

She justified it to herself saying, "Me and the other women have been subjected to this sort of harassment and brutality for years I'm delighted to see them get a bit of their own medicine back."

She spoke to Helen about it and discussed how else they could help. A few weeks later they set up a help service for people who had relatives lifted and held in different barracks throughout Belfast and the surrounding area.

They brought in other women to assist them but only Helen and Tess supplied information to the IRA: the less that knew what they were up to, the better.

The programme they developed for helping the families was very simple but efficient. They researched solicitors who were good with prisoners and families involved in the Troubles and had a list available for many areas. The main criteria for them was that, they had to be empathic to those they were helping, knowledgeable and willing to go the extra mile which was often needed. They researched the law and policies for holding those arrested and often became a thorn in the flesh to the authorities.

Because of their attitude they got away with a lot more than others would. They trained the other women to smile and joke with the security forces in order to get their own way. Sometimes this was difficult but they knew it worked better than aggression.

The number one rule among the women was; "Keep your friends close and your enemies even closer" and was often heard recited among them.

All the women dressed conservatively and acted professionally and one of them always went with the relatives to check on how the prisoners were being treated. They set up legal counsel and arranged transport and money.

The women knew the inside of many Barracks intimately both inside and outside Belfast and many of them ended up with large holes blown in the sides of them.

They also learned a lot about the crooked court system which dealt with Catholics one way and others another way. They knew there was a high chance of any Catholic who was lifted getting a custodial sentence whether innocent or guilty. It was just another Nationalist off the streets as far as the security forces and courts were concerned. Nationalists were proving to be a very big thorn in the side of all in the judicial realms of Northern Ireland.

34

While working with the IRA the women had continued their smuggling activities to different parts of Ireland. They would travel by train or car to Donegal, Dublin, Dundalk and all over Ulster.

Nicely groomed and dressed and often with their children, no one ever bothered them. Travelling mostly at weekends or in the holidays they stashed the money in false bottoms of their picnic baskets, suitcases or handbags and they would be met by a designated someone at a specific rendezvous, such as an zoo, tourist park, historical manor house, restaurant or cinema.

They went to Galway for a week's holiday once and met a contact there and another on a visit to historical sites in Clare. This was also how they ended up in Kerry with Margaret's brother.

These trips were not too frequent as they didn't want to take the children out of school or take too many risks of getting caught. Questions might be asked about where they were getting the money to take so many breaks and holidays although with both of them now having good jobs they could cover these queries. But going too often would only increase the risk.

Tess had smuggled some small arms to different areas of Northern Ireland while travelling for her work but she wasn't happy about this. Too many evenings found her up back roads and down boreens in the middle of the night talking to strange men. She didn't want questions being asked at work about where she was. She knew if she was caught with a weapon she would get years in jail.

Then came a day when she was asked to take a trip to Paris with funds and passports for a group of activists training on the continent. She was excited about this as she had never been to France and fancied seeing Paris.

Helen nearly blew a fuse when she heard about it. She had gone on the trip without discussing it with her. But Tess was now very nonchalant about it.

"You know something, it was a wasted trip. I was totally peed off. There I was in the middle of Paris and I saw nothing, I mean nothing, except the Eiffel Tower in the distance. The contact didn't turn up and I was terrified waiting for him in a strange place and not being able to speak the language. I couldn't leave the room in case I'd miss him."

"Are you bloody insane?" Helen asked her through clenched teeth "How long do you think you would get jail for on the continent if you were caught?"

"It's all over now," said Tess "Bar you shouting, that is. Don't get your knickers in a twist. I won't be doing that again"

"I should bloody well hope not!" snarled Helen "You've got a brass neck on you! You are getting too foolhardy. Be careful and don't take too many more risks, will you? Let them do their own bloody dirty work. You have three kids to look after. What happens if you're lifted in Europe? They won't see you for years! They will be old people when you'd get out! Can you imagine that? How would they feel with no father or mother and both locked up. I know they're in their teens but they still need you, you eejit!"

"Don't worry. Sure butter wouldn't melt in my mouth," she smiled with a little girl lost look on her face.

Helen grimaced; "I'm wasting my breath talking to you," she laughed "But, Tess, I'm dead serious. It has to stop! You can't do any more of this!"

"It was a waste of time anyway. I got word to abandon the whole lot, shred the passports and come home. The contact had spotted a tail."

"Oh! Jesus Christ! You're lucky he spotted the tail before he met you or you could have been locked up abroad along with your contact. You had a very lucky escape. I hope they don't discover you were in Paris at this time or you could be in shit!" said Helen, shocked.

"I never thought of that!"

"Well! That's fairly obvious, ye twit! It's time to pull in your horns and start behaving and start to think of these things!"

"Ah! Don't worry about me, my Angel Guardian is always looking after me," laughed Tess.

"You watch in case your Angel Guardian gets her wings clipped and she doesn't make it to the next sticky situation you find yourself in. I thought I was bad but you take the biscuit at the risks you take!" said Helen.

"The thing that really pisses me off is I was so excited at going to Paris and all I saw was the road from the airport and the walls of the hotel room I stayed in."

"Listen to me carefully, you could have been seeing the four walls of a very small cell. No more!" snapped Helen. "I couldn't even afford to go and visit you too often!"

“I agree with you! I promise I won’t do it again!”

Later the shock of what she had actually done hit her and she realised she was becoming too adventurous. She was going to have to clip her own wings as advised by Helen.

“From a wee, naïve, quiet woman who hardly left the house, to someone who found it exciting travelling alone to France with funds and passports for the IRA, you really take the biscuit,” one of her IRA contacts told her.

No one thought nice women like Tess or Helen would be involved in such activities, especially not with five kids between them. They were very careful not to speak to anyone about their activities except to those who were in the need to know.

But now Tess knew in her heart she had to stop taking chances and to be careful or her children would be left without either a mother or father. The Paris trip had seemed like something too good to miss but now, with hindsight, she knew the reality of the situation and knew it was madness. Any other romantic ideas she had went out the window. A grotty hotel in a backstreet of Paris was not her idea of adventure or romance.

“Next time I’ll check the accommodation and itinerary before I go,” she laughed.

“There’ll be no more trips like that for you anymore, my girl!” said Helen. “Even if I have to tie you to the table leg.”

She believed she was fighting for the future of her children and all those other children around the Province; now she knew those same risks could lose her those children.

There was also the fear that loose tongues would let slip information on their activities and it would not only get back to people they knew but to the security forces. As far as they knew from the outside their reputation was squeaky clean, except as known Nationalist sympathisers. No one ever thought they were anything other than good Samaritans but the risk was always there.

“There are too many touts around Northern Ireland,” said Helen. “They have very loose tongues and are too fond of saving their own skins or getting a few quid for the next bottle of cider or packet of cigarettes!”

“That is obvious to everyone,” replied Tess. “It is getting worse each year. We need to be very careful.”

“Who are you talking to?” said Helen. “I’m tired of preaching at you to curb your activities.”

“I think I’ve finally started listening to you. There have been so many caught reporting to the security forces its surprising and shocking the hell out of me! It's one of the reasons I am curbing my involvement. I have done nothing for a few months now."

"Maybe it's time for both of us to make that permanent and let someone else take over. We've done our bit, we've nothing to be ashamed of; we tried to help and did our best. Now might be the time to call a halt to it all."

"Maybe you're right?" said Tess, surprising Helen when she realised she was serious. "I'm getting tired of it all and is it really changing anything?"

The two friends sat quietly together with their own thoughts. It felt like the end of an era but also a huge relief. They had made their decision, their war had been fought and now it was over. It was time for someone else to take up the baton. They were getting older and tired. Now they needed rest and less stress.

35

Community groups developed and expanded and came very much to the fore in the 80's and 90's. Belfast especially saw them emerge in the Nationalist segregated enclaves. The Catholics knew they could not rely on getting jobs through family connections in the mills, shipyard or factories, a lot of which had closed down by now anyway. They needed to educate their young people in order to find employment elsewhere. Even the Catholic men were coming out of prison with degrees in various subjects. Education was seen as very important.

Many of the centres were education focused but would have gone under if so many women had not volunteered in them. They knew there was nothing for it but to look after themselves, no one else was going to do it for them. Everywhere you looked there were women in one guise or another trying to keep body and soul together in the communities. They were the glue that kept them intact.

People were very wary about leaving their own areas; it was too dangerous for a Catholic to be seen in a Protestant area and vice versa. Communities and families were split because of mixed marriages. Some families lost touch with loved ones for many years as it was too dangerous to visit them.

If you married someone from a different religion you made your choice. You were either one religion or the other and you lived in the area of the religion you had chosen or left the country. Although, it was not always that simple: people were often burned out or run out of an area because they dared to marry someone of a different religion.

Fear and worry were close companions of most people living in these culturally partitioned areas. You could not flit from one cultural side to the other. If you did, then it was seen as though you couldn't be trusted! Maybe you were carrying information? One night you might find yourself with two holes blown in your kneecaps or worse.

Destruction was all around with burned out cars and buses, bombed premises and debris from riots littering the streets.

It was said that even if you were a Jew in Northern Ireland you had to decide if you were a Catholic Jew or a Protestant Jew. You had to nail your colours to the mast for one religion or the other, no matter what else you were!

Houses on one side of the road could be Catholic and the other Protestant and riots with petrol bombs and shootings continued between the two cultures regularly.

Drinking clubs were another invention at this time in both Catholic and Protestant estates. They sprang up overnight in all forms of buildings because it wasn't safe to socialise outside your area. Some were little more than shacks and often seen as the headquarters of the local paramilitary group. Cheap drink, dances, music and paramilitary meetings were the order of the day.

Young girls were not allowed to associate with British soldiers or they would find themselves stripped, tied to poles and tarred and feathered.

There were many other incidents of young women going to parties and ending up in the wrong place with the wrong people. A few days later their bodies would be found badly disfigured in isolated areas. There was very little respect for life.

Through the years of the Troubles children were sent out of Northern Ireland for breaks all over the world. Funding was being accessed from Europe, America, Canada, New Zealand and Australia to organise the trips. Some of the women, including Tess and Helen, went as leaders and their children also got to go once or twice.

Tess and Helen's horizons broadened further when they went to Canada and the US to speak to anyone who would listen about the hardships and brutality that was being meted out to the Nationalist side in Northern Ireland.

"I would have seen none of the world if I hadn't got involved in supporting the Republican position," she told the women "The height of my vision would've been my own street. My kids are now like globe trotters because of their travels. You hear them talking about 'my friend in Calgary or my amigo in Andalusia' as though it's the most normal thing in the world. It has opened up a whole new world for them."

The Troubles continued to have a huge impact on the women's lives. Many women survived only because they were numbed by Valium or other sedatives.

The cruelty meted out to the young and old by the security forces continued with the usual results, more fodder of young people for the war machine and more heartache for the mothers of Northern Ireland.

36

One thing that worried Tess most was what was happening between men and women when the men came out of prison. She was regularly listening to women who were finding it hard to cope with relationship break downs as a result of them and their husbands growing apart due to the long separations. On top of this there were many disagreements between the fathers and children who couldn't cope with living with each other again.

She decided she would have to talk to Barry about it as she felt he was looking at his future release through 'rose tinted glasses' and needed to change his idealistic perception about stepping into family life again when he eventually was freed.

Having spent years away from Tess and the children she didn't think he realised how different everything was. Everyone had changed. The children had grown up and were becoming independent young adults and soon they wouldn't need their parents to tell them what they should be doing. Tess could see problems with how they would relate to Barry coming home and taking back the role of father again, a role they were too young to remember him ever having in their lives before.

It was one thing to tell a person about what was happening but it was quite another thing to have lived it. Tess did not believe Barry understood the full impact the Troubles had on her, the children or the community they lived in. As time went by the problems with families increased and she knew she would have to try and deal with it.

"Nothing is the same. Many of the men spend their lives in pubs with the other men and the families are neglected. Marriages are breaking down all over the place and there is a high volume of domestic violence," she told Barry "People are finding it very hard to cope and there is no outside help for them to access. They need post-traumatic-stress therapy but there is none for them. The powers-that-be don't give a damn enough to provide funding for it."

She knew what she told him was having very little impact on him and she was wasting her time.

"I'm worried," she told Helen "I know I most certainly have changed and I will never be the same again. I'm sure he must have changed too."

"That's the problem," replied Helen "The women all say that the men have not changed at all. They haven't grown up. They have had no responsibility for years and they certainly don't know the problems we've experienced. They haven't had to pay a bill or worry where the next penny was coming from. Everything was handed to them. It's like they never developed and matured. Why would they, when they had nothing to worry about? The outside world is a remote place to them, not relevant while they are inside."

"I can understand that," mused Tess, "They all look as though they only went in a few weeks ago. The women have all aged through the effect of what they've had to deal with in this hell that is Belfast, in their absence."

"That's about it!" said Helen, "And how do you explain all that has happened to us to someone who wasn't there and get them to understand how it's affected us?"

"Look around you and the men all look well dressed and the women are going about in cheap worn out clothes," remarked Tess. "I don't know how many women I know who have had their husband complain about how worn out they look! I think they are still looking for the young woman they knew before they went in even though they have seen her age down through the ages."

"No understanding! Just no understanding!" moaned Helen. "And the pubs are full of these men consoling each other. I'll kick my boy's arse if he thinks for one moment that he's joining them when he comes out."

"I think Barry is like a young fella who can't wait to get out. I don't think I could put up with much shit from him after what I've been through. I'm certainly not the wee women he left behind! She would probably have been grateful for any attention she got from him."

"You can sing that again," laughed Helen. "If he thinks you are soft little Tessie, his wee hand maiden he left behind, boy is he in for a surprise?"

They laughed about it but deep inside Tess worried. Having been on her own so long and done so much, she had become very independent.

What worried her most now was that she wasn't even sure if she wanted to live with a man again, any man, never mind Barry!

Next time she went to visit him in prison she tried to get him to think about what he would do when he got out. She spoke to him about the lack of work and the danger of going outside their own area and what was happening with the men who came out and the high percentage of marriage breakdowns. He didn't want to know. He dismissed all her worries as not relevant to him and he didn't seem to think there would be any problems.

Tess wasn't impressed with his attitude and felt he was burying his head in the sand. He had a dream that he was going to fulfil and he wasn't going to let her ruin it for him while he was still inside.

"I suppose I can understand that," she thought. "It is probably one of the ways that helped him cope inside and kept him going but he should have a more realistic view or at least give it some thought."

He'd spent too much time with men who had given little thought to their wives or their children. They spent all their lives planning a war or looking forward to a good time.

"It sounds like most of them are aiming at reclaiming their youth when they get out," she stormed angrily to Mary after another pointless conversation with Barry. "Well! This is one woman who is not going to take any shit from him when he comes out or anyone else."

She, Helen and Mary were now being left pretty much on their own at their chats around the kitchen tables. Margaret wrote once or twice a month and sounded happy. Lucy was engrossed in her new relationship and her play writing which was going well. They often went to see the plays when they were staged and were impressed by how good they were.

One night after seeing one of them Tess told the women; "It's like looking at events that happened to one or other of us over the years, isn't it, except she makes them funnier!"

"It is all about us!" said Helen, "I never thought I'd see my life story on stage, did you?"

"No! And it makes you realise the place the women have in the history of this city. I'm delighted she is writing it all down, nobody else will," said Tess.

"Good for her," said Mary. "I hope she's making a few pound out of it too."

Their children were now in their late teens and early twenties and doing well. Tess's two girls were in third level education and Jimmie was finishing secondary school and she was delighted. She'd always promised herself she would educate them as she'd educated herself and drummed into them the importance of education and they were now determined to graduate.

Life had improved in general for both Tess and Helen except for a few minor worries about their men.

Reminiscing one day Tess remarked to Helen, "Do you remember when we were travelling with the children and doing wee jobs for the IRA? I was terrified the children would find something and inadvertently spill the beans.

Can you imagine one of them rooting through one of the bags and shouting at the top of their voice, 'Oh Mammy, I found a pile of passports and a load of money in with the sandwiches!'"

"I've imagined a scenario like that many times as I lay in my bed at night" laughed Helen. "The sweat would run off me. But at that time getting our own back on the security forces was more important. We were so angry. When you're young you don't think so much of the risks. We were lucky!"

"We did our bit when it was dangerous to do it and we took an awful lot of risks I don't know how we got away with it. I'm glad we recognised it was time to leave when we did and left the rest to others. We had pushed our luck far enough," Helen remarked

"I'm glad it's over and we've come to terms with walking away from it all," said Tess.

"So am I! At one time I thought I was going to have to lock you in a room to stop you taking chances."

"I know! I think I was so angry for so long I was verging on insanity! I felt so unable to do anything to stop all the injustices that were going on all around us and I needed to do something to get my own back."

"I know exactly how you felt but it was getting too dangerous and we had too much to lose. It was time to stop!"

"I'm glad we did but I don't regret a minute of what we did!"

"That's my wee rebel!" laughed Helen as she hugged her.

37

The Trouble escalated in Northern Ireland and Belfast was very much a war zone. Almost every day there were riots in one place or another and the pressure from it all continued to take its toll on everyone, especially the women. You saw worry and stress etched in their faces as you walked down the streets. Homes were in turmoil. Communities were at war with each other and with the security forces. Women did their best to keep their children safe but it was very difficult.

Tess went overboard getting her kids involved in different activities to keep them occupied and away from the riots or any other trouble.

The other women teased her about how she was protecting them and laughed about her having the fittest children in Belfast. They were at every sport she could get them involved in. When they weren't there, they were at language classes, both Irish and French or at art and music courses. This was on top of their college work.

Helen would laugh and tell her she was going to have the best educated recruits the IRA ever had in another few years.

Tess wasn't impressed.

"I'll ship them all off to Dublin to university if I get one whiff of them having paramilitary tendencies or I'll send them to Margaret. I might even go myself," she told Helen. "I'll be out of here so fast there will be sparks flying from my heels and I will kidnap them if they don't want to go. I'll go into their bedrooms when they're asleep and tie them up and carry them off."

Helen would laugh but knew she meant every word she said. She was so determined they would not get involved with the paramilitaries.

They had got Barry and they had got her but no way were they getting her children.

"My two get their extra exercise running from the British soldiers when they escape my beady eye and end up in the riots. You're lucky yours listen to you and your father has a tight rein on them."

"I'm making sure my lot are not fit to get up to any mischief. By the time they get home in the evening they are exhausted," laughed Tess "Or their brains are frazzled with all the different classes I send them to. The two girls are really into their music which helps."

"I hope they don't turn out like them kids up the street! Their mother begged, stole and borrowed to educate them until they thought they were too good for her. Now they are living in big houses in Tyrone and she never sees them and she lives in poverty down the street."

"At least they're alive and safe!" returned Tess. "But I will make damn sure mine have a good grounding and remember where they come from, even if I won't let them join the IRA. Can you imagine my lot putting on airs and graces and going into my mother's house? They'd never get away with it."

"I can see your father looking at them if they put on posh accents and saying; 'Don't speak when you have something in your mouth because I can't understand you.'"

"Or my brother; "Ye better lose that accent if you don't want a strip torn off your backside with the toe of my shoe?"

"He would make a show of them on the street every time he met them until they learned to appreciate where they came from, no matter who they thought they were or where they were going," laughed Helen.

"My father would have them out in the back yard digging the spuds until they would be grateful to act normal and respect their family and culture again. Can't you see him with his gentle but firm voice, "And where do you think you're going lassie with another two stone of spuds to be collected?"

"I can't see them being stuck up," said Helen. "They're great kids! They're like my own, good craic and get on with everyone."

"Here's hoping it lasts!" mused Tess, lifting a cup of tea and toasting their children.

38

Even though they were no longer involved in paramilitary activities Helen and Tess were still plotting and planning.

Now it was what event, project or course they could develop, where could they access money from for the projects they planned or how to extend childcare facilities or build another room onto one of the centres.

They spent so many years running around from pillar to post trying to fix things for people they didn't know how to slow down or stop.

One year, just after Easter Tess decided they all needed a break away from the oppressive atmosphere of Belfast.

"I think we should go on holiday," she told Helen "We never go anywhere anymore! We arrange for others to go now but we don't go ourselves. We need to get away from here for a while."

"Bloody great idea!" laughed Helen. "When? Where were you thinking of going? We could get our holidays off from work together and me, you and Mary could head away somewhere with the kids!"

"Wouldn't it be great to just get out of the city for two weeks, two whole weeks away from here?" Tess said. "How about July which is three months away and the weather will be better and the kids will be on holidays from college.

"That's eleven children and three adults. It's some undertaking. You haven't started to print your own money, have you?" laughed Helen.

"No! But that's an idea! You don't know any auld boy with a printing press he could lend us?" laughed Tess

"Have you anywhere in mind to go to?"

"Do you know where I think we should go! I think we should go and visit Margaret!"

"Oh! I would love to do that! But it's so far away with so many of us. She lives in Kerry for God's sake!"

"It's not that far! We can do it! It's only a matter of planning," said Tess. "I have it all worked out. Our Sean has a mini bus and he can take us there and come back for us. We'll give him the money for petrol. He owes me a few favours. Margaret and Barney will put us up if we take sleeping bags with us. We will bring a pile of food from here, it's cheaper. We'd have to buy it anyway to feed our lot here. All we'll need is spending money and a couple of dozen bottles of wine and we're elected."

"Remember our lot are not kids anymore, do you think they would come with us!"

"To go and see Margaret and her lot? Of course they will. Aren't they always talking about them?"

"You have it all worked out, don't you, Professor!" exclaimed Helen "And it could work!"

"Of course it will work because I'm a genius!" smiled Tess "And Margaret lives in the middle of the country away from the town so the kids won't need much money because there's nowhere to spend it. They'll have a great time exploring the countryside. They'll love it."

"It just might work indeed," Helen mused.

"Of course it will. The kids will be delighted to get away. And what's eleven kids to three great women?" laughed Tess. "We'll all look after our own lot. We're well fit for it! They're old enough to look after themselves really, they'll be grand and we've three months to save for it!" said Tess. "It would be so good to have the break for us all."

"It would be great to see Margaret's lot again!"

"So it's sorted. We're going?"

"We're going!" laughed Helen.

Tess started the ball rolling the following morning by ringing Margaret, who could be heard squealing with delight three streets away.

She kept saying; "Are you really coming, are you really? I thought I'd never see you again!"

She was thrilled they were willing to make the trip to Kerry and she didn't have to go back to Belfast to all her bad memories to see them. She chatted about where she lived and how much she loved it.

"I'm dying to show it all to you. It's a beautiful area," she went on enthusiastically, "The scenery is great and the children will have plenty of places to explore. My lot will look after them all."

"If you take sleeping bags we have a huge big attic room where all the boys can sleep. Barney and my boys will partition it off for your boys. The girls and the women can have the bedrooms. Some of my children can stay in Barney's house," she told them, getting more excited by the moment at the idea.

Everyone was on a high at the thought of getting away. The young people couldn't stop talking about it. The women could hear them chatting to their friends about what they would be doing. Animals, swimming in the sea, making hay and collecting apples seemed to be some of the most exciting things they could think of. Cycling the country roads, dances and fishing were also mentioned. They were on the phone constantly to Margaret's children about what they needed to take and what they could expect.

"Imagine we can collect apples off the trees and my Ma says you can collect blackberries and wild strawberries too," said Grainne to her school friend.

"Jimmy said he is going to learn to milk a cow and a goat," said her friend with the sound of disgust in her voice. "Can you really milk a goat?" she continued.

The most exciting part of the trip to the boys seemed to be that they would be sleeping in sleeping bags.

"The boys are all going to be sleeping on the floor in a big room and us and the mammies are going to sleep in the beds," Grainne told everyone.

"None of them have had much to do with animals, except dogs or cats and they're really looking forward to it. But what have we let ourselves in for?" Tess asked Helen one evening, "Can you imagine the racket with the boys all on the one floor?"

"It isn't a problem, they are all old enough to look after themselves," laughed Helen "And if we have enough wine we'll be anesthetised enough not to notice them. Anyway they'll be in the middle of the country and no one will hear them so they can make as much noise as they like. It will be good for them to go around screaming if that's what they feel like, after all they've been through."

"That sounds like a great idea. I'd nearly go around screaming myself if I didn't think they would lock me away!" laughed Mary.

"Maybe we should have screaming sessions every morning in one of the fields just to get all the frustration out of our systems?" laughed Tess "Don't you feel like it sometimes?"

"Nearly every day," sighed Mary. "We could start a new trend, "The Screaming Jennies!"

"And be run out of Kerry!" laughed Helen.

39

Eventually, the morning of departure arrived and they woke up early with great excitement and there were no more questions of; "How many days are left now?" The day had finally arrived.

They had packed the mini bus the previous evening with the roof rack full of cases and covered in a tarpaulin in case of rain.

When Helen saw Tess and her children hauling case after case onto the roof of the van she remarked, "Is the kitchen sink in there too?"

Mary laughed and said; "I think it's in that ancient brown case with the bumps on the lid of it."

"You'll be glad of a lot of the contents of my cases before we come back," chuckled Tess. "I have everything from medical supplies to medication for us to soothe our nerves at night."

"She means wine!" laughed one of Helen's boys.

Tess's daughter Grainne said; "I don't know how you drink that stuff. It tastes awful."

"See!" said Helen to her sons. "And you think I enjoy it?"

The other women laughed. With gathering excitement they piled into the mini bus and they were off, headed for Kerry.

You could touch the delight in the air. Adults and young alike were looking forward to two whole weeks out of the oppressive atmosphere of Belfast and in the open countryside of Southern Ireland in County Kerry.

The teenagers couldn't stop chattering and planning what they were going to do. For half the journey they sang every song they knew encouraged by the older ones. Then the women told stories about their childhood. They stopped half way and had a picnic with the food they'd cooked and brought with them.

After a good stretch of the legs and a walk around they once again boarded the bus and were on their way to Dingle, their next stop and where Margaret was to meet them.

After a while, with the heat and excitement, some fell asleep while the others read or chatted quietly. When they passed the border of Kerry, Tess rang Margaret, as she had promised, to let her know their progress and help her judge what time they would arrive at their destination.

"You'll not miss the bus," she told her "It is packed solid with young ones, women, bags and cases and a big green tarpaulin over it all."

Margaret laughed and replied; "Well! I'm glad to see you're being patriotic anyway."

"You didn't expect an orange one now, did you?" laughed Tess.

Peace reigned in the bus with the young people now playing cards and the women chatting. Others dropped off to sleep again.

As they neared Dingle, Tess decided they should wake everyone up so they could see where they were going and enjoy the scenery. Gradually excitement began to escalate and fill the bus.

All heads were staring out the windows, including the older ones, looking for the first sighting of Margaret as they drove into Dingle. As they approached the Main St they started to shout; "I can see her! I can see her!"

The windows went down and a chorus of voices was sent up the street; "Margaret! Margaret!"

Sure enough, along the street Margaret stood, looking around her, obviously searching for who was shouting her name and where the noise was coming from.

The children shouted her name louder, waving frantically. She finally saw them approaching through the traffic and started to jump up and down, waving and shouting back, as excited as the young ones. The mini bus had hardly stopped when they'd all tumbled out and ran to hug her. She was lifted bodily into the air by some of the boys and swung around. By the time the women got to her she was fending off hundreds of questions.

She beamed at them with a huge grin, walked to the three of them and hugged each of them tightly to her. Her face glowed with pleasure and she laughed; "I think they're happy to see me!" she smiled then she threw her arms around the three women again.

"I'm so happy to see you all!" she laughed with tears in her eyes. "I thought I would never see you again. I was so delighted when I heard you were coming for a holiday."

"Good God let me look at you!" said Tess. "What have you been doing with yourself? You look ten years younger, doesn't she, girls?"

"I don't know what you're using but I'm getting half a gallon of it before I go home!" laughed Mary.

"Me too!" said Helen. "You look amazing. You've lost about two stone and you are glowing."

"Good country air is the answer," said Margaret "And very little to worry about. I'm out in the fresh air every day and grow my own vegetables and fruit. I have a goat and a couple of cows I milk, I keep a few pigs and I have chickens to lay eggs. I'm almost completely self-sufficient now and I get plenty of exercise."

The change in Margaret was remarkable. She wore blue jeans that she couldn't have got into the last time they say her, with a white t-shirt. She had grown her hair which she now had in a ponytail and her skin looked flawless and toned. On her feet she had a pair of Moses sandals. There wasn't an ounce of spare flesh to be seen. She definitely looked ten years younger. The strain that had been on her face in Belfast was gone and she looked completely relaxed.

"You're a new woman!" exclaimed Helen smiling at her. "Kerry seems to certainly agree with you."

Tess turned to Helen and Mary. "Have you ever seen such a change in a woman?" she asked, amazed.

"As I said it's all the healthy fresh air and the work on the farm and not a whiff of gas or the sound of gunfire or a bomb," replied Margaret. "I love working on the land and looking after the animals."

"Is this the same woman we used to know? The same women from the depths of Belfast who didn't even have a cat? asked Mary.

"I'd nearly move myself if I didn't think I wouldn't have withdrawal symptoms from the smell of traffic, bomb fumes, the sound of rubber bullet and live rounds lulling me to sleep at night," laughed Helen.

When the younger people heard about all the animals, the excitement rose a few more decibels.

"Are we really going to stay on a real farm with real animal and can you really milk a goat?" asked Tess's daughter Triona. "I told them at home you could milk a goat but they wouldn't believe me!"

"Goat's milk is very good for you. It's full of herbs because that's what they eat. I drink it all the time," Margaret told her.

"That's probably what she is getting her glow from!" claimed Mary.

Then came a chorus! "Can we learn to milk the goat too?" Everybody laughed.

The women were delighted to see her looking so well. It was like talking to a new woman. Gone were the nervous outbreaks and she seemed to have found her confidence and her place in the world and could only be described as a happy woman.

"There must be a man in the equation," said Mary.

"Oh for God's sake," Helen laughed. "She would look more stressed if there was."

The other women laughed.

For the next two weeks they discussed everything that had happened since she had left Belfast.

"There is no need to ask you if you regret leaving," said Tess one evening during the following week.

"I don't think I would be alive today if I hadn't left," she replied "I was in a very bad place mentally especially in my last six months in Belfast. It wasn't until about a year after I arrived here that I realised just how bad I was. It took me two years to pull myself out of it and it was hard work. Thanks to Barney and his family, I made it."

"One day I was walking along the lane about a year and a half after I arrived here it just hit me that I didn't have to deal with my ex again or the Troubles or Belfast. I didn't have to worry about the children getting involved with the paramilitaries and I wasn't going to get raided again. At that moment a big worry seemed to lift off my shoulders. I felt lighter and I straightened my back. Reality hit me like a bolt. I felt such a relief and joy I danced around the lane. I couldn't stop. I spun around and around with my arms in the air and I hugged myself with the sheer disbelief that I had got away from it all."

"I kept shouting to myself Oh! Oh! Oh! And dancing up and down. It felt unbelievable. Then I cried with relief and washed all the worry away. It was then I started to live again. I got Barney to buy me the goat and teach me to milk her. I got the hens and I built the hen run myself with instructions from him. He gave me a calf and I hand reared her. The boys all have jobs with him and they spend the rest of their time helping around here or over at his place. They may go out at the weekend but they are often playing football on a Sunday and they mightn't bother."

"You're really like a new woman," exclaimed Helen, awed but so glad for their friend.

"I am a new woman," laughed Margaret "The woman that was in Belfast no longer exists. I love this life. It's sheer freedom after what we went through.

Every morning I get up with a spring in my step and so much gratitude in my heart for getting away from the awful situation I was in."

"And the sixty thousand dollar question!" laughed Mary. "Is there a man?"

Margaret looked pensive and said seriously; "You know something, I don't want one. I discovered since I started my new life that because I have to answer to no one, I do far more with my life. Nobody to control me and I don't have to justify anything I do, to anyone. I don't think that living with a man again would suit me."

The women looked at each other. Margaret looked at them and continued pensively,

"This is something I have been thinking about a lot lately. I think men and women should live apart. It's always a problem when we live together. I think boys are very close to their mothers and as they become adults they go looking for someone like her to replace her and look after them. But they will never find anyone like her because a wife cannot be a mother to him. She has to be a mother to the children they produce. The men then resent this and mayhem ensues. We should definitely live apart and only come together to procreate. He can go back to his mammy and visit his children on occasions and we can get on with what we do best, rearing our children and looking after the home."

"Sounds all right to me," laughed Tess. "But you forgot one bit we should be doing. If we didn't have to put up with all the other hassle, we'd be ruling the world."

They laughed together and Helen became quiet; "You were the quieter one of us in Belfast, with not much to say, but when you do say something you often surprise me."

"And you could be right, Margaret," laughed Tess. "It sounds like a good arrangement to me. I have become my own woman since Barry was locked up and I know for a fact I would have continued being the quiet wee mouse if he hadn't been jailed. I would never have evolved like I have if he was still at home."

"And I know I would never have got myself educated if Mick was still around," said Helen. "I would have continued to see him as the breadwinner and the one to be educated."

"Me neither," agreed Tess. "Barry would have thought it a waste of time. He does even now. All this makes me realise even more so that I will not tolerate any shit from him when he comes out. I have a feeling that all the men have some kind of an idea that when they get out that we should worship them and they can do what they like and we will put up with it."

"The evidence sure seems to point that way," said Margaret.

"Well! My boy is in for one hell of a surprise if he thinks this baby will put up with any messing," said Tess.

Helen laughed. "I nearly feel sorry for him."

"I wouldn't bother," said Margaret. "Look at that man of mine. He felt so sorry for himself he had a breakdown the first time we were raided. Did he feel sorry for me and the dozens of times I was raided when he was locked up or for the children and all the times they were turfed out of their beds? Did he hell? I hear he's living with another doll now. She's welcome to him. Neither I nor the children are interested in what he does and he's certainly not interested in us!"

"All right girls! That's the end of chatting about men for the next fortnight. We can't let them ruin our holidays. They have taken up enough of our lives for the last twenty years," said Tess. "They are now off the agenda. This is our time."

In a chorus they all agreed.

40

Later Tess finally realised just how much things had changed for all of them. Now they had a better quality of life than ever before. She and Helen had more money than they ever had, they owned their own homes which were nicely furnished and drove good cars. Their children were young adults getting their educations or doing well in work. They had good clothes for themselves and the family and they could go out at night for a meal when they felt like it.

All were cautious with money, never wanting to return to the bad old days when they had to depend on charity shops to cloth their children or borrowing from their families who could ill afford it.

Margaret's life had changed beyond recognition in Kerry and Mary's children had grown up and were fending for themselves and they looked after her too.

"I look back now and it's as though I came out of a nightmare. A very long nightmare!" Margaret told them.

"I don't recognise myself now," said Tess, "God but I was innocent and I've certainly changed out of all recognition!"

"You were a bit of an eejit all right but by goodness you were a fast learner," laughed Helen teasing her "I used to think I was the smart one but today I have to run to keep up with you and sometimes I've had to yank your chain to make you slow down or you'd have got us all killed."

"What's she up to?" queried Margaret.

"She's not too bad now but she used to be in and out of police barracks and houses she shouldn't be in and out of and she says she is just doing her job. That's her night job by the way, not her day job. She doesn't get paid for it either! Sometimes she comes up with ideas I have to sit on her to quench!" laughed Helen as she shook her head at Tess.

"What are you up to, Tess?"

"I'm a good girl now!" she replied with a grin.

"And you better stay that way or I'll clip your wings!" laughed Helen.

"I'm an angel now, aren't I?" she asked the other women

Mary kept quiet as she often did when she wasn't sure she wanted to hear what was being discussed. She had known for years the other two women had some involvement in the Troubles but she never asked questions. She knew all she needed to know, they were her friends and they supported her in all she did and that was all she needed to know.

Helen continued, "Yeah! Right! You floated too close to the wind too many times for my liking. I still have to yank that chain to stop you and make you think and remind you what you have to lose."

"I'm better now," laughed Tess "Really, I am!"

"You'd better be!" said Helen. "I don't think my nerves could take much more."

"Look after yourself, Tess," said Mary quietly with a smile. "We'd hate to lose you now, after we've been through so much together."

"Come on, girls!" said Margaret, "Spill the beans. What have you been up to, Tess?"

"That's for another day further down the line," smiled Tess.

Margaret and Mary were not silly women and they could read between the lines. They had known for years they were involved with the IRA and often worried about them and they were always in their prayers. They never asked questions, which you learned quickly not to do in Belfast. They just hoped they would stay safe.

As the holiday came to an end no one wanted to go home.

"I can feel such a change in my attitude since I came here. I'm beginning to think like you, Margaret. Maybe we should all move to Kerry. It was great to get away from everything. It's like another world here," said Tess.

"You'll not get me to leave Northern Ireland!" retort Helen "It's my home and where they'll bury me."

"Yeah! In the City cemetery, where the Catholics are segregated from the Protestants with a wall that's built underground to keep them apart," said Tess.

"Doesn't that say it all?" remarked Mary.

"Belfast is still my home and it has been battered and broken but I still love the place," said Helen.

"She'll leave Belfast when I get my dream house in the country," laughed Tess. "She can come and live up the road from me."

"I'm safe enough then. I have been hearing about that dream house for as long as I can remember and not a move towards it have I seen," said Helen. "But wouldn't it be nice if we could get away from the Troubles for a few weeks every year and recharge our batteries?"

"I'm here any time you want to come back," said Margaret "You will only see me if you come and visit me here because I have no intentions of setting foot in that city again if I can help it. I can't bear the thought of it."

"You had a bad deal, Margaret, but it's not all bad," said Tess.

"Maybe!" she replied. "But it's how I feel."

"But you have family there; do you not want to visit them? I know they miss you a lot," said Helen.

"I'm here when they want to visit. I've asked mum to come and live with me now dad has gone, she was down a few months ago and said she would think about it. She loved it here. My sister wants to come too but she can't get her husband to agree. He's up to his eyes in the IRA so he won't leave."

"She's on tenterhooks all the time in case he gets lifted and jailed. She would be delighted to get him out of there, like a lot of other women. I think that's her main reason for wanting to move here, that and worrying about her children."

"I hope things change soon. We keep hearing rumours of talks between the IRA and the British Government but the British are denying it," said Mary.

"Yeah! My brother was talking about that last week but he still thinks it's a long way down the line," replied Margaret.

"Maybe if things get better you will come back to see us?" said Helen.

"Maybe! Maybe not!" said Margaret, not committing herself to anything!

"Personally speaking, if I looked as good as you and a place was instrumental in my doing so I would be reluctant to leave it too. But we miss you, Margaret, and we would love to see you anytime but we'll be back," Helen promised.

The next day a mini bus loaded with some very sad people left Kerry on the journey back to Belfast. They'd all had a great time and enjoyed the holiday immensely. It was so totally unlike anything they had done before. The young people were fascinated with the animals and the countryside and had fun trying to milk goats, feed sheep, cut hay and silage and many other farming jobs. All got stuck in. Helen's Chris and Kieran mastered the milking in no time and had to be stopped from scooting the young ones with the milk from the cow and goat's teats.

The hay loft was a haven for many of them when it rained which, luckily for them, wasn't often. They brought their books with them and read tucked up in the hay. Grainne wanted to bring some hay home with her because she loved the smell!

Tess could imagine a stack of hay in the corner of the bedroom and Grainne sleeping on it. Helen laughed and told her it would save her washing bed clothes.

"All you'll have to do is fork it out the window and replace it with a clean bale."

Margaret's children taught the older boys and girls to do lots of different chores on their uncle's farm including driving the tractor which they loved. Every hour had been filled with something different and things they would never have got the chance to try back home. It opened up a new way of life for them.

If they weren't working on the farm they were attending football matches or the youth club, making new friends, with a small romance or two thrown in. There was fishing or walking through woods nearby, tracking deer and spotting pheasants and other game birds.

As with all young people, new visitors to the area caused a stir and they became the centre of attention. Both the girls and boys revelled in it. It was like a different world to them. As Belfast city kids and all they brought with them the Kerry people were as fascinated with their experiences as they themselves were with the novelty of the countryside.

It took them a while to come to terms with the accent and the peace and quiet but as they got to know and understand the area and different people they came to love it. Every morning there was something different even if it was only to help build walls.

They loved it when the women took tea in flasks and sandwiches out to them in the fields where they were working and they would all eat in the fresh air with the sun shining on them and nothing but the sound of birds and the lowing of cattle in the distance.

Everything was peaceful and Belfast seemed a million miles away. There was a lot of laughter.

Now as they travelled home a deeper quietness descended the nearer they got to Northern Ireland.

"Will our place always be like it is?" asked one of the younger girls as the city came into view. "Why can't we have a nice quiet place to live in like Kerry with no soldiers on our streets like Margaret and her family?"

"Maybe one day!" sighed Tess. She was feeling the sadness too.

"I'm going to ask Barney if I can work with him!" said Brendan, one of Mary's boys. "I could learn a trade and I think Margaret might let me stay in her attic and I wouldn't need very much money."

"That's a good idea," said Mary.

"I wouldn't mind going too!" said Pat, another of Mary's boys.

"I'll ring Barney and check with him. He was saying the building trade is picking up. Maybe he will have enough work for you soon."

"Thanks, Ma! It will get us away from here and give us a trade."

"Aye! That would be good," sighed Mary, hating the idea of her sons going away but glad to see them leaving the 'Troubles' and all it meant.

The freedom they'd experienced in Kerry had been wonderful for them all, with no worries about soldiers, checkpoints or wandering into the wrong area. All involved were going to miss it. Mary's two boys wanted more of it and were going back.

"Will we ever get the soldiers off the streets?" asked Triona.

"We'll get rid of them one of these days," replied Helen's son Chris, who was now eighteen.

"Never mind the 'we'." snapped Helen sharply. "You keep your nose out of all that and leave it to others. I have lost enough without having to worry about losing either of you two."

"We all have to do out bit", remarked Kieran. "Or nothing will change."

"If I have to lock you up I'll do my best to keep you safe," replied Helen angrily.

Chris laughed; "Cool it, Ma! I tower over you now. So which army are you going to get to help lock me up?"

Kieran, who was nineteen, laughed, "Maybe she'll get one of those fishing nets Barney uses for trawling on the boat and throw it from the top of the stairs? But there are two of us and we'd have to be standing close together. Or maybe she could get you first if I was out and then wait for me to come home," they teased Helen.

"But then the Brits would come raiding and would ask questions about why she had tied such lovely boys up. They'd do her for cruelty to her little boys and lock her up," laughed Chris.

"You're not too big to get a clip in the ear yet!" laughed Helen.

"Ah! Ma! You'd have to run and jump to get to our ears if you wanted to clip them," they teased her.

Helen and Tess laughed with them but each knew that there was a very serious side to it all. Both boys had been involved in a lot of the riots over the last few years. Lately they had been disappearing for long tracts of time with no explanation of where they were.

They would tease Helen about being an over-protective mother but she was worried sick. She was now having rows with them on a regular basis and she didn't know what to do to stop them being involved in the IRA. She had tried arguing and talking to them with no satisfaction.

It was obvious that neither of them wanted her to know what was going on and she worried about it all the time. She caught tail ends of conversations and whispered telephone calls and she knew in her heart they were active in the IRA. She was very afraid of what could happen to them and she knew it would break her heart if anything did.

She spoke to Tess about it on many occasions but neither could think of a solution. They treated her like they treated their mother, with laughter and humour. She had asked a few men if they would stop them but was told there was no stopping some of the young people. They were running their own units and carrying out their own operations. They were listening to no one.

All on the bus had now fallen quiet with their own thoughts and worries of what they would find when they arrived home.

They were old enough to understand that the environment they lived in was not normal and they wanted better. Kerry had been like a different world and a vision of how things could be.

What they faced now were check points, aggro on the streets from all sides, neighbours and family being shot, riots, arrests or murders and the thought sickened them. It was no way to live and all had to find their own way of dealing with it. Some ignored it as best they could, others vowed to leave as soon as they could and the rest vowed to get even.

They could feel the gloom descend as they turned off the M1 and entered West Belfast. Nothing had changed, the streets were still covered with graffiti, murals and burned out vehicles and the very air smelled of oppression and depression.

The women looked at each other and their shoulders seemed to droop. It was back to the hard slog of everyday life and trying to keep everyone safe, it was back to working in the community and trying to make a difference against strong odds. It was back to fretting about their husbands and dealing with all the hardships and atrocities that faced them daily. No one was looking forward to any of it. But all would go on to deal with it in their own way, some with tragic results.

Pat and Brendan left a few weeks later and broke their mother's heart even though she knew it was for the best.

41

Although Tess and Helen had ceased all activities with the IRA a few years previously, their beliefs hadn't changed. They wanted the British out of Ireland and felt it was the only way to restore a lasting peace in the Province. They believed they had to contribute to finding a solution to the problem.

The atmosphere was starting to change and people were talking about looking at resolving the conflict by more peaceful means. They hoped that something would happen soon to bring a cessation to the violence.

On the other hand, there were lots of others who believed, as history had shown, that the British could not be trusted to keep their word. They felt the only way to deal with them was with violence. They believed that violence was the only way the British knew how to deal with the 'Irish Question' and they would have to hit back as hard, if not harder, to achieve anything.

This was the hard liner's way of thinking and there were still many of them around. There was also the element that had made names for themselves and a lot of money by inciting violence. Maintaining the Troubles in the Province was very much to their benefit.

The women now believed there had to be another solution. The violence could not continue.

As they talked one morning Tess asked; "How in God's name can you get all the factions in Northern Ireland together to agree on a peace process? You have the Provos, the Stickies, the Real IRA, the Continuity IRA and others on the nationalist side, then you have the UVF, the UDA, the UFF, the LVF, the Red Hand Defenders and the Orange Volunteers on the other side. What are you supposed to do to sort out that lot? And that's only the paramilitary groups. After that you have the British army, the RUC, the Northern Ireland politicians and Dublin and London politicians. Just how, in God's name can you find a solution to the Troubles among all that?" asked Tess worriedly.

"Then there are the ordinary Catholics and Protestants in Northern Ireland and the Republic Catholics and Protestants, who also have a say. It's worse than a hornet's nest. Good luck to anyone who can do it!" said Helen.

"I don't care who does it or how they do it but I hope they do it soon and not leave it too late for our children!"

Day after day, more young people were being shot dead, blown up by bombs or jailed. Helen was at the end of her tether not knowing how to protect her sons or what could be done to keep them safe.

"You know that saying 'the apple never falls too far from the tree?" she asked Tess one day "I keep thinking that. No matter how you try to protect your children when they become young men and women there is very little you can do to stop them doing what they are hell bent on doing. That's what makes me worry so much about my boys. Both their father and I have done our bit for 'The Cause' so how can we expect our children not to do theirs too? But I so hope and pray they stay safe."

"Face it," said Tess. "We'll always worry about them. I'm just glad my lot have shown no interest in being involved and that I know where they are most of the time and that both of my older ones are girls. In a year or two it mightn't be the same when they get out of college. They will want to do their own thing without the Ma interfering, like all young ones. Now I can still grab them and march them home if there is a riot or anything else going on. They would die from embarrassment if I did but they know the chances I would, are there. My father has them under his thumb too and seems to be able to control them. He just has to put up his finger and they do what he says. I hope it lasts!"

Both women found themselves still busy attending meetings and talks looking for solutions to the thirty years odd years of war.

"The biggest problems I have at these meetings are the egos of men wanting to make a name for themselves with very little thought to the impact their words or decisions have on the community we live in." stormed Helen one night on the way home again from another of the many meetings they had attended that week.

"We have to keep talking! But maybe we need to stop those who are spouting violence at the meetings. We need to look at other areas too, especially the impact on our youth by what is reported in the news." retorted Tess.

"Maybe that is what they are relying on. Let the young ones do their dirty work and make them big men in the process," said Helen. "I'm finding it all sickening."

"And they are getting our kids killed at the same time!"

"We did the same for them. We threw the balls when others made them and we helped others throw the balls too," said Helen. "Were we wrong?"

"That was different," argued Tess. "If we didn't do what we did then or if the men didn't do what they did we would still be under the thumb of the British tyrants with no civil or human rights for Catholics here. The men we worked with weren't getting their names in the papers with statements encouraging further violence while they were supposedly looking for peaceful solutions to the problems!"

"And they are worse on the other side," lamented Tess. "There is so much hatred and vitriol spewing from them, it is dreadful! The only thing them boys care about is lining their own pockets. They don't care about our children or our homes or even the Province."

"The worst is that the radio, TV and other media are broadcasting this hatred from the other sides although Sinn Fein and anyone with Nationalist connections are banned from the airwaves, so our views are never heard."

Behind closed doors discussions continued but no one knew exactly what was happening. Rumours circulated and died until another round started.

But it was better to keep talking, they decided. Many arguments ensued. Reports went out but there was little feedback. They talked to anyone they could who had any influence in political areas. They were part of a think-tank of women ex-activists looking for solutions and continued to work diligently in one way or another for an answer to the problem that was Northern Ireland.

42

Into the 90's the hardships continued. Tess visited Barry in prison regularly but her children had no interest in seeing their father anymore and often refused to go. She would try all her powers of persuasion to get them to change their minds and to go at least once a month but it was an on-going struggle.

They could not remember him being at home or being a father figure. He was a stranger to them. She worried how things would work out when he eventually got home and knew it would be a difficult time for all. Barry was still totally oblivious to future problems. Life in prison was now his reality and he didn't think further than getting out the doors of the prison sometime in the distant future.

Helen's children were in their late twenties and often went to see their father. Being older than Tess' children, they had very fond memories of him.

Helen knew this had a big influence in deciding their behaviour. He was their hero. They had always resented him being taken away from them and wanted to do what they could to avenge this.

Every day she continued to worry about what they might be up to. As time elapsed she grew more afraid for their safety and realised that if she knew of their involvement in the IRA then the British Army probably knew it too. Each time they left the house she begged them to be careful and worried herself sick and prayed until they came back.

Since they had been young teenagers they'd been subjected to a lot of harassment on each visit to Long Kesh from the security forces. This only made them more determined to seek revenge and get their own back. They felt it was a matter of principle that they be allowed to visit their father without harassment and also the visits, which were frequent, were another way to get up the noses of the security forces. Walking into their lair while they continued to fight them on the streets and in the countryside gave them great satisfaction.

Helen was terrified they would follow in their father's footsteps and be locked up for years with their young lives passing them by or worse. The boys had heard stories of jobs their father was involved in when he was in the IRA years before and they were very proud of him.

"If those barstool Fenians would shut their mouths and stop making such a hero out of their father, I mightn't have so much trouble reining them in now!" Helen stomped one day after she had heard the boys had been seen with guns on a side street during a riot on the Falls Road.

Nothing she said to them changed their opinions. The boys grew up believing it was their duty to carry on their father's work and nothing was changing that.

She had even begged them to emigrate. Begged them to go to her relations in England or America or even go to Margaret in Kerry. Nothing worked!

Then one morning her worst nightmare became a reality. It was a few minutes after seven thirty and she had got up to make a cup of tea and on the way down stairs she had checked the boys' rooms and realised their beds had not been slept in. This was very unusual because they always came home or if they were not going to make it home they would ring her to tell her they were delayed or staying with friends.

She began talking to herself; "Stop thinking the worst! They'll be home soon," she thought.

She went into the kitchen and was waiting for the kettle to boil to make the tea when the doorbell rang. At that moment a wave of nausea came over her. The sweat started to pour off her and she had to hold on to the worktop to steady herself. She knew no one who would ring her bell at that time of the morning. The boys had their keys and Tess would telephone her if she wanted anything.

She was afraid to answer it. Slowly she walked into the hall. There was a tall shadow silhouetted in the stain glass on the door and she gulped as she recognised the shape of the uniform of a policeman with another standing behind him.

When she opened the door an RUC men were standing there with a jeep pulled up at the front gate. She could feel her blood freeze and her face stiffen with fear. Before the one in front said anything she knew her worst nightmare was about to come true.

"Please don't say anything," she whispered. "Please don't say anything!"

She knew if he opened his mouth and spoke, her world would fall apart.

His first words confirmed her worst fears,

"I'm sorry," he said. "I'm afraid your son Kieran was killed in a car bomb explosion last night."

There was a sound like a huge wind in her ears and her mouth filled with water. She staggered and the RUC man caught her as she fell. He took her inside and put her on the couch.

After a few minutes she came around and she asked where her other son, Chris, was.

He told her that her eldest son, Kieran, had been blown up transporting a bomb to a hotel in the city and her youngest son Chris was seriously injured from the same bomb. They were travelling together. He was now in intensive care in the Royal hospital and the doctors didn't know if he would survive.

"The two of them," she whispered, and her mind screamed in despair.

The RUC men were kind enough about it and asked if they could do anything for her or get anyone to come and stay with her. Helen couldn't speak. She shook her head and eventually told them she would be all right and they could go. She wanted them away from her.

They reluctantly left and she closed the door after them. Her legs gave way under her and she had to sit on the stairs. She tried to breathe properly and stop shaking enough to get the strength to lift the phone and ring Tess.

She tried many times to ring but she was shaking so much she kept hitting the wrong numbers. When she finally got through all she could say was; "Tess! Please help me!"

"I'm on my way. I'll be with you in a minute, Helen!" Tess shouted down the phone, hung up and ran to get dressed.

She was worried sick at the sound of Helen. She knew she wasn't just sick or something simple like that. She sounded as though she was dying, she asked no questions; there would be time for that later. She had to get to her best friend as fast as she could, that's all she knew, something was very wrong!

She pulled on a pair of jeans and a jumper, shouted to the children that something was wrong with Helen, ran down the stairs and out the door as fast as she could move.

She arrived within minutes to find Helen slumped on the stairs, crying helplessly. She helped her into the living room where she wrapped her in a blanket to try and stop her shaking. Then she tried to find out from her what had happened. Eventually the story the policemen told her came out.

Helen kept repeating; "Oh Tess! Kieran's gone and Chris might die too!"

Tess was stunned by the dreadful news. She called the hospital to check on Chris while she waited for the kettle to boil to make her a hot, sweet cup of tea, as Helen was obviously in shock. When she got through she handed the phone to Helen but she was unable to deal with it.

Tess took the phone back and explained to the nurse that Helen was in shock and couldn't speak. Could she please let her know what was happening? The nurse put her through to the doctor who was on duty when the young men had been brought in the night before and he explained what had happened.

"I'm very sorry but the older of the two young men was dead on arrival. He is now in the mortuary. Christopher, the other young man, is very badly injured and on the critical list. He has lost half his left leg. He has many other superficial injuries and we are checking for internal injuries. We have him in intensive care at the moment after a six hour operation. I will speak to his mother if she comes to the hospital this evening. He will be unconscious for some time yet so no one will be able to speak to him."

Tess' children arrived to see what was wrong and they began ringing around relatives and friends to tell them what had happened. Grainne got the car to bring Helen and Tess to the hospital to see Chris, as neither felt able to drive. When they got there he was still unconscious and they were told it could be hours before he came round.

Helen said desperately to Tess, shaking her arm; "I need to see Mick. Can you arrange it? I need to get to him, please!"

"We'll get you there, Helen! Of course we'll get you to him," she said as she held Helen in her arms.

Tess rang Sean, her brother, and got him to take Helen to Long Kesh.

She kept saying; "I hope they don't tell him until I get there! He'll be devastated!"

But he knew before she arrived. You couldn't keep such dreadful news from getting out and 'the powers that be' decided Mick should be told before another visitor spilled the beans. The priest who attended the prisoners had told him a little while before Helen arrived and he was waiting for her with him. When going into the visiting room Mick walked towards her with the desperate look of a shattered man. He held out him arms to hold her, despite the warden shouting "no touching" at them. They stood holding each other for as long as they were allowed, in shock and mutual grief.

"They thought they were invincible," Mick cried as he held her. "No one could talk to them! I tried to tell them it was not a game that there were dire consequences to waging war against the British."

"I know, Mick," she wept "I know you did your best to stop them. I know you loved them dearly. But they wouldn't listen to anyone!"

Both loved their boys so much, not least for their wicked sense of humour and their wildness but because they knew they had good hearts and loved their parents in return.

Kieran with his wicked sense of fun was now gone and Chris might not live to speak to them again, his injuries were so serious. How would they survive this?

43

For the next few days Helen moved as though in a trance. When she wasn't needed to make decisions for the funeral she was in the hospital at Chris's bedside where she clung to his hand willing him to survive. At first the security forces weren't going to let her sit with him but the surgeon interceded and they relented.

The doctor told them; "This young man is going nowhere and this woman has lost one son already. She needs to be with her remaining son!"

Helen was severely shocked. She'd always feared that one of them might be killed but as she told Tess; "It is not until something becomes fact that you really know the impact. How can I deal with losing my sons? What would I have to live for if they were gone?"

These two larger than life characters were her life. Now one was gone and there was a strong possibility she would lose the other one. Even if Chris didn't die, he had lost a leg and was bound to end up in jail for many years.

The women had to almost carry her through the next few days. Along with Mary, Margaret and Lucy, Tess was worried sick about her. Margaret had arrived from Kerry a few days before the funeral, even though she had vowed never to return to the city. She moved in with Helen for a few days to support her and help her cope.

Tess and she took Helen to the hospital and collected her afterwards. The rest of the time was spent helping with the funeral arrangements and the wake, making sandwiches and looking after people arriving regularly at the house to show their respect and express sympathy.

Ensuring she ate a little, they provided copious amounts of tea and titbits and they made her go to bed at night, even if she only lay there crying. They coordinated people to spend the night vigils with Kieran's body as was the custom as a mark of respect for the dead. All of their children, with the exception of Margaret's, stayed close and looked out for their mothers. Mick was allowed home on compassionate leave for the day of the funeral, albeit handcuffed to an RUC man. Helen and he clung together as though seeking strength from each other.

The morning of the funeral arrived and the coffin was removed from the house with the Tricolour over it. A guard of honour marched with the hearse to the church and afterwards to the graveyard with Helen, Mick, Tess and the other women coming immediately behind with all their relatives after that. As Kieran was buried a salvo of shots rang out over the grave.

"Is that what he died for?" said Helen to Tess at the graveside cynically, "A few shots over his grave? I suppose, at least, his name will go down in the history of the 'Troubles'. I just have to find some way of believing that losing him was worth it. You don't expect to see your child go into the grave while you stand at its side watching and knowing that you will never see him again! He was only twenty eight!"

"He fought for a lot more than that and he believed he was doing the right thing and it was the only thing he felt he could do," Tess told her.

"I can't see that now. I can't see that anything was worth me losing him, Tess. Nothing!"

She remembered very little of the funeral afterwards. Thousands had attended the removal from the house to the church and after the funeral mass to the graveyard. She remembered none of it.

44

For a long time afterwards her only focus was Chris and Mick. If she wasn't with one she was visiting the other. The women rallied round but felt helpless and guilty for being glad it wasn't their children it happened to. Although Margaret had come up for the wake and funeral, she refused to let her sons come.

"They're so angry! They loved both Chris and Kieran and looked up to them. All I hear are 'Them bastards have to be got out of Northern Ireland. If they weren't there Kieran would be still alive!'" she told the women "It doesn't matter that Kieran and Chris were transporting a bomb, they were only fighting for their country as far as my boys are concerned. I'm so scared they'll head back here and get involved with the fighting too!"

"After you go back and things settle down they will get back to normal," said Tess "Barney will sort them out. Their lives are in Kerry now and they love it. They won't come back here! I don't believe they have any heroic ideas about the Troubles as far as I could see after speaking to them the last time we visited."

"I keep telling myself that but this could be the trigger for them! It's worrying. Barney promised he will keep an eye on them until I get back. He'll keep them busy and leave them little time to think. Then when I return I'll get them through the next few months and years, hopefully."

Since their first trip the women and many of the children returned year after year. Mary's two sons, Pat and Brendan, had settled there now and had married. Everybody loved it. The young people argued about having to do many things but the one thing they all agreed on was: every summer for a fortnight they went to Kerry if it was possible.

It was their haven, where they renewed their souls working on the farm, playing, watching sport or running around the countryside. The women caught up on their lives, cooked, walked, drank wine and relaxed.

Now Margaret was heading back and felt she was deserting Helen.

"Maybe I should stay another week to try and get her through this," she told

Tess "Maybe we should get the doctor to give her sedatives"

"No! You go home and look after your family. They need you now. Helen is suffering from grief and only time will heal that. She doesn't want to take sleeping pills or sedatives because she wants to be alert to look after Chris. She is a strong woman; we just need to give her time! Margaret, you need to go back, they need you! We'll look after her."

"I know you will, Tess. I just feel so helpless that I can do nothing for her!"

"We all feel the same way. That is what happens with a sudden death, especially with a tragic young death! It is so final and we all feel helpless but it is too late and we can do nothing but wait."

They were all very worried. Helen was losing weight and looked so frail. They got a doctor to come to see her and his verdict was as Tess said: "She's a strong woman, give her time. She has another son to stay strong for. He needs her now and she knows that!"

For many weeks a desolate Helen sat by Chris's bedside, wishing and praying for a miracle. Gradually he rallied and began to improve but without the bottom half of his leg. He was heartbroken about Kieran but spoke very little about the night he died.

When she wasn't at the hospital Helen spent most of her time with Tess talking or in long silences. She couldn't bear to be alone. She claimed her mind would return again and again to her beautiful dead son lying in a cold grave and her other son, lying injured in the hospital, who might never see a day of freedom for many years to come. On top of that Chris had now to deal both mentally and physically with life after losing his brother, his leg, and with whatever the courts would dole out to him.

Tess was practically force feeding Helen, buying tasty snacks to try and get her to eat. Meanwhile she kept repeating that she had to keep up her strength to look after Chris and to do that she had to eat. Gradually she was adding a little more to her diet of cigarettes and coffee and was regaining some of her strength.

"She's strong and she has a good survival instinct. She will get back to us again one of these days," she told Mary.

"I hope so but this is such a devastating blow for anyone, no matter how strong they are! I wish Chris's trial was over and she knew what was going to happen to him."

"At least while he is still in hospital she has him near her. It gives her a reason to hang in there," retorted Tess.

"I suppose you're right," murmured Mary as she left to check on her own family. Everyone was on tenterhooks in case one of the other children would decide to take revenge for Kieran and Chris. Margaret reported from Kerry that she was keeping her sons very close to her for the time being also.

Chris spent the next few months in hospital due to the amputation, internal injuries and other complications. Helen spent so long in it she was developing the pallor of the hospital. Tess would tease her that she was almost institutionalised. Even though she made fun of it she was worried Helen would never get back to her old self – the strong independent woman she knew and loved. She looked haunted with a look of deep pain in her eyes.

After a few weeks of being off work on compassionate leave her boss arrived to see her one evening when Tess was with her. He wanted to find out if she needed more leave or did she feel like coming back to work. Tess begged her to go back but Helen was very hesitant.

"You need the money, Helen," she told her. "And you need to start living again. Chris needs you to be strong for him."

After a few days pondering, she decided to return. Apart from anything else she enjoyed her work, she knew she needed to get out into the world again and there was no one else to bring in money. She needed every penny she could get her hands on to look after the house, herself and Chris. It had been months since she had been anywhere except the house and hospital. Tess did all her shopping for her so she didn't go to the shops.

The first few weeks back were difficult and Helen would break down in the toilets on a regular basis. But gradually her fighting spirit returned and her old sense of the irreverence wasn't far behind.

One evening she told Tess, "I'm nearly glad he has lost half his leg if it means he will stay out of trouble and stay alive. He can't really run around with a gun under one arm and a crutch under the other, can he? The thing is they will probably stick him in Long Kesh as soon as he's ready to leave the hospital"

"I'm afraid you may be right," said Tess.

"They don't go in too much for rehabilitation in there, do they?"

"No! I can't see them being too sympathetic."

Surprisingly the court let Chris home on bail until his trial. Helen was ecstatic. "Well son! They probably know you can't run away," she told him

"No!" he said pensively. "But I could hop pretty quickly," he laughed.

She looked at him for a minute and then said seriously; "You know you could, son, you really could!"

He looked at her and he knew immediately what she was saying. They said no more but Helen prayed he wouldn't have to go to prison.

He started physiotherapy the following week and a few months later he was fitted with a prosthesis. He worked hard to cope with it and gradually learned to walk on it with little discomfort.

He began to visit some of his mates' houses in the evenings and they would come back to Helen's house to keep him company. They were very good to him, drawing him out and helping him talk about Kieran. Eventually Helen heard them laugh about some of the escapades he and Kieran had been up to and she was glad he could now speak about him as his brother and not as a dead person, gone but to be eternally grieved over. The sound of his laughter gave her a real boost.

After this they would sometimes sit in the evening together and chat about their childhoods and the antics she had caught them at. It was getting easier for both of them to remember and speak of him. Even though the loss of Kieran would never ease, the pain was not as acute. His name could now be used without tears.

"Thank God to hear him laugh again!" she told Tess. "This house has been so empty without their laughter"

Watching his friends help him walk or examine the prosthesis to see if there was a better way of stopping it hurting his leg, she was very grateful to them for all for their care, even the teasing he got from them about being hop-a-long. This was all part of getting back to normal.

Within another couple of months, he was walking well with only a slight limp. Sometimes he suffered from inflammation on the amputated leg but he took care of it immediately and efficiently before it got worse. He was determined to get back on his feet as best and as quickly as he could.

She was very proud of him and how he very seldom complained of the pain and stress he had to go through in his programme of recuperation and she was glad he had the time to catch up with everyone. She couldn't bear the thought that soon all this would be lost to him and he would be behind bars for a long time.

She prayed nightly he would find some way out of it. Somewhere at the back of her mind she had the idea that Chris and his friends were planning something. It was like when she knew the two boys were involved with the IRA even though she hadn't been told.

She told Tess, "It's a mother's instinct!"

"Well! Whatever it is I hope it works," said Tess. "Get him to the other side of the world but keep him out of prison is all I pray."

45

One night, after she had been asleep for a few hours, Chris came to her room. "Ma! I need to talk to you," he said. "Can you sit up? This is very important!"

She looked at him and said, "Are you going away now, son, so soon? Where are you going?" she asked shocked that her premonition had come around so quickly.

"How did you know I was going?" Chris asked surprised.

"Ah! son! You wouldn't want to spend your life inside a gaol cell, would you? Sure I knew that. Have you sorted out your bail money and got it paid back?" she asked.

"Yeah! We had a bit of a windfall and it's all paid back," he said and laughed.

She had heard about a bank robbery in Armagh a few weeks before, supposedly by the IRA and they had got away with a large sum of money. She didn't ask if this was the windfall but she was pretty sure it was. It would be just like the IRA to use British money to aid Chris's escape. They would love the irony of it.

"Good man!" she told him as she got out of bed "Is everything arranged and you know where you're going"

"Aye! Ma! It's all arranged! You don't need to know where I'm going now but when I can I will be in touch," he said as he hugged her tightly to him.

"Let me know where you settle and me and your Da will go and see you when he gets out."

"I will do that, Ma!" he said as he put his arms around her again. "Give me a hug and we'll say goodbye. I love you, Ma! I couldn't have a better mother. I'm so sorry we brought all this on you! I know how hard it is going to be for you but it's the only alternative I have."

He hugged her tight again as though he didn't want to let her go; "Now we don't want any tears. This is the best for all concerned!" he said as he kissed her forehead.

"I know, son!" replied Helen with tears rolling down her cheeks. "I'm glad you're doing this, even if it's only for a few more years' freedom. You just get on your way and we will see each other as soon as I can arrange it. Get a bit of a life for yourself out there and be careful. Breathe the air of freedom and appreciate it. I love you, son!"

"I've no doubt about that, Ma!" he said "I love you and Da, too! Give him a hug from me."

"I will son. We'll be praying for you."

"I'll be grand, Ma! Kieran is with me," he told her as he placed his hand on his heart. "He always looks after me. We'll get through this too."

They hugged each other again and said their goodbyes. She stood and looked out the window until he was out of sight; within minutes he was gone, secreted off into the dark night to God knows where.

There'd been no car collecting him at the door and she knew this was so she wouldn't know who was involved and she couldn't hassle them for news later.

She sat down heavily on the bedroom chair. "I feel so ancient!" she thought as she cried and held herself. "I feel as old as the earth itself, like my life has walked out the door with my poor Chris."

She had given birth to him when she was only twenty years old and he was now just twenty five and now she had lost him, all because of this awful war that was raging around them. She couldn't lift a hand to help him or herself, she could do nothing to change their circumstances. Although she'd insisted on him taking the few pounds she had saved, that was all she could give him or do for him.

Both of her children were now gone. One was dead and the other gone to God knows where. She didn't know. Maybe he would never return.

Much as she had told Chris they would go and see him when his father got out of Long Kesh, she knew this was only a pipe dream. Mick would be allowed into very few countries abroad with a prison record. How could they go anyway? They would probably be followed by the security forces or someone and Chris would be arrested and taken home to an even longer jail sentence for absconding. Where would he go and how would they know where he was without the security forces finding out? Would he be caught by the police or the army even before then? Or even now, were they watching him? Would they arrest him before he got away?

Pulling the blanket off the bed she wrapped herself in it and sat looking out the window. She spent a sleepless night sitting there worrying about him. She prayed he would get away; then she prayed for a miracle that he would be able to come home to her safely without a prison sentence hanging over him. But she knew this was futile: miracles like this do not happen in Northern Ireland.

Early the next morning, just after sun rise, she pulled her jeans over her pyjamas and threw her coat on and crept along the street to Tess's door and knocked! She knew she wouldn't mind and she couldn't stay on her own any longer or her heart would break and it would never be put back together again.

When Tess saw her she took her in her arms and guided her into the living room. She tucked her up on the couch with a few blankets and made her a hot sweet cup of tea. The cure for all ailments!

"Is he gone?" she asked.

"You knew he would go too?" Helen whispered. "I feel as though I've been waiting for it for months. I now just don't know how to cope!"

"What else could he do, Helen?" replied Tess "They were going to throw the key away when they got him to court. He would have been an old man when they let him out!"

"I know! I knew he would have to go too but it's so hard to take. After Kieran dying it is so hard to bear the loss of my only other child!"

Tess sat with her arm around her as she cried; "You haven't lost him. Let's just hope he gets out of Northern Ireland safely and then we will work on how you will get to see him again. Things are changing and maybe there is hope for the future of our young people," said Tess.

She sat beside Helen and smoothed her hair as she fell into an exhausted sleep with her head on Tess's knee.

Tess rang work for her and said she was ill and wouldn't be in; then she rang her own work and told them the same.

"There is something else we have to think about," she told Helen. "When the security forces hear he's absconded they will be down on you like a storm," she told Helen when she woke up.

"Let them come!" said Helen "I'll deal with them. I've had to deal with them all my life. What are they going to do to me? I knew nothing about it. He didn't plan it with me. All I know is that one night he didn't come home. I don't know who helped him. I can tell them nothing."

She went back to work the next day and took the idea of the security forces arriving like a fighting Amazon. She waited each day and night for them.

A couple of days passed after Chris should have signed on in the police barracks and they arrived at five o'clock in the morning. She heard them approach and rang Tess immediately who arrived within a very short time.

She'd rang her brother and he arrived shortly too.

Helen had the door opened before they broke it open and was sweetness itself chatting about young people.

"You don't know what they are up to these days! They tell you nothing. I'm so worried about him. How is he going to cope with only half a left leg? Isn't it very foolhardy of him to go off like that? Feel free to search the house although at six foot there aren't many places he could hide here."

There was nothing controversial in anything she said but they looked at her as though they knew she was being sarcastic but she was smiling at them as though she was being sincere.

"I may not be able to fight them physically but I can mentally and I will!" she told Tess. "I suppose this is the beginning of the raids on my house starting again."

Sure enough she was raided on a regular basis for the next six months but they never found anything and she enjoyed bettering them. She felt she was fighting a mental battle for Chris with them.

46

Nothing was heard from Chris for a long time and Tess would tell Helen, who worried constantly; "No news is good news! It means they haven't caught him!"

Then about fourteen months after he left, Tess got a phone call from a very polite anonymous female voice who asked, "Will you deliver a message from a mutual friend of ours, please? It's for a friend of yours. You've been friends since you were at school!"

"Of course I will but would you not ring this friend direct yourself? If you want her phone number, I will give it to you!" she told the voice, confused.

The voice replied, "I can't ring your friend as it would be too dangerous for another friend of ours."

Tess realised immediately who the message was from. "Oh my God, of course I'll deliver the message!"

The voice continued, "I have to read you this and you need to listen carefully, please. Our mutual friend has made it to America. He's with a surfing crowd and other thrill seeking headers somewhere on this continent. He has changed his name, grown his hair and sports a beard and he is a very tanned, good looking dude, speaking in a 'bastardised American/Irish accent'"

"Can you read that again? I have to write it down," smiled Tess.

"I would like to stress this language is his not mine. He insisted I read it out to you so you would know it was definitely him"

Tess laughed at this. "I can just hear him saying it," she sniffed back the tears "Thank you so much for this, you don't know how we have waited to hear something. Everyone will be delighted!"

"I'm glad to do it for you all," said the voice gently.

She then said, "This message is straight from our friend and he stressed to impress on your friend that he is very well and thinking of her every day and give her partner and her his love. I'm hope you can understand what I am telling you?"

Tess laughed again and said; "I can hear him clearly in every word!"

The caller continued "You have to give the message to your friend and tell her to burn it when she has read it in case others find it."

"I will do that. Please give him all our love. We miss him so much and we all love him. Tell him everything is all right here and our friend is coming along fine. Please call again."

"Yes! I will! Thank you. Goodbye!" and the phone went dead.

Tess ran up the street to Helen immediately she put the phone down. The two of them danced with joy around the kitchen when she read the message. They were delighted to have confirmation that Chris was safe. For the next half hour Helen read and reread the message. They laughed at what they imagined Chris sounded like with his broad Belfast accent going American.

"I wish I had spoken to her," Helen said "I want to send a message to him!"

"I sent your love to him and said you were doing well," said Tess. "I'm afraid that is all the time I had to say anything. Maybe now he has made contact we will be able to arrange for you to be there sometime when she rings again?"

The caller rang again about six weeks later. She told Tess that everyone thought Chris had lost the leg in a shark attack when surfing and he was living on the story.

"That son of mine was always cheeky," Helen laughed after hearing this "That's a good idea being in America with surfing guys. Who would expect to find a guy from the middle of Belfast in that crowd? He'll never be noticed with all the other 'head the balls' that you would find there."

Tess informed her it was good that her 'Gallows Humour' was still intact but sometimes it left a lot to be desired.

'The Voice' agreed to call again in five or six weeks on a Thursday night around nine o' clock and she would talk to Helen who was so relieved she felt a little of the grief she had been carrying lift from her shoulders. She couldn't stop smiling. Now she could imagine her son some place, where before she had not known what to think.

She laughed out loud with relief and twirled around the kitchen.

"She's lost it!" Tess said as she watched her.

Helen retorted, "If I didn't laugh I would spend my life crying"

She still found it very hard to deal with everyday life without breaking down at least once a day but she was getting better. This news would definitely help her to deal with things.

Then Chris's court case came up and he was sentenced to twelve years in his absence. A warrant was issued for his arrest and her heart was broken all over again.

"Now!" she thought "He can never come home again. Now he is a wanted man and they will lift him as soon as they see him!"

Tess told her; "Be grateful! I thought he would have got a lot longer and they have to catch him first. And he's alive and well!"

"Oh! Believe me, I am grateful. Even if he's caught he would probably be out in five or six years!"

"Exactly!" replied Tess.

"I don't think I would have survived if I had lost both of them. Having Chris, no matter where he is, is a blessing. As long as he's not in jail, I will be happy!"

"I know that, Helen," said Tess gently.

"The only problem I have now is that empty house," Helen mused. "And Mick still in prison! I need him to come home!"

"You're a strong woman, Helen. I'm sure you have the strength to go on, if only for Mick and Chris' sake. You will find another cause to work for and you will keep going," said Tess.

"I believe Chris got away and is living a good life in the sunshine and I think he was spared for a reason. It's just a feeling I have and it helps me through the day. I have to think positively! I will hang on to any thought that will unite the three of us again on this earth. Unfortunately I will have to wait until I get to the other world to be with Kieran."

"That's the way to deal with it, missus. We'll get through all this together and one day we'll sit in peace at one of our kitchen tables and look back at this time from afar and thank God we survived it all.

"I look forward to that day!" breathed Helen.

47

A few months later and a lot earlier than anticipated, Mick was released from Long Kesh. The morning she got the news he was getting out Helen broke down and cried her heart out with relief.

She raised her hands to heaven and prayed, "Thank you God! Oh! Thank you God! I won't be on my own to deal with this awful burden anymore!"

Immediately she rang Tess, "Guess what! Guess what!" she shouted "Mick is coming home!"

"Oh God! Why? What's happened?"

"Nothing!" shouted Helen "Nothing at all! He is getting home for good on licence!"

"That's brilliant!" returned Tess nearly as excited as Helen. "I'm so delighted for you!"

"Not half as delighted as I am, I can't wait," laughed Helen.

She couldn't believe it. She was sure they would have made him do the full sentence because of what the boys had been involved in.

"Maybe the Brits think he'll go looking for Chris as soon as he gets out and lead them to him?" said Tess. "Nothing would surprise me with that lot!"

"God! You are such a suspicious person!" laughed Helen. "But you're probably right! They don't really know Mick if they think he would risk Chris's capture by leading them to him. But we couldn't anyway. We don't know where he is."

Updates on how he was continued to arrive to Tess every few months and 'The Voice' gave them little bits of information on his life. She wouldn't say where he was, only that he was happy and loved them and other general news. He wanted all the news from home and they would keep notes to remind them of things to tell 'The Voice' for him.

Typed notes also came in plain brown envelopes with no signature to Tess, posted in Dublin but no one had any idea where they originated except from the tone they knew it was Chris writing it.

Helen often said; "I hope to meet the person who is sending those notes and making the telephone calls one day. I will buy them a slap up meal and a bottle of champagne. They probably have no idea what a good deed they are doing and how great it is to hear about him. I might even lobby to have them canonised," she laughed.

"Maybe we should write to the Pope now and prepare the way?" laughed Tess.

News travelled fast that Mick was being released and many neighbours called to congratulate Helen as she was getting ready to head to the prison to collect him. She had many offers to take her but she wanted to go alone and have him to herself on the way back. It was so long since they had really been alone together, just the two of them.

The only other time was when Mick got compassionate leave for Kieran's funeral. They had gone up into the bedroom for a couple of hours just to hold each other and mourn. The RUC man had sat outside the door and the rest of the house had been full all the time. They'd had very little peace or quiet.

After she left to collect him, men who had spent time with Mick in prison or had been with him in the IRA started to arrive on the street. By the time they got home the street was packed with men, women and children with banners welcoming him home and the cars were all blowing horns. It looked like all of Belfast had arrived to welcome him. They had bonfires burning in barrels and barbecues in gardens. The whole area joined in the celebrations.

Mick and Helen couldn't believe it when they drove into the area. The car was stopped at the entrance to the street and they had to walk along the road to the house. Men and women they hadn't seen for years stopped them to shake their hands and hug them. Everyone knew their story and their joy was tangible at seeing Mick home with Helen. They were a popular couple.

Tess eventually got to speak to them and said she was sorry they didn't have the time they wanted to be alone together but the community was determined to show their support for both of them.

Mick laughed; "Don't worry, Helen! It's only for tonight. I will make sure we have the time to ourselves from tomorrow on. The boys, he said, nodding to some men across the road, "will make sure we're not disturbed after tonight. It's really a night for Kieran and Chris too. It's to commemorate their young lives and to recognise all they gave to their community, Northern Ireland and their country!"

"It might have something to do with you and Helen too," laughed Tess as she turned to take a burger from her son. Musicians had appeared on the street from nowhere and Mick ended up playing with them.

"It just might indeed, Tess," he laughed. "Thanks for looking after Helen for us. She has told me what a support you are."

"No thanks needed, Mick. We look after each other!"

Later that night he and Helen went into the house with a few close friends and chatted for hours. He spent the time asking questions although he knew most of what had occurred in the area from Helen and through the network of notes in and out of the jail. Hearing it all first hand from other sources was a different matter.

"Now we need a little peace in our lives. I think we'll shut the world out for a while and try and find ourselves again. What do you think, Helen?" he asked as he put his arm around her.

"Please!" she replied.

The next morning the curtains stayed closed in their windows and Helen and Mick locked the world outside their door. For weeks they hardly left the house. Helen told Tess when she rang that they were doing their mourning together for the boys.

Mick found it very hard to come to terms with the two of them gone. He had never known the house so empty before. All the years he spent inside he dreamt of coming out and spending time with the boys and Helen. Now there was only him and Helen.

As the weeks went by Tess called most days for a few minutes to make sure they were OK. Helen had gone back to work but Mick was still sticking around the house a lot.

"He had so many dreams for them together," Helen said "Some of the young fellows who are friends of the boys have started to call and that's helping a bit. They are chatting about what they got up to and he is getting to know more about the boys through them."

Then one day she arrived and found no back wall to the old kitchen and a couple of young fellows with Mick working away. She was shocked to see him with a lump hammer in his hand and hammering away at a wall.

"Good God, Mick! Have you gone mad?" she asked him.

"No! Tess! I think I have finally got my sanity back and we are doing a few renovations on the wee house. We decided to extend the kitchen out the back," he replied.

"Good man! When you're finished there I've some jobs you can tackle in my house."

"I'll give you a shout when I'm finished then," he laughed.

He and Helen had found comfort in each other and now they had begun to regain a little of their old spark and to get through their grief and face life again. They were beginning to emerge again like the pair everyone remembered and loved before he was locked up. A little older and a little greyer, a little less sparkle but with the same good humoured personalities.

Tess was delighted to see Helen was getting back to her old self. One day she remarked; "I have one of the best toned men in the country. I was expecting all the biceps and triceps to have drooping after being so long inside!" she laughed.

"Ah! It makes me sick at how well the men are looking when they come out and we women all look worn out," murmured Tess.

"I don't think myself and yourself look too bad!" said Helen "We've kept ourselves well. Maybe because we worked hard both inside and outside the house and never stop running around. But other women who were not as lucky and didn't have jobs or the money to keep themselves looking well found it much harder to cope."

Mick had never been much of a drinker and always interested in sports even before he went inside. He kept himself fit while in jail too.

"It kept me sane to exercise," he told them "I ran keep-fit classes in the H Blocks, even when we were locked up I would shout instructions from my cell to the others. It kept us going and our morale up."

He laughed and said; "I'd imagined Helen in my arms. I was determined to keep well and when I got home I would be able to keep her happy and she wouldn't be tempted to wander."

"When I didn't wander when you were inside, I'm hardly going to start now!" she laughed as she threw her arms around Mick's neck.

"Stop it, you two! You're making me jealous!" Tess laughed, she was delighted they seemed so content together. "You should start training some of the young fellows on the street around here," said Tess. "It would keep them out of trouble."

"That's an idea, I just might!"

Tess smiled as she thought of how close they were; "I suppose she never left him in any doubt that she would break both his legs if she thought for a moment he would stray when he came home. It also helps that she is the best looking woman on the street and they have the house to themselves and only themselves to worry about."

Still devastated by the tragic death of Kieran and missing Chris a lot, the tragedies seemed to have brought them closer together. They had reconciled themselves to getting updates on Chris and to being grateful that he was still alive, free and safe, even if they couldn't be with him. They lived for the day they would see him again and they firmly believed they would.

48

Mick got involved in the local community centre running keep-fit classes. Not only was he teaching young men but he was running classes for women, young and old, to protect themselves also. Helen would help him when she could.

He then began to teach guitar to teenagers in a small music club he set up in one of the centre and he brought in a few other ex-prisoners who could play different instruments. They eventually had groups of young people playing different types of music from country to ballads to pop. Once they realised the young people found they could play modern music they became interested, some discovering talents they never knew they had.

Between the keep-fit and the music they were keeping a lot of the young ones off the streets. Mick was good at dealing with them and in its own way it helped him to cope with losing his own two sons.

Helen was always with Mick making tea and providing buns and biscuits for those taking part. Sometimes she would sit in playing guitar and singing along in the background with the musicians. One of them thought she had a very decent voice and mentioned it to Mick who started to encourage her to sing with him.

After a hesitant start she realised she enjoyed it and they and some of the other men began to play in clubs. Initially it was in a corner with impromptu sing songs but soon they were asked to play at different events and paying gigs. Most weekends they could be found in different clubs entertaining anyone who wanted to listen. It gave them a new lease of life and extra income.

Some of the youth began forming bands and Mick with some of the other men got them gigs around the area and over the Border. They would do unpaid roadies and managers if they weren't playing weekend, keeping an eye on the young ones with Helen providing the sustenance and advice. After a while it was as though Mick had never been away; he fitted right back into the community again.

49

Mary's husband Owen was the next to be released, which surprised Mary. As far as she was concerned he was the last she expected to get out. He had never denied being a member of the IRA and was involved in most of the protests in the jail.

Shortly it became apparent after being released that the reason for it was due to ill health. His heart had been giving him trouble for a while and now he needed a triple bypass operation which he had a few weeks after returning home.

Owen was ill for a long time and everyone was worried about him but gradually he began to improve and regain a bit of colour but could still do very little.

Mary laughed; "At least now I won't have to worry about what he's getting up to!"

He wasn't impressed when she kept threatening to use a magnet to set his stints or pace maker haywire; "Or whatever other hardware they've put into you, if you attempt to step out of line again"

She told Tess and Helen quietly,

"I think he's really glad secretly that he has an excuse to take it easy. Otherwise he would feel he had to be doing something for 'The Cause' if he was fit and well."

One evening after he returned from hospital they went to see him and Mary was laying down the law about what he could and couldn't do.

"Good God, woman!" Owen said to her. "We had a screw in Long Kesh and he was nicer to me than you are!"

"The only difference between me and the screw," she retaliated, "is that he was probably trying to kill you or get you to kill yourself, I'm trying to keep you alive."

"I think I want to go back inside!" he declared.

"Naw! You don',!" she laughed. "You love me fussing over you really!"

"Mary! You're a hard woman!"

"I suppose it's one way of putting manners on you," laughed Helen.

"Oh! Don't encourage her," laughed Owen. "I'm looking for you to get her to ease off a bit."

"You know, I think this must be the quietest time I have ever spent with him," said Mary. "And you know something else I could get used to it. The only thing I have to worry about now is keeping him healthy and alive and I think I can do that."

The doctor had recommended Owen should walk a few miles a few times a week and both Mary and he could be seen heading off most mornings in their runners and track suits.

"Rain, hail or shine I have him out!" Mary declared "And it is doing us both the world of good. I have never been so fit or felt so healthy. Even our diets have changed to what the dietician recommends. We're both on vitamins too. I feel like a young one!"

Tess laughed, "You better watch that Owen doesn't start feeling like a young one too if he gets any fitter!"

"No chance of that. He knows I have the magnet," she laughed as she walked away with a spring in her step.

She was older than Tess and Helen by about fifteen years and a tough wee women. But at five foot one, what she lacked in height, she made up for with her strength of commitment and perseverance. Her family of six were everything to her.

Helen teased her about the iron rod she wielded over her children. She was very strict but fair and they clearly loved her.

Years before she caught one of her sons throwing stones in a riot, when he was about fourteen. She was on her way home from shopping! She put the two bags of shopping on the ground and unnoticed by her son she marched over to where he was, grabbed him tightly by the ear, dragged him back to where her shopping was, where she lifted her bags in one hand and dragged him by the other one all the way home, still holding on to the ear. He could be heard squealing four streets away.

"Ah Ma! That hurts!" he squealed trying to break away from her but the more he pulled the more she held on.

"Not half as much as a rubber bullet in the eye or a live round in the back of the head would," she told him "After this you may live to see another day but after what the Brits will hit you with you may not."

He was grounded for a week.

"With hard labour," she laughed as she told the women "He had to mop all the floors every day, take in the coal, light the fires and clean all the family shoes. He may think twice next time he goes to lift a stone to throw it."

Her son claimed many years later that he could never lift a stone after that because he remembered the humiliation of his mum dragging him along the streets.

"She left my ear longer than the other for years," he claimed.

"It was better than your head being ventilated," she would reply.

But it was not always that easy and one of her other boys did a few months in jail for taking part in a riot along with other local youth. Later he was to get involved with drink and drugs and then disappeared for years.

"It broke my heart that I hadn't kept them all safe and together! I miss the two in Kerry too but at least they're safe."

It was very difficult to know where your children were all the time. You had to give them some kind of freedom to teach them to look after themselves but it was hard sitting at home worrying about them.

Now with the other three of her family grown up and married in their own homes not far from her you could hear her call; "Have youse got no homes to go to? Every time I turn around another half dozen of you are coming in the path. Yer Da needs his rest instead of you all jabbering to him!"

"Ma! Go on with you! If we weren't here you'd be coming looking for us and giving out because we didn't come to see you," laughed her daughter.

Even the youngest of Mary's grandchildren knew they could twist her round their finger, as long as they stayed out of trouble. She was as strict with them as she had been with her own children. Any trouble in the area and she was on the phone to see where they were and then she would scout the area in case any of them sneaked out.

Tess and Helen teased her and told her it was time to slow down and let her children do the work.

"It wouldn't be in me," she claimed "I'd have to make sure myself that they're all right. I couldn't bear now if anything happened to any of them. We have come so far!"

The women nodded and knew what she meant. They needed no more heartbreak.

50

Not long after Mick and Owen were released, Barry got home.

When Tess was told he was getting out she went to the gates of Long Kesh to collect him only to discover he had been sent to Belfast in a Paddy Wagon. She was spitting feathers. It was like a repeat of what had happened when he was lifted.

"They were probably worried that he was going to get a welcoming committee like Mick," she stormed.

Getting back to the house she let herself in to find Barry standing in the kitchen boiling the kettle.

"Do you want a cup of tea, missus?" he smiled.

She laughed and hugged him. They sat down at the kitchen table, chatted and drank their tea. It seemed strange to have him in the house again but she felt she could get used to it.

He looked at her after a while and asked her; "Is this all I get after all these years, a cup of tea and a biscuit?"

She smiled, reached out and took him by the hand and led him up the stairs. Barry had been her only lover and it was so long since she had even thought about sex, never mind taking part in it, she felt really awkward but tried not to show it.

Before he had been lifted they'd had a very healthy sex life but all sexual inclinations left her after he went inside. Now she didn't even know if she wanted to make love to him; it felt strange. But after the initial fumbling's they laughed, relaxed and things got better.

Later they went to her parent's house to see them. They chatted for a while, left and called on neighbours on the way home. Barry was amazed at some of the changes in people and he kept saying; "He/she is like an auld one!" or "Haven't they got really fat or thin?"

Tess would reprimand him saying; "They had a rough time in the last twenty odd years around here!"

But he continued, “My God! He’s the same age as me, am I that old looking?” he asked about a school friend he met “Am I looking as bad as that?”

He seemed obsessed with how he looked.

“Funnily enough,” Tess pacified him. “You have hardly changed at all.” And it was true. He looked about ten years younger than he was.

“That’s because he had no bills to worry about when he was inside or worry where the next penny was coming from,” remarked Mary.

When they got home the children were very subdued and didn’t really know what to say to him and he didn’t know how to deal with them either. They were in their late teens and he had missed their growing years.

Instead of getting better over the following months things got more difficult. As with most relationships, theirs needed to be worked at but Barry didn’t see this. He thought he could step into the role he vacated all those years ago and give orders to Tess and the children and they would jump and obey him.

He was struggling to find his place in the family; everyone did their own thing and none seemed to need his direction. His old fashioned ideas of being the dominant male were still with him but the rest of the family had moved on.

“He has picked up some nasty ideas about a woman’s place,” said Tess to Helen. “He still has the old idea of a woman’s place being in the home, tied to the kitchen sink and at his beck and call.”

Tess had been manager of the electrical store for many years at this point. She ran it very efficiently and was excellent at her job with a couple of dozen staff under her. As well as this she’d the responsibilities of the home and the children while he’d been in jail. She was a long way from his way of thinking.

On the other hand the children were grown up and were used to answering to only Tess or Granny and Granddad. To all intents and purposes Barry remained a stranger they had only seen across a table every so often when they visited him in jail, which hadn’t been too often in recent years.

Now he was living in their house which they found strange. They knew he was their father but a father who had never been there for them. What were they supposed to think or do?

One day, Jimmy said to Tess, “Can’t he go and live somewhere else? I don’t like him around, he’s always bad tempered!”

She tried to explain to both them and Barry that they had to try harder to get used to the situation and make the best of it but even though the children tried Barry clung to his old fashioned ideas of being the man of the house and they should do as he told them. She was getting very frustrated by his attitude and his lack of understanding of their feelings.

51

Much as she tried to make things better, the more she was being blamed for the situation. He claimed she was taking sides with the children against him and the children thought she was siding with him against them. She was fed up with the whole lot of them.

He continued to throw his weight around and Tess was getting more incensed with him as the days went by. He wasn't like this before he went inside, they'd always made decisions together and he would never have done anything without discussing it with her first. Now he had taken to ordering her about as though she was a skivvy. The penny didn't seem to drop that she was her own boss and wouldn't take his behaviour for much longer. She'd had to answer to nobody for many years and was certainly not taking orders from someone who had been absent from the home for well over a decade. She had no intention of reporting to him every step she took as he seemed to expect.

Eventually she decided to have it out with him. Initially he listened and changed for a while; then he went back to his old ways. Finally she exploded and told him, "While you have been lying about in prison I have been out here rearing our children, who, by the way, hardly know you. With your attitude towards them they now don't want to know you. As well as rearing the children I have held down a responsible job for the last eleven years, I went back to school and become the manager of a business I now successfully run. I returned to school again to complete other courses so I now work at night with young people and potential prisoners who treat me with a lot more respect than you do. As well as all that, I was an activist for the IRA while you were swopping cigarettes you don't even smoke and I had to supply, from the very small budget myself and your children had to live on, so you could use them to play cards. Now you think you can come home here and start to throw your weight around and get me and the children to toe your line. Why? Because you think you're a great man? As far as I am concerned, if it had been left to you, your children would have died of starvation and I would have been destitute. Now pull in your horns and start treating us with a bit of respect and understanding or get out"

This caused a huge row. Even the children became involved telling their father that he had no right to shout at their mother. There were a lot of orders being thrown about such as Tess having to give up her job now he was home and stay in the house unless she was going out with him.

Tess laughed; "Who the hell do you think you are?" she asked "Hitler?"

She refused point blank to do any of the things he was ordering her to do and asked him if he realised what he was saying and the stupidity of it.

"Who is going to bring in the money to educate the children and for you to go to the pub?" she asked him

"I will, I always did before," he snarled

"That was nearly thirteen years ago and you don't have a job now! I met other boy like you in the IRA and they didn't impress me either," she stormed out.

At first he wouldn't believe she'd been active in the IRA, apart from passing notes to them from him. She told him she didn't give a fuck if he believed her or not. He demanded to know what else she had done for them and she told him she couldn't discuss it with him. This drove him silly; he started to shout about his involvement in the 'Struggle'.

"You were never in the 'Struggle'," she told him "You just happened to be in the wrong place at the wrong time and you got lifted. If you had used you brains and stayed away from Owen that night when you knew he was involved I wouldn't have spent the past decade or so of hell out here raising our children on my own and being harassed by the security forces!"

He ignored anything that she said, just kept insisting she had to give up her job and stay at home. Again she asked; "Where's the money going to come from if I give up my job, which I have no intentions of doing, by the way, after struggling hard to get where I am today? Where's your job to replace mine? And where will this leave me and the children if you ever get lifted again?"

"You will do as you are told!" he roared at her, making no sense as far as Tess was concerned.

He stormed out of the house and didn't return until the following morning.

After this he started drinking three or four nights a week in one of the clubs and stopped looking for work. He spent his days in the bookies with his mates instead. If Tess tried to speak to him about his behaviour he would walk out. He was taking money out of her purse, sometimes quite a lot and Tess was very annoyed at this. She took to hiding it from him and this caused further rows.

She was at the end of her tether and didn't know what to do. She felt sorry for him being locked up for so long but he was not going to bully her. She had to make sure the children were being looked after. She needed the money she worked for and wouldn't tolerate anyone stealing from her or ordering her about. She refused to give him any more money to spend on drink, horses and his mates. She'd earned that money and it was to make life better for them and to keep their home running properly, not to throw across a bar or to the bookies. She couldn't trust him and if there was no trust in their relationship she couldn't continue to live with him.

The final straw was when rumours reached her that Barry was seen kissing a woman and walking up the street holding her hand outside a club one night.

Tess was furious. She could put up with almost anything except him cheating on her. For years she'd given him everything she could and she and the kids had done without and scrimped and saved to make sure he had the best. Now, when she expected him to help her carry the responsibilities of the home and family, he was doing this to her.

"No way!" she vowed to herself "He will not do this to me!"

After speaking to Helen she decided to do a little sleuthing. Helen was very upset for them all. She had listened to the children telling her how impossible it was to live with him and she didn't know what to say to them.

Now this was happening. Mick had seen him with a woman a few times but they were hoping Tess wouldn't find out and it would all blow over. She hated to see her so upset after all she had been through already for him. But Tess had come to the end of her patience and this was the final straw. He had completely disrupted their home, the children were very upset by his behaviour and now this.

After convincing a few men she knew to watch him, she discovered he was seeing a woman who lived a couple of streets away from her.

"The ungrateful bastard!" she shouted at Helen one morning. "After all I did for him when he was locked up! We lived in poverty because of him!"

"Calm down, Tess," pleaded Helen. "You'll give yourself a heart attack."

"I'll not have a heart attack!" she stormed "I wouldn't satisfy the bastard! But by God that boy is in for one hell of a surprise!"

"Please Tess! Think about what you are going to do!" pleaded Helen.

"Oh! Helen, I've thought about this long and hard. I've had twelve months of hell from him and so have my children. I know exactly what I'm finally going to do and I'm going to do it now. After the last year, I've had enough to do me a lifetime and I'm putting a stop to it. Enough is enough!"

With that she stormed home yanked open the doors of the wardrobe and packed a case with some of Barry's clothes and hid it.

She watched him get ready that evening and knew he was looking for some of the clothes she'd packed but he said nothing and neither did she. He took what was available and left without saying a word to her or the children.

A couple of minutes after he had left the house she pulled on her eldest daughters parka jacket with a hood and followed him at a distance to see where exactly he was going. As she watched him he turn into the street she knew the women he was seeing lived on, she waited at the corner and peered around it. He stopped outside her house, reached up and knocked on the door. The woman opened it and greeted him with a long lingering kiss. She then stepped out and closed the door after her. He put his arm around her waist and they walked up the road together entering a pub a few hundred yards further on.

Tess turned on her heel and headed back to the house. She climbed the stairs and dragged the suitcase down them to the front door. She then hauled it out to her car and threw it in the back seat.

Going back into the house, she combed her hair, put on her good coat, high heels and a bit of lipstick and shouted to the kids that she wouldn't be long. They were so engrossed in the TV they didn't pay much attention to her.

"My life is falling apart and their only interest is what is on the telly," she muttered to herself.

"I'll be back in fifteen or twenty minutes," she said again as she went out the door.

"All right, Ma!" Jimmy called back.

She pulled down the mirror in the sun shield and checked her lipstick and hair.

"Now breathe deep and calm down. You have to look your best when you are making your exit," she smiled at herself in the mirror "You don't want to look like a tramp when you face him. And he can't accuse you of letting yourself go either. You look good, missus. Now breathe!"

Taking a few deep breaths she turned the key in the ignition and started the car. A calm came over her.

"Keep breathing deeply," she told herself "You'll be fine. Let's do this with a bit of dignity and finality!"

Carefully she drove out of her street and within a couple of minutes she arrived at the pub. Hauling the case out of the car she pulled it along behind her and pushed her way through the front door.

Passing the doorman she handed him the keys of the car and said,

"Look after the car for me for a few minutes, will you, Joe, please? If it needs moving will you move it? I won't be long!"

"Of course I will, Tess! But I don't think you should go in there, not at the moment anyway," stammered Joe, surprised and looking at the case she was dragging behind her. He was worried because he knew both her and Barry and he knew he was inside and who he was with.

"Oh! I definitely think I should go in there, Joe! And no better time than the present! But thanks for trying to protect me," said Tess smiling sweetly at him. Then she patted his arm "Don't worry, I already know he's there."

He looked at her and said, "I'm sorry, Tess! Are you alright? Can I carry that for you?"

"No thanks Joe," she replied. "This is something I have to do myself. I'm afraid it wouldn't be the same coming from you."

He smiled at her.

He was very fond of her, she'd always been decent to him and he wanted to help her now. He knew she didn't deserve the treatment she was getting from Barry.

"All right Tess! Take your time and don't strain yourself," he said.

"Give me five minutes. I'm just getting rid of some unwanted baggage," she smiled, nodding her head towards the bar, she walked on.

Barry was sitting comfortably with a pint in front of him with his arm around the other woman's shoulders as Tess walked towards his table. He was so engrossed chatting to her he hadn't noticed Tess at first. Then he saw her cross the floor and obviously heading in his direction with the case dragging behind her. He looked completely stunned and sat staring at her mesmerised.

She stopped and said; "Nice to see you've got company, Barry. Obviously you have decided the children and I are no longer relevant in your life so I packed a case for you. Hand me the keys to the house: you won't be needing them anymore!" she demanded holding out her hand

He hesitated.

"Now!" she insisted loudly

He took them out of his pocket and handed them to her.

She then lifted the case on to the table and emptied the contents on top of him. She then poured what remained of his pint on top of that.

"Don't come back to my house," she told him "Neither I nor the children want you near us. Maybe your bit of stuff on the side here will put you up, though I doubt it. I don't care what you do or where you go anymore as long as it's not near me!"

"Jesus Christ Tess! What are you doing? You don't understand!" he started.

"You won't insult my intelligence anymore either. I understand very well! I have watched you men come out of prison and try to recapture your youth. Well! If that is what you want, don't let me stop you. I will not be sticking around anymore watching you make a fool of yourself, me or your children. You even stole the price of that pint from my purse, didn't you? I assume my money paid for your girlfriend's drink, too. Don't come back to the house again, I'm warning you. It is not your home. It is mine, I paid for it and everything in it while you were inside and it's the children's. We owe you nothing!"

Then she turned to the woman; "You know who I am and you know I have three children and what I've gone through to rear them on my own and you betrayed me. You should know better than to give your loyalty to a toe-rag like this. Instead you should go home and look after your own children."

With that she swung on her heel and with as much dignity as she could muster she walked out of the pub with her head high. As she crossed the floor she heard a round of applause from the other punters and calls of, "Well said, Tess!"

As she passed Joe at the door he held open for her, he smiled at her and said, "Well done Tess and the very best of luck to you!" He handed her the car keys.

"Thanks Joe," she smiled nervously. "I feel a whole lot lighter now after getting rid of that baggage."

Joe laughed and said; "I bet you do. Take care, girl!"

She quickly walked on to the car, swinging her arms and feeling a whole lot better. Still a bit nervous but relieved.

"Wait Tess, please!" she heard a call as she got into the car.

She paid no heed. She didn't look in the rear view mirror as she drove out on to the street and home.

"There'll be no looking back for me!" she thought to herself as she stared ahead.

When she got to the house she rang Helen who arrived ten minutes later with a bottle of wine.

"You all right, Tess?" she asked as she came into the house.

"I am now. I just feel relief and a wee bit shaky," she replied and leaned back on the couch with a sigh.

She'd had enough of carrying Barry. She had done everything she could for him and this was how she was being repaid. Maybe other women were prepared to put up with a total lack of respect, manners or thought but she wasn't.

52

She didn't hear from him for a few weeks until one evening he knocked on the door and said he would like his clothes. She told him to come back the following evening and they would be in plastic bags outside the front door.

He then asked if he could speak to her. She told him she had nothing to say to him and there was nothing for him in her home except his clothes and after the following evening that would be the end of it.

He said he wanted to see the kids.

"Why?" she asked him "The last time you spent any time with them you kept telling them to "shut up" All you wanted them to do was to be quiet and sit like mice. My children are young adults and they will be allowed to act like young adults as long as I have any say in their upbringing. Go back to your girlfriend. There's nothing for you here!"

"I'm not seeing her anymore," he replied.

"So she dumped you, did she? She discovered what a prat you are, did she?"

"Yes! I mean no," he stammered.

"I couldn't care less what she or you did or do!" she said and went to close the door.

He put his foot in the door to stop her closing it. She opened it wide and told him; "If for one minute you think you can use violence here to get your way you'd better think again. You won't get away with it!"

She kicked his foot out of the way and slammed the door closed.

He left that evening and she didn't hear from him for another fortnight. Then he rang her to beg her to speak to him. She refused. After many more phone calls she finally relented.

That evening he came to the house and he sat like a whipped pup in the corner. Tess felt nothing but disgust.

"I'm sorry, Tess," he told her "I've been a fool. I don't know what came over me."

"I'll tell you what came over you," laughed Tess cynically "You think you're a big hero and we women should all lay down the red carpet for you. You think you can treat us like doormats. Well! This is one woman who is having no man wipe his feet on her. You were only in neighbourhood watch when you were lifted. I'm more of a bloody hero that you are for rearing our three children on my own while you were safe and warm inside Long Kesh. You come back here and think you can lord it over me. You are very wrong there because I have discovered I'm worth more than ten of you. Go away and leave me alone. I'm not putting up with any more of your shit."

"I was wrong, Tess," he said "I shouldn't have treated you and the children like that."

"You're damn right you were wrong and you will never do it again!"

She continued, "Look at you all, all you boys inside sitting there chatting to each other and believing your own publicity! Little legends in your own minds! Making yourselves into big men with no respect for the wives who supported you all the way through the years you were locked up. Well! This wee woman wasn't sitting at home feeling sorry for herself while you were away. She was educating herself and making money to rear your children and boy did she get an education! This wee women will go through hell and high water to protect herself and her children and from where she is standing at this moment you are a threat to both her and her children. Now get out and don't come back!"

With that she walked to the door, opened it, gave him no choice but to go and she closed it after him. She didn't know this man and she did not want to know him.

Barry realised he had made a big mistake. As he looked back at the house where he had once been so happy he realised he didn't know the woman in that house. He had taken Tess for granted all through his time inside and thought he could control her and do what he wanted when he came out. He believed all the rubbish some of the other men had spouted and thought she was still the same timid wee woman he'd left so many years before.

The clarity with which he now saw the situation was a shock. He saw what he had lost through his own stupidity and couldn't believe he had thrown it all away for a bit of craic in the pub. He didn't know what to do to make it better.

He walked to his parent's house, instead of to his mate's where he had been staying for the previous few weeks. Entering he asked if he could stay for a while.

His father grunted but said nothing.

His mother looked up from her knitting and commented; "She's thrown you out again, hasn't she? She's not taking you back! I knew she wouldn't put up with your behaviour! She has more sense."

"How do you know what I've been doing?" he asked, surprised.

"The dogs on the streets know what you've been doing and what an idiot you've made of yourself. Your children come here regularly and talk about you all the time. We know how you've treated them and Tess and we're ashamed of you!" snorted his mother.

He'd thought he had kept what was happening from them. Obviously he had failed.

"I suppose you knew all along?" he asked.

"Yes! Ever since your children came here crying about how hard it was to live with you a short time after you got out. What the hell's happened to you, son?" asked his father. "How could you treat Tess and the children like that? She was so good to you when you were inside and she reared them children all on her own and they're great kids."

"I know! I know! Don't preach!" he pleaded.

"If you know, then why did you make such an idiot of yourself and lose them. For what? A slapper who goes out with anything?" said his mother.

He was shocked. They knew everything.

"I should have known better," he sighed to himself. "Everyone knows what is going on around here. The grapevine is well and buzzing!"

"Doesn't the whole street know about your carry-on?" sighed his mother "I hate to say it, son, but you've become a bloody eejit. You weren't like this before you went inside. You were a good husband and a good father. What happened to you? You have probably lost the best woman who ever walked these streets, for what? So you can fly your kite?"

"Ah Mother! I know what an idiot I am. I don't need you to tell me! Give me some peace until I find out what I'm going to do."

"If you've lost that woman for good, you're a bloody fool. You better start fighting for her or you'll regret it for the rest of your life!"

He headed up to his old bedroom and threw himself on the bed. He knew they were right but he couldn't bear having it rubbed in anymore.

"What am I going to do? I've just thrown away my family and everything that meant anything to me! All for a few drinks and sex with someone I feel nothing for, just a bit of fun."

For hours he thought about what he had done and what it meant to him. It was as though, for years, his clarity of vision on his life and his future had been dead. Now it seemed to open up before him in very clear pictures of what he wanted, what was most important to him and what he had done to throw it all away. He felt like he was having a panic attack.

"What have I done? What have I done?" he asked the wall.

He couldn't understand how stupid he had behaved and felt as though he had been taken over by some kind of demon that made him do the exact opposite to what he wanted. Now he could see it clearly and he was a very sorry man.

It had all occurred to him a little too late.

53

He got a part time job in a club he didn't usually go to a few days later. One evening, while it was quiet, a man he knew from years before came up and sat down at the bar. Everyone knew this guy was an old IRA man and very well respected in the area. Barry had a feeling he had come specifically to speak to him and he was a bit wary about what he wanted.

"Well, son!" he started "You've made a bit of a mess of things since you got out, I hear!"

Barry knew there was no point pretending he didn't know what he was talking about. "You could say that, I suppose," he replied.

"There is no supposing about it, I would think," the man continued. "She threw you out again, I hear."

It was on the tip of Barry's tongue to say "You hear a lot," but decided against it. He knew he got all his information from his own father who had been a friend of his for years. He didn't want to blot his copybook any more than he had with his parents, especially now he was staying, under sufferance, in their house and they were still angry with him for his treatment of Tess and the children. He knew he would have to grit his teeth and listen.

He told him a lot of things he hadn't known and was amazed at the life that was being portrayed to him of his wife's activities. How she had scrimped and slaved to keep him in prison, how his children had to do without, how she had to rely on charity, how she had started various projects with Helen, how she had helped so many families of the prisoners, how she had educated herself, how she managed the home, the children, her work and the community projects.

The man spoke to him at every opportunity throughout the evening and built a picture of a Tess that Barry had known very little about. Or if he did, he'd ignored it.

He was shocked at how much she had done. He knew she had told him most of it down through the years but it hadn't impacted on him until now when he saw it through this man's eyes.

"And I tried to treat her like she was a nobody! She is a hero to this man and I'm sure to others. She will never take me back," he berated himself.

"You have a woman in a million," the man told him. "She had never stepped out of line and was totally faithful to you the whole time you were away. She worked like a Trojan rearing your children and working full time. You arrive home and treat her like shit and forget all she did for you when you were inside. She was one of the best women we ever had and we're looking after her now."

"What the fuck do you think you are doing cheating on her after what she has been through and done for you? You're only been out of Long Kesh over a year and you've made a pig's ear of your life already. I wouldn't mind but she is a fine looking woman too and any man would be delighted to have her on his arm. What the hell is wrong with you, son?" he asked Barry.

"I don't know!" replied Barry rubbing his hands over his head. "I just don't know! And don't think I don't know how much I messed up. Big time!"

"Well! You have a lot of work to do if you want to make things better between you. Don't think for a minute that a few words of sorrow will make Tess change her mind about you. She is a tough, intelligent woman and she doesn't need you. She was coping grand on her own. You have years of crawling to do, son, if you want her back and you better start with easy steps and you better start soon!" the man told him "If you think it's too much work then let me know, I know many good men who would love to have the chance to be her partner."

"I know what you are telling me. I know you're right too. But I just lost the head and was totally stupid," said Barry.

"You're like a lot of boys who came out and only thought of themselves. Now they're sitting at bars wondering where it all went wrong with nobody to go home to and no one who gives a damn about them. A lot of them once had it all but they didn't recognise it and they threw it away for a few drinks and a bit of skirt. Don't let that happen to you, son. You have a good one, look after her, if you get the chance," With that he left, clapping Barry on the shoulder as he went.

Barry had a hard job to think of the Tess he knew before he went into Long Kesh as the woman this man was talking about. In a way he resented her changing, she was no longer the quiet, dependant Tess he had married and he thought he was coming home to. On the other hand he really admired the strong independent woman she had become.

"Maybe I'm afraid I won't live up to her expectations now."

He now realised he was really proud of her, he was proud she was his wife and he wanted to keep it that way. He felt totally ashamed of his behaviour to her now he saw it through the eyes of others and there were many others who wanted to make sure he saw it that way.

But how was he going to get her to take him back? All he knew was that he would spend the rest of his life trying if necessary!

54

For the next two years Barry stayed in his parent's house. He went to and from work and did very little drinking. He told his mother, "I need this time to get used to being back living on the outside again."

He spent more and more time with Mick who helped him settle back and he was very grateful to have him and Helen to talk to and help sort his head out.

After a time the children agreed to meet him one evening each week and a few hours at the weekends. Barry knew this had a lot to do with Helen's influence. Initially, they weren't interested in anything he had to say or do and treated him as though he was the enemy. It was an uphill struggle to engage them in any conversation but over time it got better.

If Tess was going out of an evening, he would go over and stay with them until she got home. Not that they needed a babysitter but he felt he needed to be with them in the family environment to get used to them and for them to get used to him. Of course Helen had arranged and explained all this to him and to the children. For a long time Tess could hardly bear to speak to him when he came to the house but gradually the sentences between them got longer until they could speak to each other with more ease.

He now had a full-time job working with a construction company and making good money. Tess's father had retired years before but a mate of his was looking for workers and with a little prompting from Mick he proposed Barry for the job. The building trade had picked up and he started to contribute more to the children's upkeep.

Still, Tess could not trust him completely though their relationship was not as strained as it had been. She had disliked the man who had come out of jail and what he had done to her and the children and it kept preying on her mind. She tried to remember the man he was when he was lifted years previously but could see very little of him in Barry initially. Who could do what he did to his wife and children if he cared for them?

"The man who went into prison all those years ago would not have dreamed of cheating on me. He would have put the family first and foremost. What happened to him inside?" she wondered. "Is that man still buried inside him and will he or can he surface again?"

Helen told her she had to speak to him honestly about what had happened and eventually she admitted if they were to live in peace whether together or apart, it had to be discussed.

He felt he was walking on eggshells around her but he was more and more determined to get her back. He saw everything differently now. He loved how she was with the children and he was very proud of her for rearing them so well. He was also very proud that the three of them were his and he grew to care about them more and more.

When her animosity towards him abated a little, she began to speak to him about what the children were doing and sharing their achievements with him. Gradually she realised she enjoyed chatting to him about their everyday lives and sharing her pride in them with him and he was doing his best to make up for his former behaviour by always being there for her and them.

"After all, he is their father!" she told Helen.

She admitted to herself, "for all his stupid actions and attitude when he came out first, there is still an intelligent, decent man inside there somewhere."

They started taking the children out for meals together and in this way they began to discover the old Tess and Barry that attracted them to each other in the first place. It was easier to relax in a social environment.

55

Over the following months they began communicating more honestly. He spoke of all that went on in his life during his time in prison and she began to see why his sense of loyalty to her and the family had been eroded.

"The 'Struggle' to get the British out of Ireland was all that came to matter to us. We, the prisoners, were 'The Boys'. We could do what we wanted or so we thought. I forgot all that had been important to me before I went in. When I got out I didn't recognise anybody or the area I had been born into anymore. Everything had changed. I got annoyed because I'd missed out on all my 'normal' life and I felt everyone owed me. I refused to recognise all that you had done for me on your own. I didn't want to know. It wasn't important or relevant. It didn't come into the equation at all! It was like we, the prisoners, were the only ones who suffered. I know different now. I'm sorry."

The talk had been about the craic they would have when they came out and how they would catch up on all they missed. He started to forget he had a family and his responsibilities to them. Emotionally he hadn't developed as he would have outside.

Tess feared he had changed too much to change back to the man she had known, loved and married. How could she think of trusting him? She didn't ever want herself or her family to be abused again. Little by little she could see traits of the old Barry emerging.

"Let me tell you, Barry!" Tess told him one evening. "Unless you learn to put me and the family first, before everything else, from now on, I don't want you here. I don't want to hear of you going to clubs or pubs boozing your hard earned money. I work hard for my family and they come first and I expect you to do the same. You have given up enough for the war and so have I. Now is the time to make something of our lives."

"I know you're right!" he said "I know what I want now. I want you and the children. You mean everything to me!"

"You better be prepared to put everything you have into our future. I want a better quality of life for us than what we've had up until now. I want to leave

Belfast when they are all educated and live in the country in a few years' time. That is my dream and I'm working for it and unless you want it too there is no point in you being around us."

He agreed to do everything she asked. He was just glad she would even consider taking him back.

"You'll have to work hard to prove yourself to me!" she told him. "I've my own life to live and I intend to carry on with all the work I do. You'll just have to fit in with it."

"I know I've to prove myself to you and I will," he promised. "I'm determined to find a life for us together and do whatever it takes to make that happen."

"If you ever cheat on me again, that will be the end for us, with no going back! I hope you understand that?"

"It will never happen again. I know now what I have to lose."

"I still don't trust you but maybe that will come with time. We'll play it by ear for the moment and see how things go," she told him. "I need more time to make a definite decision about us, I don't want you moving in here with me and the children and then throwing you out some months down the line."

Barry didn't care how long he had to wait as long as there was a chance she would take him back.

But she still had a mental block about having him live with her. She was afraid. A lot of the time she couldn't think of one reason why she should let him return. But the one thing he had going for him, that no other man had, was that he was the children's father and her husband.

"He can still be the children's father without living with us and he can continue to see them regularly," she told herself.

Gradually the friendship grew stronger between them and there were times when she'd even forgot for a little while what he had done. She realised she was growing to like him again. Maybe that was a good first step.

One night, sitting alone and watching television she realised that she was constantly thinking, "I must tell Barry that!" or "I must tell Barry this!

"Not too long ago it would've been Helen I wanted to tell everything to," she thought surprised. She was surprised also how she had begun to look forward to spending time with him again.

"Maybe there's hope for us!" she smiled to herself. "But I'm making no commitment to him yet. We have a long way to go."

Barry continued to work hard on building his relationship with the children and Tess and most of his spare time was spent with them. The children accepted him as part of their lives now and communication between them had improved greatly.

Coming up to Christmas and over two and a half years after she had thrown him out, Tess invited him to dinner. Afterwards she informed him that although she didn't know if she wanted to live with anyone again, she was willing to give it a try as long as he knew he would not and could not control her. She was not going to be ordered around by him and she was not answerable to him or anyone else. If he agreed, he could stay over that night.

Barry was delighted that his dream was being realised and smiling he agreed to all her demands. That night he stayed with Tess and for the next few days he didn't leave. He collected his clothes on Christmas Eve from his parent's house so he could be with them all on Christmas morning. He moved back in permanently and he was glad to be home.

"I never thought this would happen," he thought to himself. "I'm a bloody lucky man. This is where I belong and want to stay. Happy Christmas Barry! You have received the Christmas present of a life time here, boy! Protect it!"

The women teased Tess about the perfect way to tame a roving husband but Tess knew they had a long way to go before they were as close as they had been before Barry had been lifted. The good thing was that they were both willing to work at it.

56

In 1993 the Downing Street Declaration was issued by the British Prime Minister John Major and the Irish Taoiseach Albert Reynolds with statements which included the following

"The English government had no "selfish strategic or economic interest" in Northern Ireland and the British Government would uphold the right of the people of Northern Ireland to decide between the Union with Great Britain or a United Ireland"

It added; "The people of Ireland, North and South, had the exclusive right to solve the issues between North and South by mutual consent. A United Ireland could only be brought about by peaceful means. In 1994, talks began between the SDLP and Sinn Fein which led to joint statements going out on how the Troubles could be brought to an end.

Rumours had it that the British Government had been in talks with the Provisional IRA since the 1980s but the British Government denied this. It would not have gone down too well with Loyalists that the British would speak to what they saw as Fenian enemies of the state.

In 1994 the Provisional IRA announced a three day ceasefire to run from the 6th to the 8th April.

Five months later, on 31st August, the Provisional IRA announced a "cessation of military operations" from midnight.

The Taoiseach Albert Reynolds said that he accepted the IRA statement as implying a permanent ceasefire was taking place.

A framework was proposed with a ninety member Assembly to be elected by proportional representation to create a Government for Northern Ireland. Many Unionists were sceptical. The proposals were not welcomed by them or the DUP who described the process as a "one-way street to Dublin and a joint Government programme for Irish unity."

The Good Friday Agreement was signed by the British and Irish Government and endorsed by the Sinn Fein political wing and most Catholic and Protestant parties in Northern Ireland. The deal was brokered by US

President Bill Clinton, Senator George Mitchell, British Prime Minister Tony Blair and Republic of Ireland Taoiseach Bertie Ahern.

It created a semi-autonomous Government with both Catholic and Protestant members and called for the disarmament of all paramilitary groups, the release of all prisoners who had been involved in the Troubles and the reorganisation of the RUC. It also stipulated that Northern Ireland would remain part of the United Kingdom until the majority of the people voted otherwise.

57

This brought hope to a lot of people. They were tired after thirty long years of the Troubles and despairing of ever solving the problem that was Northern Ireland. Three generations had known nothing but violence and it was leaving a terrible legacy.

Not everyone agreed with the ceasefire. A lot of people on the Nationalist side didn't trust the British Government. They had broken too many promises to the Irish people in the past to engender trust now.

Many prayed that this was the end of the terrible conditions they lived in but they were sceptical. There were mixed feelings within those involved on the Catholic side.

Some prayed that it was the end to all active IRA military operations, others prayed that it wasn't. They thought it was another scrap from the table of the British Government and not worth the paper it was written on. They wanted complete surrender by the British and a united Ireland and nothing less would do.

Many men and women had been involved in active rebellion since their teens and for the first time they discovered what normal life was like and most wanted it to continue. They knew if the ceasefire broke they would become active again and involved in the fight to rid Northern Ireland of British control because that is what they believed in.

Others on the National side thought the IRA were giving in to the British Government and it was difficult keeping some of these groups from returning to action.

But for the first time in over thirty years people began to really hope.

Many parts of Belfast were still sealed off in segregated areas with barbed wire and the so-called Peace Wall. This structure of concrete, steel, wood and barbed wire had increased in height three times over the thirty years of the Troubles and stood between Protestants and Catholics in the working class interface areas of Belfast.

In places it was three miles long with the aim being to keep the two cultures apart. It created an insular mentality and some people never left these segregated enclaves. Because of the lack of integration and on-going segregation the animosity between the cultures was still alive and festering.

58

The interfaces, the areas where the Peace Wall was built between the two cultures, had once been patrolled by paramilitaries but were now patrolled on both sides by community workers trying to keep the peace. Mobile phones came into use with patrols on both side of the ‘Peace Wall’ ringing across ‘the divide’ to inform community workers on the other side where gangs of youths were gathering. This was a sure sign that trouble was kicking off. The message went out to keep a look out on the opposing side of the wall and try to stop the violence from escalating.

Tess and Helen would join others patrolling along the partitions. It was an on-going struggle to stop the youth from creating trouble. The young people saw it as a bit of craic but it was not very pleasant for those who lived in the houses close to the Peace Wall when a hail of missiles came over the walls raining down on their roofs or through their windows. Their yards and streets were littered with missiles all along the interface.

Through working together on different projects, many young people were taken off the streets, educated or brought on holidays in an attempt to teach them a different way of life. This included taking joy-riders off the streets and teaching them to drive fork lift trucks, often bringing their training up to the level of rigid and articulated lorries.

Rioters were taken off the streets and taught to play music or make musical instruments, young girls and boys taught to cook or work on computers, others were taught languages or did foundation courses for college. Children who once believed college wasn’t for them discovered a love of education and a new life opened up for them.

There were many success stories through this medium but then problems struck. Once a project was working well and the kids were taken off the streets the ‘powers that be’ in the funding agencies and government thought the problems had been solved and pulled the funding.

But nothing had changed except the projects which were taking the kids off the streets and changing their attitudes were now having to close due to lack of money.

For others waiting to get onto the courses in the centres everything remained the same. When there was nowhere for the youth to go, the rioting, hijacking and carnage began again. The scallywags were back on the streets and mayhem ensued once more. To change this mind set would take generations and a lot of on-going education.

It came to a point that when the kids saw what they called "the holiday people" (the funding agents) coming up the street they would start a riot. When this happened the funding would be reinstated in that area and the kids got to go on a holiday again. This was solving nothing.

The 'powers that be' did not understand that they had to keep these projects and programmes in place to keep the kids off the streets until the mind-set of the people changed. You had to teach the communities the benefits of education and until that happened, there would be no permanent change.

Next thing that came was a surge of IT courses, exclusively. Two things developed from this; as one woman said to Tess, "they were spewing out boys with briefcases as fast as you could blink as though they were on a conveyor belt but you couldn't get a plumber, electrician, welder or a carpenter for love or money!"

Community people were sick at the illogical actions of those who were supposed to know what was needed in the communities. How could they know what was needed when they didn't come from the communities or consult those living there?

Another worker told Tess when she asked if she got a lot of help from local politicians: "We try to stay away from politicians, they only do what they see will bolster their votes. Often this is detrimental to the community work we are carrying out. Many times I hear them screaming violence on the TV and know that tomorrow I will have trouble in my centre with one religion taking the other to task about what was said the night before. Some of these people thrive on hatred. The politicians need to learn to look at what is best for their people not what is best to line their pockets. How can we get youth from different religions to work together when politicians are spewing hatred at each other and encouraging segregation?"

For many years people in the communities ran successful projects with very positive results. Then the 'powers that be' decided they would make these projects 'legitimate'. That's when things began to fall apart. You had funding agents sitting behind desks and not interacting with the people on the ground to find out what was needed. One woman who had been a volunteer for many years in her community asked; "Can no one see what is happening? All we get are Government offices with men and women sitting behind desks developing policies, not for the good of the communities but to keep their own jobs? They are strangling the community and the volunteers with red tape and bureaucracy. Justifying their jobs by writing new policies or six pages of guidelines which communities cannot adhere to! Nothing in it relevant to the people who need their help! It has stopped a lot of volunteers from working in the community. They are burnt out fighting it all!"

This was the fight the women were engaged in now and it was a lot more frustrating than what went before.

The rioting and hijacking continued. Gangs were taking control in the segregated areas and this time drugs and crime were their main interests. It suited them to keep the people down, afraid and separated behind the 'Peace Wall' as it created a marker for the area each gang controlled. The women worried about how they could change this. It was like jumping from the frying pan into the fire, from the paramilitaries to the drug pushers.

"When we had our own boys protecting us at least we knew we were safe from the other side but who is going to protect us now from the druggies on our doorsteps?" an old lady from one of the worst affected areas asked.

They worried about the impact this was having on their children and grandchildren and were anxious to do something about it. The police force was seen as the enemy in Nationalist areas. The IRA were gone and were now more interested in politics and peaceful means of solving the problems of Northern Ireland, leaving behind a big void and no community policing to protect the people.

In November 2001 the Royal Ulster Constabulary (RUC) became the Police Service of Northern Ireland (PSNI) after many complaints from the Nationalist side on discrimination in the force. Many believed that only the name had changed and everything else remained the same, the discrimination and the harassment of the Catholic community continued.

"Except they now have a few more Catholics in it!" said Mary, "The token half dozen or so!"

59

Tess and Helen were tired of fighting the war? Once it had been against the unfair treatment of the Nationalist community now it was the drug dealers and other unsavoury characters. They longed for peace.

It occurred to them the best way to change anything would be through the women from both religions, starting with the mothers, sisters and grandmothers. They would educate them and get them to bring the message back to their children and families. Change the family's attitude and control what was happening from the kitchen sink, was their new plan.

Helen moaned, "I can see a long, long journey with very hard work before us if we want to do this."

"We're not going to do this! We're going to delegate!" laughed Tess. "We get it started and we get the younger women to take over. I will give it two years and then I'm getting out of 'Dodge'."

"Ah! Listen to her. She still doesn't realise she's a control freak!" laughed Helen. "I can see her when she's eighty directing projects from a Zimmer frame in some nursing home! God help us all!"

Tess knew some Protestant women through work but was reticent about broaching the subject with them. Her first surprising discovery when she finally began to have in-depth discussions with them was that they were very like her, all looking for peace and a decent life for themselves, their children and grandchildren. Over time some of the women became her friends and through her, Helen came on board. They began meeting up and going for meals or drinks together.

The conversations varied and were often hilarious but they also discussed the 'Troubles' and the impact it had on their lives. The Protestant women were shocked on hearing of the Nationalist women's experiences and hadn't known what was happening with them but were also surprised at the similarities between them.

Throughout her life Tess thought the Protestant community all had plenty of money. This, she discovered to be completely untrue. They, like her, had to work for everything they had; nothing was handed to them any more than to the Catholics.

One of the main differences was that a lot of jobs were given to young Protestants, not because of their ability or education but because of the influence of their family who already worked in the businesses.

This often led to Protestants youth, especially the young men, thinking they didn't need education. If they were sure they could walk into a job when they left school, why bother? Therefore the standard of education in young Protestant men was a lot lower than in the Catholic areas. This worried the women and it was a cyclical thought process they found very hard to break.

Tess was surprised to find they lived in similar houses to the Protestant women who had the same problem with the Corporation as the Catholics did, trying to get anything done. Many lived on very low wages or social security.

One woman informed her, "Our parents were told by the Corporation that we should be grateful for the great wee houses we had, that the people of the Catholic areas were living in hovels."

"I remember that!" said another woman. "My Gran use to say, 'If those women on the Falls Rd are living in worse houses than us, then I don't know how they survive!' As I got to know Catholic women from the Falls Road area I discovered the houses were almost identical and with the same problems. We were being fed rubbish. It was just a case of divide and conquer! What we didn't know, wouldn't worry us!"

Another Protestant woman told them of the hassle she had at home when she was younger with the security forces because her brother was involved with the UFF. "Because he was involved with the paramilitaries and in jail they would raid our house whenever they got bored."

"The soldiers never cared about anybody. If you were born on Irish soil you were Irish to them. It didn't matter whether you considered yourself British or not. I got terrible abuse from them because I objected to the treatment we were getting. One day I said to one of the soldiers after objecting to their treatment of us 'especially as we are on your side'. He called me a traitor to my own country because I didn't consider myself Irish and I lived in Ireland. It seems we couldn't win with them!"

Tess thought this was a much different story to what she had heard down through the years and now knew that though the abuse was on a much larger scale in the Catholic areas, the Protestant women suffered in some ways too.

"A few years ago, I swear, I thought those women would all have horns when I met them. Now I find that they are just ordinary mothers and wives like ourselves. Some of them had someone close to them murdered, bombed or shot too!" Lucy exclaimed.

"Isn't it terrible the things we believe without questioning the origin of the belief?" remarked Tess.

"All that propaganda we believed to keep us separated and at each other's throats!" agreed Mary.

"Another example of divide and conquer and politicians and governments thriving on it."

60

After much discussion Tess, Helen, Mary and some of the women from the Protestant areas decided they would set up a cross cultural network, to see if the women could work together to make their lives better.

The aim of the network was to dispel the myths, misinformation, prejudices and propaganda that both sides believed about the other, to open up dialogue between different groups and shatter the lies. It would be based on open and honest discussion among the woman who wanted to move forward in peace together.

Helen told Tess, "I never thought I'd see the day when I would want to live in peace with Protestants in Northern Ireland."

"Isn't it funny how life moves on and we evolve and get rid of prejudices we didn't know we had?" asked Helen.

Many nights and days of hard work with plans and ideas set up and torn down again led to them finally deciding to apply for funding to run with a simple programme of talking to each other in order to build trust between the women of the two cultures.

A name for the group was the first thing they wanted. Many ideas were thrown back and forward until one night the CD "A Woman's Heart" was brought in and played at a meeting. Immediately they agreed on 'The Woman's Heart' as the name of the group.

It started small with five officers on a committee and a few others sitting around the community centre table drinking tea and talking.

As Tess laughingly said, "Discussing the war".

It quickly escalated to a room full of women chatting about their lives and come incredible stories emerged.

One woman told them, "I got engaged in Crumlin Road prison where I was jailed. I was one of the first to get married in Long Kesh when my husband was in there. I married a "lifer" and do you know what they bloody did? They let him out. I didn't sign up for that lark!"

Along with the laughter came the tears.

Another told how she was coming down the street with her niece in a pram to see her brother; "He was the wee one's daddy and working in a shop along the street. As we neared the shop a huge explosion occurred and my brother's body came flying out through the window and across the railing at the side of the road. We were about twenty yards from it. I was so glad my wee niece was too young to remember or realise it was her daddy," she said.

More women from both sides joined the group and continued to turn up week after week. They arrived with scones, biscuits, pieces of home craft, a homemade remedy for some other woman's complaint or a bottle of wine they got from someone. Everyone mucked in and made tea and cleaned up afterwards.

The one thing that shone clearly through the tears, laughter, anger and despair was the support the women gave each other. Protestant for Catholic and vice-verse!

For some it was the first time they had a chance to voice their opinions or air their feelings about what happened in their lives during the Troubles. Each one was listened to with respect and given the support they needed.

For many it was an eye opener. They had their own hardships and traumas but others were worse off. Many lost close relatives in horrendous circumstances, were caught up in bombs, in house raids or riots. And of course there were the many women like Tess, Mary, Lucy and Helen who had to cope with their husbands in jail for long terms, leaving them to deal with life alone.

Soon there were over sixty members.

"What the hell are we going to do if they keep coming?" asked Helen.

"Get a bigger room!" returned Tess. "We're turning no one away!"

Seed funding kept them going for a while and paid for room hire. Then they applied for money for speakers to come and talk to them and to let them run workshops and Art and Crafts. This was granted. Some of the women were interested in social policies and empowering themselves and they ran a couple of courses on this.

One laughed, "I've done all the sewing and patching I want to do; now I want to work on my mind before it leaves me!"

One night Helen remarked, "We often hear the men's stories from the Troubles but never the women's. We may as well have never existed during the Troubles and we were the ones who held the families and communities together through it all."

A debate ensued on what they could do to ensure they were seen as part of the history of Northern Ireland and highlight their place in it. Books, brochures and storytelling were all mentioned. Then it was suggested they develop a DVD with their stories, the good, the sad, the funny and the ridiculous.

The first surprise was when they got funding to continue running the group itself or what Mary called the 'gossip shop'. The next surprise was when they got further funding to develop the DVD. The women were ecstatic.

"Good God!" said Helen one day. "We can really do some work with this."

One of the women's daughters was doing Film and TV in College and she agreed to do the filming. Everything was falling into place.

They ran workshops to help the women decide on experiences they wanted to relate and public speaking workshops to help them tell them simply. The effect was as good as counselling for some of them. It let them take ownership of their personal history and feel proud of it.

"I was embarrassed to say where I came from" was one reaction. "It was like I felt the trouble in my area was my fault. Now I feel I am bloody great for coming through it all and after what I suffered it's amazing I'm still sane. That alone is an amazing feat for me, fair play to me!" she laughed.

"I feel I'm no longer on my own. All the other women here went through the same hell as I did and none of it was our fault!"

"I wish I could get over what happened to me. I was interned for a year for something I didn't do. My husband was interned for two years. Then my home was raided regularly and my son was shot dead. My children all have some kind of medical complaint and I blame the stress of the Troubles. It seems as if it is never going to end in my house. I'm so tired I just want to lie down and die. I think I suffer from paranoia, I'm constantly waiting for the next bad thing to happen."

"Paranoia!" asked another. "What's that? I can hardly say it nor spell it, never mind suffer from it!"

This kind of humour kept them going.

Another laughed. "Don't you miss the hammering at the door? At least someone came to see you then. They left a bit of a mess but sure it kept you occupied! My house is like a morgue during the week now since the auld boy died. At least he used to mumble and grunt at me. Now there's only silence."

"Mine is like an asylum at the weekend when the whole family lands on top of me."

Helen smiled at Tess; "This what makes us great!"

Tess asked a Protestant woman what she wanted from the meetings.

"If I can do anything to prevent my children and grandchildren from going through the terrible experiences we've had, then I'll do it. That's all I want!"

"That's what I think too."

Do you know what annoys me? We were the backbone of the communities when the men were fighting their war or inside and we were put through hell. They came out and were given our jobs in the community centres and now, once again, we are the ones who must pick up the pieces and influence our families and we have to try and prevent it ever happens again."

"Exactly!"

Tess's opinion of the Protestant women had changed completely by now and she was often surprised to find herself fighting on the same side as them. But now it was for peace.

"We are human beings with the same failings, it's time to stop fighting and start building a future for our wee Province," Helen told them one night.

One old problem kept raising its head when they discussed their cross cultural women's group with politicians, particularly the men.

Tess informed them one evening; "Their attitudes are, to say the least, patronising. The other evening at an award ceremony I invited to one man took my hand and patted it and said; 'It will be all right. Leave the peace building to us, little lady' I was astonished at his remark and said, 'We've left it to you for the last thirty years and I know what we got!'"

"He nearly choked because I has answered him back, he was so surprised," she laughed. "His good humour very quickly vanished and he told me in a seething voice, go home and don't rock the boat!"

"Is he still living?" laughed Helen.

"Unfortunately, yes! And it seems there are a lot more of his kind around. What hope have we got if that is what's running Northern Ireland?"

"Feckers buried in the past, without the brains, balls nor imagination to change or improve things!" snorted Mary.

"I feel sorry for all us women if that is an example of what we have to put up with," returned Lucy.

"We better get our act together then and try to change their thinking from our end!"

61

"I've been doing a lot of thinking lately," said Helen one day in the centre.

"So that's what that churning sound was?" laughed Mary.

"Was it painful?" asked Lucy who was now working with the women through drama.

"Shut up! You two are like a double act out to torment people!" said Tess. "Go on, Helen."

Helen continued, "The more I think about the wars that occur the more I believe they are all orchestrated by Military Brass and big Governments to keep them and their buddies in jobs and funds."

"Sweet Jaysus, we're going to get a lecture!" snorted Mary.

"Shush Mary! The prophet is about to make a proclamation!" laughed Lucy.

"I agree with her," said Tess. "It wouldn't do that the arms factories closed down or there wasn't a war to keep them going. Can you imagine how much money the Governments would lose?"

"And the backhanders and little brown envelopes that are passed around! What would they do without them?" Helen remarked cynically. "It's not the ordinary people who are causing the trouble around here. It's the ones who want to feather their own nests. They come in, create havoc and mayhem and stand back and watch it explode."

"They did that all through the Troubles in the jails and on the streets. Set one side against the other so they would get overtime and stay employed. Barry told me they were always saying things to the prisoners to get their backs up, against the other side. Some of the fellas made knives to protect themselves and they would lie waiting for the other crowd to come charging through their cell doors. None of it was true," said Tess.

"What's the value of a few thousand Irish lives to those people?" she retorted. "Nothing. They don't care about our little homes being torn apart and the hardships and trauma we went through. This is just the acceptable casualties of their war games. It won't affect their peace of mind. They can always find someone else to blame."

"Off they go to their country estates with their buddies who are also cleaning up on our backs and discuss the horrendous problem of 'those awful fighting Irish," said Mary.

"All through the Troubles, Government representatives have been warmongering and encouraging their followers to create havoc. Then the army supposedly comes in to sort it all out!"

"Or came in and created further havoc, which was more like it!" said Tess.

"That certainly happened here and all over Northern Ireland!"

"When I think about it, the more I believe it was all orchestrated by the 'powers that be' in Governments. The many atrocious incidents carried out by the army throughout those early years could only have had one reaction from the Irish Nationalists and that was to encourage more people to join the IRA and fight against those who carried out the atrocities. I don't think the Government or the Army Brass could be so stupid not to know this would be the reaction. They had to know what the outcome of their actions would be!"

"I believe we were all used as puppets to ensure some big boys somewhere far away from our little Province kept their jobs and shovelled money into the appropriate pockets. The more I think about it the more I feel this has to be the answer," said Helen.

"I believe it is even worse!" returned Tess. "I believe there is a policy out there to create conflict in countries all over the world to ensure the Arms Industry survives. There're probably Top Brass all over the world in their pay to create trouble through insidious propaganda to ensure they have somewhere to sell their ammo, grenades, AK47s or Kalashnikovs and it's poor sods like our husbands, sons, daughters and fathers who are the fodder and the collateral damage for it, completely disposable to these faceless men in uniforms and expensive suits."

"There's big money in arms and a few bribes here and there to the Government and the army could orchestrate any conflict or war," pondered Lucy. "They'll always get a few hotheads to do their bidding."

"Money speaks all languages. Get a few people to stir things and you have the embers. All you have to do then is blow on it and fan the flame," mused Helen.

"That's an interesting theory and not beyond the realms of possibility!" mused Mary "Any other theories?"

"Divide and conquer!" said Tess. "That is what was done here in Northern Ireland! Separate the Catholics and the Protestants and set them against each other."

"They certainly did that!"

"One woman told me when she was younger she lived on the Shankhill Road and they were always being told about atrocities the Catholics were carrying out against Protestants which never happened," said Tess.

"Protestant women thought that the Catholics women hated them because we lumped them together with the security forces because they were British and they saw themselves as Unionists, Loyalists or British subjects."

"I had a discussion with a Protestant woman and told her I couldn't understand how she could see herself as British when she lived on the island of Ireland! She said she couldn't see how we could see it otherwise when Britain had ruled the North for hundreds of years. We laughed, shook hands and agreed to differ."

"Sometimes you have to tell the truth to move on. She understood how I felt. She thinks its men acting like turkey cocks strutting their stuff, defying the other turkey cocks across the yard!"

"Turkey cocks, is right! Causing mayhem? Sounds about right," snorted Mary.

"I'm amazed at the change of attitude in the women, on both sides," remarked Lucy.

"I believe the women on both sides had a lot to put up with all over the years and often had to keep their mouths shut in fear of repercussions, even when they disagreed with what was happening," said Tess.

"The only way is let us believe what we believe and allow each other to do the same and learn to live in peace together," said Helen.

62

"I'm tired! I've lost count of the people shot on our streets over the years," said Mary. "I've lost count of the relatives and friends whose funerals I attended. I should be shocked but I just feel so tired. I want it to end now!"

"We have been subjected to too much, too many bombs, bullets, riots, the whole damn lot they threw at us and we had no say in anything. We had to put on a brave face and pretend we were getting on with things and that it didn't hurt like hell when we went into the prisons to visit the men or the soldiers raided our wee homes. You're damn right we're tired," sighed Lucy.

Mary continued; "I just feel I need rest now!"

Helen looked across at Tess who had always been her strongest ally and thought of her journey, which was so like her own. Their conversations and support through years of hard slog, pushing each other to keep going when either of them faltered. They were proud of themselves for getting so far.

Most of the problems were never mentioned to the men. Even though she loved Mick with all her heart there was a big part of her life she could never share with him and he would never understand. That was why her women friends were so important: they had been through it together.

The men would never know what it was like to have their homes 'Kango hammered' and to then have to pick up the pieces time after time and try to make a normal life for the children. No matter how many times you told them the stories, they were, to them, always just that, stories.

They hadn't experienced the helplessness at not being able to stop the destruction, the hatred for those doing it, the loss of pride at begging officials to help clear up the mess or replace children's allowance books that had been destroyed deliberately in the carnage, pleading with other officials to give you more time to pay a bill or borrowing money from family to buy shoes for your children because their feet were getting bigger so fast you couldn't afford to buy another pair, there were too many other bills to pay.

Then the night's waiting for your sons to come home and you so afraid they wouldn't and then, as in Helen's case, the night when they didn't come home.

“No! The men would never understand what we went through. You needed to experience it first hand to know and understand,” she sighed.

“Are Governments the same in other countries? Is there so little respect and credit given to the work we women put into our families and our communities elsewhere?” asked Tess. “Do they not understand that families make up communities and the population of the world? Mothers rear those families! We are the lynch pin they work from!”

“Can you remember how many times you cried when you were alone rearing the children? I can’t, there were too many. I must have cried a couple of rivers!” sighed Helen.

“And we are still fighting for peace.”

“There is still propaganda being thrown about,” said Tess. “They have people terrified about the Peace Walls coming down because the drug gangs want to preserve their territories.”

“A lot of women are terrified at the thought of the Peace Wall coming down and many think the ‘other side’ will come in some night and attack them in their beds,” Lucy said.

“If it’s not one thing we have to worry about, it’s another,” remarked Mary. “I’m just glad my family are all old enough to know not to be influenced by drugs.”

“Them boys in the drugs cartels have a captive market in the segregated areas, as do those who want to promote themselves in particular political quarters. This is now what we have to fight. Until they take down the Peace Walls that separates us we will never learn to live together!” said Tess.

“Oh! Hell! She’s on the war path again!” shouted Helen holding her head.

“No!” said Tess. “I’m on the Peace Path!”

“Oh! I can see it all now,” laughed Helen. “She will be mustering all the women on both sides and we will be marching down the Springfield Road with lump hammers and chisels, with her probably driving a digger she borrowed and tackling the Peace Walls some morning around six. She’ll get us all killed by the druggies wanting to preserve their territories!”

“That’s what the people did with the Berlin Wall. It was only up twenty nine years. Our Wall is up over forty. It’s time it came down! Then the people would know their fears of the unknown are groundless and the druggies will be out in the open,” retorted Tess.

“And the women will be able to see their neighbours.”

“One girl had never spoken to a Catholic before she met us nor had ever stood in a Catholic area, she'd been scared to meet us. She thought we'd look different and she would be able to tell us apart. She was worried too about not knowing who was a Catholic or Protestant. I told her, that's good, you will now treat us all equally. She wasn't too sure about that."

"It's the propaganda that's spread to keep us in our place and scare people," said Mary.

"It's terrible that someone can get to their twenties and admit to not ever speaking to a Catholic," said Helen. "We're all over the place; there must be at least a few hundred thousand of us in Northern Ireland. You would think that she would at least have spoken to one of us?"

Mary said, "A couple of our women who have become good friends were chatting about where they lived when one said, you live a few minutes from me. If the wall wasn't there it would take me five minutes to walk to your house. But with the 'Peace Wall' it would take me nearly half an hour."

The other women replied, "I would love if you would visit me but I don't know if it's safe. I would do my best to look after you but you don't know what others on the street would do."

"Arragh!" said the other woman. "It's the same with our boys, there are still some stupid hardheads who want to prove a point and they don't care how they do it!"

Tess said, "That is so sad. These women really like each other and could be great friends but because of outside influences it can't be."

"Maybe we could visit each other's community centres at Christmas to celebrate the season and invite the others back. Isn't it time we did something positive?"

"We'll take a couple of bottles of booze with us, I'm anybody's after three vodkas," laughed Mary.

"You may forget that!" laughed Lucy. "At your age it's praying for a happy death you should be doing!"

When Christmas came that's what they did.

At most meetings there were important discussions on what the role of the women should be and Helen asked question; "What would you like to do now?"

One night one of the women said in exasperation; "I would like to get the hell out of Northern Ireland and get a rest from the bloody oppressive air around here. I want to get away from the Peace Wall and the Interface and every other thing that reminds me of the Troubles!"

"Imagine being able to walk by the sea and the wind blowing in your hair and not a soldier in sight and to go to a bed where you can sleep without having to worry about it all for a few days?"

"I want to lie on the ground and look up at the stars and not see a street light or anything else obscuring my view," mused another woman.

"Imagine that?" said another. "You couldn't really do it in the middle of the Whiterock at ten o'clock on a Tuesday night, now could you?"

The women laughed.

"There's a dream to hold on to," said another. "We could take a blanket to the nearest beach and just lie there."

"Knowing our bloody luck, we'd have a weekend of thunder and lightning!" snorted another.

"Or an Irish tsunami!"

"I don't care what the weather is like, if we get there I will be out on that beach having every cobweb blown off me," laughed another. "I've heard there are projects which get big money to take women to the Republic of Ireland for workshops and they stay for a couple of nights."

"Right!" said Helen. "We'll look into that and if it's possible it will be the next thing we apply for!"

"Chance would be a fine thing!" said Mary. "Especially with us asking for so much. Forty or fifty women for accommodation, food and travel, I don't think so!"

"And money for a couple of women to run the project and open an office thrown in," laughed Tess. "Go the whole hog. All they can do is say no!"

"I suppose it's always worth a try," retorted Helen.

63

A few months later Helen received a brown envelop through the letterbox. There was no one around as she opened it. Thinking it was another piece of junk mail or a bill, she was prepared to throw it in the bin.

She read and reread the letter before she could fully grasp its content and then had to grab a chair to steady herself.

It read; "We have great pleasure in informing you that you have been successful in your application for the above project and a cheque for £185,000 will be lodged in the group's bank account shortly. The funding is towards the opening of an office, the hiring of two part time staff and to bring forty women to Donegal for six two day workshops over a period of twelve months. The money will appear in your bank account in due course."

The blood drained from her face and she almost fainted. She was shocked. "Breathe, breathe!" she commanded herself.

Then she read the letter again. It still read the same.

"Bloody hell! I need a cup of tea. I think I'm in shock!" she said to herself. "I better ring Tess and the rest of the women."

She shook from head to foot. This was a lot of money! They could do so much with it. It would make a huge difference. They could plan their workshops and get the women out of Belfast.

As she boiled the kettle she had calmed down a little but she was still amazed. The longer she thought about it the more excited for the women she became.

"This is brilliant," she said to herself. "The women can get to the beach. Wait until they hear this. They'll go ballistic."

She hadn't really believed they could do it. She felt she was just chancing her arm in applying for so much. Now she could hardly speak as she made the phone call to Tess.

When she answered the phone she asked her quietly, "Do you remember that application we filled in for £185,000 to open an office and bring Protestant and Catholic women across the Border together for workshops?"

"Yeah! Did you get a letter back that said 'catch yourself on'?" laughed Tess.

"No!" said Helen. "We got a letter back saying we were getting the whole lot. The whole £185,000, to do what we applied to do with it!" she shouted.

"What are you drinking this morning? What do you mean the whole lot?" asked Tess confused.

"The whole bloody lot!" squealed Helen. "All £185,000 of it!"

"I don't believe it!" said Tess very quietly.

"Believe me, it's true!" exclaimed Helen. "I have the letter here in my hand and I'll show it to you in five minutes if you come over. I have the kettle on."

"I'll be there. That means we will really have to do all the work we planned," murmured Tess. "How are we going to do this with us both working?"

"They have given us the money to hire two people to run it part-time!" exclaimed Helen "They are giving us salaries for a part time Coordinator and an Administrator."

"This is amazing! We need to tell the women!" laughed Tess as it finally sank in.

"I'm ringing the committee after I get off the phone and we'll call a meeting. If nothing else we will make a difference to two women's lives when we create two jobs for them."

That evening two very excited women met with the others and told them the news. Some had already heard and came prepared to celebrate with bottles of wine.

One woman sat and cried, "This is the first time we've ever been given anything decent! We can get away and maybe find ourselves again!"

"Oh! I think I'm so lost I don't think a mechanical digger would find me!" laughed another.

"A good psychiatrist might, though. Maybe you should book yourself in to the Big House?"

"Good idea! I could be doing with someone making me three decent meals a day and not having to look after our gang! Maybe I will!"

An impromptu party took place with lots of excitement and laughter. No one in that room that night cared if the woman she hugged was Catholic or Protestant. They were celebrating their luck, all of their luck and they would share it together.

The joy was empowering. Tess and Helen looked around and knew they had to keep working for another while to ensure the support among the women would grow and spread out into the communities.

It was brought home to them how insular some of the women's lives were when they discovered how many of them had never left Belfast, ever. Some were afraid of travelling to the Republic in case people there would realise they were Protestants and attack them. They didn't believe that many Protestants lived in the Republic or if they did, they were different to them.

Tess promised she knew a few Protestant women in Donegal and would get a couple of them to come and meet them. This seemed to put them more at ease and they began to look forward to the trips.

Within weeks two women were employed to run the office. Both of them had lost jobs when they'd been given to released prisoners.

One of the women, Maggie, was told her job was no longer available as they were moving forward and needed qualified personnel. This woman had developed the centre she worked in from nothing and this was how she was treated, to make room for a man coming out of prison who got himself a degree while he was inside.

"She is capable of doing the job," said Helen. "I know Maggie and I can vouch for her. She's a great worker. I would do referee for her any day."

Weeks later they offered Maggie and another woman the jobs.

They were on their way.

They rented premises with easy access for women of all creeds, bought computers, printers and a photocopier, put articles in the local papers advertising their services and opened for business.

The two new employees trained some of the women in office techniques and researching information for those who dropped in. In fact they helped anyone who dropped in, including men. Their spare rooms were rented to agencies who dealt with family matters and through this they had income coming in to pay for stationary and overheads.

64

The much awaited day arrived and on a bright September morning, forty women from many areas of Belfast boarded a bus and travelled to Rossnowlagh, Co Donegal. Some couldn't wait to shed the city for a few days but others were apprehensive at the reception they'd receive and feared crossing the Border for the first time. This all disappeared quickly when the staff at the hotel welcomed them and chatted easily to them.

Tess remarked, "They discovered people were only human on the south side of the Border too."

The women from the Protestant areas met Protestant and Catholic women from Donegal as promised, who took them under their wings and looked after them. No one asked anyone what religion they were. They didn't care.

The weather was beautiful and they were only minutes from the beach which stretched for more than three miles. By the second day, strong Cross Border contacts and friendships were forged.

On the evening of the second day Tess and Helen inveigled rugs from the hotel and called all the women together. They handed the rugs to them and walked them to the beach where they were all spread out on the strand. The women then lay down as instructed and Tess and Helen called for silence.

The day was coming to an end with a beautiful pink, orange and red sun setting over the water now resting on the horizon. Soon it would be dark. All that could be heard was the wash of the tide and a few birds by the water side. The air was balmy as in the best of the fabled Indian summers.

A young girl sat on a rock near Tess and Helen and she lifted a bow to her fiddle. Out of the blue the sound wafted over the strand and through the air. A slow haunting Irish air floated like an eerie voice from the past. You could hear a deep sigh come from the women as they lay on the rugs gazing at the darkening sky as the last of the sun sank into the sea.

Tess and Helen looked on from the rocks.

"They will remember this moment for a long time!" whispered Helen.

"Can you see?" asked Tess tugging Helen's arm "There are Protestant and Catholic women lying on the same rugs and they are at peace together," said Tess.

"Maybe through this we will build something that will make that peace last."

"If those women have anything to do with it, it will!"

"Amen to that!"

They had met, Eileen, the young woman, playing the violin the previous night and had told her about the women's wish to lie on the beach and gaze at the stars.

She'd told them; "I'm playing in the hotel bar tomorrow night and if the weather is good and you get something for them to lie on I'll come down about nine o'clock and play a couple of tunes for them. I can't guarantee the stars or the weather though."

When the tune came to an end none of the women moved. The violinist started to play again. It was now dark.

"This is a beautiful moment," sighed Tess "Look at the sky. The stars are starting to appear!"

"Somebody up there must like us," whispered Helen.

"Yes! We must be doing something right!" smiled Tess.

"Oh! We are! We are!" replied Helen. "You have to believe that."

With another couple of slow tunes Eileen told them. "I'm afraid I'll have to go soon. Do you mind if I play a couple of lively tunes and see what happens?"

"That would be great," agreed the women.

With that she put the bow to the fiddle once again and out over the strand and the water a lively tune danced. After a few seconds some of the women got up, helped others to their feet and danced to it along the strand. Little by little they were added to, while a few more lay as they were, listening.

When the music finished the women clapped and cheered and it began again. There were bodies silhouetted all over the strand dancing in all forms.

Eventually it was all over. The cheering could be heard for miles. Gradually some very happy women lifted their rugs and walked back to the hotel with faces glowing and shoes in their hands. They were to talk of this moment for many years to come.

After that first trip, a change came over the women and they relaxed more. During the workshops they opened up and honesty was the name of the game. Some very awkward questions were asked and the women were brave enough to truthfully answer them.

Friendships were solidified that would last a lifetime. The trips over the Border continued for the coming year with very positive results but none quite as poignant as the first trip.

After this Tess and Helen pulled back from community work and concentrated on their families and employment more, determined to finally have time for themselves. They were tired.

Tess said; “We’ve done our bit! It’s time now to give a wee bit of attention to us.”

“I’m so looking forward to it,” replied Helen as they walked away from the office one dark winter’s evening. “Myself and Mick have so much planned.”

65

Helen and Mick became well known on the entertainment scene at home and abroad. Their relationship went from strength to strength; they had forged a strong unit and worked well together.

She, jokingly, was heard say; "The woman who works with her man always knows where he is and what he's up to!"

Tess would laugh at her; "Don't you trust Mick?" Knowing full well Helen knew he would die rather than hurt her.

"Of course I do," she would answer laughing. "as long as I can see him! None of them groupies will get their grasping greedy little hands on him while I'm around. They are unbelievably predatory and a temptation to all red blooded men. Give a man a guitar and he's irresistible to some young women. It's easier for Mick to refuse them when all he has to do is point to me and I turn on them with a smile that would curdle milk."

Tess laughed, teasing her; "Poor Mick can't decide right from wrong and needs you to be his conscience, is that it?"

"Men are weak! It's a precautionary measure, keeping my beady eye on him."

Tess laughed; "There she stands, long brown hair down her back, tight jeans, size ten figure, doesn't look a day over forty, usually surrounded by cables as she dismantles the sound system, throws an amplifier over her shoulder and away she goes to the van with it all. Meanwhile the band members are tucking into the food she cooked for their supper. Bloody super woman! Why would any man leave a woman like her? She doesn't seem to age normally like the rest of us. What is this magic elixir she is on?" She looked around at the rest of the women.

Helen laughed out loud, "You make me sound like an idiot or a slave to my man and I am neither. As well you know!"

"Aye! And you know you're everything to that man of yours so don't give us all that blarney about keeping an eye on him! He wouldn't think of stepping out of line because he adores you!"

"That's one of the reasons we are best friends!" Helen laughed as she put her arms around Tess' shoulder. "You never let me down! Never mentions the lines or the drooping jowls. I'm still only forty in your eyes. Bless you!"

"Of course you are! Aren't we the same age? Only I have aged a bit more than you!"

"You'll never see it again! Either of you!" laughed Lucy.

"Keep the mirrors away and I'll always be forty," laughed Tess.

"Look at you, only a slip of a thing who takes on the world every day! Men look at you and think they have a soft touch. Then this little blond woman in the fitted black skirt and almost see through white blouse that shows just a glimmer of cleavage, turns them into jibbering wrecks as she smiles her way to get what she wants. They leave the premises wondering what happened and where they went wrong and why they bought the cordless drill with the masonry bit when they live in a wood framed house and have another drill in the shed anyway."

There was a lot of laughter from the other women.

"They're running their own fan club, you know!" came Mary's input, full of sarcasm.

"Sure we're brilliant, the lot of us!" laughed Tess as she put her arms around Helen and hugged her. "And so are you all too and don't forget it."

Tess knew Mick adored Helen but maybe, she thought, part of it was because he knew she would 'have his guts for garters' as Mary was prone to say, if he stepped out of line.

Helen very seldom lost her temper but anyone who knew her knew she didn't suffer fools gladly.

"Nobody takes the piss out of our girl if he values his health. If he tries he could end up parked on the nearest roundabout, hoisted on the nearest pointed object," laughed Tess.

On the other hand Helen was like the proverbial earth mother to all the young people they worked with. She'd now retired from work claiming she was burned out but Tess teased her; "You? Burnt out? I don't think so! You retired because it's better craic running around with Mick and the bands."

She laughed and agreed. "I've given enough of myself to others now it's time for me. I like this work; it keeps me alive and young!"

"You're nearly as busy now as you ever were," said Tess.

"Ah! But its work I enjoy. I've got it all now, a good pension, young enough to still enjoy it and the craic and I travel all over with some lovely young people and of course the auld boy," she laughed.

And the young musicians were a way to substitute her loss of Kieran and Chris and they thrived under her and Mick's attention.

They played gigs most week-ends in different venues throughout Ireland, England, Scotland and sometime mainland Europe. Mick kept talking about making contact with guys he knew in the US and the group could go there for a few weeks each year to play. The big problem was that Mick couldn't go as he wouldn't be allowed in because he's been in jail.

"But you and the rest of the group could go," he insisted.

She knew his aim was getting in touch with Chris if possible. It was also her dearest wish but she didn't want to go to the US without him.

66

The contacts with 'The Voice' continued. But it was very frustrating as Mick and Helen were never sure when she would call so they weren't always there to speak to her. Nevertheless they were grateful that they were still getting updates on him and what he was doing.

Eventually Mick had enough and decided he was going to do something about it and he hit on a plan. He rang some friends in the US, arranged for them to set up gigs and the group would fly over to play there without him. He insisted Helen should go, as someone had to try and see Chris.

He told Tess to tell 'The Voice', when she rang that the group was going to be in the US in the next few months to play some gigs. She would give her dates that suited the venues, and 'The Voice' would get Chris to come and see them at one or other of the gigs. If he thought it was safe, he would speak to his mother; if not, then they would make other arrangements.

The man Mick got in touch with was delighted to help him and he got a list of phone numbers and dates to give 'The Voice' for Chris to pick from. Passports and visas were arranged for Helen and the group for six months ahead. The phone calls from 'The Voice' came every two or three months, so that would give them time to arrange everything.

Chris agreed to meet them in an Irish pub in Chicago where Mick arranged that he would be protected as would Helen and the group. The weeks leading up to their departure seemed to drag and Helen couldn't wait for it to arrive. She couldn't believe there was a chance she would finally get to see her son but on the other hand she was terrified it wouldn't work out.

They told no one about the meeting with Chris except Tess as they were afraid someone would let it slip. Helen was excited about travelling to America but she hated that Mick couldn't travel with them. She knew how much he longed to see Chris but there was nothing else they could do. It was either she went or no one would and that wasn't on the cards.

They knew Chris had met someone and was living with her and that it was serious but knew very little else about his private life. Helen kept thinking of what would happen when he had children and she couldn't see them. They'd missed so much of his life already; she didn't want to miss something as important as her grandchildren growing up. She saw the other women with theirs and felt an aching void.

Flying into Boston a couple of days before the gig they did a bit of sightseeing but Helen's heart wasn't in it and she couldn't settle. Boston was an attractive city but she wasn't interested and sent the group off on their own to soak up the tourist hot spots, while she went back to the hotel where she paced the floor of the bedroom. If she left the hotel at all she wanted to go back immediately in case anyone was trying to get in touch.

Finally the evening Chris was to meet her arrived and she was sitting in the kitchen of the pub they were playing in waiting to go on stage and not knowing what to expect. People were in and out of the kitchen all night but she wasn't passing any remarks on them. She said later, "I was praying so much that I would see him, I didn't care about anything else and I didn't expect him to arrive until after the show!"

That's when she heard a voice; "Hey Ma!"

She lifted her head slowly, her heart was in her mouth not knowing if she had imagined the voice or not. But it was not her imagination and there stood Chris, her son, with the great big smile she always remembered. His hair was sun bleached, he sported a great tan and he was dressed in light coloured cargo pants with a white t-shirt under a khaki coloured shirt.

"Very changed!" she told Mick afterwards "Very American looking. I'm not surprised he could hide for so many years among the surfing crowds. But I would have recognised those eyes anywhere even though they were surrounded by a beard and a deeply tanned face. He looked what he was meant to portray, a surfing dude."

Chris scooped down and lifted her in his arms and hugged her. All he could say was; "Oh Ma! Oh Ma!"

She caught his bearded face and kissed it all over. Both were crying like babies.

"At last!" she jabbered on "You're alive! Thank God! You're alive! You're here! I was so scared I would never see you again. Or that someone would shoot you. I've missed you so much! I'm so glad to see you!"

He laughed; "Ah Ma! I'd have got to see you some way!" he replied softly.

He let her down and they stood with their arms around each other staring into each other's faces. Helen could see he had aged but had the same glint in his eye that she remembered so well.

Within seconds the old Chris emerged; "Jaysus woman, you've been looking after yourself," he laughed in a broad Belfast accent. "You don't seem to have changed at all. I better keep my friends away from you!"

"Hey! I was told you had an American accent but you sound as though you never left Turf Lodge now," she laughed.

He laughed too as he hugged her again, "I have an American accent when I need one. But I practise in front of the mirror every night in case I get back to Belfast. It's still my dream, you know! To walk up that street again and say hello to all the neighbours before it's too late and then walk into my own home. I couldn't walk up to Tess or any of the other neighbours with an American accent. They'd never let me live it down."

"They would be only too glad to see you."

But she knew he was right. It wouldn't be the old Chris without the Belfast brogue and that sense of humour that was definitely Belfast.

They spoke twenty to the dozen for the next fifteen minutes until one of the group told her it was time to go on stage.

"Come on, woman! You're here to work and the place is full and everyone wants to meet you, the Belfast mammy. Most of them know Chris's story now and they want to meet the mammy now."

"Go on Ma! I'm dying to see you strut your stuff!" laughed Chris.

"Oh! My God! You've never heard me sing in public!" said Helen "And I feel as though I have been doing it forever. You've been away a long time, son!"

"I know I have Ma," sighed Chris. "Maybe it's time to come home."

"Not yet, son, it's not safe yet but hopefully one day soon!"

"I hope so, Ma! I miss you and Da and the old place!"

She hugged him, "And we miss you, son!"

As she walked on stage the other guys in the group now knew the story and they hugged Helen. The rest of the bar gave her a standing ovation as she moved to the microphone with tears in her eyes.

"I have waited many years for this night," she told them. A huge cheer went up.

"This first song is for all my fellow Irish men and women out there tonight, it's 'A Song for Ireland.'"

A thunderous clapping and cheer went up again. And as Helen started to sing from the heart the noise subsided and you could hear a penny drop. Her soul filled voice drifted over everyone in the bar and there were many tears, each one thinking of their homeland and what it had been through for the last thirty plus years, the people and the places that they missed and most of them would never see again. The concert continued for a couple of hours with many requests of old Irish songs which Helen did her best to oblige.

Afterwards Chris was amazed at how good Helen was. "Good God! Mum! I never appreciated how good a singer you are! I didn't know you could sing like that!"

"I've improved with age and practice," she laughed.

"I could get you gigs in loads of Irish bars here and I could see you when you come over!" he said excitedly.

"We mightn't be good enough for them. We got the gig here because your Da knew the owner."

"You were great! Did you not hear that crowd tonight? Sure, you're great at everything you set your mind to!" he told her. "Especially as a mum and a wife."

Helen smiled. She was a very happy Irish mammy that night.

67

The next day Helen was introduced to Chris's partner, Leah and she finally met 'The Voice' whose name was Carrie Mc Loughlin.

Helen hugged her tightly to her and cried as she told her how important her voice had been in their lives over the years and how much she had done for their family.

"Without you I would probably have died. You kept me going when my boys were gone. You were the only thing who kept me hanging in there when I was left on my own. I had to know how he was doing and I knew as long as he was alive I might one day get to see him. Now here he is with us and it's all thanks to you."

"Don't be daft! I only made a few phone calls. It was nothing!" she replied.

"It was everything to me and his father!" Helen insisted, as she hugged her again.

Carrie Mc Loughlin was a young Irish woman and a cousin of Leah's. She travelled back and forth to the US working as a Public Relations Manager for a range of hotels, which was how she could give the three monthly updates. The company she worked for owned hotels in Dublin, Chicago and Miami where she met Chris and introduced him to Leah.

"She stole him from me!" Carrie laughed.

Leah pushed her and said, "Those two couldn't have a relationship. They don't know how to behave or be serious. You need at least one adult in a relationship and I'm obviously the one in ours. They never stop joking. It must be the pure Irish in them. I can't keep up with them."

Chris laughed and said, "She's right, apart from Leah, Carrie's my best friend. I will never forget what she has done for me. Tess told her all you lot were up to and she used to write it down in shorthand and read it to me. I then got her to type it out and I would read it over and over just to make me feel nearer to you. She used to give me the gossip too so I knew who got married and who died and who had a child. I know everything about the street and all my old friends and neighbours. I have read it all so many times. I don't know what I would have done without her."

"Neither do we!" Helen exclaimed. "You kept us living for this day."

"I'm going to start charging for this service if I'm that great!" laughed Carrie.

"Don't I buy you a beer every time you get in touch with Tess?" asked Chris.

"Yeah! A lousy beer! Skinflint!" laughed Carrie. Chris threw a cushion at her.

Leah said, "See what I mean? Children!"

But it was obvious she loved them both.

Chris had a large social circle of friends, with many impressive people in it. While she was with him, Helen met politicians she had read about at home in the newspaper, stars of the theatre and screen, business men and many others. She wasn't a bit surprised at his popularity as she knew he could charm the bird off the trees.

Carrie told her; "That boy could talk himself in or out of anything. It's a pity he couldn't talk himself out of a jail sentence and you could get him home for a while. It's all he really wants to do, you know, go home!"

Helen sighed and thought to herself; "those are my dearest wishes too."

She couldn't bear the thought of leaving him although she felt so much better knowing he was happy and had a good life. A few days later when they boarded the plane that brought them back to Belfast she vowed she would return soon.

Every year afterwards she contrived to meet up with him at least once or twice a year. Although Mick couldn't go, they felt happier now they knew for sure he was safe and well. As the years passed he became the father of two children, a boy and a girl and having expanded his business in publishing he was becoming a very wealthy man.

Mick found this worrying as the more attention Chris brought to himself the more likely his identity would become public knowledge and he would leave the security forces with very little options but to lift him. As time wore on and the group continued to fly back and forward to the US he was convinced they must know who they were visiting and why. The guys in the group all knew Chris's story and he felt sure it was being spoken about.

Chris started an International water sports magazine a few years earlier and it was becoming famous worldwide and it often had his picture on it. He was also growing more frustrated with not being able to return to Ireland.

As he said; “I can have anything money can buy but I can’t return home.”

His business continued to spread; he was making a lot of money and looking at options to expand. Ireland became one of the big names in surfing and water sports worldwide and he wanted to branch out here and he wanted to do it himself. As time went by his desire to return home grew stronger and he became fixated on the idea.

Mick worried the security forces might just be biding their time until Chris came nearer home where they could lift him without having to go through the US extradition system. After returning from another trip to the US Helen was convinced that Chris would do something stupid, like give himself up.

“After all he has been through I don’t think he would do something like that, Helen!” remarked Mick when she told him how she felt. “Would he?” he asked doubtfully.

“I have a feeling he is planning something and when I asked him he refused to discuss it with me.”

Then one morning Mick got a call from Dublin that answered all their questions. Carrie was on the other end of the phone and the news was not good!

“Chris flew into Dublin airport yesterday and handed himself over to the security guards. He’s now in one of the Dublin Garda stations and rang me to tell you what he has done. He told the Gardaí he wanted them to hand him over to the PSNI in Northern Ireland that he’s a wanted man.”

“Oh sweet Jesus! Is he mad?” asked Mick.

“He wants it sorted out one way or another. Can you and Helen come down here and see what you can do?”

“We’ll be there in a few hours. We’ll meet you.”

“Everything is moving fast here and he could be handed over tomorrow,” said Carrie.

“I could kill him!” said Helen when she heard what he had done. “Why has he done this?”

“Maybe he has a plan?” said Mick anxiously. “Our boy is not silly. He wouldn’t do it unless he had a plan!”

Two very worried parents packed their bags and headed to Dublin. In the past they had pictured many scenarios of Chris being arrested, shot, betrayed, tortured or some other dreadful fate or the preferred option of being granted an amnesty but never once had they imagined he would give himself up voluntarily.

“He must have a plan!” Mick kept repeating.

"I don't know what he was thinking but I keep remembering him telling me that he wanted to marry Leah but he couldn't get his birth certificate or letter of freedom without the chance of him being detected. It's something that really bothered him."

"Couldn't he have got the whole lot forged in the name he uses now? With his money he could buy anything."

"He didn't want to do that. He wanted to get married as Chris Mc Fadden and not as Charlie Foyle. He wanted it to be all right and above board."

"Well! He certainly can do that now because the world will know his real name. It will be plastered all over the media. He won't be able to keep this quiet and he will never be able to hide behind any alias again because now everyone will know his face."

Sure enough, the next day, his picture and story was on the front page of every newspaper and on every TV channel.

"Wealthy businessman arrested at Dublin airport" "Wealthy business man is escaped bomber" screamed the papers with photos to go with it.

When Helen and Mick arrived at the Garda barracks, the press were camped all over the street. Carrie met them and brought them in. Only one of them could get to see Chris so while Mick went in to see him Helen and Carrie met with his solicitor who told them what was happening and the full story came out.

Chris wanted to come home and sort everything out. He was tired of being on the run and always watching his back. He didn't want to wait until his parents were too old or the children more aware and wise enough to know what was happening. He decided he was going to bite the bullet and do the time. There were amnesties for political prisoners now and he hoped they would go easy on him. He didn't care if he did three or four years for absconding but he hoped it wouldn't be any more.

68

With some very influential friends working on his behalf they believed because he had stayed out of trouble for so many years now and made something of his life, the law might look at his case differently. He was going to appeal his sentence citing extenuating circumstances.

The solicitor informed Helen, "As you know he has made a lot of friends in high places in the US who can pull strings for him and he may come out of this with a much shorter sentence than originally handed down. I have had a few of them on to me already and some are indeed very influential political figures with a lot of influence the world over and they are speaking to those in charge. A few words in the right ears in the British Government could work wonders!"

Helen was worried sick. She couldn't see beyond the fact that the security forces were getting their hands on him again. She could understand what Chris had done and why he'd done it but she wasn't too sure how successful an appeal would be. With his father being an ex-prisoner and his brother blown up by a bomb he was carrying, it didn't bode well for Chris in her eyes.

They debated it back and forth well into the night for many nights. Mick was sure his plan would work and as he pointed out;

"It was the Diplock Courts that sentenced him and they were discredited worldwide years ago! He was only in his twenties when it happened and he's in his forties now and he gave himself up! They have to realise he's a changed man. Didn't he suffer enough losing his brother, who was his best friend, and his leg at the same time. They would look very hard hearted giving him a long sentence."

"We'll get the media on his case when he is back in Belfast and play for sympathy," decided Helen.

"Now you're talking, missus! You're the grieving mother who had to wait on word from a stranger for years to know how your son was and you couldn't see your grandchildren because Chris was on the run. Any tear jerker you can come up with will do. You must get the world press behind him. You want his partner and children home here in Belfast and Chris wants to get married here.

The war is over and Chris has suffered enough. He has been a pillar of society and worked hard since he ran away. This must mean something."

Chris was handed over to the PSNI and taken into custody a few days later. He spent months in jail before his appeal came through. Helen spoke to the International Press whenever she could. Leah did the same both in Ireland and the US as she came back and forward to Belfast to see him and staying with Helen and Mick. The family story was all over the press around the world.

"It doesn't hurt that Chris has a gorgeous glamorous mother and a wife that the press love either," remarked Tess laughing. "You slew them on the BBC with the story of the night Chris left and what Belfast was like to rear two boys in at the time. When you spoke about your home being raided and dug up on a regular basis, you shocked quite a few people who thought things like that only happened in foreign countries. If that had been a plain wee woman worn down by it all, it wouldn't have had as much impact as coming from an attractive, intelligent woman. They even got a bit of a video of your show in which you're singing a ballad."

"You didn't do so down badly yourself, telling them of all the times you and I waited at night for weeks on end to hear "The Voice" tell us if Chris was OK. You looked so petite and helpless; every man who saw you will want to protect you."

"As long as no one finds out who "the Voice" is and gets poor Carrie into trouble!"

"Nobody knows but us and we're not telling."

"And as long as nobody finds out either that Tess is not the innocent little angel she portrays on the TV, we'll be okay!" laughed Helen.

"And the glamour mum is her accomplice in whatever devilment she gets up to!" remarked Mick. "You're two tough women, fair play to you both and you're doing a great job with the media. The campaign is gathering strength all over the world. The American politicians are playing a blinder too."

"James Mahooney is such a good liar with his "No Siree! I never knew Christopher was a member of the IRA. He was only a hard working family man when he was in the US. Everyone respected him and all the work he did for those less well off than himself. He gave many young Irish men or women jobs here and he didn't care if they were Protestant or Catholic. He's a good human being and him with his leg amputated too!"

Everyone was lapping up the story of the young Irish man who made good against all odds in the US even though he had lost his leg and was on the run.

They courted the newspapers, TV and radio stations appealing for leniency for a wonderful son, father, friend and partner. Yes! He had made mistakes when he was very young but he had changed completely and now he employed thousands throughout the world. What was going to happen to them if he went to jail? He was going to open a business in Northern Ireland too and Northern Ireland needed all the business it could get in the economic times that were in it.

Finally the long awaiting came to an end and his appeal came up. The world media crowded the court room and building along with politicians from the US, Northern Ireland, the Republic, Britain and the rest of the world. Influential men who wanted Chris to bring business to Ireland were in attendance. Everyone wanted to be seen and heard.

It was all over by the end of the first day. Chris had become too big a figure to mess with. The British didn't want any further bad publicity on their role in Northern Ireland. They knew they would not come out of it very well. Women were lining up to tell the media of the abuse they suffered during the time Chris was lifted and the world could understand their hatred for the security forces which led to the two young men taking to the gun and the bomb.

The judge announced his final verdict and Chris' sentence was brought down to two years. Eighteen months were suspended. This meant that with the time he had spent in jail waiting for the appeal he could walk away from the court that day a free man.

The cheers went up in the courtroom and it spread down the corridors to the steps outside. Most of their neighbours and friends from West Belfast and many other parts of Ireland and the world waited on the steps of the Court House. As he walked out he was greeted like a hero. Hugs and kisses were distributed to the whole family and Chris, Helen, Mick and Leah were hoisted on shoulders while Tess and Carrie hugged each other.

All Helen could say was, "I've got him back now! I've got him back now!"

Chris stood and spoke to the press for a while and then got into Mick's car with Leah and Helen with a cavalcade following behind them. As they neared his home in West Belfast he got Mick to stop.

"I'm walking into my street and I'm walking in a free man and I'm going to prove it to myself." He grabbed Leah's hand and pulled her out of the car with him and they walked down the hill into his street with many others joining him. This was the street he had been born and reared in and where he spent the first twenty three years of his life. He hadn't seen it for a long time.

He called on houses he used to run in and out of as a boy and hugged and chatted to everyone he knew. They all shook his hand and hugged him back, welcoming him home.

Tess had made it home before them and she was standing at her door with bottles of champagne; she poured a little into as many glasses as she could and celebrated his freedom. Food and bottles of beer and wine started appearing from everywhere.

It was a couple of hours before he stepped into the family home.

"Arragh Ma!" he said. "You changed the whole place!"

"Of course I did, son! It would be in some state now if I hadn't."

"But it's not the same!" Chris said quietly, sounding disappointed. "I always pictured it in my mind the way I left it."

"Son, nothing's the same and neither are you, me or your Da!" replied Helen. "We've all moved on and so has life. And I know you are trying to find Kieran here but he's not here except in spirit. He will always be with you in Spirit, even in America. You didn't have to come home to find him, son."

"I'm losing him, Ma!" he said as he put his arm around her, "I can't hold on to him anymore!"

"Let him go, son! You'll find him again later, when it's time."

"I don't hear him anymore when I talk to him."

"You don't need to hear him anymore. You can go your own way now!" said Helen. "Just say goodbye. See you later! And you will."

He bent his head and stayed silent for a while. The tears were dripping from his eyes. She hugged him.

"He's always with us, you know that. You can't lose him. He may not be as clear as he used to be but he is still here. I'm sure he has been looking after you all down through the years, look how well you have done. Could you have done it without him?"

"No! I couldn't but I don't want to lose him!"

"Maybe it's time to let him go. He got you through it all, now you're a free man and you can do the rest on your own."

Helen walked away from him and carried on making the tea as tears ran down her face.

After a while he came over and hugged her, saying nothing for a minute. "I know you're right! Thanks, Ma! I knew you'd understand. I think it may be time to say goodbye to him for a while now and try and let him go."

Helen held him in her arms for a minute and then let him go.

"Tell your Da and Leah their tea's ready," she told him gruffly as she brushed away another tear.

"Will the hurt of losing Kieran ever cease?" she asked herself. "But thank you God for giving me Chris back."

He headed back to the US again a few days later. Unlike his father the way was cleared for him to do so.

Mick teased him that money could buy anything and with Chris's influence in high places, it did. A few months later Mick got a visa to go and play in the States and they went twice a year. Chris returned frequently to Ireland to where his heart would always be, Belfast.

69

Home life for the women carried on with its usual ups and downs but without any major problems. Children and grandchildren came and went. Mick and Helen continued playing a few gigs here and there but not as often as they used to. Now they preferred just sitting in a corner of a club with a few friends and having a sing-song.

They travelled to the US a few times a year to visit Chris and the family who also came home regularly. He developed the publishing company he had dreamed of in Northern Ireland and it was doing very well. They rented a house up the Antrim coast and when he was home Helen and Mick would spend a lot of time there with him and the family. They grew to love the countryside and dreamed of moving away from the hustle and bustle of the city and all the memories of what had gone before. Even Helen was heard to wax lyrically about living in the country.

Barry and Tess lived day to day with little excitement. The kids had all graduated, got well-paid jobs, settled down, married and had children. They loved their grandchildren dearly and spent as such time as possible with them.

"Our house is fuller now of kids than when we were rearing our own," said Tess.

"Sure, it's great! What else would we be doing if we didn't have them? Twiddling our thumbs?" smiled Barry.

One of Mary's sons, who had taken to drugs when he was in his late teens had left home and hadn't been seen since. The last they heard about him was when someone saw him in England a few years before. She pretended it didn't matter but everyone knew that Mary wasn't happy when one of the nestlings wasn't accounted for in the nest by the mother hen.

She fretted every now and then about him to the women but after a few years of not being able to trace him she seemed to give up. Tess thought she had not just given up on finding her son but also on life. She wasn't the same feisty woman they all remembered, even though she tried very hard not to show her heartache.

Then one morning her life was thrown into turmoil. At about six o' clock she awoke to find Owen in agony on a seat beside the bed.

"Call an ambulance!" he told her. "It's my heart." With that he collapsed.

She jumped out of bed and threw a blanket over him before she ran downstairs to ring an ambulance. It arrived almost immediately and after a few checks on Owen, the paramedics connected him to oxygen, put him on a trolley and rushed him out the door and to hospital.

Mary's son, Nick, whom she had called, arrived just as Owen was being carried out of the house and he and Mary followed in his car.

When the ambulance reached the hospital Owen was unconscious and rushed into emergency where they began to work on him straight away. By the time Mary and Nick arrived his vital signs were not good. He was deteriorating fast and they weren't allowed to see him. One of the nurses explained the situation to them and asked them to sit in the waiting room. Half an hour later the cardiologist came to speak to them.

She knew what the he was going to tell her before he opened his mouth and she gripped the arms of the chair waiting for him to speak and kept whispering, "No! No! No!

She knew when he opened his mouth and spoke, all would change and her life would never be the same again. But no amount of wishing could stop the cardiologist's pronouncement.

Owen had a massive heart attack and died on the operating table. He told them there had been no hope for him once he got that heart attack and it was a miracle he had survived so long. He told Mary that Owen had known how bad his heart condition was and he had asked him, at his last appointment, not to tell her as he wanted the time they had left together to be as normal as possible. He didn't want her to worry.

She was shocked she hadn't known and couldn't believe he had kept it from her. "I thought he was better. For God's sake I walked the feet off him every day!"

"That's probably what kept him living so long, the way you looked after him!" the cardiologist told her.

"I could have supported him more if I had known!" she said.

"Ma! You supported him in every way you could all your married life. He wanted to save you the worry. Give him that much! He knew what you were like. He chose not to worry you," said Nick. He hugged her.

She patted his cheek and said, "You're a good son."

"Can we see him now?" she asked the doctor as she cried quietly.

"In a little while!" he said. "A nurse will bring you down to him."

In the meantime they rang around the family who arrived in a very short space of time.

"All I felt was very tired. I needed to lie down," she told Tess afterwards. "I felt as though I had come to the end, as though all my life I had been working for Owen and now he was gone there was nothing left for me to do. First I married him, then had his children, worried about him being in the IRA, then kept him happy in Long Kesh and then came his sickness and I did my best for him. I thought we had years more together, now it's all over. I want to lie down and be at peace. I can now stop striving, working and worrying. I've done my best! I can let go now, my job's done!"

She looked as if someone had deflated her. All her energy had dissipated as though she had nothing left to give. Life seemed to have left her completely.

"Ah! But sure I knew really, when I look back!" she said. "I think I just chose to ignore it, not believe there was a chance I'd lose him! I could see him fading but I knew if there was anything he could have done about it he would have done it. He loved us and he would've wanted to stay with us as long as he could. No! He'd no choice. It happened the way he wanted, with no fuss."

It all seemed to be over so quickly, everyone was stunned. The grief of the family, friends and neighbours was obvious. Owen was a family and community man who touched many lives. Hundreds attended his wake and funeral to say their final farewell and then he was gone, completely, from their world.

Mary moved through the days quietly. No one or nothing seemed to have an impact on her. As she passed the children she patted their backs or heads but if they spoke to her she didn't seem able to respond. She walked on or sat staring into space.

The family were worried but thought she would improve when all the activity of the funeral was over and the initial phase of mourning passed. This seemed to be true as a few weeks later she began talking to them again as though nothing had happened.

She would interrogate them as to their future plans and what they should be doing with their lives. She pushed at the grandchildren and encouraged them to try something new. Then as quickly as she started this phase she stopped and became quiet again.

70

The lives of the five families had always been fairly insular and although some of them travelled to different parts of the world holidaying once or twice a year, the majority of their lives were lived out in West Belfast. Over the years of the Troubles they had developed the habit of keeping to their own areas and to the same close family and friends. Even now they seldom ventured into other areas, particularly not to those seen as Protestant areas.

What happened to one family in their group was felt by all and Owen's death was a shock to everyone. Mick, Barry, Jim and he had become like a support system for each other and for many more men in the area after they got home from jail.

They claimed they didn't have much choice as their wives were in and out of each other's houses so much they didn't know what house to go to bed in. Now one of the main links in the chain was missing and he would be sadly missed.

Tess worried about Mary and how she seemed to never really recover after Owen's death. She felt something had died in Mary too when she lost him.

She and Owen had been a very close couple and Tess expected a more emotional response from her. She was eating very little and not leaving the house. The family were now very subdued around her and not their usual boisterous selves and she had stopped complaining about the 'tribe' as she called them.

Deciding to keep a closer watch on her, Tess called every morning before work to see if she wanted anything from the shops. She didn't drive and Tess would often take her shopping or get something for her on her way from work although she knew she wasn't eating much of anything she bought.

Helen thought she was worrying unnecessarily and that Mary had been through so much over the years she was now past being dramatic about anything.

"For God's sake Helen! She's the most dramatic of any of us. She was always making a drama out of the simplest situation. Have you listened to her about the family? She has written about ten short stories in her head about each of them. They could be put on stage and she could act them all out and make a fortune, they're so funny and only half true, if that. She exaggerates everything. Now you only get that quiet smile and no drama at all. I miss the old Mary!"

"People grieve in many ways, Tess. This is her way. She's accepting Owen's death philosophically."

"Mary doesn't do philosophical. I know something is wrong with her. I think she has decided to die and be with Owen. She is so thin!"

Helen was shocked at this statement from Tess. "Now who is being dramatic? You don't just die because you decide to!"

"I think Mary will!"

She couldn't put her finger on why she thought this but she was worried. No matter what Helen said she felt in her heart she was right.

When Tess enquired how she was, Mary's reply was always the same; "I'm fine. I'm glad I had the last few years with him and he didn't suffer. It was quick. He would've hated being bed ridden. What more could I ask for?"

"Dammit!" stormed Tess to whoever would listen "She should have had more time with him after all they've been through. It's terribly hard for her to lose him now. He was only in his late sixties."

"Mary's at peace with herself and life," said Barry "That's all she needs now. Leave her be. Stop worrying."

"I don't want her at peace, when was she ever at peace before? I want her to create drama like she did with every little thing that happened over the years. I want her scolding the children and grandchildren and to listen to them teasing her back the way they did."

"Tess, you have to stop worrying about her! You'll make yourself sick!" Helen urged her.

"I know! But for some reason I can't. There is something niggling away at me and I don't know what it is! I may laugh at this sometime down the line but for now I know there is something wrong with Mary, no matter what anyone else says. I firmly believe she has decided to die and she will!"

Mary started to lose a lot more weight and even when Tess made dinners for her she only picked at it. She was eating like a bird. Tess would nag her but all she would do was smile and say quietly, "I'm fine, stop worrying."

One evening about three months after Owen died Tess called at her house but got no answer. She opened the door and walked down the hall and into the sitting room calling her name. No one answered. As she entered the kitchen she found her slouched on the chair, barely breathing. Her colour was bad and she was very cold.

Tess rang for an ambulance immediately and got a rug from the settee and wrapped her in it. Then she tried to bring her round but there was no response.

While waiting for the ambulance she rang Helen who arrived with Mick in tow. The wait for the ambulance seemed like hours even though it was only about five minutes. Helen was shocked to see the condition Mary was in, even though she had seen her a few days before. She seemed to have aged into an old woman overnight and looked very ill.

After the ambulance left with the lights flashing, they rang her family and then headed to the hospital to see what was wrong with her. They knew it was serious as she looked like death. Pacing the waiting room with the family they had to wait for more than an hour.

Finally the doctor came to see them. He couldn't tell them what was wrong with her. She had a very high temperature but no signs of infection. All her vital signs were normal but she wasn't responding to treatment. They checked for injuries which could have occurred from a fall or a bang to her head but there was no evidence of bruising or internal bleeding. They checked for an overdose of medication but they found nothing. They were keeping her in for further tests and observation.

When they got in to see her she was all wired up to machines, still unconscious and looking very frail and ill.

Helen looked at Tess and frowned. She could see from the look on her face that she now believed she had been right all along, Mary had decided to go to Owen.

For the next two days the women and family visited her as she lay unconscious with her breathing very shallow. It was as though she had already left them. Everyone wanted to know what had happened or what was wrong with her but there were no answers. The doctors and other specialists didn't know what was wrong and couldn't or wouldn't make a guess.

The doctors informed them they didn't know if she would get better, she was deteriorating all the time and not responding to medication.

None of the family knew what to do and they were heartbroken. It had all happened so quickly. This was the woman who had controlled their lives from when they were babies, now she was slipping away from them.

"What will we do without her if she dies?" was the refrain repeated many times over the next few days.

"She is the one who runs the family. She kept us all in line," they told each other.

Mary's son asked Tess, "Did she know she was dying, is that why we all had an interrogation about our futures? Was she checking if we'd be all right when she was gone? Is that possible, Tess?"

"I don't know!" Tess replied. She didn't want the family to think that Mary didn't want to stay with them but she had no doubt she wanted to go to Owen and she'd given up and was now on her way.

All were stunned that this strong wee woman had come to this.

Tess spoke to them, "You're mum's very tired. Her body is weary with all she's been through. You may have to let her go."

"We can't!" they cried. "We couldn't cope without her!"

"Yes! You can. She taught you everything she knew!" Helen said. "You are all strong people and you have to let her know it is all right for her to go. Let her go in peace with your blessing. You will all see her later when it's your time. Let her go to your Dad."

That night the family had a meeting and next evening all came to the hospital with their local priest. He said a few prayers and one of Mary's girls sang the hymn 'How Great Thou Art', which Mary had loved to hear at family parties and celebrations over the years. Then one by one they bent and kissed her, said their goodbyes and went out into the corridor where they held each other and cried.

Helen and Tess said they would stay with her that night for a few hours and let the family get something to eat and sleep.

When they were alone with Mary later, Lucy joined them and they kissed her gently and said their goodbyes. They spoke to her about what she meant to them, thanked her for being their friend and all the support she had given them through the years.

Tess said, "Go on Mary! Let go, he's waiting for you. You've done your bit here. You were a great mother, grandmother, wife and friend. It's time to go to God and Owen. You'll find a better place there than what you had here. Just keep an eye on us poor mortals down here struggling on."

They sat with her until the family returned.

The next morning Mary left them.

Helen and Tess spoke about her and how they now both believed she'd decided she didn't want to go on without Owen. She just stopped living. Helen couldn't get her head around that she had done it just by willing it. Tess wished she had done something about it before it was too late.

“Hindsight is a great thing,” said Helen, “I wish I’d believed you when you told me!”

The doctors found no reason why she died and put it down to some kind of virus or allergy she may have had. The two women knew better but said nothing.

The family spent the next two days searching for Tom, their brother who had disappeared. They got in touch with anybody and everybody they knew in England who might have information on him. The Irish are always running into each other abroad and catching up on what’s happening at home. They finally located him on the outskirts of Liverpool and phoned him that evening to tell him of his mother’s death. He was heartbroken but happy to speak to them and that they’d got in touch with him. He immediately caught a flight and arrived home just in time for the funeral.

“I knew we would find him,” said Rachel one of Mary’s grandchildren. “Nannie made sure we did, from Heaven. I bet she is bossing everyone about up there too. She is probably ordering St Christopher to sort it out and send the lost traveller home. I hope there are children up there for her to look after, she would like that.”

The family were expecting a down-and-out hobo, who’d probably been sleeping rough for years as they waited for the ‘Prodigal Son’ to return. But when he arrived he looked very respectable, clean and well-cared for. It was obvious he had been looking after himself or that somebody had been looking after him. Of course the family had a lot of questions.

His story was like a lot of other Irish stories. He’d carried on taking drugs and drinking for a couple of months after he arrived in England but decided to get his act together after he got a job in a hotel. He worked his way up from dishwasher and handyman to the bar, then on to the dining room and reception and a year preciously he had been made manager.

“Why didn’t you contact home? Mum longed to hear from you. She never stopped missing you!” they told him.

“I always meant to get in touch with her but the longer I put it off the harder it got. What excuse could I make to you all? Then I used the excuse to myself that I would wait a wee while longer until I had more money so me Ma would be proud of me and how well I was doing. Unfortunately I waited too long.”

His sister told him, “Mammy would have been proud of you for just giving up the drugs, never mind making a good life for yourself. You would have made her world if you had just phoned. One phone call was all she needed! She just wanted to hear from you, just to know you were well.”

It broke his heart to hear all this.

Mary's youngest son said, "Well! You're here now! Ma is probably instrumental in that too, so you're going to have to stay in touch. If there is nothing too important to take you back to England maybe you could look for a transfer here? That hotel company you work for has a hotel in Belfast, maybe you could get a job there and you could stay here in Ma's house. You could look after the house and we would still be able to come and torment you, like we did Ma!" Everyone laughed.

"It sounds as though she is still giving orders from the grave. I wonder if I could do that for her?" said Tom.

"Of course you could!" laughed one of the girls "She's probably working on it as we speak!"

Tom found all that had happened a lot to take in and had some thinking to do when he returned to Liverpool. Gradually the idea planted at the funeral took root and he couldn't shake it. He wanted to go home. He went back to see the family again a couple of months later and while he was there he went to see the manager of the hotel in the city.

"Mum is definitely looking after us!" he told Tess. "When I spoke to the manager he told me that he was transferring back to London in a few weeks' time. That is where he comes from and they are advertising for applicants for his job. He said he'd ring me and let me know what was happening and as I worked for the sister hotel in Liverpool, I would have a good chance of getting it as I've had lots of experience and I know how they operate."

Just months after Mary died he returned to the family home and Mary's wee house remained the base for them all to get together. He looked after it as though she could still see what he was doing and there were times he felt she could, that she still flitted here and there about the house.

A few months after he returned home, he and Tess' daughter, Grainne, started dating and within a short time they were married.

"She is certainly weaving her magic from up there," laughed Tess one evening after the wedding.

"She always had to control things," smiled Helen back.

They continued to live in the wee house and eventually they added their own two children to Mary's ever expanding family.

71

Tess and Barry continued on life's way, with no great excitement or problems, looking after the family and home, working and enjoying each other's company got them through the days. If she had been asked how she felt she would have said content.

She once told Helen, "I love him but not in the way I loved him before he was lifted and jailed. Something died in me the day he turned against me and the children when he came out of jail. I never got it back. It is still sitting in the back of my mind somewhere and I will never quite trust him again like I used to but I've had to deal with it for all our sakes. I've forgiven him but I will never forget. We're good friends and I really like him and I think that is enough. I'm not looking for shooting stars and fire crackers, so we're okay! I'm too old now for that kind of craic anyway."

A few years after the crisis in their marriage and after he'd returned home they were out for a meal one evening and she spoke to Barry about how she felt. He reached across the table, took her hand and spoke softly to her; "I know how you feel and I know what I did to you and I know I destroyed something that will never be the same again with us. I also know what I nearly lost. When I was out of the house and I came to my senses I was terrified by where I found myself. It all became terribly clear to me. I knew I needed to get back to you and the children or everything good in my life was gone forever. I still believe that. I love you and our kids. I love talking to you and them. I learn all the time from you and I feel as though I'm now in a safe place where all the love I need is. All I need from you is to let me stay here and I know our relationship will grow and strengthen. Will you do that?"

Tess was surprised by how clearly Barry saw their situation and agreed to settle for what they had.

"It's more than a lot of other people have," she thought.

She loved him to the best of her ability and they worked hard for their family and home. They were good friends, went on holidays abroad and had the same friends since they were teenagers. They renovated the house again and built another extension.

That house in the country was still on the agenda and still their dream. As Barry said smiling, "As soon as Tess slows down enough to look for one we will move."

But often, like a lot of good plans, the 'Powers that Be' had other ideas.

Barry became ill and had to take time off work. He was back and forward to the doctors at first with fatigue and infections and was swallowing medicine, vitamins and herbal remedies by the handful. Then he started picking up more serious infections and antibiotics had no impact on them. Nothing was helping and he began to deteriorate rapidly. He went back to work a few times but had to leave again as he found when he cut himself it was very difficult to stop the bleeding.

Initially the doctors didn't know what was wrong with him and started tests to pinpoint the problem. Within days he was diagnosed with leukaemia which eventually gave rise to problems with anaemia and bleeding. He was hospitalised for weeks because of infections he continued to pick up and became very frail.

The family were in shock. It happened so quickly, within a matter of weeks.

As Tess said, "Leukaemia is what other people get; you don't think it will affect your own family."

"It can affect anybody and cancer has become very common in our area," said Helen.

Shortly after Barry's diagnoses there was chemo therapy and radio therapy. He would be well for a few weeks but then the problems reoccurred.

One day as Tess spoke to the doctor on how Barry was getting so many setbacks he told her that because the strain of cancer he had was so acute it was taking its toll on his immune system. He was finding it very difficult to beat the disease and each infection was making him weaker.

Tess came away devastated. She knew it looked very unlikely that Barry was going to make it. The doctor had practically told her so.

"I'm only fooling myself! He has told me as diplomatically as possible that I'm going to lose him!" she told Helen.

Helen held her as she cried. She'd known he was very ill and it would be a miracle if he survived as he had told Mick about it and was worried how Tess would cope. Mick reminded him of how she'd coped when he was in jail and convinced him she could do the same again. She would miss him but Tess was strong and would rally on. After that he seemed to become more peaceful.

"Isn't it funny how you never know what you have until you are on the verge of losing it?" Tess asked Helen. "He's such a good man and we've had a very good life together the last years."

The doctor told her there was a large number of men in Northern Ireland who'd been in Long Kesh at the same time as Barry suffering from different cancers. This was the same time as the British Army had dropped the CR Gas on them and they were now suffering from leukaemia, throat, breast, testicular, prostate and many other forms of cancers along with diseases of the lungs and the heart.

Tess was shocked and asked, "Could this be the reason he has developed leukaemia?"

"It's very possible," he informed her.

She began research on the use of CR Gas in Long Kesh and whether it could be the cause of Barry's illness. At the time it was more for something to do as she felt so useless at not being able to help him recover, more than anything else. She was shocked by what she found and couldn't believe that a so called modern nation could commit such an atrocious act on human beings.

"Have you forgotten exactly what happened during the Troubles?" he asked her, Barry laughed weakly and said "CR Gas was just one of the many atrocities meted out to Catholics during that time."

With a lot of the diseases the men were developing some specialists believed it was in all probability as a result of being subjected to the CR Gas. All these men dying from various forms of cancers, throat and chest diseases and heart attacks were too many for it to be put down to natural causes. Especially as they had one thing in common, all had been subjected to the CR Gas.

Tess visited some of the men she knew from when Barry was in Long Kesh and spoke to them about the problem. Most agreed that it was probably the reason for what was almost an epidemic among the men! She got in touch with others who were lobbying the Government regarding it. They were getting very little satisfaction from anybody.

"Don't go there!" Helen begged her. "You have enough on your plate. You will make yourself angry and sap the energy you need for yourself, the children and Barry. Walk away from it, please!"

"But I feel I should do something!" she said.

"It's too big a fight for you to take on and it could go on for years. Leave it!" pleaded Helen. "You haven't got the energy to start another fight."

Tess thought about it seriously and finally agreed with Helen. She had little time and energy left to give while working full time and looking after Barry in the evening. She wanted to give up work but because hers was the only wage coming into the house and Barry insisted she should continue. Not that Barry was letting her look after him much. She felt he was insisting on her keeping her job just so she would get out of the house and lead some kind of a normal life instead of being with him all the time.

He continued doing what he could for himself but as time went by he became so weak he found it hard to walk across the kitchen. Trying to make dinner for Tess coming home in the evening he would have to sit down many times before he was finished. Eventually he agreed to stop pushing himself so hard.

Helen, Mick or Lucy would drop in during the day and the children were always calling over. They had a good support system to feed and look after him and Tess usually found her dinner made by one or other of them when she came home.

He was visibly getting weaker each day and they were all worried. Only in his fifties and a strong, active man before this awful disease he should have had many more years in him. Mick especially was heartbroken about it and did all he could to help. Being such good friends, he felt helpless that he couldn't do more.

"The Brits are still killing Irish men even years after the fact!" he said to Helen one evening as they discussed Barry's illness.

"Mick, it's over! Let it go! It's not our fight anymore!" pleaded Helen.

"I want to get out of the city. I want to go and live away from here when Barry goes!" Mick told her, "I need to get away from all this. I need to live in peace somewhere. I need to live in open space where I'm not reminded of what has happened!"

"Maybe that's what we should aim for! Forget about all the rest," exclaimed Helen, relieved that she found something to keep Mick's mind away from seeking revenge. "We will talk to Chris and see what he says."

72

Eventually Barry's body could take no more and he gave up the fight one evening as he lay on the couch in front of the television. Tess was in the kitchen making tea and talking away to him. Sometimes he would be too weak to answer so she wasn't too worried when she didn't hear his voice. She went in with his tea and was putting it on the coffee table chatting still, when she turned to look at him. With one glance she knew immediately he had gone. Her partner, friend and father of her children had left her.

She sat beside him for a few minutes, held his hand and spoke to him.

"We were some of the lucky ones Barry, we survived to have a decent life for ourselves," she told him. "Thank you, I'll miss you so much. You were a good man and I loved you. You gave us everything you could, you made life so much better for us all!"

She was glad he was no longer suffering. He had hated being ill and helpless and not being able to pull his weight in the home or with the family. She bent and kissed him and caressed his cheek with her hand and then with tears in her eyes she went to the phone and rang the children. "Daddy's gone," she told them as she quietly cried. "He passed away peacefully just now as I was making tea for him."

"We're on our way, Ma! We'll be with you very soon."

Even though the situation had been difficult initially when Barry came out of jail the children had learned to love him again and had the greatest respect for him. He was always there and would do anything for them. When the grandchildren arrived he was available for babysitting or taking them for walks. They were heartbroken and they would miss him terribly.

Next she rang Helen and Mick who arrived within minutes and then the other women.

As in most Irish communities news spreads fast and the neighbours called in to see if there was anything they could do. Plates of sandwiches, biscuits and cakes materialised out of nowhere, as did a boiler for water and neighbouring women making tea and coffee for the mourners. Tess didn't know where anything was coming from. It was a typical Irish wake.

The children with Tess greeted people as they arrived and the house didn't empty for three days. They talked about Barry and as the stories were told, the family saw another side of him they didn't know. The respect and love that many outside the family felt for him, was evident and all the kind deeds he had done to help people were many over the years. Tess wasn't surprised as the Barry she knew was a good man. At night friends sat up and kept vigil until morning. During the evenings the house and front garden was full of men and women, some who had not seen each other since the Peace Process began.

Mick took Tess aside and told her that Barry had given him papers with all his funeral arrangements which he'd made through his solicitor. Tess had known nothing about this.

"He knew you didn't want to discuss his funeral with him so he felt it would be better if he did it himself. He'd wanted you to have as little as possible to do when he was gone. He told me to ring the solicitor when he died and check that the arrangements were carried out and for any other things that you needed doing. I want to do this but I don't want to do it behind your back. I think you should have a say in the funeral too."

Tess told him; "Go ahead Mick and do what he wanted. It is, after all, his funeral! It will be so much off my mind and I would be very grateful if you did as he asked."

The next morning the solicitor arrived and she found everything organised and paid for. He'd ordered white lilies for peace for his coffin. He'd loved the ones outside their kitchen window and had said as long as they grew they represented peace in their home if not in the Provence. He left the Tricolour with the solicitor for over his coffin but insisted he didn't want any gun salutes.

"There's no need for guns when we are trying to build peace," he wrote in a letter to Tess.

The family agreed, although some neighbours felt the salute was recognition of the time he'd spent in jail as an innocent man and all the work he'd done for the Nationalist community before and since he left jail.

Three days later Barry was laid to rest. He was in his mid-fifties. Another one of the group gone!

When Barry's estate was sorted, Tess discovered to her amazement she was going to be left very comfortably off. This was a total surprise to her. Although they'd never discussed money matters in great depth, she'd assumed they were like everyone else, getting by, just a bit more comfortably off because of her job and Barry being his own boss from the time the building trade had improved.

She only spent money on what she needed in the house or for the kids or holidays, the rest was saved and she believed Barry did the same. But it appeared he was making a lot more money than she thought when the building trade was going well and he was a lot more astute than she was with it.

Although he'd never said what he earned and Tess had never asked she didn't think it was too much more than her. Now she discovered when his will was read how wrong she was. He'd been making quite a lot more than she had. He didn't drink much, gamble, buy many clothes or spend foolishly. Instead it had all gone into different savings accounts, several insurance policies, shares in safe commodities and playing the markets. He'd had good advice and made a nice little fortune. Tess was shocked for days after this was revealed. She'd never known what he was doing and to her astonishment she found she was now worth a lot more than she could ever have dreamed possible. All she'd ever worried about was if there was enough to look after the family and the home. Barry always said there was plenty but she thought it was a throwaway remark and his 'plenty' was the same as hers, a few thousand.

"Maybe he wanted to surprise you when you finally got around to buying that house in the country you always dreamed of?" said Helen.

"And we never thought he wouldn't be around to see it!" said Tess.

She couldn't get her head around having so much money. To her the poverty she'd experienced when Barry was interned first was still strong in her memory. Not knowing what to do with it all, for months she did nothing.

Having not got around to buying their dream house, it was bothering her now. She knew Barry had wanted to move for years but she'd always been too busy with her job or something else to think about it. She couldn't seem able to walk away from it all. He'd brought the subject up often but she always found an excuse for not doing anything about it.

Now it was too late for him. Realising that sometime would never come for him now and if she ever wanted her dream to come true she'd better do something about it soon. Tomorrow may not come for her either if she waited much longer. With the money he had left her she could pay outright for a very nice property and have a considerable nest egg left over to live on.

"If I'd known how much we were worth, would I have moved earlier?" she asked herself. "I probably would have! I've wanted to give up work for a long time. But there's no point in 'if onlys' now."

Within weeks her decision was made, she was retiring and selling all. She converted the majority of stocks and shares into cash except for those her auditor advised her to keep.

A few weeks later the house went on the market and she went looking for a place in the country with a bit of land to keep a few animals. Some of the family came along each weekends and they had a great time spending many hours searching for properties and arguing over what she wanted or should be buying.

Tess had a picture in her mind and she was determined she was settling for nothing less. She wanted a few fields, big enough to build barns to keep animals, to fence off ground for those that were not compatible living together and with enough grass in the spring and summer to feed the animals. She needed a large meadow where she could cut silage or hay so she wouldn't have to buy fodder for the stock in the winter and she needed barns to hold the food stuff.

Helen laughed many times as she made her lists. "You sound like a farmer already, with fodder for the stock and bales of this and that."

Researching everything, many evenings were spent in front of the computer on organic farming, animals keep and much more. She didn't envisage a huge number of animals, just enough to keep her occupied. About thirty acres would suit her fine.

"God be with the days," laughed Mick, "when a quarter of an acre was a decent amount of land to you!"

"I know!" she replied laughing, "I'm getting a bit big for my boots, aren't I?"

"Barry would be proud of you!" he smiled.

Her criteria for the house were a different kettle of fish altogether. It had to have character but newly renovated or built. She didn't want to be running looking for a handyman every week to fix this, that or the other. The kitchen had to be spacious with place to sit and eat with a view of the sea. This was definitely not something she was compromising on, it had been her dream for as long as she could remember and the dream was as clear as if it was real to her.

She was in her element. The freedom of getting out of the city and wandering through open spaces with the belief that one day she would live out there permanently was almost too much for her. She felt elated and all the bad things that happened to her over the years were now firmly behind her. She could plan for a peaceful future.

Often she'd hug herself and wonder, "Is all this really true or am I dreaming?"

She could see the goats, the small breeds of cattle, ducks, cats, dogs and of course her llamas all in the picture. She'd never seen a real llama but that didn't stop her dreaming, she'd seen pictures and she thought them beautiful.

From her large warm kitchen she'd cook, hold conversations, throw Christmas parties and watch the sea. Her grandchildren would run around outside in the fresh air and she'd invite everyone she loved to stay with her.

Tess claimed she would know the house when she saw it and a few months after the search began that is exactly what happened. They had been looking at different properties since early morning and she was on the verge of giving up for the day when Jimmy coaxed her to see just one more.

They had pulled off the main road and driven up a wide country lane which was running parallel to the sea. She began to get a very good feeling about the area and then about the house as she looked around at the location. As they approached the house and drove around it she realised the coastal view could be seen from three sides. It was situated on a short peninsula that jutted out from the land. A large veranda surrounded the house and a beautiful garden, with green fields sweeping down to the sea and out behind the house, all belonging to the property.

It had thirty one acres of land. The house was newly renovated with a large open-plan kitchen and living room. Large picture windows ran along the front and the sides and were insulated in triple glazing which kept the cold Irish wind out. There were four large bedrooms, big enough for the grandchildren.

Upstairs the first floor was surrounded by a veranda also with a view of the sea. She smiled as she imagined herself sitting there on an evening with a mug of tea or a gin and tonic in her hand. It was twenty miles from Belfast, near enough for the kids to get to it at weekends.

She turned and smiled, "I think we've found my house. It's like someone read my mind."

"It's a great property. I wouldn't mind inheriting a place like this" laughed Jimmy.

"There might be a few more waiting in line for a bit of it too," she laughed, hugged him and smiled at Triona and Grainne, "I have a good feeling about this place."

Unusually they were all there that day; "It's fabulous!" they agreed.

She gathered the kids up from around the house and told them she was going to buy the house. There were screams of delight all round.

When she got it at a bargain price she was convinced it was meant for her. The little home which had supported them for so many years in Belfast sold quickly for a good price and she prepared to move. She couldn't wait to start her new life.

Helen was as excited as she was, even though she couldn't imagine her not living down the street from her.

Life was changing for them all. She and Mick were spending more time up the Antrim coast. Mick was always on call to do one thing or another for Chris, who claimed they were his encyclopaedia on Northern Ireland. Every day he was on the phone three or four times looking for information on where he could get this or do the other. If Mick didn't know immediately he found out from his myriad of contacts.

Tess's children were astonished at how quickly she was decamping. When it came to the last day they all stood in their old home and said a tearful goodbye to all that had gone before and a prayer for a happy and healthy future. Turning the key in the door for a last time she whispered a heartfelt goodbye and thank you.

The signing of all papers was completed and she moved in to her new home that evening. Within days she was ordering supplies to build sheds, patios and paths and getting men to carry out the work.

"I've waited too long to buy this dream, I'm going to get it the way I want it and then I'm going to enjoy it," she told Helen.

A few weeks later with the sun shining, the countryside looking wonderful and the sea lapping peacefully at the shore she drove along the road to collect the first of her animals, a dog, a neighbour had to give away.

Every morning she arose with a feeling of adventure and she'd never been so content. Now she'd made her mark on the house it was beginning to feel more like her own and she was surprised how quickly she was becoming accustomed to it. Her days were spent planning what she was going to do and where everything was going to go.

Green fields, wild flowers and the sea were all around and it brought peace to her soul. The fabulous green foliage on the trees along the road sides and the animals in the fields made her heart swell with joy. The air smelt and felt so fresh and healthy.

Returning along the road with the pup in a cardboard box in the boot she decided she needed a kennel, food and a lead for the pup she now called Lucky. She headed to another farm up the road where she heard kennels were made. When she got back to the house the grandchildren had arrived and they and the dog spent the rest of the day running from room to room showing the pup his new home.

Tess put the kettle on and when it boiled she poured herself a cup of tea and stood at the open French-windows, looking out at the sea. She lifted her eyes to where she assumed Heaven was and prayed; "I don't know how I got here but

I'm grateful I did, it's like being set free. Thank you God for it all and please let me live a healthy and happy life here in peace for a long time to come so I can really enjoy it."

She smiled as she bent down and took one of her wellingtons from the pup and said, "And please God help us to train this pup so he stops chewing everything he can get his teeth on and peeing all over the place!"

73

Almost every weekend, the family were down helping her decorate, putting up sheds for chickens, donkeys and cattle, sectioning off parts of the garden for different beds for vegetables and flowers, erecting gazebos and putting in paths. Tess had very definite ideas of what she wanted.

"Thank God Jimmy has taken after his father and can turn his hand to anything. He's nearly as excited as I am about developing the farm and garden and it is saving me a fortune," she told Helen.

Some other men from the local area were working with him but Jimmy was planning, supervising and leaving instructions on what had to be done while he worked in Belfast during the week.

Helen and Mick would arrive and stay over during the week if they weren't playing or doing something for Chris. He mucked in with the other men while Tess and Helen worked on plans for decorating the house or building walls on the periphery of the grounds.

An elderly neighbour, Jack, from up the road, asked her if she would look after two donkeys he had as they were getting too much for him to care for. Tess thought he gave them to her because the children were always going up to the wall and talking to them and petting them. They were ecstatic when they arrived one weekend and they were in her field. They loved feeding them and combing their coats and Jimmy's son could often be found on their backs.

Jack stood with her at her window drinking tea and watching as the donkeys following the children around; "They've never been so well looked after and they're thriving on it. I don't think they ever had their coats brushed before. You can see they're fond of the young ones and the attention they're giving them."

"You're kind of fond of their company yourself," smiled Tess, "from what I can see."

"Indeed I am! They've brought new life to the area," he told her.

"They're kind of fond of you too, Jack!" she laughed.

He called in most days for a cup of tea and a chat and Tess enjoyed seeing him arrive. He was a mine of information on the area and Tess loved his company.

That was the beginning of her menagerie. Hens were given to her by a woman in the next village and a kitten arrived a few days later. Then a lamb whose mother couldn't feed it landed in her kitchen with a farmer's wife who heard she was collecting animals. Tess tried to stop the rumours that she would take anything, as she was afraid of what would arrive next at her door.

Her grandchildren loved it all. From never having pets they now had puppies following them around, kittens on their knees, chickens pecking through the fields, pigs grunting and trotting after them and the donkeys who loved their company and let them brush them.

As Tess liked to tease her children; "The big kids are always out there with them too and just as excited as the younger ones."

All were curious to see what else she would have when they arrived each weekend. She tried to stop the animals coming but she loved having them too. It gave her a purpose in life and she never had a dull moment. It was a great change and a new life for everyone. Now her children were talking about moving out of the city into the country and buying houses near her. The clear fresh air, peace and safety to move around, was a new phenomenon for all of them. On Sunday evenings they hated going back to the city and all it entailed.

Helen and Tess sat at the kitchen table one evening with a glass of wine each and looking out over the garden to the sea. "Well kid. Life has taken another turn for us!" said Helen.

"Isn't it wonderful? Though it's a pity Barry had to die for me to do it!"

"I think Barry could have a hand in orchestrating it from above. Everything is going so well for you."

"It sometimes feels like he is standing behind me and urging me on. It's weird and feels so real sometimes that I think if I turn around quickly I will see him."

"Maybe he is there! What do we know?" said Helen. "And Chris's problem has been sorted and he is here so often now it's like he lives here. I'm so happy when I see him. But when I wake in the morning I still get that feeling of tension, you know the feeling that something is not right and there is something to worry about. Then the relief comes and I realise that he is a free man and we have him back with us. But it's getting better and is not as bad as it was."

"That is such a blessing for all of us."

"He's doing so well and loves being able to come home and he's talking about moving back permanently. His business is doing well and he can fly back and forth to the US when needed! He wants the children to live and grow up in Ireland so they have the best of both worlds."

"Life is good, my friend!"

"Indeed it's bloody amazing when you think of what we've been through!"

"Come on, we have the livestock to feed. Isn't that what you're here for anyway?" Tess laughed as she grabbed Helen and pushed her out the door.

74

She'd been in the house a few months and standing at the French windows, in what had become her favourite spot, with a mug of tea in her hand, when a large lorry approached down the road. As it arrived into her lane she went to meet the driver who informed her he had a delivery for her. She thought he'd made a mistake and it must be meant for another house. Nowhere in her mind could she consider a delivery so big it would need a lorry this size. The driver produced a delivery docket and sure enough there was her name on it. She became very worried.

"My God, what is going to come out of this truck? They don't allow you to keep elephants or hippos around here, do they?" she asked the driver.

"No! You have to have a special license for them! But maybe someone has arranged that for you too?" he laughingly teased.

"Oh! Please don't even joke about it. I'm afraid of what my children might think is a good idea to keep next."

Completely intrigued but scared stiff she waited as the driver reached up to open the lorry doors. What would he reveal? He had sounded very mysterious. Was someone playing a nasty trick on her?

"I was told not to tell you what was in here until you saw them for yourself," he told her "I have to put them in with the donkeys for company."

"They? There's more than one?" she asked looking startled.

He just smiled and stayed silent; he seemed to be enjoying her dismay. All she could do was stand back and wait while he undid the latches and unloaded the truck. As the first door came slowly down she strained to see what it held but it was too dark to see inside.

Just before he opened the second set of gates Helen and Mick arrived up the road.

"This has something to do with you, hasn't it?" Tess accused them.

"Indeed it has not! We wish we had thought of it but we didn't. It's like a present from heaven via Chris," laughed Helen.

The lorry driver hauled back the wooden gates of the truck and out from its depths strutted two llamas. Tess was astounded. As she got her breath back she cheered and clapped her hands when she realised what she was seeing.

"Oh my God! I don't believe it! I have always wanted llamas since I was very young and read about them in a magazine. They were part of my dream of having a house in the country. I'd forgotten about them! Oh! Aren't they wonderful?"

"We know!" laughed Mick, "Barry told us about it and I told Chris the story and he got these two for you. This rogue here is Kevin," he said pointing to the driver. "He and Chris are good friends. He rang us and warned us to be here when they arrived."

She couldn't believe her eyes. She walked to the first one that came off the truck and rub its coat.

"Oh! You beautiful thing! My grandchildren are going to love you," she sighed. "It is like a present from heaven. I have to ring Chris and thank him."

"He would've loved to be here when they arrived but couldn't make it," said Mick.

"What are you going to call them?" asked Helen.

"Well! One of them will have to be Barry and I think we'll call the other one Chris," she said.

"I think you should call one of them Kesh because it's the one thing that's had the biggest effect on your life and family. And maybe you'll break the jinx it has had by naming something so beautiful after it," retorted Helen with a laugh.

"You could buy another two from me and call them Kesh and Maze," laughed Kevin.

"No!" said Tess. "That's all behind me now and I don't need any reminders."

"Well! I have a few dozen more if you ever change your mind," he laughed.

"Ah! So it wasn't from the goodness of your heart you were making the suggestions? You were trying to flog me another couple of them. What sex are they by the way?"

"One female and one male," he laughed. "That's what the man ordered. You can't have one without the other, now can you?"

"I don't know about that!" laughed Tess. "I'm doing all right on my own."

"A good looking woman like you shouldn't be on her own!" he smiled.

"Are you offering to keep me company?" laughed Tess finding herself amazed at her cheek. She couldn't believe she was flirting with this man.

"You'd never know about that! I could think of worse things I could be doing!" retorted the man. "There's my card, if you ever feel like a bit of company or a few more llamas give me a ring."

"You're a fast worker!" laughed Tess.

"With someone like you I think I'd need to be. Don't want to give you time to make excuses. I've a feeling you could find plenty if you started."

She turned and gave him a serious look over and was surprised to think she quite liked what she saw. This was the first time since she got married she'd even thought of having another man in her life. Barry was dead just under two years and she'd been married over thirty years to him.

"How extraordinary," she thought. "Here I am fancying a man who has just delivered a present which has come indirectly from my dead husband. Is Barry delivering more that the two llamas here?" she wondered.

Then she heard Mick say, "I'll do a referee for him. I've known him for years. He's the father of our Chris' friend, James, and he's a widower. A good man, a hard worker and good craic, will that do for starters?"

"Now you've got my pedigree," laughed Kevin. "What do you think? I've heard loads about you so I know you could be a handful, but I like a challenge!"

"Now there's a recommendation and a proposal for you," Helen laughed. "All in a matter of seconds and he has other llamas on his farm if you need more too. What else could you want?"

"Or I can come without the llamas," insisted Kevin laughing.

"Good God!" laughed Tess. "Am I being ganged up on?"

"You could be doing with getting out and having a social life and Kevin has a great social life. He could be the man to take you out and show you around," laughed Mick.

"There would be no pain there as far as I'm concerned," laughed Kevin.

"We're playing in the local rugby club at the weekend and you both should come and get to know each other a bit better," said Helen.

"So now that's arranged, are you making tea?" laughed Mick, "I could be doing with one."

"Put my name in the pot too," said Kevin.

"And cheeky too!" laughed Tess.

After they had put the llamas into the paddock with the donkeys and watched them for a while, the four of them went into the kitchen and sat around the table chatting as she and Helen made tea. After an hour or so while Kevin told Tess about looking after the llamas and much laughter, Helen and Mick left. She took Kevin around the farm to show him what she had done with it. He gave her a few tips on looking after the other animals, their shelter and feeding and ideas for growing plants so near the sea.

"The only thing you're missing is a goat and I've one who is lost for company at my place. You can put her in with the donkeys and llamas. Her mate died a few weeks ago. I'll drop her up to you at the weekend," he said.

"What do I need a goat for?" she asked.

"Every farm needs a goat and donkeys and llamas love their company. Then you could open up as a wee farm for schools to visit. The children would love it and I'll give you a hand."

"I don't believe this!" laughed Tess, "I retired from work and now I find I'm taking on more responsibility than I've ever had."

Kevin laughed, "I've got a feeling you thrive on responsibility and couldn't be idle."

"I thought I was going to have a quiet life in the country when I bought this place but there is nothing quiet about it."

"A friend of mine has peacocks and ducks and there's loads of room here for them too."

"Take it easy. I'm not going to have enough room for any more!"

"You have loads of room and old Jack up the road has that field next to you and neither chick nor child. If you ask him nicely he might sell or lease it to you," said Kevin. "You could get him to give you a hand, he would love nothing better. It will give him something to live for."

Tess looked at Kevin and found it strange how easy she felt in his company and how exciting it was planning with him as though he was going to be part of the future of the place.

"Maybe it might be worth my while taking him up on his invitation for the weekend," she smiled to herself.

75

Tess rang to thank Chris for the llamas and they discussed his coming wedding which was taking place in Belfast in a few months' time. Even though they had lived together for many years and reared their children he and Leah had never got around to making it legal until now. They were also looking at houses around the same area she was in and he'd seen some he really liked. He hoped to have it all sorted before the wedding.

A mixture of many nationalities was coming to the wedding. It was to be a big affair. The hotels were booked and the invitations had already gone out to the American and other foreign contingents, who had to make plans to travel and find places to stay.

The following week the invitations arrived in Belfast and every house in the old neighbourhood with connection to Mick and Helen got one. It was the gossip of West Belfast and all over the local papers, 'Local boy made good and doesn't forget his roots.'

The next surprise came a few weeks later when Helen and Mick arrived saying they had something to show her.

"Not more bloody animals, I hope?" said Tess, as she took off her wellingtons and raincoat after coming in from feeding her own.

"No!" said Helen. "Stick on your shoes, we have to take a wee run up the road a couple of miles. And hurry up, I'm so excited, I can't wait!"

"Are you sure it's not more animals?" queried Tess worriedly. "I'm taking nothing more. I have enough mouths to feed. I don't care what it is."

"No! It's not more animals, I promise!" insisted Helen excitedly. "Come on!" she exclaimed as she dragged Tess out to the car.

"What else could be a couple of miles up the road?" she wondered.

They headed off along the main road for a few miles and then veered to the left along a side road for another half mile eventually stopping at a two storey ivy covered Manor house down a tree lined avenue. It was a beautiful house in a beautiful setting. As they got out of the car Tess looked around and sighed.

"What a beautiful place? Whose is it?" she asked.

Helen looked at Mick and they both grinned; "It's ours! Isn't it amazing? It's ours! We're going to live here!" laughed Helen, hugging Tess and swinging her around.

"I don't believe you! It's Chris's. I know he is buying a house somewhere around here."

"No! It's ours! Chris bought it for us," laughed Helen, overwhelmed with excitement.

"Chris has bought a farm house about five miles from here," said Mick "We were with him when he went looking. We wanted him to buy this one because we loved it but he wouldn't. We were really disappointed when he didn't because we thought it was beautiful. It is so full of character. Last night he arrived at the house and handed us the deeds with our names on them and the keys. It's ours, lock, stock and barrel. All paid for."

Helen danced around in front of the house.

"Isn't it amazing? Isn't it a dream house?" she asked.

"For God's sake, woman, open the door and let me see inside it. I've never been in a place like this before!" said Tess, amazed "This is brilliant, you're going to live up the road from me again. This is amazing!"

They hugged each other and as they wandered around from room to room the women talked about how they could decorate it and what they could use the rooms for.

"Here we are in a house I couldn't even fantasise about and we own it. The deeds are in our names. Isn't that amazing?" Helen repeated with her eyes as wide as saucers with delight.

"It's a dream! I'm so delighted for you," laughed Tess hugging her again.

"I may never get to live in this place, I may have a heart attack from all the excitement and shock," exclaimed Mick.

"I know the feeling," replied Tess, "I have to pinch myself at times I am so content with the farm and the animals. I feel like I have come home. As I walk the shore line in the evening with the dog at my heels and chatting to the llamas, donkeys and other animals along the fence I feel very sure that God is in his heaven and looking down on me and mine."

"You deserve it! You worked hard for it," said Helen hugging her.

"And so do you and Mick, my friend. We've been through so much hardship and trauma."

A few weeks later Helen and Mick moved in and after they'd settled and decided on the décor she left Mick to do the work with a few of his mates and she came over almost every day to help Tess on the farm.

One day Helen said to Tess, "I have a four bedroom house with four reception rooms, three toilets and a big kitchen and I can leave the central heating on all day if I like and I don't have to worry about paying for it as Chris insists on paying our household bills. They are all sent to his company. He says it's the least he can do for us. We wouldn't take anything from him before. It's a long way from the days we walked the streets worrying where our next loaf of bread was coming from. Look around you here at your animals and your home; we're a long way from those streets now. Isn't life amazing?"

"It certainly is, and I'm actually making money with my little farm now and I'm delighted."

Tess had taken up Kevin's suggestion and advertised with schools who were delighted to bring the children to her farm with so many different animals. They came from all over and she loved showing them around and had at least one or two tours a week and getting busier.

"And we're still living just up the road from each other," she beamed.

"You didn't think you were going to get away without us, did you?" Helen laughed "No! We're going to stick together for the duration, my friend, however long that may be!"

Tess didn't argue with her, she was thrilled to have her near again.

76

Chris and Leah's wedding day drew near and people started arriving from all over the world. Helen and Mick hadn't sold their house in Belfast and some of Leah's family were staying there and were thrilled to be staying in the middle of Belfast after all they had heard about it down through the years. The neighbours made sure they were looked after and they were never short of home cooking, gossip and information on the area.

Each day they took a trip to places they had only heard about in newspapers, TV or from Chris. Long Kesh was a place they all wanted to see and Mick was convinced to be tour guide for the day although it was the last place he wanted to see again.

"It didn't look the same," he told Helen. "There was no noise and nobody I knew there. It's no longer relevant to me. I'm glad I went! I needed to purge it from my life and expel any demons I had about it. I will never forget it but I don't care about it and it can't hurt me anymore."

Helen was relieved. She had worried when she'd first heard he was going on the visit but it seemed to have lifted a load off his shoulders and done him good. There was an extra spring in his step for a few days after. He seemed a different man since moving out of Belfast into the countryside. He loved walking through the fields with a collie dog he'd got and was spending hours reading up on wild flora and fauna and fishing in the area. He's finally at peace, was Helen's description of him.

Margaret arrived, a couple of days before the wedding and stayed with Helen and Mick but most nights all of the women got together. Tess, Helen, Lucy and Margaret sat around the kitchen tables alternatively in Tess and Helen's houses, chatting about everything and putting the world to rights as usual.

Lucy and Jim came out to visit regularly and give them updates on what was happening in West Belfast. There was many a reminiscence, tear and laughter. All were conscious of those missing and Kieran, Barry, Owen and Mary's ghosts often flitted across their minds.

Margaret still lived in Kerry with her children close to her and her grandchildren in and out all the time. She only came back to Belfast occasionally, for weddings and funerals and could never see herself living there again.

“I have all I will ever need in my wee home in ‘The Kingdom’. I don’t need anywhere else,” she told them.

77

The day of the wedding finally arrived with everyone at the church in their finery and delighted to be catching up with people they hadn't seen for a while. Tess looked around at her children and grandchildren and felt very proud of her little family. They looked beautiful.

Deep in thought and smiling she contemplated the day ahead. What a blessing it was that it could take place in Belfast without having to worry about the Troubles anymore.

Lately everything that had brought her to this moment was slotting through her mind. The young innocent girl she had been when Barry had been lifted. The lone parent raising her children who had done so well and the poverty and hardship they had all endured. The changes these events had made in her. The raids on their homes and all that had happened to Helen, Mick and their boys. Chris's amazing life in America and his return home. Barry's death and the catalyst it had been to make her sell up and move to the country, loosing Mary and Owen, Lucy's life and her relationships and her own and Helen's involvement in the Troubles. As she thought about it today it was as though it happened to another person who was either very brave or very stupid.

"I wonder which I was," she pondered to herself. "But it doesn't matter now, it's all over, in the past and the truth lost in the mists of time."

She hugged herself as she realised she was very happy where she was now! For the first time in her life since she married so many years before she was only responsible for herself. She loved her family but they were no longer her sole responsibility. She could do what she wanted and that is what she was doing. She was finally happy.

A rustle of noise could be heard at the church door and she heard familiar voices and turned to watch Mick and Helen walk up the aisle, dressed to kill.

"My God, look at you, girl, well into your fifties and you still look like the young woman you were many years ago running around in jeans and t-shirt, just much better dressed today. I remember you, from so long ago." She smiled as she reminisced.

"You look fabulous. I'm so proud of you," she whispered as Helen stopped to speak to her and give her a hug. There were tears in both their eyes as Tess caught her hand and winked.

"No problem! We could always do it, you and I! You look wonderful," she smiled at Tess in her classic shift dress of deep blue, large picture hat in navy and matching accessories.

Tess watched her with pride as she continued up the aisle, Mick by her side as usual. After he handed her into the seat at the front of the church he walked over to stand beside Chris. He was the best man. He put his arm across his shoulder and gave him a hug of support. Chris beamed a smile back at him.

The bride arrived, only five minutes late. She made a beautiful picture as she glided up the aisle in an elegantly fitted ivory lace dress carrying a bouquet of red roses. Behind her came Carrie and their two children, Kieran and Teresa.

Chris, standing at the altar at the top of the church, turned and looked down the aisle smiling at his approaching family. It was obvious he was a happy man as he watched them walk towards him. Mick held his arm with a big grin on his face clearly proud of them all.

As the procession reached them, Chris kissed Leah and took her hand with tears in his eyes. It was like the end of the hard road of anger, hurt, worry, loss, uncertainty and fear he had trudged for so long and the beginning of the happy-ever- after.

A prayer went up from many minds at that moment that this would be so.

The church was packed with all those he cared about and it was a wonderful day. Like, everyone else who knew his history, there was one name they all remembered; Kieran. He felt as though he was there with him saying, "haven't you all done well, brother?"

Chris smiled as he hugged Leah and thought to himself, "I have done well, against all the odds and I've been so lucky. I think you must have had something to do with that brother!" Leah was finally his wife and as they walked from the church with their children in a jubilant procession they were almost dancing with joy.

Later as Tess and Helen stood and looked around them at the reception, Helen remarked in wonder, "How the hell did we get here?"

Tess laughed, "In a very roundabout, precarious way but we got here and that's what matters. It's been an amazing journey. Aren't you proud of us?"

"Too right I am!" exclaimed Helen laughing. "I'm so very proud of us and so happy we got to this stage. Even if there are many who I wish were here, not least Kieran, Barry, Owen and Mary. I'm sure they're hovering above us somewhere. They couldn't just go and forget us, they were such strong characters. Today I feel they're very near."

"I was thinking that myself earlier," smiled Tess

"I'm so glad we survived and got to this place in our lives! Not bad for two wee women from West Belfast!"

"Not bad at all, even if we do say it ourselves," Tess giggled, "I don't think I have ever been as content as I am now," she remarked as she looked across the floor at Kevin where he played with one of her grandchildren.

She'd seen a lot of him since the day he'd delivered the llamas. They went for a meal and a drink with Helen and Mick that weekend and he'd used every excuse since to come back to see her during the weeks that followed. She enjoyed his company, he made her laugh and she wouldn't object to him becoming a permanent fixture in her life.

"Kevin's a good man," said Helen as she noticed her gaze.

"I know," smiled Tess

"I'm really happy for you both." She lifted her glass and toasted her; "To you, my friend! You go for it! Life is too short and he will keep you young!"

"Yes," laughed Tess, "I think he will!"

They smiled as they stood together surveying their world. Peace reigned.

"We deserve a few years of it after what we've come through," sighed Helen contentedly.

It had been an amazing journey for all but now was the time to enjoy the here and now and hope for good things in the future. Who knew what tomorrow would bring?